# DAWN OF DOVES

## TIL KINGDOM COME
## BOOK TWO


## ABIGAIL BRIER

BLACK SEA
ORO
USHOLK
VALLEY OF THE SHADOW
EDMA
INK VALLEY
DEAD WOOD
NORTHERN WOOD
THE
BRUNTS
OZANNA
VESTELE
SUNSTONE FOREST
ADULLAM
BRINLAND
HOLLOW COVES
DAWN PRISON
SEA OF DAWN
THE DAWN ISLANDS
TABRANA
ORIANA

THE ISLES OF VOLCANIA
CRYSTAL SEA
ESWEN
REMONT
ARRESIA
Z.W.

*for those lost in the darkness—you are never too far gone for His light to reach*

# PLAYLIST

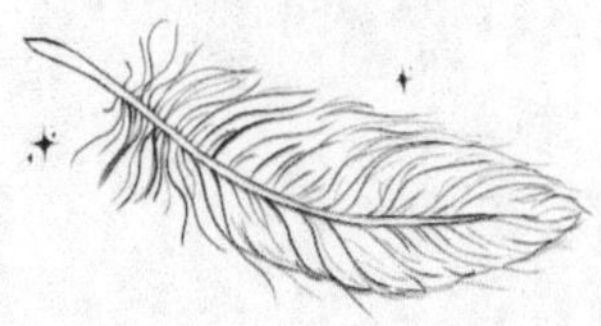

For those of you who want the reading experience to be like a movie in your mind, visit the "listen while you read" tab on my website.
www.abigailbrier.com/listen-while-you-read
There you'll find free, downloadable cinematic playlist guides for each book and the links to the Spotify playlists for easy listening.

# DAWN OF DOVES
## ABIGAIL BRIER

# PROLOGUE

## GALEN

**Five Weeks Ago, The Night Ravenna Broke the Stone**

*Keep our hope alive.*

Galen sent Zephaniah into the darkness with a waning torch and closed the door. Her mind raced, but the wooden rocking chair she now settled in kept a slow and steady pace. Her fingers drummed against the arm as she watched out the window, his silhouette shrinking as he wove through the streets of the kingdom slums, nearing the entrance to the tower where Ravenna was being held. The healer watched him disappear into the night, and then she prayed.

Galen prayed that the Father would protect him. She begged for His Light to cover Oro—even all of Arresia. She pleaded guilty for her part in keeping the Dove from the Light, and she asked the Father to do what she had just asked of Zephaniah—to keep their hope alive.

About a half hour later, when the kingdom rattled with an

1

explosion and the hand painted dishes were knocked from her walls, Galen fell to her knees beside the bed where Ravenna had once laid. She knew Zephaniah would die if it meant protecting Ravenna, and she was coming to terms with the fact that he would not be returning to her. She had sent him into the darkness with a dwindling flame, and he would not be able to find his way back to her before the shadows inside that castle swallowed him and Ravenna whole.

The guards outside her home began flooding the streets, running every which way, unsure of what force had shaken the kingdom. Unforgiving winds and cries of confusion infiltrated Galen's home through the crevices around the doors and window. The guards knew not what was occurring, but Galen felt the hope of Arresia withering, and she understood.

Ravenna had broken the stone, and the destruction that came with it was a warning. Galen should have realized sooner. Ravenna had laid claim to the birthright given to her by her parents, but it was not the birthright given to her by the Father of Lights. No, the power the princess had awakened was anything but Light.

Galen rose and braced her hands on the window frame as she peered out, watching as the gray clouds thickened over the trembling castle. Her breaths became shallow as she witnessed a whisper of light dissipating into the skies. In response, the wind howled relentlessly against the windowpane. The mark on Galen's ankle seemed to burn now, urging her to action, to prepare for the war that was surely beginning.

Her stiff hands smoothed her apron as she turned from the window and shoved the table in front of the tapestry on the wall. Galen had not thought it possible that the kingdom could fall any further, but it had. Zephaniah was in that castle when the explosion had happened, and Galen would venture to guess he had been right there with Ravenna, as he always was.

She swallowed, fighting every urge in her body to march across the kingdom and into the castle to rescue the closest thing to a child she ever had. But the Light within her was telling her she could not risk it. *Someone has to live. For Ravenna. For the daughter of the Barren Queen–the Dove of Ozanna–whose title is scattered about the prophecies as one who will bear Light but is now chained in darkness.*

Galen quickly urged some sprouts up through the cracks in the dilapidated walls of her home and used them to make a skin-toned paste, as she had many times before. Propping her foot on a stool, she raised her skirts and rolled down her stocking, hurriedly patting the paste over the faint lightmark at the pulsepoint on her ankle. She threw the remnants of the concoction into the fire and then restricted the near constant flow of power that went out from her to keep the herbs and vines that hung from her rafters alive. She watched through teary eyes as the plants dried up, turned brown, and life was sucked from the room.

*Oh, Zephaniah.*

Her breath extinguished the candle flame on the windowsill–the one that discreetly announced to other Embers that her home was a safe house. Galen threw the unsent messages into the fire–the ones that would reveal her identity as a spy. She also burned the feather signum, and when she had destroyed every remnant of Light that would incriminate her, she waited in the rocking chair by the door. She prayed that Zephaniah was alive and would find the strength to continue in the path she always knew he had been chosen for.

It was daylight before she finally heard the king's men approaching. She rubbed her tired eyes and inhaled deeply. Before she could rise, and without so much as a knock, they kicked open the door of her haven. At the king's guard's arrival on her doorstep, Galen conjured a look of surprise and ducked her head in quiet greeting.

"Wh-what can I do for you?" she asked, rising at once. She did not have to fake the stuttering of her words.

"Galen Bauer?" one of the Despiri guards asked. His hand rested on the sword at his side, and Galen took note of the brass raven pin on his chest. He was from Zephaniah's battalion.

"Yes," she said hesitantly. "That is my name." Her eyes shifted nervously to the witch at his side. Galen guessed her to be Jara, who because of her shared bloodline, slightly resembled Galen's old friend, Ashreya Ozanne.

"Then you can come with us right now," the Despiri grunted, motioning her to the door.

Galen spoke with as much innocence as she could muster while she straightened her apron. "What is this about?"

Jara gave her a sly smile. Her hair was in an updo, pulled tightly back from her porcelain face. Her jaw was like glass, sharp enough to maim, and her thin frame was swallowed up by an expensive fur cloak that blended her into the night. "I think you know what this is about," she sneered.

Galen's eyebrows sank in a facade of confusion as she looked from Jara to the half a dozen soldiers that faded into the fog behind her. She narrowed her eyes against the mist, searching for a hint of that familiar, gentle face in the crowd where he had never fit in. But Galen only allowed herself to hope for half a second before she turned her attention back to the witch. Zephaniah was not here to help her, and the ravens were descending to begin their ravagings.

"Search her already," Jara spat, nudging one of the Despiri forward into Galen's home. Galen staggered backward, barely dodging the hands of the largest soldier.

"Search me for what?" she asked in aggravation. The wind roared outside; a ruthless rush of air that traveled from the southern territories. It tore Jara's hair from her pin and sent some dark locks wisping into the air around her sculpted face.

The witch chuckled, brushing the loose strands back at once. "Step aside. I'll search her mind. It'll be quicker than maneuvering around all those. . ." Jara paused, surveying Galen's linen stockings, dress, and apron, "layers."

Galen braced herself, pushing every non-condemning thought to the top of her mind, just as she had taught Zephaniah to do when he had first come into this kingdom.

Jara's bony fingers crept around Galen's skull, and she fought the urge to draw back as dark tendrils of pain worked to coax thoughts and memories to the surface of her mind. Instead of letting her anxieties dwell on the incriminating mark on her ankle, Galen fed those tendrils with nonsense questions that she suspected she already knew the answers to. It was the only cover she could manage in the presence of the witch's dark magic.

*What are these people doing in my home?*
*What do they think I have done?*
*What is it she is searching me for?*

Jara struggled against Galen's subconscious for a short moment and sighed. "No lightmarks."

Galen's heart thumped back into a steady rhythm, and she rolled her shoulders as the witch released her. Her body was stiff as she watched one of the soldiers rummage through her cabinets, and as another kicked a rug from the floorboards where the table had been.

Finally, one of the shorter men with pale skin and dark hair like Jara's announced across the room, "The house is clean. Shall I check her mind too?" Galen's breath caught in her throat as she felt the slight prodding of his strange power against her mind.

The witch rolled her eyes, stepping between Galen and the Despiri. "Degare trusts me, Jio. You should, too. I am tired of you trying to steal my place as his favorite. Just accept your position as his most favored *Despiri* and move on," she said with a shrug. "What can I say? Witches are just–better."

Jara paused for a moment, acknowledging the mess they had made of Galen's home, and flashed her uncanny, orange eyes in Galen's direction. "Apologies for the intrusion. But the king has a new position for you. We need a healer, and Faxon here," the witch gestured to the Despiri next to her, the one from Zephaniah's battalion, "assured me that you were the best healer we would find." Galen's eyebrows lowered in genuine confusion as she studied the witch and the Despiri. The castle was full of healers that were certainly more experienced than her–surely, they even had Despiri healers. Jara explained further. "He said Zephaniah Wilmore brought the redhead here on the verge of death, and she left still breathing."

Galen's heart thundered in her chest. *Is Ravenna still*

*breathing now? Is Zephaniah? What is happening inside that castle that has landed the witch on my doorstep?*

Jara looked around the mess one more time, at Galen's possessions which had been scattered and thrown about. Her ocher eyes fell to the two cups of lukewarm tea that sat on the table—one of which had been Zephaniah's just hours ago. Galen's breaths came rapidly.

The witch's gaze lingered on the cups for only a moment before she took a deep breath beneath raised brows and redirected her attention to Galen. "We had to be sure you were trustworthy, since the boy you basically raised by order of the king turned out to be a traitor." The words slithered off Jara's tongue like an accusation, but Galen said nothing—did not dare ask what the witch meant by *traitor*. Traitors did not typically get to live, and Galen was sure now that Zephaniah's true allegiance had been discovered.

"You are a healer, right?" Jara prodded, and Galen barely heard her over the sounds of her heartbeat in her ears. She blinked.

"Yes," Galen answered tentatively. She knew how to use herbs to make natural remedies and salves. She was a healer in that sense, and because of her gifts from the Light, she could grow what nature had to offer. The witch could not know that, though. The witch could never know that the power that dwelt inside Galen used to be much more. Galen may not have stowed her gifts away through dark magic like those in Vestele, but she, too, had grieved the Light within her all these years, suppressing it, and not allowing it to grow. She should have stayed in practice, no matter the risks. But because she had grieved the Light, her healing gifts had weakened, and the lightmark on her ankle had faded significantly. Where she was once able to weave light and life through torn flesh–as she had for Willa after Ravenna's birth–she could now only offer relief from the herbs she now focused her powers on growing. It was why she was unable to do more for Ravenna when she had first arrived in Oro, but somehow, Zephaniah had still recognized her as Ravenna's only chance.

Galen was once considered a castle healer in Ozanna, and then here in Oro, when she had come here after the war and taken the opportunity to work as a spy for Ashreya. Galen had only held that title for a few years before she moved to this home in the slums, thankful she had been replaced by seemingly more talented healers. Why did they want her back now?

"And you can cook, I presume?" Jara's gaze swept over the many pots, pans, and jars that cluttered every flat surface.

Galen nodded slowly.

"Perfect. When you are not practicing healing on your patient, you'll work in the kitchens. You'll be in the castle living quarters with the other servants from now on. You will attend to whomever you are assigned." Galen's hands fidgeted with the skirts of her dress.

"I have only one patient?" she dared to ask.

Jara smirked. "Follow me."

Galen followed Jara and the Despiri by the name of Jio through the empty streets of Oro toward the black castle. She was allowed to take nothing but her bag of medicines, and it weighed down her shoulder as they traveled through the slums, where not a single window glowed with any promise. The castle guards were on high alert, and after Jara muttered something to the ones outside the entrance of the west wing,

Galen entered into the throat of the beast, led by Degare's witch and surrounded by his men.

They maneuvered recently fallen rock, and Galen's eyes wandered up the snaking cracks of the arched hallway at the damage that must have been caused by the bursting of the stone–the stone Galen had hidden within Ravenna's flesh. Galen's hands shook at her sides. She should have told Zephaniah about the necklace the moment he had first come through her door with Ravenna, when Galen had recognized it for the noose that it was. She knew it was what Degare searched for, and she should have known that the power inside would not be of the Light. Light cannot be inherited or transferred from one to another–not even through the bloodstone staff. The powers held by Despiri were only weak mockeries of what had once dwelt in the hearts of those who had chosen the Light.

If she had only realized, they could have formed a plan, and none of this would be happening. Galen never should have promised the Ozannes she would hide the truth from Ravenna, their only heir. The heir they had prayed for, had waited seven years for. The heir that would usher in the war against darkness and bring Light back to Arresia. The heir that did not even realize the hope she held in her hands, if she would only place her trust in the Light.

Orange torchlight led the way to their destination at the base of the towers where Jara gestured to a door. The mark at Galen's ankle burned beneath the paste and her stocking, and she held her breath as she considered who her patient might be. The door slowly swung open with a lengthy *creak*.

"You'll find your patient inside. I trust that you can keep him alive so that we can continue our session tomorrow?"

*Him.* The eerie sound of water dripping echoed through the tunnel that was lined with tools. Galen swayed.

She staggered forward at the witch's nudge and walked into the torture chambers alone. She knew who she would find on the stone altar that had been stolen from one of the ancient Temples of Light, but knowing could never prepare her–not for this.

PART ONE
THE RISE

# CHAPTER I
# THE DAWN OF IT ALL
## ZEPHANIAH

**Four Weeks Ago**

In the torture chambers, Zephaniah measured time by the *drip, drip, drip,* of his blood pooling around the altar.

*Seven thousand, eight hundred, and fifty-three.*

*Seven thousand, eight hundred, and fifty-four.*

*Seven thousand, eight hundred, and fifty-five.*

How many drops would he lose before the Light called him home?

*Just a little while longer,* he assured himself. *Then you'll walk in Eternal Light.*

With no lightmark, there was a time when he had worried where he would end up after death. Where he would spend eternity. Whether that be among the shadows or under the reign of the Father of Lights. Zephaniah worried no longer.

*You are hidden by the Father for a reason,* Willa had said to him.

*Yes,* he thought. Because had the Father of Lights not placed him here for a reason, free of lightmarks in a kingdom of darkness, in the path of the Dove who had yet to hear of His Light? The very Light which would return and fill Arresia one day, defeating death and darkness once and for all?

Zephaniah's lips twitched upward. *My purpose.* What he had always wanted was right here in front of him the whole time.

*I got to tell her. I got to prepare the Dove.* Perhaps his purpose had been fulfilled after all.

"Thank you," he whispered to the Light that surrounded him now.

His eyes stayed closed as he awaited the peace that death from this life would bring.

*I have seen the dawn of it all,* he thought, breathing a sigh of relief. Soon, he would be reunited in Eternal Light with those who had gone before him. His mother and father. His older brother, Samuel, whose unwavering faith Zephaniah had always admired. The selfless, elderly mapmaker who had given far too much when he had so little.

*Seven thousand, eight hundred, and fifty-six.*
*Seven thousand, eight hundred, and fifty-seven.*
*Seven thousand, eight hundred, and fifty-eight.*
Zephaniah flinched against the sudden touch that grazed his hand.

A strangled voice followed. "Zephaniah. It's me. I'm here." He knew that voice. It was the voice of a worried—no, a broken—mother. One who was looking at her son, body bruised and cut upon an altar of stone in a kingdom of unrelenting shadow. For her, he forced his eyes back open to the darkness of Arresia.

"Galen," he said on a barely audible breath. She was stout, hovering over him in the light of the torch flame, and if his vision hadn't been unclear, he would have sworn tears fled down both of her cheeks as she looked upon him. Zephaniah's chest rose and fell in an involuntary, shuddering motion.

"I've been by your side every day," she said quickly, wiping her face on her sleeve. "But I've been giving you a sedative to help you rest between. . .sessions. Zephaniah, I am s–"

"Ravenna," he said slowly, not recognizing his own voice. At the name of the Dove, Galen glanced behind her, toward the winding hall and the door Zephaniah had wished to escape through a hundred times.

He blinked, recalling the events at the top of that tower that had brought him to these chambers. He remembered the king's staff shattering as it was thrust toward her, and he remembered being dragged down every last step of the tower, until his back was on this very altar. He did not know how many days had passed since then, or how many of them he had spent in these torture chambers. The days spent under the knife felt like years, and the minutes like days.

"She broke the stone," he said, remembering the way the castle and the grounds of Oro had quaked as the power was awakened as something completely different than what it had been created to be. He clenched his eyes shut as he replayed the memory of her skin, painted with darkness. "She's shadowmarked. They took her."

"Worry about yourself right now," Galen said, palming a jar from her bag.

He had told Ravenna of the Light. He had told her what she would do for the Embers, and how it was told that she would be one of the many to usher the Light back into Arresia.

But he had not told her enough, had he? He should have realized it would be darkness that lay inside that stone spelled with dark magic. He should have done everything in his power to stop her from breaking it. Had he fulfilled his purpose, or not?

"Is she alive?" Zephaniah tried to sit up, but his body did not obey him.

Galen placed a gentle hand on his bare shoulder and nodded. "She is alive. Been asleep for days, according to the rumors. The blonde servant is in and out of her chambers." Zephaniah relaxed slightly, and he watched Galen's face grow gaunt as she took in the mutilated state of his body. She collected herself, for his sake, continuing in conversation as she shakily administered aid to his wounds. "She's quiet, that one," Galen said about the servant. "I don't know her well enough to ask questions. I only know what I hear from the other women in the kitchen, and it is all purely speculation. You know how rumors spread here. Ravenna's name can be heard across the kingdom—but still, few know her true identity as the heir of Ozanna."

"I need to talk to her," Zephaniah choked out. "There is so much more I have to say—so much more to tell her. She doesn't know, Galen. She doesn't understand."

"We need to focus on getting you healed," Galen said as gently as she could through the fit of sobs that left her throat. *Again*, Zephaniah thought. *Healed again.* Galen had been in these chambers with him daily, if not multiple times a day, keeping him just off of the brink of death. But she had no power to heal, no ability beyond offering herbs and salves that would only chain him to this life for a little while longer. Soon, she would have to let him go.

Galen could not seem to keep her eyes from darting up and down his body where he lay on that altar. He watched them leap from wound to wound, unable to find rest. His fingers lethargically grasped the air until they found hers, effectively drawing her gaze back to his.

*Seven thousand, eight hundred, and fifty-nine.*

*Seven thousand, eight hundred, and sixty.*

"If I don't make it through this," he coughed, "and Ravenna does, promise me you'll be there for her. Remind her that she is the Dove. Despite those shadowmarks–she can still be redeemed. She needs to know that she is never too far gone. She needs to know she still has a choice."

Galen shook her head. "You will tell her yourself. We will get you out of this. We will–"

"Galen, promise me you'll remind her of the Father's love. Help her understand. She needs someone to help her understand." His requests were turning to desperate pleas. Just minutes ago, he had been content. He had felt confident in the work he had done for the Light. But now, as he felt his breaths fading, he was pleading for Galen to complete it for him. *Prepare the Dove for Arresia where I have failed.*

Galen looked at him for a long moment, heavy expression clouding her eyes.

"I will. I promise." At those words, he let his head droop to the side.

*Seven thousand, eight hundred, and sixty-one.*

*Seven thousand, eight hundred, and sixty-two.*

"No, Zephaniah. Stay awake." He heard Galen rustling in her bag, searching for any way to help him. "I cannot lose you." Zephaniah knew that Galen had been sent here to keep him alive so that the torture master could continue day after day, but that was not why Galen pleaded with him now to live. Zephaniah could not help but wonder, if he were to die, would there be any reason left for them to allow her to live, or would they kill her? He knew it would be the latter.

So Zephaniah clung to his fragile life for Galen, and for Ravenna, and he did not allow himself to sleep until the *drip, drip, drip* had been stopped by the healer.

Somehow, after a number of days strapped to that altar, Zephaniah found himself alive, crumpled against the same wall where Ravenna had been in the weeks prior. The cell door had been reinforced from where the blast from the breaking of the stone had bent it, and above him, the tall, black ceilings of the cell held new cracks. Bits of stone littered the floor around him, and a layer of dust had settled atop the blood stains on the ground. He ran his fingers across the floor beside him, fighting the soreness in his body. He blinked against the shadows and tilted his hands toward the torchlight that glowed just across the narrow hall. The tips of his fingers were covered with dust, but there was no fresh blood.

They were allowing him time to heal. *Why?*

He flexed and unflexed his fingers then tried to extend his legs. He winced against the searing pain that traveled up his spine.

"Zephaniah? Are you awake?" Galen's voice echoed up the tower and was followed by hurried footsteps. He tried to sit a little straighter, but the air was cold, and he curled back into himself. He said nothing, just waited for Galen's troubled face to appear on the other side of the bars.

His head leaned against the wall, face toward her. "Why you, Galen? Why do they have you taking care of me?" Galen looked down at the tray of steaming food in her hands, and a lock of her light, coppery-brown hair fell in front of her dull eyes as she bent to hand it through the door. They did not trust her enough to give her a key, then. He frowned. "They are onto you, Galen."

"Don't worry about me," she whispered, squatting by the bent door of his cell. He mustered all the strength he had left to scoot toward the platter of food she had set on the floor. She nudged it toward him, and he nodded his thanks.

"The witch and Jio have both been in my head," he said as he pulled the tray onto his lap. "They searched my mind again and again." Galen took a deep breath, and Zephaniah tried not to dwell on thoughts of the torture for too long. "I think they are searching for something on you, and I am weak. It is hard telling what they know. You need to get out of this kingdom while you can."

She shook her head. "I am not leaving you, Zephaniah. Besides, I could not leave if I wanted to. I must report every two hours. That would barely be enough time to make it to the Dead Wood."

Zephaniah shook his head. "They know enough to be suspicious, Galen. They are only keeping you close so they can watch you. You are not safe here."

She smiled softly, reaching for him through the bars. "They have nothing on me," she assured him. "Let's not take for granted this time we have together." Her hand found his stitched cheek as her eyebrows knitted together, and she blinked back the tears that had welled in her pale blue eyes.

"You're right," he said, pulling her hand from his face and

cupping it within his own. He offered her the only smile he could muster, which was the slightest twitch of his lip.

"Eat, it will help you heal. I am not allowed to provide you with medicine or any more sedatives, but I carefully selected the herbs I used in your soup. It should bring you some relief." He smiled softly, bringing the spoon to his mouth with an unsteady hand.

She watched him sadly, and her head fell as she spoke. "I overheard some of the guards talking at the base of the tower. With everything that has happened, and with Degare's staff breaking and having to be remolded–"

"They were able to rebuild the staff?" Zephaniah asked hopelessly. Zephaniah's mind was clouded, but he remembered that evening quite clearly. Zephaniah had watched in utter desperation as the king had placed his bloodstone weapon to Ravenna's chest, hoping to steal her power, only for the staff to be fractured into a hundred pieces by the immense amount of power within her.

The corners of Galen's lip turned downward as she nodded. "The Delle Witch Clan agreed to help him rebuild it in exchange for bloodstone. But to rebuild the staff, he had to use all that was left of his own cache. His search never stopped, but now he is reopening many of the once inactive mines in hopes of gathering every last bit. I do not know if the witches have been fooled again, or if he truly plans on providing them with the stone found in his mines. But something is brewing, Zephaniah."

"There is no way he will hand over anything that could make them more powerful than he is. Degare would never do that. He knows the witches draw power from bloodstone."

"That is not all," she said with her eyes cast down.

"What else aren't you telling me?"

"Ravenna is awake now, according to one of the ladies in the kitchen," Galen said. "She began stirring this morning." Zephaniah's heart began thrumming in his ears.

"What is he planning to do, Galen? I need to speak with her. I need to tell her–"

"There *is* much she has yet to learn, Zephaniah. The Father will make a way if that person is to be you. But I believe you have done your part," Galen said gently. "Let me do mine."

"What do you mean?" he asked tightly. He did not take his eyes from her for a second.

"Even if you could make it out of this cell, you have done enough. We cannot force her to choose the Light. You have presented her with a choice. You have given her the hope she needs to make it through this. What she does with that hope is her decision. Nothing you do can change the fact that in the end, it always has to be her decision. If it is prophesied, we know it will come to pass, but we cannot force the *when*. You have not failed," she assured him.

Zephaniah looked to the wall beyond her, blinking away the sadness in his eyes.

Galen's hand found his through the bars. "You take the Light with you wherever you go, my son." Her eyes sparkled then, and she reached into her pocket reluctantly. "Just because you are locked in here does not mean you can't share that with her." She pulled some folded parchment from the pocket of her apron and offered it to him with a stick of lead.

Zephaniah looked at her curiously.

"The witch watches me closely, but write to our Dove, and I will do my best to deliver them. Tell her whatever you must. Be the light, even if it is the last thing she knows."

Zephaniah sat a little straighter each day, and his stick of lead grew shorter as the small pile of parchment grew taller. He wrote by the dim light of the distant flame, letters of encouragement to Ravenna, words that the Father of Lights Himself seemed to speak onto the paper. Zephaniah knew she would need a friend when he was no longer here for her. These letters were his last chance to tell her everything he wished he had shared sooner. He shared with her what he could remember from the Light Scrolls he had access to as a boy. Prophecy, wisdom, and scriptures that would provide hope in the midst of darkness–so she would know she did not have to walk it alone.

As many hours as he sat in that cell, Zephaniah never ran out of words, but he did run out of pages. Galen was not permitted to see him aside from meal times, but he looked forward to the few minutes each day they were allowed when she brought the chowder and bread. Night fell, and with the lack of luminescence coming from the high windows, it was clear to Zephaniah that the crescent moons had faded to black. It was the first set of new moons since the week of The Darkening, and the night seemed eerily similar, though tonight, the stars still shined through the thick fog above.

Galen snuck in some more parchment with a late dinner, and as he reached toward the bars to accept it, she spoke quietly. "Ravenna's been awake for three days now. I cannot imagine they would let her go much longer possessing all that power. But Zephaniah, if she were to turn to the Light–"

"As the Dove, she would be strong enough to overthrow Degare," he said. "That is what I have been telling you. I just need to speak to her one more time. She needs to choose the Light before it is too late." Zephaniah truly believed it to be that simple. All Ravenna had to do was make a conscious decision to put her hope in and live for the Light, and she would become an heir to the Kingdom. Her shadows would be surrendered, and she would have the power to reestablish Ozanna.

"I have no way to get you out," Galen said, shaking her head. "It will be dangerous, but I think I should try to get these letters to her tonight. I fear our time is running out."

Zephaniah nodded, gathering up all of the letters he had written to convince Ravenna to embrace her title. But Ravenna wasn't the only one he wrote letters to those days in the cell. There were a thousand words that needed to be said. To her, and to any who would hear them. Specifically, to Magdalene in the back of the library, who he thought of often. *How was she faring without my rations? Has she been forced to venture out into the shadows yet?* He pushed the stack of parchment through the bars and into Galen's outstretched hands.

Zephaniah watched her closely, the way the dull blue of her eyes seemed to be pools of sadness, the way the wrinkles at the edges of those pools seemed to deepen right before his eyes. Galen loved him just as much as his own mother had.

"I will speak to her if I can. I will try to convince her." For him, he knew she would do anything. "I will—"

"I love you, Galen," he said, cutting off her flow of words. Her eyes softened, and her hand found his cheek through the bars. She said nothing, only looked at him with the warmth she had always possessed. "I never thanked you," he whispered. *For taking me into your home and reminding me of a mother's love.*

*For helping Ravenna, and for helping me, always. For being a light for me to see by when the fog rolled into my life.*

"You never had to." Galen's eyes stayed locked on his.

"Degare tried to leave me without a family. But you–" Zephaniah wiped a tear. "You made sure that did not happen."

Galen smiled. "You are my son," she said softly. "I love you too."

A few hours later, in the middle of the night, Zephaniah heard the many footsteps ascending the tower. Without a word, he knew they were coming for him. He had been given time to heal, and his bruises, though still there, were fading. He understood this type of torture. He had seen it done to Ravenna's parents, Gerrin and Willa. Torture until the victim was acquainted and comfortable in death, only to be brought back, never allowed to find relief. Tortured. Healed. Tortured. Healed. It was a torture so cruel that on that altar, even Death itself wept in its longing to free him. Zephaniah guessed it was coming time for the torture to begin again. Today he suspected such a fate, but it was not that fate he spoke of in the letter he hastily scribbled on his last piece of parchment now. His words foretold an eventual fate much more carefully crafted by his tormentors. A torture meant for someone else. As the soldiers' footsteps ascended the tower, he clung to the stick of lead in his hand and could not stop himself from sinking into the shadows of the corner in his cell, praying they did not see him.

Zephaniah pretended to be asleep as the soldier's keys turned in the lock. He kept his eyes closed as the air in the cell fell stale and footsteps entered through the door. Perhaps they would mistake his trembling for discomfort in the cold, or perhaps they knew he was awake, quaking at the feet of darkness. The cracking of rocks and dirt beneath boots sounded around him, and only when he felt the hands on his arms, did he open his eyes.

"King's orders," a familiar voice said. He dropped the stick of lead, and it clanked against the floor.

"Faxon?" Zephaniah asked, and he was unable to suppress a cough as the words trickled out of his dry throat. Faxon was the leader of Zephaniah's battalion.

"You're a traitor, Zephaniah. You were never one of us. You can't talk your way out of this one," Faxon said before guiding him out of the cell toward another soldier Zephaniah recognized. They shackled his wrists and prodded him down the steps toward the bottom of the tower, where he suspected the altar awaited him.

He wondered if Galen had found an opportunity to slip the letters to Ravenna yet, or if she would still be keeping them concealed in the pocket of her apron when she came to heal him again. As they neared the base of the tower, he could see that the halls were swarming with guards, and he guessed it was the latter. It would be difficult for the healer to deliver such things under the watchful gaze of a dozen men.

The door to the dreaded chambers neared, and Zephaniah held his breath against his fate. Galen would get Ravenna those letters. He knew she would. And as long as Zephaniah could give Ravenna one last ounce of hope, as long as they could bring her one more spark of Light, he would be okay.

So he did not fight as the guards pulled him toward the torture chambers, nor did he fight when they dragged him right past the door.

# CHAPTER 2

# THE COLOR THAT STARTS AND ENDS IT ALL

## RAVENNA

**3 weeks ago**

R*ed.*

Followed by the words spoken by her sire, the red came pouring out, trickling down to fill the cracks between her fingers where they clung to the staff.

Red, a single shade of death: bright, slick and condemning.

# THE LIGHT SCROLLS
## THE BOOK OF PROPHECY

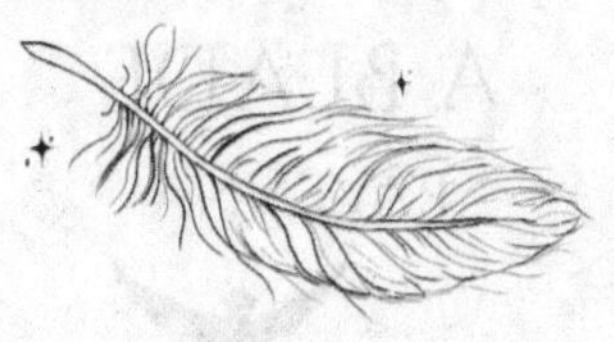

*She who bears wings of sin, his death ushers in.*

CHAPTER 3

# A TORTURE CRAFTED LIKE A BLADE

RAVENNA

**Present day**

"*Ravenna, kill this man for treason.*"

Ravenna stared aimlessly across her expansive new chambers as her mind circled around one name, one face, one life. His was the first of many she would take for her sire. Zephaniah Wilmore. Her friend. Her hope.

Her hope was gone.

Those six words spoken by the king on that evening in the throne room three weeks ago had marked hope's last breath. Those six words were the only ones that echoed through her mind as she sat in the silent darkness of her room. Below her window, the streets of Oro were silent for the first time in days. The Summer Ember Trade had been held in the coliseum the week before, and with it finally over, most of the travelers who had once littered the streets with greed were gone. Ravenna had been lucky to remain hidden in her chambers, tucked away

28

from the misery of the trades. She did not think she could handle any more death.

Ravenna had not even bothered to light a candle when the sun had gone down hours ago. Because the darkness always clouded her vision, day or night, she had seen no point. She could not bear to look at her reflection, which had paled and become little more than flesh and bone. Freckles had once been scattered over her nose and cheeks and across her shoulders, but the little spots that came out with summers spent in the sun were now absent from her shadowmarked skin. Even her hair had changed. With the lack of pure light in the kingdom, the malnourishment she had suffered through the winter in Vestele, the confinement to her cell, and now her chambers, her lengthy locks had darkened to a red tone that was almost as deep as the blood she had spilled.

She tried to shake the memory away, and her eyes clenched tightly until her head pounded in protest. But the image had already set in, and it would not go. It spiraled down into her soul and took root, determined to make her remember that night from three weeks ago. Again. And again. Her mind did not obey her, and it relentlessly wove and stitched the memories together with such precision that even the minuscule details she had nearly forgotten came rushing back.

*The Despiri guards brought Zephaniah before her and pushed him to his knees. His hair, though short, was messy, and the ends dripped with sweat. A bruise spread across his left eye. Not his right. But his right eyebrow had a cut across it, and the blood trickled down so slowly, until a single drop hit the floor between them. She heard it as it landed against the stone, and then she heard the clank of the bloodstone staff against the floor—*

*so close she thought she could reach out to touch it. Somehow, the noise was deafening, yet muffled all at once.*

*She sank further and further into that darkness, and the Light that had once reached for her was long gone. Against her will, as if her hand had a mind of its own, her fingers wrapped around the hilt of the staff that the king had so carelessly tossed to the floor next to her. The golden metal wrapped around a sliver of bloodstone, and slowly, she traced a finger down the red. Cold to the touch, just as she had expected.* Just as it always was every time this memory took her prisoner. *Her heart thundered in her chest as her body moved involuntarily through the next several, agonizing seconds.*

*Zephaniah's gaze held her own. No moment of recognition spread across his face, as if he had come already understanding what awaited him. It was like he already knew that she did not have control of her own movements. He watched her fight the command held in those six, condemning words, and he offered her a smile of sympathy. He, who was about to die, offered her sympathy?*

*"Ravenna, kill this man for treason." Again, she heard the words repeated in the back of her mind. A silent command whispered into the sire bond. This new, unfamiliar tether between a supposed, prophesied Daughter of Light and Darkness Incarnate. Again, she felt her heart stop cold in her chest and then sputter back into a thundering rhythm.*

*No.*

She gasped for air and her eyes burst open. She stood before the vanity, needing to distract herself, to stop her mind from spiraling as it did when she was awake and when she was asleep. Every single moment of every day, she remembered what she had done to him.

She traced the dark, sunken skin beneath her eyes with her pointer finger. Palming the brass comb, she brushed through her hair, carefully avoiding her mother's braid and averting her gaze from the sinful reflection in the mirror. The comb did not pull easily, and she withdrew it from her locks, removing clumps of brittle hair from its teeth. Her shadowmarked hands trembled, from lack of sleep or from the dark power that ravaged her body, she did not know. She brought them to her face and then started tearing.

Hair came out by the handful as she yanked and ripped through it. A scream of frustration and agony and pain sounded before she found herself tossing the vanity onto its side. One of the wooden legs snapped, the mirror shattered, and the metal comb clanked onto the floor. In an instant, Ravenna was back in the throne room.

*It was now the staff that bounced on the ground beside her, bloodstone glinting with the promise of death. Her body betrayed her, slowly, as the sire fought to control her. Her hands wrapped around the metal weapon, shaking uncontrollably with fear. Zeph was before her on his knees with that look of sympathy and sadness. But not for himself. For her. She collapsed onto her own knees before him as the dark power of the sire bond briefly released the grasp that had kept her upright. She wanted so badly to bring a gentle hand to Zephaniah's cheek, to tend to the bruises that painted his face and to the wounds that had spilled the blood that stained his clothes. She wished to draw him up to his feet, to take him and run as far as their legs could carry them. But what Ravenna wanted did not matter. What she wanted was impossible.*

*Perhaps in another life—a life more gracious—she could have fled with him. They would have built their friendship under different circumstances—not in this kingdom where death clawed at their heels. She could have taken him home to Vestele, where her people would be waiting. Vestele never would have burned, and her mother never would have died. The Vestelians would be hesitant to welcome him into the clan, as they never did accept outsiders, but Zephaniah carried the Light with him, and it drew people in. The Vestelians would have come around, and Zephaniah would have gained the family she knew he longed for. He would have no problem making friends with the warriors and Xan.*

*Zephaniah was gentle and kind. But Degare was neither of those things, and he controlled her now. His words were a vise around her spine, urging her to extinguish the only light she had ever known.*

She deserved this pain. She deserved to remember what she had done. As Zephaniah had been tortured in his last days for defending her, Ravenna would torture herself for killing him.

*So, she watched him as he wrapped his fingers around her hands, which held the weapon that would take his life. He spoke soft words that only she could hear. His gray eyes were dull, and his voice was different. Broken. Ravenna knew days of torture would do that to a person. Ravenna felt the darkness within and around her, but as Zephaniah spoke, it was as if the room grew brighter for a short moment.*

*"You must forgive yourself, Ravenna. Not just for this, but for everything else, too." And then, despite the sharp metal of the staff beginning to break through his skin, he smiled another sad smile and lifted his shackled hands to her face. Ravenna struggled against the sire, as she did every time she was brought to this place in her mind, but each time, she was unable to stop her body from sending its strength toward the staff. A tear slipped*

down her face as Zeph held her cheeks in his palms and said words that were far too kind. "Thank you for giving me a purpose." His thumb gently swept her tears away. "Promise me you will find yours."

He had wished her well while she was taking his life. Worse, she knew he had meant it. The genuine hope that he had for her made her sick. Could he still not see that she was not deserving of forgiveness, or hope, or love?

She said nothing. Only stared into his gray eyes, utterly consumed by the sire and her despair and rage that could find no vengeance. Then, he added whispered words that she had clung to, words that could maybe offer her a small piece of hope, unlike the previous sentences he had spoken, which required her to forgive herself for something utterly unforgivable. She knew there would be no redemption for this sin, so these were the words she had held tightly to.

"There will come a time, when seven bloods from seven kingdoms will come together in the Light, and no weapon formed against them shall prosper. Not even you, Ravenna." At that moment, Ravenna's eyes saw the breaking dawn, though she knew it to still be night. A strange ray of golden sun shone on him through the tall windows of the throne room, and Ravenna wondered if anyone else had noticed or if she had only imagined it. The Light seemed to encompass him as the words flowed from his mouth like prophecy. For some reason, she believed them. She had to believe them. Because the alternative was believing she would be stuck under Degare's sire for the rest of her life. And still, maybe she would be the king's to control until her last breath. But these words Zephaniah had spoken, they gave her hope that her breaths would be few.

The staff shifted in her hands, and she glanced down to

*where its sharp tip had broken the skin on his chest. Fighting the sire did nothing except summon insurmountable pain. Her arms burned as she struggled against the king's command, as if they were melting beneath flames, but still, they continued to add more pressure to the staff. "I am so sorry. I am so sorry. I am so sorry." She repeated the phrase over and over as the weapon plunged through him and he swayed. "Zephaniah." She could not stop the desperate words that poured from her mouth. "I am so sorry. I am so sorry. I am so sorry."*

*He held her gaze until his last breath, until his body slumped to the side and lay lifeless on the floor, drenched in red. She only stared at him, repeating those four words, wishing that she could join him.*

*I am so sorry.*

*The sound of Degare's satisfaction rumbled through the darkening room as Ravenna released the staff and retreated backward, trying to put space between herself and her lifeless friend. Her heart fell silent, and the vision of breaking dawn dissipated back into night. The throne room spun, and the voices around her felt distant, like she was under the water in the Edmarian River once more, and her name was being called from above the ice.*

*I am so sorry.*

*"Very good!" Degare clapped. Clapped, while her friend lay dead by her own hands.*

*Ravenna vomited.*

*She heaved and clutched her chest against the unbearable pain that had taken root in her soul. The king spoke again and ordered the Despiri guards to remove him. They moved at once, obeying his order just as she had. But Ravenna knew they still had free will while she did not. The Despiri guards chose to be* here. Just as they had chosen to kill innocent Embers for their gifts.

Both Jio and Jara were smiling at Ravenna from beside Degare's throne, and anger took her at the sight of the guards dragging Zeph away, at the sight of his blood smearing across the floor. They carried him with such carelessness, with no regard or respect for the life his body had just parted with. Ravenna wiped her mouth with the back of her hand, and her stare did not leave Zephaniah until he was on the other side of the wooden doors. Only then, did she turn her face to her sire with unruly rage. Her entire body began to tremble, starting at her very core, like a shockwave ready to burst the seams of the earth.

The power she had acquired when Jara finished the spell was strange. What had come from Degare felt different than the power from the stone she had once worn around her neck. This power was even darker than that from the bloodstone, and Ravenna did not wish to touch it, but she tunneled into it with all her might anyway, burrowing down into its depths with all the strength she had. With no knowledge on how to use it, let alone control it, she expected the explosion would bring utter destruction—an earthquake from within. She saw no other option than to fall into this darkness—to destroy the king.

The river of power begged for release, and she would burst the dam on the king, who sat satisfied on his throne amid her ruin. She did not know what would happen when she released the hold she had on her power; she did not care. She was certain it was enough to kill him, a king who now held no special gifts or power to defend his frail human body. A deep breath flooded through her, and just as she readied to send her new, wild power toward the throne, a malicious female voice rang out into the air around her.

*"I would not do that, Ravenna, dear." The power stalled for a moment. In all her rage, Ravenna had nearly forgotten the witch existed. Jara tilted her chin as a smug smile painted her thin lips. Ravenna looked back toward the wooden doors, which had just swallowed the body of her last friend in the world. The power swelled just under her skin, and she could feel it pushing and pleading to be freed from the new body which now encapsulated it—but there was a hint of something else there. An emotion that was not her own. An emotion that had some level of control over her.*

*She turned back to the witch, who stood tall next to Degare's throne. Her long, skinny fingers moved against the velvet back of the chair, and her orange eyes crawled with complacence. Ravenna's eyes slid to Degare's, where that strange emotion of smugness seemed to be coming from. Jio and Degare looked to be having an internal conversation, Degare sitting seemingly satisfied on his throne. Perhaps he was learning the details of this new arrangement.*

*Jara directed her prideful stare to Degare, who seemed delighted with her. Ravenna almost laughed as she readied to send her power toward Degare. Nothing happened, but that emotion she had pinpointed as Degare's spun into something new: a fear for his life.*

*He feared her for only a moment before Jara began again, cackling, and the sound sent Ravenna's jaw tensing with anger. "You foolish girl. You do not know how to use your power yet. You'll need training." The witch picked at her fingernails as she spoke. Ravenna spied the dagger that she had planned to kill Degare with—before everything had gone so wrong. She refused to live as his slave. In a swift motion, she grabbed the weapon and brought it to her own throat.*

*As she started to swipe, and a warm trickle of blood slipped down to her collar bone, that same fear returned to her as if it were her own. The king's voice yelled out in worried haste. "Do not harm yourself!" Her hand stiffened. She watched in shock as the dagger clanked against the stone at her feet. For a moment, her eyes studied her hands as if there would be physical signs of their betrayal. Then, she bent to quickly collect it from the ground. "Do not harm me, either," said the king. Her backup plan was immediately halted by his spoken command. She could not comprehend it. He had physically lost his power, but he controlled every nerve in her body. She was his power. He now feared for her life as much as he did his own.*

*She fell to her knees again, without restraint, and her bones crashed into the stone. There would be no escape. The king's demands and rules were barked toward where she crumpled onto the floor. She could barely hear the commands over the sound of the guilty blood rushing in her ears. She felt nothing and everything all at once. Brokenness. Hopelessness. Grief. Guilt. Guilt of such intensity that she could not breathe.*

*"You will not end your life."*

*Breathe.*

*"You will not harm yourself unless I command otherwise."*

*Breathe.*

*"You will not harm me."*

*Breathe.*

*"You will kill anyone who tries to do either. You will not try to escape. You will serve as my guard, my weapon."*

*Breathe.*

*"Whatever is asked of you, you will follow each one of my orders, until your last breath."*

*Stop.*

Jara tapped her fingers at the back rest of his throne. He looked to her once, and added, "And you will not harm my witch." Jara's wicked eyes flashed at those words, and she held her head a little higher.

Ravenna only stared at the king with cold, calm rage as the guards pulled her out of the throne room, toward her future of utter darkness. Under Degare's reign, she would become a messenger of death to all Light, and there was no way out. The King of Oro stared back at her in satisfaction.

Her hope was dead, and Degare had won the war.

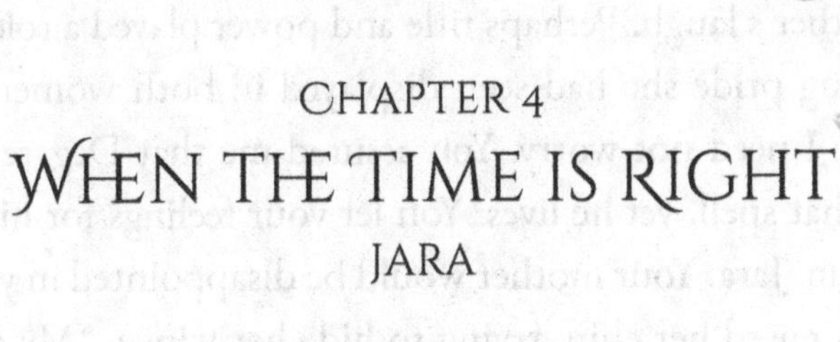

# CHAPTER 4
# WHEN THE TIME IS RIGHT
## JARA

Jara sat atop an onyx mare, its hooves clicking against the dark stone streets of Oro as she rode toward the Black Temple. She tugged her cloak over her head and traveled east until she saw the flash of silver hair and the face of the Delle Witch Queen. Jara had been anticipating this meeting since she had set it up over two weeks ago via handwritten request.

Norell stood with her back to the wall, silver threads encompassing the majority of her cloak. She did not bother hiding her identity in this kingdom, but Jara hid her own. Being seen scheming with the Queen of the Delle Witches, when she was supposed to be loyal to Degare, would end with her in the gallows. What had her devotion to the king gotten her? She had gained nothing but a bedroom chamber and a job without reward.

"If it isn't the traitor herself," Norell said as she pushed off the wall, her silver hair flowing out around her shoulders, seeming to blend with the shimmering threads of her cloak. Norell crossed her arms and waited for Jara's excuse. At Jara's silence, Norell let out a wicked laughter that reminded Jara of her mother's laugh. Perhaps title and power played a role in the bellowing pride she had seen displayed in both women. "You told me I need not worry. You assured me that Degare would die in that spell, yet he lives. You let your feelings for him stop you again, Jara. Your mother would be disappointed in you."

Jara raised her chin, trying to hide her wince. "My mother would understand once she saw the grand scheme. I have a plan."

"A plan you could not tell me of weeks ago, when you lied to me and told me Degare would die?"

"He will die," Jara said. "But the time was not right." That statement was a lie. Jara had been too weak to kill him. But after the fact, she regretted letting him live. She regretted gifting him life with Ravenna as his weapon. But she had not been so foolish as to give him all the power. Because of her quick cleverness with the spell after someone—perhaps Galen Bauer—had broken into her chambers to alter it, there was a way for Jara and the witches to claim Ravenna as their own.

"You are a snake," Norell hissed. "You've requested to meet with me, for what? To offer me more empty promises? Do you not know that your words mean nothing to me?"

Jara handed her a letter and prompted her to read it. She hoped this would be enough proof of a plan to convince Norell to trust her again. She only needed one more chance. Degare would not manipulate her again. "What of those words? Do they mean something to you?"

Norell examined the broken seal and opened it. When she

finished reading the message, she looked at Jara skeptically. "Okay. So you have a plan," Norell acknowledged. Jara nodded. *A very good one at that.* "Since you're the rightful queen of the clan, it's only sensible for you to be the one to find us a place to call home." Jara nodded. "However, unlike you, I do not care about the title but the safety and continuation of our clan. It seems you are only after your mother's throne. What of the indestructible weapon you've just made for Degare?" Norell asked. "That rumor is true, isn't it? Are you a fool? How will we fare against Oro with her on his side?" Jara was a fool for love, but she had never been too deep in love to protect her own interests. She always knew the way out of the messes she made. Whether or not she was ready to act on them, was another story.

"I did the spell and I created one way to break the sire. I know how to claim the weapon as my own when the time comes. The throne is mine, Norell. And I intend to deliver the witches more than a home. Once they are settled there," she gestured to the letter, "and can gather to prepare for battle against Degare's Despiri soldiers, I intend to deliver them this entire kingdom."

*And then the world.*

Norell studied her, as if trying to figure out if she could trust her. If Jara was honest, she was not even sure if she could trust herself. In order to break the sire, she would need to set aside all feelings for Degare and view him as little more than a means to an end. She would play his games until the time was right, and she would have to guard herself against his influence in the meantime.

Norell spoke with sternness. "Only when my clan sets foot

in this land, only when we *rise* as you have claimed we will, will I hand my title over to you." Jara nodded in understanding. She would reclaim her mother's throne. It was all she had ever intended to do, before she had met Degare. "Do not let that man make a fool of you again, Jara Delle."

# CHAPTER 5
# THE DARKNESS THAT SURROUNDS US

### RAVENNA

"Let me in, dear."

Ravenna said nothing. Felt nothing.

"You need to eat. The power will take every ounce of nutrients your body has left. I have breakfast. Open the door."

*Silence.*

Food would not fill the void within her. Nothing could fill the black hole that had cracked open inside of her soul. Ravenna heard rustling outside as Galen's hand slid down the other side of the door frame in defeat. Ravenna winced at the sound of her breakfast plate clanking against the floor, where it would go untouched until the servants collected it at lunch time.

Her stomach growled, but she did not move from the window bench where she sat staring into the dreary kingdom square.

There was another rustle, and Ravenna slowly turned her attention to the crack beneath the door, where she'd watched dozens of mice scuttle over the past few weeks. A small stack of ripped parchment slid into view.

Still, she did not move.

"He wrote those for you. From the tower, before. . ." Galen's voice trailed off. *Before you killed him.*

Ravenna allowed no breath to fill her lungs until she heard Galen's footsteps retreating down the hall. Only then, did Ravenna inhale slowly. But still, she did not move toward the letters. Not when the servants came and knocked in the afternoon, and not when the sun had set beyond the cliffs that hung over the Black Sea. She did not move until it was time for bed and she could feel the nightmares approaching.

When the room was filled with darkness, and she felt she could use a little light, she unfolded the letter from the top of the stack. She struck a match and lit the candle beside her bed.

The warm glow illuminated the page, and she could read his quickly scribbled writing, as if he had been afraid to get caught.

*Ravenna,*

*If you're reading this, that means Galen was able to get my letters to you, and I am probably still in the tower. I've not received a sentence yet, but if I had to guess, it is one of death. Still, I do not regret any of it. You have to know that. I don't want you to worry. I am confident in the Father's plans in all of this.*

*It is killing me, not being able to come to you. There is so much more I wish I would have said. Things you have to know. A love you need to understand. But I am realizing now, that it was never my duty to break through to you the wonder of the Light. Though, perhaps my hands have sown a seed in you, and I pray one will come along and water it—to make it clear to you that you are never too far gone. But Ravenna, you must open your eyes and see that the Light is all around you. It never left, but it cannot dwell within you until you allow it. Do not let the darkness blind you.*

Ravenna's throat tightened. He had been hopeful. But that was before she had done the unforgivable. She doubted Zephaniah would cling with such certainty to that same hope now. Because she was too far gone. She felt it at her core.

Ravenna wiped her eyes and continued reading the letter.

*They are holding me in your cell. I've spent more time in the torture chambers this week than I ever did as a soldier, but I now find rest in the tower, no matter how cold and hard the ground is. You were right. It is quite uncomfortable. They confiscated our books, and the cloak disappeared, too, so the nights have been cold.*

Ravenna looked to the scraps of his raven embroidered cloak on her dresser. It had been here when she first woke after the breaking of the stone, and it had served as a reminder of him every day since.

*They had to reinforce the door because of the blast when you broke the stone. Galen brought me the supplies to write with. As long as my hands work, I'll write to you when I can.*

She unfolded another one.

*Galen says Cove is in and out of your chambers. I met her once—I think she'll take good care of you. You're on my mind daily, and I pray you'll come to the Light. Do not let the shadowmarks worry you. You are never too far gone. His Light shines through any darkness. My hope is to see you again someday with the coming Dawn.*

If the Dawn he spoke of was the day when the Light would come to burn up every shadow, he would not see her. No, because if all of it was true, she would burn up with the darkness on that day. The judgment she would fall under was deserved. Ravenna crumpled the letter and unfolded yet another.

*Do not blame yourself for any of it. Not for my fate, not for anyone's. You cannot. It will tear you in two. None of it is your doing. It is of the darkness that surrounds us. So, fight it, Ravenna. Fight it with everything you've got.*

*Your friend,*

*Zephaniah Wilmore*

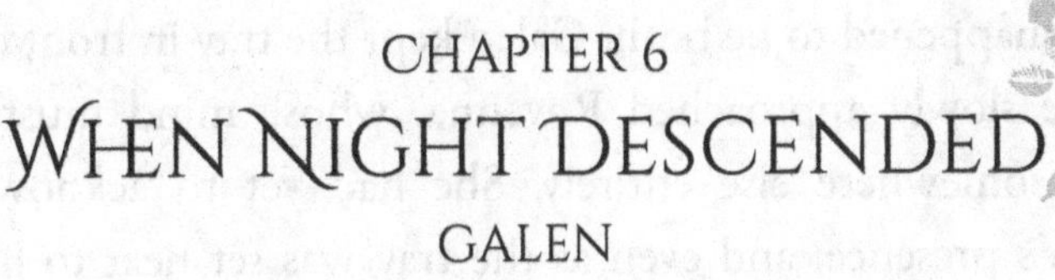

# CHAPTER 6
# WHEN NIGHT DESCENDED
## GALEN

Day after day, Galen returned to Ravenna's chambers, just as she had to Zephaniah's cell—until the morning she had climbed the tower to find it empty, with only a stack of parchment and a quickly scribbled letter left on the grimy floor. That was one of the letters she had not given to Ravenna, but had delivered to the loft in the library under the cover of night. The cryptic words on that page had broken her, and she would not allow them to break Ravenna too. If Galen was being honest, though, she did not think there was anything in the Dove left to break.

Galen cleared her throat from where she lingered in the hall, trying to keep that knot from forming. Currently, there were no guards posted outside Ravenna's chambers, and for that, Galen was grateful. She collected herself and wiped her eyes before knocking twice on the door. As usual, there was no answer. Galen pushed the door open slowly, scanning the room to find the mourning Dove of Ozanna sitting on the window bench. Her red hair cascaded down her back as she stared out into the square below. Galen swallowed as she surveyed the new cuts and bruises on the Dove's body.

"I brought lunch," she said. She was only sanctioned by the witch to come during mealtimes or after torture sessions, and today happened to be both. Galen kept the tray in front of her as she slowly approached Ravenna, whose mind must have been somewhere else entirely. She had yet to acknowledge Galen's presence, and even as the tray was set next to her on that bench, she remained silent and still, staring emptily forward, wrapped in bloodstained clothes.

Ravenna flinched as Galen's gentle hand found her arm. "Let's get you to the tub, dear," Galen said, smoothing her hair. "Come on," she said, offering Ravenna a hand. "Let me help you." Ravenna's near colorless eyes blinked back into reality, and she peered down at her once-white linen dress, where red now festered.

She rose violently at once, and Galen backed away as the tray was shoved from the window bench in a fluid motion. "Get this off of me!" Ravenna screamed, tearing at the stained garment. "Get it off!" Ravenna yanked at the clothes, aggravating the wounds on her arms and stimulating more blood flow.

Galen stepped forward with her hands low as her heart broke. "I will help you. Let me help you," she said gently, speaking through the quake in her voice. Ravenna looked up at her in a way that suggested she had not fully realized she was there, and her eyes softened for only a moment before she began grabbing at her clothes again. "It's okay. You're okay," Galen said as she unlaced the back while Ravenna fidgeted. Galen guided her into the tub and then gathered water from the buckets near the fireplace.

One by one, Galen lifted the buckets and spilled them into the tub. The water turned pink around Ravenna, and before she could look, Galen got to her knees to be eye level with her. "Just close your eyes. You are safe with me. As long as I am here, I will not let the darkness touch you." Galen choked on the lies, and the guilt she bore became tangible as she peered on Ravenna's wounds and shadowmarks. The darkness had touched her already. It was taking its hold, and there was nothing Galen could do to stop it. She could offer her no true healing. This was a matter of devastation that only the Father of Lights could mend.

Galen arrived in those chambers day by day, always afraid to look upon the ruin that breathed within, always unable to create a spark in the Dove that Arresia so desperately needed. Too quickly, the bones in Ravenna's shoulders became visible. The hair on her head became brittle and dull. Shadowmarks plagued her, and her freckles faded into the skin that was now void of color. Her voice rarely sounded, and her gaze was empty. Over the following weeks, Galen watched helplessly as the mourning Dove plucked her own feathers, as she cracked her beak and refused to eat, and as she perched on that windowsill without a song.

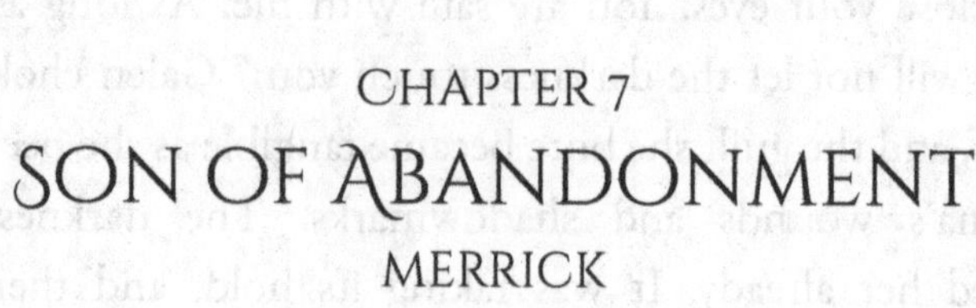

# CHAPTER 7
# SON OF ABANDONMENT
## MERRICK

Merrick watched silently from against the wall as his father, King Idris of Edmaria, tore his brother's chambers to pieces. This room inside the Sand Palace had been empty for months now, and Andreas had been dead for half of them. Merrick's brother, the eldest prince of Edmaria had traveled to the Dawn Islands and never returned.

"My son is dead, Jamila. Killed by one of *them. An Ember.* They must pay." His father turned his face toward Jamila, revealing his creeping shadowmarks and a hateful stare. Merrick stiffened.

"And they will," Jamila said gently, eyes sweeping to Merrick, pleading for assistance. "At the trades. You'll go and you'll kill as many as you can afford." Merrick swallowed as his father's new wife tried to talk him off one cliff and onto another. She was far too young to be dealing with such things. She was a year younger than Merrick, and had her engagement to him not been broken by his father's wishes to claim her as his own wife, she would have lived comfortably, as royalty, with no true responsibilities. Because Idris had never intended for Merrick to take the throne. It had always been Andreas. "You are a king, Idris. You can afford a fine selection," Jamila offered.

Idris waved her off. "I will not limit myself to rely on Degare's quarterly trades to repay what one of their kind has done to Andreas. It is not enough. I want the very Ember who killed my heir." Merrick chewed on the inside of his lip, watching carefully as Jamila–the young duchess to whom he was once engaged to–took the place that was once his mother's, comforting his father with a soft caress. The Duchess of Matuk, Brinland was a strange choice for his father. Merrick had not expected his father to remarry after his mother had abandoned them, but he had, spitefully making a wife out of his own son's betrothed.

Merrick did not allow himself to think about it. He had pondered on the subject enough these past few months. He shifted on his feet, and the king's eyes flashed toward him, trailing up his arm and landing on his face. The face that resembled his mother's. "Get out!" his father screamed, and Jamila winced beside him, offering Merrick an apologetic glance. He breathed tightly as his gaze dropped to her neck.

His father's hatred for him was a tale as old as time. Merrick was a disappointment, and Merrick was now his only heir. Merrick turned on his feet, thankful for the permission to leave. He never felt so much anger as he did in his father's company, and he hated the feeling that brewed in his bones, the thoughts that took him captive as he stood wishing it was his father and not his mother who had left him.

"That boy is weak!" Idris's yells followed Merrick around the corner. His father used the term *boy,* because in his eyes, Merrick was not a man. There was a thundering crash as

Merrick assumed the bookcase was tipped over by his father's uncontrolled Despiri power. Merrick took a breath as he imagined Jamila cowering in the corner. But she was no longer his responsibility, so he continued forward, leaving her with his rageful, grieving father.

The kingdom was better off without Andreas, and his death had, at the least, delayed an alliance with the Dawn Islands that would have further rooted Edmaria in darkness. Perhaps this *Light* the Embers so worshiped was beginning to creep back into the lands. If it was, both Merrick and his father would be doomed to Eternal Darkness.

Among all the weapons, the sword felt most unnatural in Merrick's hand. But he practiced daily, if not to impress his father, then to pass the time.

"You can do better than that!" Kenan yelled, advancing forward and pushing his thick hair out of his eyes. Sweat trickled down Merrick's brow as he took two steps back, avoiding the swipe of his friend's sword.

Merrick ducked and swung low until his blade clashed with Kenan's silver armor. Kenan pushed back until Merrick was pinned against the exterior wall of the Sand Palace.

"Looks like I will forever be stuck as your bodyguard since there is no way you could defend yourself against an attacker." Merrick tossed his blade to the side, and Kenan backed up, shaking the sweat from his dark curls. "What are you doing, Prince? Pick it up. Let's go!"

Merrick's gaze was fixed on the duchess, who was now

hovering behind Kenan, waiting to speak. "What is it, Jamila?" Merrick asked gruffly, stepping around his guard.

The duchess's dark hair was unbound, suspiciously covering her left eye. Her bright purple wrap contrasted against her brown skin, partially covering the shadowmarks that traveled from her neck to the top of her shoulder. "Your father has accepted the offer." Kenan looked between the two of them, and Merrick stood silently. He nodded, setting his jaw. After many months of uncertainty and rumors, the alliance was going to be official.

"Very well then," he muttered, watching the dust fill the air as he clapped his hands together.

"What does that mean?" Kenan asked, crossing his arms as he looked between the two of them, his gaze lingering on the duchess.

"It means I am to marry Princess Mina of the Dawn Islands," Merrick said, carefully watching Jamila as Kenan whipped his head back toward Merrick.

Jamila ducked her head in confirmation and spoke again. "Queen," Jamila corrected him. Merrick blinked. "King Sebastian of the Dawn Islands has finally died of the illness that plagued him, and now Mina sits on the throne," Jamila explained. "Soon after your father has returned from the trades, you shall go to her." Merrick watched her throat bob as she turned to go on her way. He started after her, reaching for the purple fabric of her gown, and then he paused, turning to his friend.

Kenan's eyes trailed her as she went. "Prepare a team for travel," Merrick said. Kenan blinked. "I'd like to visit the country home one more time before I am to cross the sea which led my brother into death." Kenan nodded, and with a sidelong glance, he started toward the stables to alert the stable masters. "I cannot spend one more moment in this palace," Merrick muttered beneath his breath, and then he sighed before pursuing Jamila.

"Duchess!" Merrick called behind her. Her steps sped up and she turned the corner, entering the east side of the palace. She slipped behind a curtain, and he inhaled deeply before going in after her.

Her hands found him immediately, pulling him into the shadows where they would not be seen. "Jamila, no. We cannot do this," he said, gently pushing her away. He turned his back to her, running his fingers through his dark, chin-length hair, which was damp from sweating beneath the heat of the afternoon Edmarian sun.

"This was supposed to be us, Merrick." She fiddled with the gaudy wedding band on her finger. "You are to marry, and once you've gone to the Dawn Islands, we will not see each other again," she said. He set his jaw. "We have waited too long," she said, her hands smoothing down his arms.

He hesitated for a moment before shaking her off. He spun in a slow circle, and then, almost involuntarily, his finger was tracing her jaw. His teeth gritted at the sight of the bruise that colored her eye, and he released an unsteady breath as she began to slip her gown off her shoulder.

"I shall not covet my father's wife," he whispered, catching the fabric of her gown and securing it with her golden broach. "You must stop with this. You are married."

Her hands wandered across his chest, and her lips grew nearer to his with each breath, her gaze fixed on his mouth.

"No," he said, backing away. *I have to get out of this kingdom.* She reached for him again, eyes pleading. "I am leaving this evening, Jamila. I am to spend the rest of my time in this kingdom apart from you."

"I cannot stay here with him. You have no idea the things he is capable of. Take me with you," she begged. It broke him, the way their friendship had faded with her betrayal, and the way he still found himself longing for her. He could not seem to escape the sense of responsibility he once had for her but was no longer required. *You can be free of her,* he told himself. *This is goodbye.* He swallowed and crossed his arms, tucking his hands away.

"You should have thought about that before you began with your antics. You are the one who chose to get involved with my father while we were still engaged." *And with my brother before that,* he thought. Were her claws in him so deep that he truly could not tear himself away from her after all of this hurt? She started toward him again, and he held up a hand, still unable to remove himself from the guilt that came with that bruise on her cheek. He shook his head, regretfully. "There is nothing I can do for you."

"He abuses me, Merrick." Merrick took a breath, refusing to look at her–at the swelling across her cheekbone that made him hate his father even more. The same pain reflected on her face that he had seen on his mother's a hundred times before she had left. Could he blame his mother for leaving, when this had been her life?

"You think I do not know that? You think anyone in this kingdom is oblivious to that? He did not marry you for your position in Brinland, Duchess. He doesn't even care enough to consider you his *queen*. He married you to spite me and that is all. I am sorry it was not for love, but there is nothing I can do that will not end in both of our slaughters. And believe me, if he can find a reason to have my head, he will not hesitate."

"He would not kill his only heir," she argued.

Merrick scoffed. "When you bear him a son," he spat, looking to her womb, "or maybe even a daughter—yes, he will."

"Not if you've successfully allied Edmaria with The Dawn Islands, though," she said.

"Well, then I guess I better not mess that up," he said, yanking the curtain to the side and leaving her where she stood.

# CHAPTER 8
# NO MORALITY
## RAVENNA

"Ravenna."

Ravenna opened her eyes at the sound of the king's gravelly voice outside of the thick, wooden door to her chambers. She winced at the twinge of pain that slithered down her spine with his spoken command.

"Ravenna, come."

She was beside her bed, curled in the fetal position on the stone floor. Her nightmare followed her into the day as she rose to her feet and limped toward his beckoning call. She had fallen asleep to the sound of witch guardians snarling in the streets below as she read letters from Zephaniah and Galen. She quickly kicked them under the chest by the window.

*Fight it, Ravenna. Fight it with everything you've got*, Zeph had written. She had read those words a hundred times these last few weeks. A deep, shaky breath entered her lungs as her hand found the bronze doorknob.

She hesitated for a moment, struggling against the invisible prodding at her back, but then pulled it open to reveal the king and his Despiri in the hall. Degare's hair had darkened significantly since Ravenna had taken the burden of his power, and the once deep wrinkles on his face had become little more than fine lines.

"Better timing than yesterday," Degare said cheerfully, tapping his fingers across the top of that wretched bloodstone staff. "Tomorrow shall be even better."

Ravenna stood in defeat as a Despiri shackled her wrists and led her toward the stone altar where Zephaniah and her parents had laid almost two months ago—where she had laid nearly every day since. She had no defiance left in her bones, no will to fight the treacherous feet that took her forward by Degare's silent command.

They passed by many curious soldiers who were overseeing the work of slaves of all ages. Not all were lightmarked Embers. Some were what Ravenna assumed to be Lumes, as Zephaniah had once spoken of. Not worshippers of the darkness, but not true followers of the Light, either. According to Zephaniah, when the Father of Lights first sent His Light to dwell within His followers four hundred years ago, the Lumes who had true faith in Him received that Light and became Embers. By definition, that would mean that these Lumes were placing their faith elsewhere, whether knowingly or not.

Ravenna understood none of it. What was the purpose of faith, and why must one have it? Zephaniah had believed in a place of Eternal Light with the Father that Embers—because of their faith—go to when they die. He had also explained that the gifted ones were those who had faith that the Father of Lights could overcome any darkness. But if there truly were a god of pure Light and all things good, Ravenna was the epitome of darkness. Even if He could overcome the darkness within her, why would He spare her in doing so? Her death would be justified in the presence of a judge undefiled like Him. There would be a need for atonement after all the wrongs she had committed, the shadows she now entertained, and nothing would suffice. She would never rest in the Eternal Light Zephaniah had spoken of.

Degare did not care about technicalities. Light or no Light within, these people were traitors to the darkness. Each one of the king's slaves strained a too-fragile body to collect the fallen rock in the halls from the night Ravenna had broken the stone. Dolefully, they loaded wooden carts and wheeled them down the torchlit halls of the castle to somewhere out of sight.

A voice bellowed through the halls. "You! Get up!" Ravenna's eyes darted to the group of soldiers to her right, where an elderly Ember man had fallen in exhaustion. He was lying flat on the stone, and slowly turned his eyes to hers. "Get up!" The crack of a whip followed, and Ravenna lunged forward as if to save him, but her chains, both figurative and tangible, reminded her that she was Degare's slave now. She broke his gaze, unable to watch any longer as she abandoned him. Ravenna ducked her head in shame as the Despiri and Degare escorted her through the mess she had made. Was it a blessing or a curse that her thoughts were still her own?

The winding entry to the torture chambers seemed to close in around her as she walked through the glints and gleams of the metal tools in the torchlight.

Quietly, she took her place on the stone slab.

Like clockwork, the guards tied her wrists and ankles.

She listened to the sound of metal scraping against stone as Degare dragged his knife against the wall. "I can feel your resistance to the bond between us, Ravenna. I need you to

submit, wholly. Whatever is holding you back, let it go."
Ravenna blinked the cowardly tears from her eyes as she stared
up at the stalactite covered ceiling. The downward spikes
seemed to tremble, as if there were a hidden vibration coming
from the uttermost parts of the earth.

The bond between her and the king had already stolen her
free will. She would do whatever he said; her body would not
allow otherwise. But that was not enough for him. Resistance,
no matter how small, frightened him. He wanted her
conscience too, and Ravenna had come to realize over the past
seven weeks that her conscience was the one thing she could
hold onto. Though he had tried, he could not simply
command her to give it up. That was why she found herself on
this altar.

Degare wanted to be sure that her obedience would never
have the chance to falter. He wanted to change the parts of her
that made her, her. The king was trying to take every last piece,
leaving no room for defiance, and she was losing hold. With
each of his commands, with each cut of a blade, Ravenna
Zenevieva Barrett Ozanne was succumbing to the shadows.
And as he wished, she was losing sight of herself—getting lost in
the darkness that tied her soul to his.

*Soon,* the sire seemed to whisper. *Soon you'll be all mine.*

Ravenna clenched every muscle in her body, fighting the
pull to become that blindly obedient weapon that Degare was
forging her into.

She had to hold on to the voice of reason within her. Just a
little longer.

*There will come a time, when seven bloods from seven
kingdoms will come together in the Light, and no weapon formed
against them shall prosper. Not even you, Ravenna.*

She clung to Zephaniah's final spoken words to her, to the hope he had offered. It was that hope that she waited for.

"I need you to serve me with no hesitation. With no hint of quarrel in your mind. When you prove your loyalty to me, when I am sure you have been broken, we can stop this nonsense," the king said, turning the small blade over in his hands. "Give in to me." The waning voice in her mind pulled her in two directions.

*Fight.*

*Let go.*

*Fight.*

There was red in every place where the blade met her skin, and the hours spent in the torture chambers were slow, but Ravenna did not break. Not today.

The Despiri guards had to carry her back to her room.

Galen found her where she had collapsed just beside the tub with her body of broken bones and bleeding skin. Ravenna could not bear to look the healer in the eyes. She deserved no healing, no relief–however temporary it may be. Ravenna knew Galen saw her assignment as torture. To keep Ravenna alive, only so she could be broken again tomorrow. The healer had been forced to do the same to Zephaniah, and in the end, Ravenna had been the one to deliver him into death–to finally release him of his misery. But like Galen, Ravenna refused to see what she had done as a kindness.

Galen removed what was left of Ravenna's clothing and hoisted her up, guiding her into the bath. As Galen rubbed a wet cloth over Ravenna's skin, blood clouded the water around her, and the healer began determining which of her wounds would need stitching. Ravenna closed her eyes. The sound of a jar opening graced Ravenna's ears, and she awaited the salve that was sure to bring a touch of comfort. She had been in this same position many times before, begging for the healer to just *let her die.* But like every other time, Galen would not.

"You're the Dove of Ozanna," she said quietly. Ravenna's head lopped to the side as Galen propped her against the edge of the tub. *I cannot let you die,* she seemed to say. Ravenna's gaze fell on her wardrobe of red fabrics just outside the door, and Galen's gentle hand gripped Ravenna's jaw, trying to gain her attention. "You must fight, Ravenna." *Fight it with everything you've got.*

Ravenna did not want to fight any longer. Her eyes avoided the healer's gaze at all costs, and she did not move. Not until Galen had attended to her for the evening and had left her alone in her pity. "Choose the Light," Galen said from where she paused at the door before she had left. "If not for yourself, for Zephaniah."

Ravenna was unsure how long she was frozen in her filth, completely silent as her mind twisted around the memory of him, before the pumice stone at the edge of the bath found her unrelenting grip. She began to scrub every inch of herself away. She rubbed herself raw. The backs of the hands that had betrayed her. The arms that had taken that staff forward, toward her only friend. The feet that willingly walked her into torture each day. Her scars, both old and new. Every bit of weak flesh that would soon completely give into her sire–she scraped them all away. Her stitches, undone, until red poured from her once more and darkened the bath. Screams of frustration filtered through gritted teeth.

*Give in,* the sire bond whispered. *Give up the fight, and you'll find relief.*

*It is a lie,* Ravenna told herself. There could be no relief. After what she had done, she did not believe that she could ever feel clean. The memory would always live on within her, whether she had surrendered her conscience to her sire or not.

She could not outrun the hauntings of what she had done. Even if she could, she would not allow herself to forget.

In the coming weeks, when she was sure she would finally give in and the sire bond would take her morality, this guilt was what she would cling to. This one reminder of what Degare had done. Of what *she* had done.

She gathered some hair into her fingers. "For Zephaniah," she whispered as she weaved a new braid of sin and guilt and shame beside her mother's.

## CHAPTER 9
# A HEALER'S PERSISTENCE
### RAVENNA

"I am not leaving until you clear your plate."

Ravenna heard the curtains being yanked, and she sighed and cracked her eyelids open from where she lay on the drafty window bench. She shielded her eyes against the afternoon light, though it was dim in comparison to the sun in Vestele. Galen stood stout before her with her arms crossed. A silver platter of meats and cheeses lay next to Ravenna's feet on top of the brown fur hide.

"Why do you even bother with me?" Ravenna asked, sighing at the decadent tray of food as she sat up. It had been two months since she had killed Zephaniah, and Galen was still here, showing her kindness.

"I made a promise long ago to protect you. This is me ensuring you survive," Galen said sternly.

"I think it is safe to say you can forget about your little prophecy that I'll usher in the Light to Arresia. Besides, I thought you were just following the king's orders. Did he command you to watch me eat too?"

64

Galen shook her head, gesturing to Ravenna's bony arms and pale skin. "You're wasting away, dear."

"If Degare could not handle half the power I possess, what do you think is going to happen to me? It is only a matter of time." Ravenna avoided her gaunt reflection in the standing mirror behind Galen and tugged the platter toward her.

"You were destined for unmatched power, Ravenna. Your body is built for it. His isn't. Almost anyone else in your position would be dead, or well on their way to it. You need nourishment. That power in your veins, it uses a lot of energy."

Ravenna turned a piece of meat over between her fingers. "My body may have been destined for power as you say, but the power that fills it now is made from death. You do not think that will take a toll on me? A toll I cannot outrun, even with proper nourishment?" Ravenna could only hope.

"Just eat, girl. I do not think your sire would like it if you died because you refused to eat." Ravenna gritted her teeth at the reminder that she was not allowed to end her life, when starving herself would do just that. She plopped the piece of meat into her mouth, chewing slowly.

"I killed him, Galen, and you're holding out for what?" Galen's eyes shot to the floor, and Ravenna did not miss the quiver in her lip. "Why are you showing me kindness?" Ravenna jerked the blanket from the window seat and stood on her feet. "Heal me so they can torture me, again and again, if you must. That, I deserve. But do not offer me anything more than a beat in my chest. Every day that I live, I should suffer. Do not bring me food, or comfort, and do not try to convince me to *hope*."

"Someone has to," Galen said, sitting down on the bed. Ravenna gave her an incredulous look.

*Why will she not leave me alone?* The healer patted the bed next to her, and though her shame was eating her alive, Ravenna reluctantly joined her.

After a long moment, Galen, staring forward, uttered the words that broke Ravenna. "No one told me, you know? No one said anything about him being taken. I didn't know that he was gone until I went to deliver his breakfast the next morning and found the cell empty." Her voice cracked. "I thought–hoped–they had sent him to the mines with the other prisoners. But that hope didn't last longer than a few seconds. Jara came to me with new orders, and I knew. I knew he was dead before she proudly told me the details." Out of the corner of her eye, Ravenna saw the healer wipe a tear away. "You are not just an assignment from the king or the witch, Ravenna." Galen's words became shaky. "I promised him. I promised Zephaniah that I would be here for you when he could not be."

Ravenna swallowed the rising knot in her throat. Why were there so many promises surrounding her? So many oaths? So much hope, when she clearly had nothing left?

Ravenna took another bite of meat, and with her mouth full, she muttered, "You seem to make a lot of promises you can't keep."

Galen only stared forward. The plate of food was between them, and the healer continued in silence as Ravenna ate. Bite after bite, Ravenna wished she could shrink into herself, to flee Galen's Light that seemed to illuminate and expose all her sins.

She begged the healer to go, but only when she had finished the last crumb did Galen leave her to wallow.

Ravenna had been alone in her chambers since Galen left and had lost track of time in a bout of dissociation. There was a knock at the door, and she looked to the window, where dusk was quickly falling over the Kingdom of Oro. *Was it dinner time already?*

"Come in," Ravenna called. An unfamiliar servant entered with dinner. Though Ravenna now considered *herself* a servant to Degare, she had been assigned her own servants as well. The only castle worker she ever saw twice was Galen. Degare had likely ordered it that way, after Ravenna had made friends with Cove—who was likely dead now. Had Degare yet learned who Ravenna had schemed with before it all went wrong, or had he thought past his newfound pride in Ravenna as his weapon? Did he suspect it had been one of his very own, a rebel in his kingdom? That a spy, posing as a young servant girl, had nearly fallen his entire empire?

The unfamiliar servant delivered a tray with a silver cloche and a glass of wine to the small wooden table next to the bed. "I'll need more than that," Ravenna grumbled, taking the wine first and downing it in a few gulps. The servant scrambled for more, and while she was gone, Ravenna checked beneath the lid of the cloche. Sure enough, there was another letter from Galen. Ravenna never mentioned the letters, and she did not tell the healer she appreciated the kind words, or that they were the only light she saw throughout the day. Galen knew, and that was why she wrote them.

*If I cannot inspire you to become the Dove you were meant to be, I fear Oro will only grow colder. You must rise to your destiny and become a daughter of Light. The Heir to the Throne of Ozanna. And yes, you have been destined for this, Child. But it is still your choice. Do not choose wrong.*

Ravenna crumpled the paper. She had been expecting something a little more hopeful, whether she would have allowed herself to believe it or not. Galen was stuck on her being this symbol for Ozanna. A Dove, which had been the crest of the ancient kingdom since the time it was established. The Dove, which symbolized peace and new birth.

Ravenna scoffed, reaching for the papers that she had hidden beneath the chest. She took the stack in her hands, and as she shuffled through them, she walked onto her balcony, taking in a deep breath. After a few moments, she found the message Galen had written about her parents. She loved this one.

*Your parents are still alive. I think Degare has shifted his focus to you for the meantime. Because of that, they have been able to rest. I have not been able to speak to them directly, but they have been eating, and both are gaining their strength.*

*I cared for Willa during her pregnancy with you. You cannot possibly understand the love she and Gerrin have for you and for each other. I hope that one day you will be able to experience such love and to know that you have not fallen too far.*

*Their love for one another has burned brightly through so many trials. When your mother was your age, her village was burned, and she was trapped in her home. She cried out to the Father of Lights for help, and Gerrin is the one who pulled her from the fire. I believe they were meant for each other.*

*Seven years they waited for you, and I know they would do it all again. All they ever wanted was to keep you safe. Ashreya was not supposed to keep these secrets from you forever. She went against your parent's wishes. They all made mistakes in how they went about it—as did I. We cannot change the past, but I am here now, and I only hope you'll let me be a friend.*

*Galen*

"Miss?" Ravenna blinked and quickly wiped her eyes from where she stood on the balcony, pondering the distance of the raging waters below.

"Yes, just set it on the table," she said to the servant, who carried three bottles of wine. Ravenna rubbed a hand down her face. "Thank you," she called as the woman left.

The bottles sat next to a platter of food, and Ravenna's attention fell to the knife that had been brought with dinner. For the next few minutes, she stood there, staring, fingers tapping wildly against the table. That blade could put an end to her miserable life, and it could save thousands of others, if only she was permitted to bring it to her neck, to destroy the weapon Degare was forging within her.

But her hand would not reach for it, and soon, her eyes could not even be moved in that direction. Sighing, she opted for the temporary numbing of the wine instead.

# CHAPTER 10
# THE FIGHT THAT LEADS TO DEATH
## RAVENNA

It was no coincidence that Ravenna's birth was followed by the darkest night of the year. Like prophecy spoken into the world, Ravenna would give way to the shadows. Degare would break her. Before the three moons aligned at the end of summer, Ravenna would be completely and utterly his to command. She could not foresee herself resisting–the torture, the sire, the urges–any longer than a couple more weeks. But if she was being honest, she was much closer than that to breaking. Just another torture session away from yielding her conscience, just so she no longer had to *feel*. Between the remorse that came with obedience to the sire and the physical pain that came with trying to fight it, she searched for a numbness that only full surrender would bring. Even her nightmares told her of the way she would soon loyally serve the King of Oro with no penitence.

His wishes would become her wishes. It was inevitable, and she felt that promise closing in with each spilled drop of her own blood; an impending oath, waiting for her acceptance.

Her braids–the memories she so badly wanted to leave behind–reminded her of who she fought for, but she could not fight much longer. Not when those people were all dead.

She was waning like the moon, giving up what remained of the light that had once been reflected upon her. Darkening, and shifting into shadow. And like the third moon, which hid through the winter until the other two entered beyond the shadows to retrieve it, Ravenna would succumb to the sire and soon become the darkest night of all.

But unlike the third moon, there was no one left to retrieve her. No one to pull her from the shadows. An eternal darkness would fall upon Arresia, and she was to be the bearer of it.

Her first few weeks in these chambers, Ravenna had not allowed herself to enjoy the bed. Zephaniah had spent his last days on the same hard ground she had slept on in that miserable cell, most nights sacrificing his own comfort to be right there with her. But as undeserving of comfort as she still may be, the window bench where she had spent many nights was drafty, the flashbacks were haunting, and she could not handle one more moment curled up on the wretched floor, begging the memories to leave her. She could not spend one more second writhing on the stone where she had envisioned Zephaniah's blood spilling over a hundred times in the months since she had been placed in this prison.

It seemed that she–like her parents–had been given a break from the torture. The past few days, when she was not soaking her sin away in a scalding hot bath, she was under the horrid red covers which provided warmth in this kingdom that was always cool and dreary in the night, even in the summer months. Her surroundings were decadent in the red of Oro and the red of spilled blood. She suspected Jara had something to do with the design choice of her chamber. She had peered into Ravenna's mind many times and had probably gathered by now that red was the color she most despised.

For Ravenna, red was a reminder. The beginning and the end. A symbol of the life she was forced to live and the life she had been forced to take.

Ravenna turned on the mattress that was far too fluffy for her taste. She would not allow herself to enjoy the grandeur that her chambers offered, but she was trapped within these walls most hours of the day. The only escape she was granted was a direct path to torture a few times a week. Degare would physically and mentally break her before risking teaching her how to use her gifts.

He had not yet trusted Ravenna enough to allow her the liberty to exit her chambers unless he was pulling her out for a lesson on compliance, so she spent most of her leisure time in bed awaiting the terror-riddled sleep that was sure to find her. While she lay awake, pondering, she replayed the same moments–a personal, emotional torment meant to fill the gaps between the bouts of physical pain she met at the whipping posts and on the stone slab.

She saw her mother's death, caused by her own foolish choices. Well, not her true mother, but the woman she had always called by that title. Ashreya of the Valley–her *mama*. Gone, because of her. She saw the night Vestele had burned with poison, and with it, all her people–simply because they had hidden her. Xan, crawling to her, reaching for her in his final moments as she was carried away to Oro. She remembered the day she realized just how much pain her parents had endured for her as they lay upon the stone altar. But these flashbacks were nothing compared to the most dreadful: the moment her volition was stolen. The moment her own hands betrayed her as she took Zephaniah's life in the throne room.

From where she lay in the bed, she had a clear view of the rich burgundy tapestry that hung on the opposite wall and the chestnut bookshelf below it, full of books she had not touched. Above her bed, the ceiling was sullied with cracks that snaked down and around the window. A constant breeze seemed to whisper through them, reminding her to breathe. Empty bottles of rum and wine cluttered the table next to her bed, and one lay beside her, staining the sheets.

A skitter on the windowsill grabbed her attention, as yet another raven landed near the open window. She rubbed her head against the dull ache left by the wine. As expected in Oro, the day was not sunny, but it was warm enough that she had asked the early morning servant to let the fire go out. The short brunette had only nodded and then opened the window that was parallel to the bed, exposing the thick fog that rolled over the kingdom and revealed the black waters of the sea to the west. Ravenna's chambers were up a few flights of stairs, perfectly positioned over the kingdom square. She paid little attention to the cavalier people that roamed below, chatting about the upcoming anniversary of the wretched Ember Trade and the ball the king was to be hosting in just over six weeks. The trades were always accompanied by a ball, but not one so extravagant. Being that Autumn marked the anniversary of the trades, Degare was promising an elaborate celebration to coax more buyers into his kingdom.

Another faint wind flowed through the chambers, and for

a moment, Ravenna was reminded of Vestele and the valley she would ride through on her horse, Fintah—who was likely dead now, like everyone else. She doubted any of the horses or cattle had escaped the stables in the fire. *Perhaps they are better off dead than living in a kingdom where I am to be the king's destroyer*, she tried to tell herself. But the thought buried itself in her chest as she thought of the loyal mare she had loved so dearly. And then her mind jumped to Xan, her best friend who had always ridden beside her—or behind her, since she *always* won the race. But this race with the king—this war—she had lost.

A dinner knife from her breakfast found its way into her hand, and without looking, Ravenna chucked it toward the raven that sat on the stone sill. The oily feathered, black bird fell a hundred feet onto the street below, along with a few dozen others that had piled up from the last several weeks. The stupid birds would not leave her alone, and after about three weeks of putting up with their incessant croaks at her window, she had begun throwing dinnerware at them. They seemed to trail her like the witch guardians did.

The golden, oval-shaped mirror that had been placed on the wall next to the window bench and above a small table reflected her exhaustion perfectly. Ravenna had destroyed the first vanity, and the next day, servants had quickly brought in the mirror and table as a replacement, though she insisted she did not need them.

She roused herself out of bed and shoved the hideous scarlet covers from her aching body. Her toes touched the cool stone, and she stepped to the rug, which provided a little more comfort for her feet. She pulled her robe on and strode to the bathing chambers, fractured body begging to be wrapped in the warmth a bath would bring. She considered waiting for her servants to bring the buckets of water, but she wished for solitude. She looked to the empty tub, then to her bony hands, and finally, out the bathing chamber window toward the Black Sea.

She opened the windowpane and concentrated on the tide, attempting to reel it in a little closer. Ravenna did not know if there were any in the world of Arresia who had the strength and control to shift the tides, but that did not stop her from trying to move the dirty sea water. She had not yet been taught anything of the power that now writhed within her, twisting and winding and aching for release. Without understanding what gifts she possessed, she doubted she would ever be able to wield such things. Learning to utilize those gifts would be fully dependent on the king's wishes and if he deemed that she could train. Though, he had not told her she could not *try* to use them. . .a mistake on his part. If he had, she would have no choice but to await his permission.

Ravenna had no clue as to what His Majesty had been up to these last two months of her misery. She imagined he had been sitting on his throne, taxing the poor villages of Oro and taking their food rations, all while stockpiling Embers in the mines and in his fortified prison here in the kingdom.

It was not that she wanted, or did not want, to learn her power. Either way, someone would suffer for it. She supposed not learning her gifts would be the better of the two options if it were her choice, because though she would remain in pain as the power swelled within her, unable to escape, she would not be a master of the many deadly gifts which Degare controlled. The gifts that were rumored to be strong enough to destroy entire villages. With her torture coming to a suspicious halt, she knew it was only a matter of time before her training started and she was utilized as Degare's new weapon of mass destruction.

She urged the water to come to her. She willed it toward her with all her might. After a few minutes when, still, nothing had happened, she turned to the glass of water next to her bed. She focused her mind on the water inside as Cove had once done. She had not seen the blonde servant since the day it had all gone wrong. The Ember had been smart to flee, or Ravenna would have likely been forced to kill her, too–right along with Zephaniah.

*What rebellion was it that Cove had been working for, anyway? What had her goal truly been in altering the spell?* Surely if Degare found out about a rebellion in his own territory, or anywhere else for that matter, he would put a quick halt to whatever games they were playing. None of it mattered, though, because Cove had failed at keeping Ravenna from the shadows, and now Degare held her as a weapon against all Light.

Ravenna blinked away her intense focus on the glass of water. It did not move as she willed it, and instead, a drop of salty water slipped down her cheek. Ravenna groaned and aggressively wiped the tear from her face then pulled her robe tightly across her torso before she melted back into the bed.

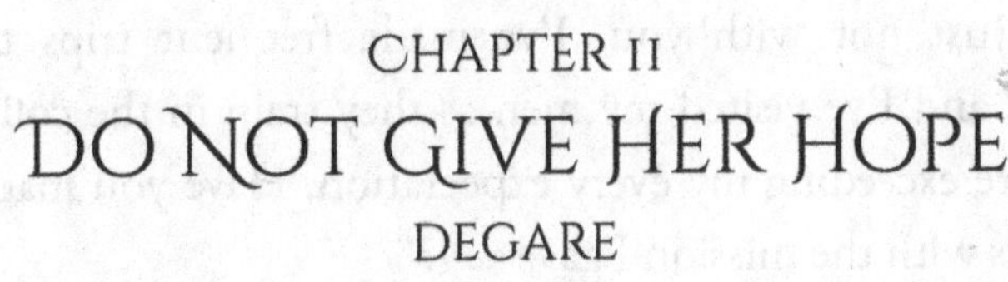

# CHAPTER II
# DO NOT GIVE HER HOPE
## DEGARE

Degare was enjoying a nice evening on his balcony, listening to the crashing waves of the Black Sea, when Jara strode out of his chambers to join him. He sighed and took a swig of rum as she rubbed his shoulders.

"I free your body from destruction after your own greed nearly killed you, and now you fill it with that muck?" she asked, annoyed.

Degare shook off her touch and breathed the cool evening air through his teeth as she took her place in the chair beside him. "By all means, have a seat." His tone was monotonous.

"You have not been out much these last few months," Jara said, prying.

"Am I not allowed to bask in my newfound health? My freedom and new power in this sire?"

Jara slowly turned her face toward him. "I just thought I would hear from you, being that I am the one who made this possible. That is all." The witch never left him alone. "You have not even asked me to join you in the torture chambers. I just thought–"

"Ravenna is mine, Jara," he snapped. His witch fell silent, and he took another drink. "Besides, I have been out quite often. Just not with you. I've made frequent trips to the temple, and I've visited my men as they train in the coliseum. They are exceeding my every expectation. Have you made any progress with the mission I gave *you*?"

Jara breathed tightly. "That is actually why I came, Your Majesty."

"Oh?" He lifted his glass to his lips and kept his gaze on the night before him.

Just as Jara began to speak, a raven swooped onto the balcony and landed on the rail. It croaked loudly, staring at him. He raised his staff toward it, aiming to shoo it from his presence. It only shifted sideways, talons clicking against the black stone.

"Wait, there is a message tied to its leg," Jara said, advancing forward. Degare squinted against the night, studying the strange parchment that had been fastened to its leg with a ribbon dipped in something red. *Blood*.

"Move," Degare demanded, rising to his feet and shoving her to the side so he could get a closer look. He tore the note from the bird, and it flew off, cawing into the night.

"What does it say?" Jara asked over his shoulder.

"I can't see," he hissed, and she lit the torch with the wave of her hand. Sometimes he missed the power that had once lived within him. His soul was still filled with shadow, but every ounce of power that had accompanied it was now within Ravenna. She would be put to use soon, when she yielded fully to him. He was close to succeeding in that; he could feel it.

"Well?" Jara prodded.

Degare read the letter slowly.

*You have three days to let Ravenna and every Ember in your possession walk free. Three days or your kingdom turns red.*

Degare's cheeks heated, and he looked out over Oro, as if he might see the perpetrator watching proudly from the streets. *What was this supposed to mean?* He gritted his teeth. "Find out who sent this," he demanded, shoving the note toward Jara.

"How, Your Majesty? It is not signed, I–"

"Don't you have a spell of some sort? I do not care how you do it. Figure. It. Out," he said with a snarl. If the power had never been transferred from his body to Ravenna, he would have sent shadows across the kingdom in uncontrolled rage. But now, he was incapable of doing anything. He was useless, powerless on his own.

He tapped his fingers against the balcony railing. "And Jara? Prepare my Raven for training. It is about time I unleashed her. I do not care if she has not fully surrendered to our bond." He set his jaw. *I am tired of feeling weak.* "Do not let her know that there is still someone out there who searches for her. Do not give her hope."

Jara's hand tightened around the written threat, and Degare watched as she downed the rest of his rum and shattered his glass before leaving him on the balcony.

# CHAPTER 12
# POWER'S BEGINNING
## RAVENNA

The morning skies were turning from black to gray when three maids barged in with less regard for her than any others had in the mornings prior. Ravenna sat up in the bed and rubbed her eyes against stolen sleep. The snarls and growls of the witch guardians that visited the kingdom in search of her at least once weekly had kept her awake. The guards had been anything but quiet as they had fought them off at the gates in the early morning hours.

The tallest of the three servants carried a set of new clothing woven of smooth, black fabric Ravenna had not worn before. In the hands of the other two were four buckets of water–not even enough to fill the tub. Their movements were stiff and confident, as if they rose and dressed noblewomen all day long. Not that Ravenna was a noblewoman–she was far from it. But the way they moved quickly about the room with a subtle confidence, she figured they were some of the more experienced servants in the castle and probably some of Degare's most trusted.

The tall one ripped the sheets from her pale legs, urging her up into the coolness of the room. Ravenna breathed tightly as her body revolted.

The black-haired woman's gaze shifted to the empty bottles at Ravenna's bedside, and then she spoke in a shrill voice as she tapped the bed and motioned Ravenna up. "His Majesty would like you to train today. Your guards are waiting just outside to escort you to the coliseum." It became clear, then, why her king had chosen the three of them to prepare her today. Ravenna was to look presentable. She would not be remaining in her chambers or forgoing continuous torture any longer–she was to begin playing the role of the king's weapon.

Ravenna was hurried into the bathing chambers and robbed of her clothes within seconds. Every muscle in her body ached, and though a small, undeserving part of her hoped for some lavender oil, she was disappointed with quickly thrown buckets of lukewarm water over her skin as she sat in an empty tub. There was just enough water for a rinse, and the servants acted as if soap was not a necessity this morning. Ravenna sighed as the thinnest maid dumped the last remaining bucket of water over her back, careful to avoid her hair. A towel was shoved in her face not more than five seconds later, and she took it with haste, yanking it away and giving the scrawny woman a scowl.

"You'll need to wear these." Ravenna took the clothes from the maid and held them up in the light coming from the window beside the dressing screen. The fabric was solid black and tight. It was breathable and quite stretchy. When the suit was on, hugging her body and accentuating every ghost of the curves she had lost in the last two months of constant vomiting, little sleep, and much torture, she looked to the servant with eyebrows raised.

"What in darkness is this?" Ravenna asked, stepping out from behind the dressing screen. The maid tipped her head downward and then turned as the chamber door opened, revealing another set of servants. They carried something of black metal and a few other pieces of black clothing. As they walked across the chambers and passed her bed, she began to make out the shoulder and breast plates, which had been designed to resemble feathers. A raven's, to be specific. She pulled a long black tunic over top of the skin tight fabric, and it fell to her midthigh. She laced up her new leather boots as the maids lifted the metal pieces over her shoulders and clasped them into place. Thankfully, the metal was thin and lightweight, making it easy to move in. She turned to the mirror, where a swallowed-up reflection stared back at her. The servants reached for her braids.

"Leave them!" Ravenna barked, catching one of the young servant's hands in her own. The woman tried to back away, but Ravenna held tightly, somehow squeezing the bones in her knuckles until they crunched. She yelped, and with a look of surprise, Ravenna released her, sending her running out the door.

*What type of strength is this?* she wondered as she examined her boney hand. The other two servants stared at her, and after a long silence, they hesitantly worked around the braids, pulling them tight into a larger one that snaked down the back of her head. One of the ladies sighed as she looked upon Ravenna, then tapped her lip as if something were missing. She then strode to the washstand, her boots clacking against the stone, and grabbed a small clay pot of black powder.

"May I?" she asked, before dabbing her crooked thumb into the substance. Ravenna nodded tightly, and the woman brought her fingers to Ravenna's face, tracing a thick line around her eyes and under her brows, until her reflection was that of a masked raven. Her eyes peered out from beneath the shadow, once vibrant blue and green, now irrevocably dull. In a way, she looked like her mother–Ashreya of the Valley.

Xan had been the last person to mark Ravenna's face, on the day she had taken her mother's place as shield-maiden. The day she had taken a vow to protect Vestele. Ravenna averted her gaze and worked to subdue the knot that was working its way up her throat at the reminder of her failure.

After the servants were finished preparing her for her first day of training at the coliseum, she stood at the open chamber door, awaiting permission from her guards to exit. Spelled shackles found her wrists, and the gruff men surrounded her on all sides. They did not push and prod at her back as they had in the weeks prior, shuttling her down to the torture chambers where Degare always awaited her with imaginations running rampant of what more he could do to break her. Some days, she had not even been able to walk and had been carried by these men all the way down to the stone altar, where they had strapped and tied her for hours upon hours of torture. With hands shaking as they passed those very chambers, Ravenna kept her focus forward, hating every bit of what she had become. She was a coward who shook with fear. She was a killer who had taken the life of her friend, and she was a slave to darkness–headed to do his bidding.

She brought a hand to the charcoal on her cheeks and examined her blackened fingertips. Ravenna of the Valley, *the shield-maiden to Vestele*, would not have stood for this. She would have fought back. Somehow, she would have found her vengeance. For her people. Her mother. For Xan, and Zephaniah.

*Fight it, Ravenna. Fight it with everything you've got.*

Those were the words her final friend had left her with.

Then and there, in the blackness of the halls of Oro's castle, she made a new vow. Even when not an echo of that resilient shield-maiden remained, she would still remember her. She would fight against the sire bond, and though there may not be hope for a true victory in breaking free, she would make Degare pay for it. He would pay for it all.

And so, Ravenna smiled as she turned on the guards with a movement so swift, none of them saw it coming. Degare had underestimated her in not demanding she not harm his men. He had thought her to be weak, without knowledge of how to use her power. He thought the shackles would be enough to hold her, but they were not. Ravenna was a warrior before she was anything else. She had fought for that title, and she had earned it.

She pulled a sword free from the belt of the guard at her right and started swinging before the two others could even free their weapons. A blow landed on the side of her head from behind, and she swayed with dizziness for a moment before pretending to fall, only to swipe her blade across the shins of the offender.

He cried out too loudly for her liking, and she hurried his last breath with a final jab. She imagined Xan at her back, going through the maneuvers they had practiced a thousand times. But she was alone, and Xan was dead. She turned on her heels and her thick braid swiped through the air as she brought an elbow down into the last man's gut, temporarily disabling him.

Another jolt of force between his legs and he stumbled backward, dropping his dagger. She bent to grab it as the dagger fell to the floor, the familiar clank sending flashbacks that threatened to claim her attention. She tried to fight them, but she was already falling. Falling into that gloom where the memories took over and into the haunting that entertained her thoughts each night.

She heard the guard rising to his feet, but she could not see him. She felt his hands hauling her up from the ground, but she was still in blackness. He pulled her back into his chest and whispered low and eerily against her head, "Did you forget who you live among? That Despiri guards are common in the king's army? I have taken your sight, Ravenna." She felt his wicked smile against her hair. "Welcome to the darkness."

Ravenna struggled against his grasp, feeling against him for a weapon, or anything to grab hold of to gain the upper hand. But there was nothing save for the memory of Zephaniah, and she was spiraling, as if sinking into the depths of the Black Sea. Air would not come to her. She was under the sheet of ice in Vestele, and someone was calling her name, but they were nowhere to be found.

As her knees hit the ground, her sight was returned to her. Ashy dust entered her lungs immediately, sending her into a coughing fit. As she brought her hand to her face to shield it against the sudden light of day, she noticed the blood that now visibly stained them, covering the shadowy marks that crept where her lightmarks may have been, in another life. And then, behind her hand, she noticed Degare standing before her with rage in his eyes and the witch at his side. The three of them were amid the massive black stone coliseum, the arena's seats surrounded by an audience of Despiri and ungifted guards alike. The Summer Trades had happened here two months ago, and just behind Degare, Ravenna could see the blood that still stained the stone near the raised viewing platform.

"You think me a fool, Ravenna?" Ravenna blinked against the unusually bright sun that had come out to shine upon her pale skin. Her bones ached, and she looked up at the king who had beat her senseless just days before.

"Since you have commanded I be honest with you, yes, I do think you are a fool, *Your Majesty*." She bowed her head from where she already sat on her knees and smirked, anticipating the physical blow. Perhaps he would whip her for all to see. Or maybe, he would allow the witch to weave her way through Ravenna's brain, bringing pain as her nerves were stimulated by the wretched magic.

But the king only said, "Then you shall enjoy playing slave to a fool." Ravenna looked up to see him motioning a Despiri toward them in the center of the arena. "Unless it is to protect myself or you, you are not to harm my men, *ever again*." Ravenna nodded at the new order. She should have known it was coming, and she should have planned something bigger if she had wanted to make an impression while the opportunity still stood, but fighting back, no matter how useless, had felt freeing.

The sun darkened as fog rolled in from the sea, and Ravenna rose to her feet as Degare began explaining what the day would entail.

"This man will be training you." He motioned to the

muscular, fair-skinned man who had come to join them. "Cyrus, wielder of fire."

Cyrus stepped forward, his long, golden-red hair swaying in the breeze. He was not particularly good looking and needed a shave. He reminded her of Roarke, whom she had nearly forgotten. His was another death she had caused. "You'll be learning to control the fire within you first," he said. *One of the more destructive of my numerous unknown gifts*, Ravenna was sure.

"I'll be watching from the stands," Degare said. "Do not disappoint me today."

"I would not dream of it, Your Majesty," her words were laced with sarcasm, and she again awaited retribution, but none came. As Jara and Degare walked to a distance far enough that Ravenna could just barely make out their figures against the shadowy stands of the coliseum, Cyrus began speaking. "I received my fire gifts a few years ago. I was one of the first of Degare's guards to become a Despiri. Kind of volunteered for the experiment."

"How noble of you," Ravenna said tartly, crossing her arms and shifting her focus to the man in front of her. She surveyed his attire, noting his lack of weapons. "You *took* the gifts. Not received," she corrected.

He shrugged, as if letting her comment roll off his shoulders. "Today we will be working on–"

"Offense, not defense, right?" She watched as he studied her with curiosity. "Degare plans to use me as a weapon, so I'm assuming he wants me ready to show off at this elaborate Autumn Ball I keep hearing about?" The wealthy chattered in the kingdom square below her window every day, about their excitement for the trades. From her window, Ravenna had experienced the nuisance of the crowds that had gathered for the Summer Trades over two months ago. She had no doubt that Degare would want to flaunt her at the next one, and with thirteen weeks between each trade, he only had five and a half weeks left to prepare her.

Her lips formed a thin line, and Cyrus's brows raised at her observations. "Let's just get to it," she muttered.

The Despiri smacked his hands to his hips and nodded. "Alrighty then." He held his palm out and nodded for her to do the same. "I won't be much help with your other gifts, but I do know fire well." A small flame danced within his palm, and he smiled.

"Have you always done Degare's bidding so proudly?" she asked, ignoring his direction again. Cyrus took a deep breath and rubbed his face with his now-flameless hand. "I just wonder why it is I who must carry out his desires to. . ." she paused, wondering exactly what Degare's plans for Arresia were, "*destroy,* when he has you and his entire Despiri Guard already."

Cyrus chuckled. "You are *very* powerful. Your power is unmatched. Like nothing I have ever heard of before. The power you must have received from that bloodstone mixed with Degare's power. . ." He shook his head. "No one could stand against you. That is why you are Degare's to control." She wondered how much this man understood of that *bloodstone*, that the powerful gifts within it had once been gifts of Light possessed by the mighty Ozannes.

But, "lucky me," was all she said. Cyrus held his palm out again, prompting her to follow. She did, so as to not disappoint the king. With her hand outstretched and palm up, he instructed her with a hint of dread in his eyes for what she might conjure. Ravenna tilted her head with intrigue.

"Using your gifts is about control. If you can't control your emotions, your power is going to let loose. Emotions fuel your gifts. You must maintain a hold on them," he prefaced. "Now, watch me." She studied his hand as a flame danced across it once more. "Now, I'll focus on anger." The flame blossomed into a small, but raging fire that began to creep up his arm. "Calm." The fire stifled, reverting to that one tiny patch in his palm. She narrowed her eyes on her own hand, wiggling her fingers while trying to focus on summoning her own.

"Visualize it in your palm," he said. She gritted her teeth and focused so intently that she forgot to breathe. "You need fuel," Cyrus reminded her. *Emotion.* She dove into that depthless well of anger within her soul. She looked across the arena to Degare, who had taken everything from her, including her own free will. Ravenna looked to the witch beside him, who surely donned a smug look. She thought of Zephaniah and the vengeance she owed him.

*Vengeance.*

Before she knew it, Degare was standing, and there was yelling from behind her, *Cyrus,* and her entire body was encased in flames. Her skin did not burn; she felt nothing more than a warm sensation as the flames entangled through the metal feathers of her armor. She spun to face Cyrus, whose eyes had gone wide. His mouth was moving as he backed away from her. "Control." She could see the word forming on his lips but could not hear it over the sound of her racing mind, that vengeance she desired so badly. But it was vengeance with nowhere to go. She could not use the flames against her sire, against his witch, or against his men.

"Control!" The command sounded through to her, begging her to get a hold on her emotions, but to release power gave her strength and long-awaited relief. The wildfire had extended to the ground and was creeping toward the stands. Cyrus shielded himself in his own flames as hers advanced toward him. As she emptied her lungs and her soul of all the pent-up shadow, she took a long, deep breath.

*Control. Control. Control. Vengeance comes later,* she promised herself, though, she was hopeful of no such thing. Vengeance would be impossible, because she was forbidden by the sire bond to harm the ones who most deserved it.

*Do not disappoint me,* the sire bond reminded her.

After a few lengthy minutes of searching for that control, the fire subsided, dwindling to only an ember in her palm. She stood there, panting, staring at the small glimmer of light, until even it left her.

Cyrus breathed a huffy laugh. "Incredible."

Ravenna's forehead wrinkled as she looked up from her now flameless hands. "What are you talking about? I had no control." She flexed her fingers. Her own power had not obeyed her, and it had struggled to obey the king.

"In my first several attempts at summoning the flame, I was lucky to make a spark." She examined her palm again. He looked beyond her, to where Degare watched. The king gave him a curt nod.

"That's enough for today," Cyrus said. "I am sure that performance drained you, with it being your first time and all." She shook her head in protest.

"I am not drained. Releasing that power was a relief. I–"

"I am sure it was. But you cannot do too much at once. Trust me, you need rest." He looked her up and down, taking in the horrid state of malnourishment her body was in. "And start eating more, or you'll never reach your full potential. *That,* would be a disappointment to the king." Ravenna narrowed her eyes. *How much did this man know about the bond between her and the king?*

"I think I shall require much more training if I am to be the king's weapon," she said. She wanted to continue in her lesson. She needed to try again. She needed to feel the pressure leaving her veins. "Degare may give me commands, but it is clear that I will be unable to fulfill his wishes without control."

Cyrus shook his head. "Soon, you'll be begging for a break from training. I am sure you'll be back tomorrow. For now," he said, looking over her shoulder toward the stands, "go get some rest."

She was not the least bit tired. From expelling power, anyway. But her body did ache, and she did not know which would soothe her more: to release more of the power that was eating her alive or to go back to her chambers and soak in a warm bath.

She looked back toward Degare in the stands, but to her surprise, he was already gone. Ravenna looked back to Cyrus. "You must've shown him what he came to see," he said with a shrug. "Imagine what you can do with all that power if you can wield fire with such ferocity on your first day. The king never gained full control over his power. He never cared to master it. He let it ravage him. With training, my lady, you will be a sight."

Ravenna searched the dispersing crowd for her sire, but could not find him. "Yes," she said. "I suppose I am to be quite the spectacle."

Ravenna was stunned that there was no punishment for killing three of the king's soldiers and especially caught off guard when her escorts shuttled her right past the torture chambers. She could not help but smile at the faint victory the day had been. While the king had tried to teach her compliance these last two months, she had found the fire within her and was rebelling in the only ways she could. Though only small acts of resistance, they were something, and they made her feel more herself again. Like maybe she had not been completely lost and remolded. A little bit of the shield-maiden still shined through, and she had finally gained a foothold against the king. There was nothing more he could do to her. Nothing left to surprise her with. She just needed to hang onto herself long enough for the hope Zephaniah had left her with to come to fruition.

*Not even you, Ravenna.*

As the guards shoved her over the threshold of her chambers, and the locks rattled as they shut her inside, Ravenna breathed a sigh of relief. He no longer had anything to hold over her. She could do this. She could fight this.

She sank into the plush mattress, relishing in its comfort for only a moment before cheers and sounds of shock echoed up through the window by her bed. She went to the bench and plopped onto her knees, letting the cool breeze kiss her sweaty skin as she looked down into the kingdom square, where *Galen* hung in the gallows.

# CHAPTER 13
# FOLLOWER OF THE LIGHT
## RAVENNA

Ravenna's body went numb as the healer's body hung limp, swaying on the rope that held her. A crowd gathered around, equal parts celebratory and astonished at the execution they had just witnessed. No one looked up to where Ravenna watched out the window of her prison. The sign above Galen read: *Follower of the Light*. It was a crime against this kingdom.

Ravenna looked down to the shadowmarks that snaked across the skin on her own hands, all the way up to her neck, and down her back. The king had bragged to his Despiri of how he had brought the prophesied Dove to her knees before him. She was slipping away into darkness, and soon, the prophecy of the Dove would be no more.

Under Degare's sire, she was only darkness. She could offer no light to the world around her as Galen had. As Cove had. *As Zeph had.* The Father of Lights did not speak to her, and she did not dare call out to Him. She hid from His presence in fear her punishment would be worse than anything she had endured thus far. She deserved a punishment worse than death, *for death would be a mercy.*

Ravenna's hands trembled as she peered out the window, as her eyes glazed over the cobblestone and then traced the angles of the gallows, all the way up to the dead healer. A tiny lightmark was now fading at the healer's ankle, where her stocking had been removed to display it. That strange strength returned to her, and the windowsill crumbled beneath Ravenna's grasp, sending pieces of stone falling to the dead ravens below. She turned her hand over to examine the tiny fragments of dust and stone that now clung to her sweaty flesh. Her eyes shifted back to the noose.

A knock sounded at the door, but Ravenna did not turn from the scene before her. She listened to the footsteps that followed the creaking of the door, and a platter was extended beside her. She took it quietly, and the servant's strangely downcast reflection in the half-open window pane caught her attention. The woman was the brunette who had helped Cove bathe her on that day in the witch's chambers over three months ago—Mirren. She looked past Ravenna and down into the square. Sadness seemed to wash over her face at the sight of Galen, though Ravenna only recognized her as Jara's faithful servant. Only when Mirren turned to leave, did Ravenna remove the letter from around the handle of the silver cloche. The parchment crackled as she unfolded it.

Inked in Oro's scarlet, Degare's scratchy handwriting read: *Do not be so foolish as to think that there is not much more where this came from. Wherever—in whomever—your hope is found, I will put an end to it, to them. Surrender your conscience to me, Ravenna. Because I will not hesitate. Until I have your blind obedience. This,* Ravenna looked to the healer again, *is the company you'll keep. The clock is ticking. I'd surrender now if I were you.*

Ravenna breathed tightly as she clung to her conscience and then opened the lid. Inside was a letter from Galen, which she had received in the form of a paper dove when she had first come into this kingdom. *I know who you are. I can help you.* Ravenna's breath caught in her throat. The small note had given her so much hope, hidden with the herbs in the small pouch under her skirt while she was in the tower. Ravenna had foolishly left it in the dress when she had been bathed in Jara's bathing chambers. The brunette servant–Mirren–had collected the note along with her clothes. It was a mistake that had cost Galen her life. Ravenna looked back down to the gallows as a tear slid down her cheek. The healer's body had stilled.

Ravenna shuddered, gripping the note in her hands. The king had been given this note, likely months ago. Ravenna doubted Mirren had held onto it for more than a day; she had likely marched it right to the king to win his favor. He had chosen Ravenna's chambers carefully, to be sure they overlooked the gallows and the square. She knew the inner workings of his mind. He and the witch had recruited Galen into the castle for a reason. He had intentionally waited to kill Galen until it could be used to break Ravenna into further obedience. Today, Ravenna had earned this punishment.

*Give in. You won't have to feel any longer.*

She collapsed against the wall next to the window seat and sobbed for Galen. For the lives of her people, her mother. Xan. Zephaniah. Everyone had been taken from her. Her existence had gotten *everyone* she loved killed. Death was the only company she kept. She couldn't handle any more guilt or pain.

She was forbidden to free herself from it, and though she tried many nights to point a knife toward her own heart or jump from the west balcony of her chambers that overlooked the Black Sea, she could not do it. Her body would not obey her–it only obeyed her sire.

She was forbidden to end her own misery, and she was forbidden to harm Degare, the witch, or the king's men. Only if one of the guards tried to harm her or the king could she kill them without orders. It was a command she must follow. She was to kill all threats to her life or the king's. Degare had made that very clear. She was not yet permitted to exit her chambers without an escort, though Degare had promised that would change very soon–when she proved her obedience.

*I would hate for you to get bored*, he had said in a tone that made her want to kill him as he scraped the dull side of a knife down her bare arm during their most recent endeavor in the torture chambers. *When you master your gifts, the luxuries of the kingdom are yours to enjoy.* She had only nodded in response, the picture of grace and respect to the king that had ruined her. But inside, *inside* she was raging.

From the window bench where Galen had woken her with a platter of food just a couple of days ago, Ravenna violently wiped the tears from her face and looked back down into the kingdom square. Something green caught her eye. A vine–the only color amid the drear of Oro–crept from just below Galen's body and snaked its way up the castle walls and into the window of her chambers, scrawling out the shape of a dove and winding into a short message that reminded Ravenna of her one last ounce of hope.

*Seven bloods.*

After a couple more training sessions, Ravenna felt she had become proficient in summoning fire. It was becoming a natural reaction to conjure her flames at the first sign of any danger, and when the afternoon servant came in without knocking, Ravenna could not stop herself from throwing up a defensive wall between herself and the quaking woman.

"I am sorry, miss!" the portly servant exclaimed, backing away from the sudden heat. Ravenna dropped the flames with just a thought. At the king's command, she would always protect herself from potential threats, whether she truly cared to continue breathing or not.

The servant quickly picked up the training leathers she had dropped and set them on the table before scurrying out into the hall. Ravenna walked over to them and took them into her hands only seconds before Jara waltzed through the door that had been left open.

"Love the new braid," she said, admiring the third set of woven strands that had been added for the healer. Ravenna took a breath and went into the bathing chambers. Jara sank into the chaise and said, "I'll wait," as Ravenna slammed the door behind her.

When she exited in her new leathers, Jara was reading a book from the shelf Ravenna had yet to touch. "You know, my king gives you all these nice things, and you do not even use them." She threw the book to the side.

"When will he provide me with something useful? Like permission to end your wretched existence?" Ravenna asked.

"Careful, girl. I will be overseeing your training today."

Ravenna scoffed. "Why do you do his bidding, anyway? It seems like he is just using you."

The witch straightened her shoulders, strutting out the door. "Follow me and shut your mouth."

Ravenna did not have to listen to the witch. The king had only ordered Ravenna not to harm her. Technically, she could have refused to follow her to the coliseum across the kingdom. But she knew she would be met with retribution, and then the king would give her another order to follow the witch's commands as well. She could not stomach the thought of being stripped further of her free will, so she followed and kept her lips pressed tightly together.

The windowless hall was dark, as expected. Candles lit the way down the three flights of stairs, and as they neared the bottom, light began to penetrate through the open windows across from the throne room. They waltzed right past the entry, and two guards opened the massive oak doors to the castle. Outside, the air was humid, but not too hot. It was likely a beautiful, sunny day in Vestele. The fog had lifted completely to the skies, leaving a rare, partly cloudy day in Oro.

Every time she set foot out of the castle, she was reminded of the lack of life in the kingdom. No trees grew, except for the few not yet drained of life in the distant Dead Wood, which would take her home if she just traveled southeast. She swallowed some of the humid air and averted her eyes from the gallows, which Jara had made a point to walk by. Ravenna's anger boiled beneath her skin as they passed by where Galen's body still hung, two days later.

The coliseum had been constructed for the Despiri to practice using their new gifts. Most of them were castle guards and king's men. There were some noblemen and even a few women who strutted around inside, using their surplus of powers on each other as they trained. One man who was no bigger than Ravenna was lifting a few hundred pounds of stone above his head and tossing it into the air. Beneath, a woman held her hand out and blasted the stone with some kind of invisible force. The rock blew to bits, and one chunk flew toward Ravenna. Without a thought, she ducked, letting it crash into the ground behind her. Jara turned, face painted with annoyance and the gaudy dark lip color she always wore.

"In here, use your gifts. Degare is tired of waiting."

"My apologies, but perhaps if he had not wasted two months cutting me open, I would have mastered my gifts by now. What does he expect after only three days of training?" Ravenna awaited the witch's response, but she said nothing. "What exactly does he have you preparing me for?" Ravenna asked.

Jara avoided the question and motioned toward a twisted piece of metal at the north end of the coliseum. "Let's get to work," the witch said.

After a few hours of sorting through the hundreds of threads of power within her, Ravenna had successfully summoned at least five powers. They remained uncontrollable, but that she was even able to access them, satisfied Jara in a way Ravenna had not expected to come so easily. "Try to open that door with only a thought," Jara said, motioning to the door at her left. "One of the powers within the stone was the ability to move things with the mind." Ravenna envisioned herself plucking the thread of power that she had located earlier. "I'm waiting,"

Jara muttered after about a minute of silence. Ravenna tried again, focusing on the door. "This one should be quite simple," Jara murmured as she walked over to Ravenna. "Use your emotions. Focus."

Ravenna narrowed her eyes on the door, willing her power to move toward it.

"You can wave your hand or something. It helps to visualize."

Ravenna did, holding her breath as she tried to keep her focus on that thin thread within her, refusing to lose hold of it again.

Finally, the door moved an inch.

Ravenna's eyes flashed at the witch, and Jara rolled her eyes. "Impressive," she mocked. "Now shut it." Ravenna clenched her jaw and focused again on the door, but drawing the door backwards was even more difficult.

Jara groaned. "Try expelling your power with great force in that direction. Do not worry about control."

"You want me to release it so carelessly?"

"If it will help you learn the way it works, yes," she said, checking her pocket watch. "And if it gives you any motivation, His Majesty says that if you are successful today, he will think about allowing you out of your chambers. With an escort, of course."

"He will allow me out of my chambers?"

"Yes, within the kingdom. If you do well today," she reiterated.

Ravenna raised her chin. It was something to consider.

She diverted her attention back to the door, and Jara shifted beside her, waiting impatiently. It took Ravenna a moment to locate the thread again, but when she did, she channeled that power and let it build inside her until her body trembled. She failed to release it on her first try, but on her second, it tunneled toward the door with force so great, the door flew off the hinges.

Ravenna smiled, and turned to the witch, who stood with her arms crossed. "Good," she said. "Now try to move the door from where it lays." Ravenna rolled her head back on her shoulders and walked a hundred feet into the street where the door lay.

Again and again she practiced, through the afternoon, excelling until she knew the king would be proud. Until she felt she had earned the king's graces and would be allowed out of her chambers. Only when Jara confirmed with the king did Ravenna rest.

# CHAPTER 14

# SOMETHING IN THE WATER

## RAVENNA

While in her chambers, she did everything in her power not to fall victim to sleep. Her fingers twisted a white feather from her pillow as she let her mind wander around thoughts of Galen's body down below, still swaying in death. They had not given the healer any sort of respect. No burial. No, they had not even removed her from the gallows, and instead, had allowed the birds to begin picking at her flesh. It made Ravenna sick, to hear them fighting over her in the night.

She could not stand it any longer. In the wee hours of the morning, she decided to make use of her reward. Because she had excelled at training, she was now allowed out with an escort. She kicked the door open and the guards backed away from it, immediately drawing their swords.

"Be careful not to appear too threatening to my life. You never know what I may do," she said as she pulled her cloak from the back of the velvet chaise and wrapped it around her shoulders. She took one last glance at the now-dead vine that the Light within Galen had given life. Ravenna had not known Galen to be lightmarked–an Ember–but it made perfect sense. Zephaniah had told her himself that all true followers of the Light were lightmarked. He seemed to have been the only exception.

"Take me to the gallows," she demanded the smallest of the three guards. He looked to the others of higher ranking, awaiting confirmation that he had permission to escort her to the square. "The king notified you that I am allowed out with an escort, did he not?" Ravenna asked impatiently. The smallest guard looked nervously between her and the others once more.

"It's about time you proved yourself around here," the man of highest ranking, a Despiri, grunted to the smallest guard.

The other high-ranking guard laughed at the fear in the smallest's eyes. "And I could use a nap," he added.

"Take her. You know the rules. Don't let her out of your sight," the Despiri ordered.

"Yes sir," the smallest, nervous guard said, turning to motion her after him.

"And Soldier, *relax*. The king has given her many rules that she has no choice but to follow. Isn't that right, Ravenna?" the other soldier sneered behind her.

Ravenna set her jaw as she followed her reluctant escort through the castle halls toward Galen.

"Lady Ravenna, may I ask why you have made this request at such a late hour? It is past midnight. You should be sleeping," he said, voice shaking. *Is it his first night on the job?*

"If you do not wish to escort me, just say so," she said, trailing him.

"It is not that I do not wish–" She scrunched her brow as he floundered for words. "I do not think His Majesty would want you out at this hour."

"Perhaps he should have clarified then, and perhaps he should not have left my friend hanging from a rope," she sneered. The petite man opened the door to the streets, glancing in all directions as she narrowed her eyes at him. "By the way you tremble, I'm beginning to wonder if you even know how to use that sword." His eyes widened as he gripped the hilt, and she advanced past him, hoping he would continue to escort her, or the rules of the sire would force her back to her chambers.

As she approached the gallows, she scared the ravens off into the night with a low yell and a quick burst of unruly flames. With the anger that swelled inside her at the sight of Galen, the flames came easily. Her escort watched their surroundings as if something might leap out of the darkness and grab him in an instant, and she rolled her eyes. "Sword," she said, holding her hand out to him. He looked at her in confusion. "Give me your sword," she repeated. He slowly handed it over. "Now, help me cut her down," she directed as she began to cut the rope that held the healer. Her escort hesitantly wrapped his cloak around Galen's body, slowly lowering her to the ground. Ravenna placed the white feather from her pillow into the healer's hand.

"To protect you while you sleep," she whispered. "I am sorry."

"I think we should go back now, Miss," her escort said.

"Would you shut up? We are burying her. Grab the cloak. The quicker you move, the sooner you get to hide inside the castle." Grudgingly, he did as she said and lifted one end of the thick cloak. They carried Galen all the way to the seaside, where the ground was no longer stone, and Ravenna knelt on her knees and began to dig. Until her fingers were raw and bleeding, and her arms could no longer move, she dug. She did not allow the guard to help her. Not with this.

Ravenna wished the grave was her own. She wanted so badly to sink into it and hide from the shadows of Oro, but she knew that there were certain things from which even death could not save her. Unlike Galen, there would be no rest to greet her upon her last breath.

After they had lowered Galen into the hole, and Ravenna had said her goodbyes and her apologies, they covered her with sand and a stone marking.

"Okay, it is time to head back now," the guard insisted. Before she could whirl on him and give him a scowl for rushing her, her ears caught a familiar, eerie sound. She closed her eyes and inhaled.

"Ah. So, you're scared of the witch guardians," she said, realizing that even after all this time, they still returned for her. There had been a few nights where she had heard the king's men fighting them off in the streets below her chambers, but she had not realized how persistent they had become. She drew the sword from his belt, leaving him defenseless as she swung on the first guardian, which seemed to appear out of thin air behind them. Her blade contacted the beast's open rib cage, clashing with bone over and over until it cut into the heart that pumped black blood. She spun and killed another with a quick jab through the spine.

This fight was different. Easy. She had power to wield against them but found herself preferring the blade for old time's sake. She had thinned and lost much of her muscle mass since her days as a Vestelian warrior, but one of the strange powers within her was strength like she had never known. She laughed as more witch guardians fabricated in the darkness around her, assembling to end her life. With swift movements and quick thrusts, she had killed four in a matter of seconds. She moved quicker than she ever had, and because she was sired to protect the king and to preserve her own life, nothing could stop her.

Before she knew it, there were eight dead guardians scattered about the black sand beach. She looked to her escort, who stood paralyzed in fear.

"How did you do that?" he asked breathlessly.

She looked to her hands, which had solely relied on her training as a Vestelian warrior.

"I am the shield-maiden," she said, looking up from her hands. *And shield-maidens do not cower.*

Dawn came far too quickly. Ravenna had not wanted the fight with the witch guardians to end. After these months with no free will, being a warrior was what she missed the most about life in Vestele, aside from the people who she once considered family. When the sun had begun to turn the skies of Oro a deep gray, and the witch guardians went into hiding for the day, Ravenna and her useless guard headed back toward the castle.

In just over a month, the Autumn Trades and its anniversary celebration would sweep through the kingdom. As they approached the square, where a dozen vendors were already beginning preparations, Ravenna heard screams coming from the direction of the commoners' well. Her guard stiffened behind her, barely stopping himself from grabbing her by the arm and tugging her away from the ruckus. She stood on the tips of her toes, moving slowly toward the gathering crowd, checking over her shoulder only once to be sure her escort had chosen to follow.

"Miss, let's head back to your chambers," he called. The commotion at the well only grew louder, and Ravenna kept going. His incessant worries followed closely behind her. "What if the king is wondering where you are?"

"I guess you will have to answer to him," she said with a shrug, weaving through a group of drunkards. All but one of the inebriated men were oblivious to the crowds gathering at the well, and as Ravenna shoved through them, a slosh of something splashed onto her front. She paused for only a moment, mouth watering at the sweet smell of rum. She breathed tightly and kept going, eyes fixed on the woman whose face had gone stark white.

"Lady Ravenna, the king will not be happy."

*The king this, the king that.* Ravenna rolled her eyes.

"I have done nothing against the commands I have been given," she said, brushing off his concern and heading straight into the mass of people. *The proven strength of the sire is the only reason the king has allowed me out with an escort as weak as you, because he knows I am unable to flee or harm his men.*

"What is happening?" she muttered beneath her breath, pushing through the crowds that had formed around the stone well. The woman was pulling up bucket after bucket from the well and dumping pure, thick *red* onto the stones.

"Blood! It's blood!" someone yelled.

Ravenna swayed.

*Red. Red. Red.*

"The water is blood!" that voice yelled again. Ravenna backed away from the sight, blinking through the unwanted memories that began forming in her mind.

A clammy hand found her arm and pulled her from the crowd. "Inside," her guard said hurriedly, and she nodded, letting his trembling hands direct her through the growing mass of spectators. Her gaze caught the massive ocean that bordered the kingdom, which she had just stood on the shore of. The once-black water was now a swirling scarlet.

Ravenna's hands found her temples, and she held pressure there, trying to force those menacing thoughts away. "The water is blood!" the crowd was yelling. Mothers gathered their children and held them close as they took toward their homes in the slums, and men gathered in groups, discussing the possible causes of this strange happening.

She continued massaging her temples, allowing her escort to pull her into the castle and away from that wretched color. If Ravenna knew anything, it was that this was an attack on the kingdom. Someone was messing with the water.

# CHAPTER 15
# KINGDOM OF RED
## JARA

"Blood?" Degare yelled. "Blood?" Her lover's voice rattled through the pointed stalagmites of the throne room and carried down the halls. Jara tapped her fingers against the back of his throne. *Does he wish for the entire kingdom to hear his pathetic bellowing? To know of the anger that rarely leaves him these days?*

Jara had done all she could to please him. She was coming to the realization that he would never be pleased. With the absence of power, through her cleverness, he had gained his health and the ability to have a long reign in Oro. She had hoped to reign beside him, but with his temper quickening by the day, the thoughts of reigning apart from him often crossed her mind. It was not what they had originally agreed upon. With the lies he had spun and the selfish greed of his heart, things had changed.

"Yes, Your Majesty. All of the drinking water. Even the sea," Faxon, one of Degare's Despiri soldiers, said.

"But not the water we give to the Embers in the prison?" Degare asked.

"No, Your Majesty. That water is clean."

Jara chuckled in disbelief. Whomever the threat had come from was quite clever, she had to admit. She placed a silver hair pin between her lips while she swept her hair back into a bun.

Degare turned to scowl at her. "Can you fix this?" he asked.

She looked at him incredulously.

"You think I have the power to turn an entire sea of blood back into water, Degare?" She rolled her eyes and slammed a piece of paper down into his lap. "This came for you."

Degare tore through the red-stained ribbon and unrolled the message. She pretended to read it over his shoulder, though she had unfurled it the second she had torn it from the raven's talons.

*This is just the beginning.*

It was a claim to the attack on Oro. It was a letter that marked the start of a war. Jara smiled faintly at the thought that, finally, someone had come to humble him. *If not this mysterious enemy, let it be me,* she thought.

Degare took a deep breath. "Bring me Ravenna!" He demanded Faxon so loudly his voice cracked in rage.

"Yes, Your Majesty," Faxon responded with a dip of his head and the sweeping of his red cloak as he immediately took toward the exit.

"No," Jara argued. Faxon paused, and Degare looked at Jara standing tall in her defiance and rose to his feet. Before he could start, she spoke again. "She is not ready."

"What do you mean, she is not ready?"

"This is an attack on your kingdom," Jara said. "You intend

to deploy her as your weapon? She cannot yet handle a mission." Jara may have been holding hatred for his ungrateful attitude toward all she had done for him, but she was not going to allow him to waste a perfectly good weapon. If Ravenna were released without proper training, this mystery adversary would have the upper hand, and Ravenna would be compromised before Degare had ever seen the wonders of what Jara had gifted him. "She possesses little control over her power, and on top of that, there is still a fight within her. She cannot be trusted. It is too big of a risk to task her with this. She is not yet fully loyal to you. Physically, yes, but I worry with that bit of defiance that there is a chance she could break free of the sire."

"Break free?" Degare asked through gritted teeth, advancing toward her.

"Yes, dear," she said, trying to calm him as a lover would.

"You fail me time and time again," he spat. He grabbed her by the throat, and she repeated to herself, *You are no failure. It is him who has failed you. It is him. It is him. It is him. Not you. Not you. Not you.* The king turned to Faxon as he lifted her from the ground by her neck. Her hands took hold of his wrists, arms straining to hold up her bodyweight.

"Disregard my last orders. You may go," he said, still squeezing Jara's throat and dismissing the general. Faxon ducked his head and left quickly.

He released her and watched in indifference as she lurched forward in a coughing fit. "It is not likely," she explained, rubbing her neck. "But I've never done a spell of this sort before, and it was all done in such haste. I do not want to risk it. As long as there is a fight within her—I advise you not trust her with the state of your kingdom."

Degare tapped the bloodstone staff on the ground as he paced back and forth.

"So, what do you suggest I do, Jara? I have taken everyone she loves." He paused his pacing to look at her. His deepset eyes harbored shadows. "You said removing the healer would work."

She cleared her throat. "The two of them were friends, and I think killing her did break Ravenna's spirits a little more, I-I watched them. It was Galen's house Zephaniah fled to the night I almost killed Ravenna. I sensed his betrayal, and I sent him out of the torture chambers. My magic trailed him to her doorstep, but it would not cross the threshold. Just as she corrupted the boy, she was trying to do the same to Ravenna. Killing her was the right move. It weakened her, I am sure."

"Is that why Ravenna coerced one of my guards into helping her bury the healer last night? Do you not see that as an act of rebellion?" Jara chewed on her lip. She had not known of that, but that fact did not surprise her. Jara and Ravenna were more similar than either would like to admit. Ravenna had endured months of torture, and Jara, years, but of a different kind. Ravenna would break because Jara understood just what it would take to break herself. When she had nothing left to fight for, surrender would not be far off.

Degare huffed at Jara's silence, and then he muttered, "Forget it, witch. I will think of some way to force her into full surrender on my own." He looked upon her in disgust. "You are dismissed."

# CHAPTER 16
# BLOOD BATH
## COVE

"The witch is headed to the library. Now is a good time," the rebel muttered from beside her in the alley. Cove did not look at him, and he did not look at her. Their hoods were up, concealing their identities in the shadows. He took a bite of stale bread from his pocket and tore it with his teeth. Rain tumbled down around them, pitter-pattering on the cobblestone, while Cove kept them dry against the alley walls where they had conspired most nights. His name was Sinley. He and Cove had crossed paths on the night she had sent the raven to the Shadow when she had nowhere else to go.

"Two and a half months in the slums has been enough for me," Cove said, pushing off the wall and heading into the downpour without a thought.

"Be careful," he called behind her, his voice hoarse. She waved him off. She was quite tired of sitting around. While the witch was out, probably on the hunt for a spell that could lift the peculiar curse of blood from the waters, Cove was going to

113

do what she had come here to do in the first place. She had not come here for Ravenna, and she had not come here for Leith.

She had come to liberate her husband. To set him free of the chains she had inadvertently shackled him with. Marriage to her had been his biggest mistake. She had the type of cursed past that followed, *stalked,* and she had seen it working against them at the threshold of their story—when they had fallen in love—her father as their adversary. *Has my father, Marinos, sent the hunters after me yet, as he always promised he would if I fled the islands?*

Cove grimaced. She could not erase the past, but she could save her husband's future. If only she could find him.

She scurried between raindrops, cloak dragging through the puddles as she approached the castle of Oro. Fear hung in the air, and children were out gathering buckets of the clean water that poured from the skies. A young mother clung to her infant, her green eyes peering out from beneath her cloak in fear as she watched her bucket fill up slowly. It was hard to tell when Oro would have another rain that brought clean water, and a pang of guilt had Cove sending her power weaving through the drops, allowing it to fall harder and fill the tin pails a little faster.

A legion of Despiri were huddled beneath a small shelter where they could often be found training when the weather was dry, and as she neared, she realized some of them were enjoying the clean water, too. Some were washing in it, and some were letting it fall onto their outstretched tongues. *Not for you,* she thought. *None for you.*

Cove hid behind some wooden crates and pretended to be waiting out the sideways rain against the castle walls. She focused on the distant sea, carefully coaxing the red water into the skies. After her final night in the Dawn Islands, when so much of her water manipulation power had been released, she had a new understanding of it. Finally, when enough had gathered in the clouds, she let it separate into a million droplets that crashed upon the Despiri.

She watched in satisfaction as they spewed the water from their mouths and clambered for their shelter. They began to glance around, and she took toward the servant entrance of the castle, careful to keep her eyes down in fear she would be recognized as the servant who had mysteriously disappeared. She had been a fool to stay in this kingdom, and she was an even bigger fool to step foot back into the castle where the heart of darkness resided.

She snuck through the halls, only catching the eyes of one lone guard. His mouth opened to question her, and her hands began to shake with anxiety as she prepared to use the gift she saw as a curse. "Hey! What is your business here?" She held her breath as she dove into the power she hated. Reluctantly, she held eye contact as she worked to cloud his mind with disinterest. He stepped toward her once, and then he shook his head, blinking, as if he had forgotten his pursuit. He waved her on, and she took a deep breath. *It worked.* Her practice was paying off.

It was the ability that opened her mind to the emotions of those around her, allowing–*forcing*–her to feel every dark crevice of this world. Using her gifts of emotional manipulation was a risk, mostly due to the fact that after all these years, she still did not understand the inner workings. It was a skill that she had not yet mastered, and one that could cause considerable damage if she misstepped. But this mission was important, and she would risk it all for him.

Cove had made a deal with Leith–the man called the Shadow: she would play spy and help him acquire the Dove. In return, he would help her get Elias back. But Ravenna was too far gone, and Cove guessed that deal no longer stood. She was taking matters into her own hands.

As she walked down the halls of the castle, her heart beat wildly in her chest. But instead of allowing the rapid rhythm to trap her in fear, she breathed slowly, cherishing the beat and letting it remind her that she was alive because of what had been done to spare her life.

"Elias, talk to me," she whispered aloud, hoping for an answer down the bond that now entwined them. "I am about to do something incredibly stupid. If you just tell me where you are, I can turn around right now. I'll come to you in a heartbeat." Nothing. The bond stayed silent, as it had for over five months. Since the moment he had given up his freedom to spare her life.

*Where are you, Elias?*

Even still, his absence was the weight of the entire ocean, pressing down on her chest.

*I will find you.*

Cove invited a gulp of air into her aching chest and pushed herself toward the witch's chambers. Thankfully, there were no guards posted outside. She had not picked a lock since the time she and Princess Mina had snuck into the king's chambers while he was visiting Tabrana. They were only fifteen, and had wanted to look through the late queen's jewelry. They had spent an entire afternoon snickering as they tried on every string of pearls and even some of her dresses. Life had been much simpler then–a time before Mina's betrayal had left Cove all alone.

Cove used two hair pins to manipulate the internal mechanisms of the lock. "Come on," she whispered as she struggled to move through the three metal pieces inside the lock. She had one piece left to set when she heard footsteps in the hall. *No, no, no.* She looked over her shoulder and took a long, deep breath before trying a final time. She inserted the hair pin and pushed it into the lock until she heard a click.

As she turned the knob, the tension in her chest dissipated. She peered around before slipping in behind the heavy wooden door. When she was safely on the other side, swallowed by the deep purple hues of the room, she turned the lock once more and waited for the footsteps in the hall to pass before heading to the desk. She had been here before, to alter the spell the witch had done on Ravenna. That had been a foolish mistake, and it was one Cove would regret until the end of her days. But her husband was out there somewhere, awaiting death for a crime she had committed, and she would do anything to find him. That, unfortunately, had included her involvement in dark magic.

The plan would have worked, though she had not put much thought into it before she had jumped into action. Elias had been the only one on her mind. Ravenna had just been a stepping stone for Cove to continue on her way to rescuing Elias. Perhaps if she had thought it through and weighed the chances of it all going south, things would be different. If Cove had left the spell as it was, and not given the witch the idea of transferring the gifts to Ravenna, the Dove of Ozanna would not be bedecked in the feathered, armored wings of a raven— she would be dead. But a dead Dove was still better than the threat that now faced Arresia with her rise to power as Degare's weapon.

Cove was a fool. She looked in the drawer of the desk, digging through papers upon papers of information on the Embers that were in the prison. Finally, she came across a few new pages she had not seen the last time she had been here. She kept her ears on the sounds outside in the hall as she scanned the list of male Embers with their gifts and assigned numbers. Thankfully, the ship Elias was on had not made it in time to be sold in the Summer Trade, but the Autumn Trade was in a month, and Cove had to find him before the king's staff found its home in his chest.

*Please, please, please be in Oro,* she thought as she looked through the list. How she would get him out of Oro before the trades, well, that plan had yet to be concocted. But at least she would know he was alive.

Her eyes quickly skimmed the page to the end of the list, but still, there was no sign of him.

*Elias, please answer me.*

She never truly expected an answer, and she never got one. She spun the silver band on her finger and said a silent prayer, begging for the sparing of the innocent life that was now tied to her guilty soul.

Cove nervously looked at the door again and began to place the papers back into the desk drawer as she had found them, but something on the desk caught her eye. A letter, addressed to Jara, stamped with the black seal of the Delle Witch Clan. A seal which had already been broken. Cove hastily unfolded it.

*Mother,*

*As I am sure you have heard, there was some trouble with the alliance between Edmaria and the Dawn Islands. Prince Andreas was killed by an Ember. Do not fret, I still work to secure the land you seek for our clan in Edmaria. With the king dead and Mina's best friend out of the equation, the new Queen of the Islands is becoming quite easy to manipulate. I have Lord Yarris of Edmaria wrapped around my finger. You will be free of Degare and lead our witches to war in no time. We shall claim a home for ourselves.*

*Beneath your leadership, the witches will rise again.*

*Celeste*

Cove's heart plummeted into her chest. *Celeste.* Lady Celeste, whom she had spent years with in the Dawn Islands serving the princess, was a witch, and she had no doubt been planted there by Jara–*her mother.* What kind of deal was it that King Sebastian had made with Celeste's mother, *Jara,* to earn her a place at Princess Mina's side? Had the King of the Dawn Islands known he was dealing with witches? Did Mina know the truth? Cove's mouth went dry as she thought of Mina.

*The king is dead. King Sebastian's illness had finally taken him, and now Mina is all alone.* Cove fought the tears that came with the grief she could almost feel tugging at her from across the seas, from the heart of the girl who had once been her best friend–her sister. *Who is there for Mina with me gone?* Cove shook her head violently. Mina had helped orchestrate Elias's capture. Cove owed her no pity.

She read the letter over and over.

*The witches will rise again.*

*Is Jara working against Degare?*

Cove was on her fifth read-through when she heard the witch approaching at the end of the hallway.

*No, no, no.*

She skimmed the page a final time, hurriedly folded it, and set it back on the desk. She took a few seconds to survey everything she had touched, to make sure nothing had been misplaced. At the rattle of the brass door handle, Cove moved toward the balcony, stumbling over a horribly placed rug. She hastily opened and shut the glass pane door too loudly. Just as the door to the chambers creeped open, and Jara appeared in the doorway, eyes cast down at a book in hand, Cove took a breath and jumped from the balcony to the red sea below.

Cove hit the bloody waters with her eyes shut tight. She held her breath as long as she could before coming up for air, and tried not to let herself think about the nights she had spent floating into oblivion. Once, when she was twelve, fleeing her parent's murderers, and another just four months ago, starting the night Elias had been forced onto that ship, when she had jumped into the sea after him.

The red ocean waves churned around her, stirring up the metallic scent of blood and the odor of dead fish. She gagged as her arms urged her toward the shore while she floated on her back, and she looked to the witch's balcony that towered a hundred feet above.

She kept her eyes fixed upward, ensuring Jara did not come out to enjoy the chilly breeze. *Celeste,* the lady in waiting that had threatened Cove's life, was a witch. Not just any witch— but Jara's daughter. *Who was her father?* Cove wondered, thoughts immediately circling to Degare. She doubted it, being that Celeste had addressed him as nothing more in her letter. Cove blinked the water out of her eyes and continued taking deep breaths as she neared the shore, trying to keep her mind occupied. *What did she mean, the witches will rise again? That*

*Jara would soon be free of Degare? That the witches would soon have a place to call home?*

Jara was scheming, and though Cove wanted to know everything about it, to protect both herself and all of the Ember people, only one Ember held her full attention. The one who had captivated her–loved her–and had willingly marched to his own death in place of hers. Before she could do anything else, before she could shift her focus, she had to make sure that death did not come.

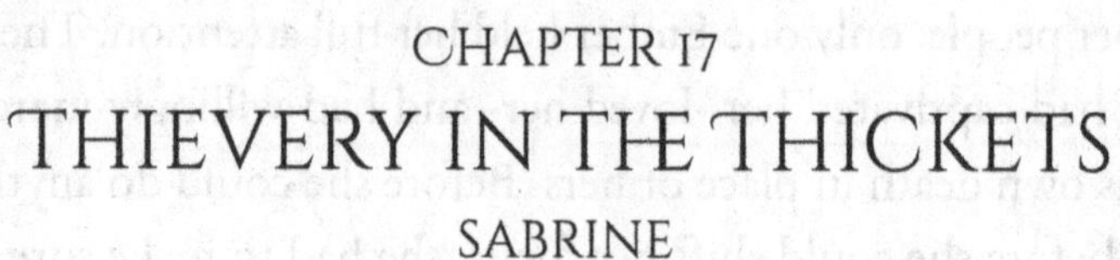

# CHAPTER 17
# THIEVERY IN THE THICKETS
## SABRINE

The dry air of Edmaria caressed Sabrine's tawny skin as she walked toward the sounds of music, which had coaxed her out of her cabin in the woods early this morning. She was in desperate need of food and money, and with foreigners traveling through the port city on their way to the Ember Trades in Oro, today's pickings were promising.

She tripped over her makeshift sandals and nearly tumbled down the hill on the outskirts of the woods. She cursed as the thorns of a thistle pierced through her feet. "I have got to get some new boots," she muttered, picking the tiny needles from her skin. *Today*, she promised herself, peeling the poor excuse for sandals from her feet and discarding them at the base of a tree.

The mossy green soil at the edge of the forest quickly transitioned into sand as she traveled east. In the heart of the Thickets down below, the small city was loud with noises of laughter and joy as townsfolk and vendors came out of their houses to meet the travelers that paraded through their village, disembarking from the docking ships. The Thicket's market collected the most profit just before each seasonal Ember Trade, when the ships docked for a few days while they collected and dispersed the stock as needed. Some of the foreigners would lose their lives crossing the Black Sea to Oro, and some would be taken by the shadows in the Valley. For them, the promise of power was worth the risk.

The sun was creeping higher into the sky with every minute, and with it, the desert sands grew hot on the soles of her feet. Sabrine picked up the pace, beelining for the little shade the city provided.

As she made it to the edge of the Thickets, where golden-toned buildings were erected in the sand, she was relieved to find the city full of men and women who wore fine jewelry and expensive fabrics. Their satchels were certainly full of more than her usual pickings of copper coins. Silver, and perhaps gold, lined the pockets of these wealthy, traveling killers. Sabrine would feel no guilt taking from them.

Carefully, she unbuttoned her navy cloak and revealed the bright turquoise of the stolen outfit beneath. It had a high neckline and left her arms bare. She thought she could use a few golden cuffs for her arm to complete the look, but those, she did not have. Dark blue beads dangled from the ends of her blouse until they overlapped the waistband of the billowy satin pants. She blended in fairly well with the people she would be thieving from. No one would suspect her. She made frequent trips to the markets to practice thievery; it was the only thing that kept her alive. She picked a group of finely dressed young women close to her own age, and as she trailed them through the streets, warm sand squished around her toes. She *hated* the feeling. Sabrine was used to the green grasses and prairies of

Brinland, where she could run with bare feet over the soft ground without fear of the hot sand burning her.

The city buildings towered tall above her, blocking the late morning sun from her face. Banners hung across the dusty streets and the sunlight caught their many colors, painting them with a brilliant glow. She looked toward the Crystal Sea, where the clear water was rippling around the docks. She stopped to observe until Embers began exiting in chains and shackles. An Edmarian soldier stood with a paper, documenting and sorting the stock of Embers. Sabrine's nostrils flared as he prodded and poked at each of them.

A man, who was close to her in age, came off the ship with his sunken eyes focused on the boards beneath his feet. His clothes were wet rags, his body, ill. He did not look up as the soldier commanded him, but after a smack to the face, he mindlessly moved to the side at the soldier's direction. Some of the other Embers stayed on the docks with him while others boarded the next ship, likely headed to Oro for the approaching Autumn Trade.

She watched the Embers as they lined up on the docks to be surveyed and sorted. Maybe the stock was being split up into two shipments—one by land and one by sea—similar to how the foreigners traveled. Some through the Valley, and some through the black waters.

Sabrine continued walking, observing the wealth around her. The owners of the stands that held breads, meats, and enough fruits for a crowd, were always kind to her. Some waved as she walked past. Most of them were poor, as her family had been. It was these types of people Sabrine could not bring herself to steal from—the ones who scavenged to survive, just like she had been made to. Because those who weren't born into royalty or wealth would never be able to climb to a higher status. They were to be stuck in eternal poverty. Each cent they made would either go back to the kingdom in taxes or toward necessities like food and rent. Sabrine was lucky in that aspect, she guessed. Because she was a thief with no registered residence in this kingdom, she saved much of what she squandered.

Despite what her parents thought of her, she did have some morals. In a city of people struggling in the same ways as her, finding a candidate she deemed it fine to steal a few coppers from was the task that usually took up most of her morning. But today, her pool of potential victims was endless.

Sabrine kept her eyes down as she strategically selected her place near a leather stand being flocked by a dozen rich noblemen. She selected a piece of leather, smoothing her fingers over it as she eavesdropped on a conversation. Two Edmarian men were chatting rather loudly on the other side of the table.

"I was at the mines last week," one said. He picked up a cut of black leather, examined it, and then tossed it back onto the table. "The Delle Witches are going mad, and none of the mines in Ozanna seem to be bringing in much bloodstone. I heard Degare's witch betrayed them again by siding with Oro." Sabrine listened closely, following them to the next stand and keeping her eyes on the intricately painted pottery on the table. "Apparently, she just made him unbeatable." *Unbeatable?*

"What do you think the weapon is?" *Weapon?* Sabrine was careful to keep her eyes down as she stayed near them.

"A dragon?" Sabrine went rigid as they both chuckled. "Nah, I don't know. But I hear it can level an entire village. I am sure we will find out what it is at the trades. Why else would he be promising such an extravagant ball than to showcase his power that never seems to end?"

The other scratched his beard. "Well, the ball is to celebrate the anniversary of the first trade," he said. *The trade that took my parents.* Sabrine's cheeks heated. "But the formal invitation did promise a surprise. I suppose you're right. I look forward to the big reveal."

Sabrine planted her feet as they walked out of earshot, and as she turned she made eye contact with a man who now stood across the table, watching her. He smiled, flashing a set of too-white teeth, and she forced a blush as she averted her eyes to the handmade pots in front of her. She traced his footsteps around the table until he was hovering behind her, and then she turned into him, acting as though he had caught her off guard.

"I'm terribly sorry," she said, moving her eyes from his, to his mouth, to the many rings on his fingers.

She was aware of the unique appearance she possessed in these lands. She was from Brinland, and her brown skin was like those in Edmaria, but her eyes were a bright blue that enticed conversation. She refrained from backing away from him, and instead, took one step closer as he surveyed her.

His deep brown eyes did not leave her for a second. She recognized the way he stood a little taller at the sight of her faux smile. She batted her eyelashes, smirking beneath the fine, stolen fabric she had pulled across her nose and mouth. *Fool,* she thought as his hand reached for hers, and he slowly placed a kiss upon the back of it.

"Where do you come from, my lady?" His skin was a rich brown, and he spoke in the tongue of Volcania. Sabrine had learned pieces of the language from her teacher in Matuk when she was young.

"Brinland, my lord," she said, bowing her head in imitation of reverence. He smiled at that, and she returned it, still flirting with her eyes and holding onto his hand.

"My family dwells in Volcania," he stated pridefully. "Come back with me." She held back a scoff at his direct offer. She was sure he had traveled across the sea to attend the Ember Trade in Oro—as every foreigner in this city had—and to her, there was nothing more abominable. She looked at him with doe eyes, blinking slowly and keeping his attention on her face as she gently worked the rings from his fingers.

*Keep looking at my eyes.* He grinned at her, revealing those straight, white teeth. When she had gotten what she needed, she pulled her hand away.

"I am married, my lord," she said with disappointment in her voice, flashing the brass, faux marriage band on her left hand.

A look of disappointment flashed across his face and he shook his head at the ring on her hand. "Return with me, and we will build a new life together. You'll replace that brass with gold," he pledged. "I will make you rich." Her brow raised involuntarily. *Ah, the promises of a marriage to a wealthy man.*

"I do not crave money or gold," she lied.

"You do not know what you are missing. One can never have too much."

That was where he was wrong. She did know what she was missing, and one had too much when their wealth began filling the pockets of the King of Oro. One had too much regard for themselves, too much pride, when they would end a human life, without remorse, for their own selfish gain.

"I am sorry, my lord. But I cannot return with you." With

one last sweep of her hand across his fingers, she smirked at him and slipped away, getting lost in the crowd as he called after her. Pocketing the luxurious rings she had just stolen from his hands, she grinned beneath her veil. Desperate men were fools, and today's profit would far exceed any other.

Perhaps the money and gold she craved, and had finally pocketed thanks to the trades, would finally be enough.

With a pocket full of fine, gold-plated jewelry, a handful of copper, and a few silvers from the pockets of the rich, Sabrine had to admit that the Ember Trade market was benefitting her in some ways. She could hardly believe the profit she had made and the fine foods she would be taking home to feast on this week. When she prepared to leave the Thickets, she would even be able to afford a hide for the chilly nights and maybe some new boots to protect her feet against the thorns and hot sand.

As she prepared to trade in her jewels for coins, Sabrine became greedy at the sight of a handsome gentleman around her age, escorted by two men on black stallions. To have escorts was a sign of great fortune. She would bet she could triple the profit in her pockets by taking what he had in his. At his side was a sword—shiny and probably custom designed for him. She had never seen one with such intricate markings. Jewels had been placed in the hilt of brushed gold. Obviously, the sword was not something she could steal, but he was bound to have something small of greater or equal value.

She removed the brass ring from her finger, and as he approached the alley she stood in, she picked up her cloak and draped it over her arm, leaning against the stones of a tavern.

When he passed by, she walked directly in front of his stallion, causing a ruckus amongst his posse. She tried to look interested in some fine spices across the street, paying no regard to the holdup she had caused. She twirled her fingers in her thick black braid as she admired the many jars and half-listened to the elderly merchant's story of the herbs that had just arrived this morning on a very-delayed ship from the Dawn Islands.

Sabrine followed the old woman's wide gaze to the man that was now climbing down from his horse and stalking toward her. As he approached, Sabrine minded her own business and reached for a jar of spice. When he arrived at her side, she paid him no mind. He towered at least a foot over her.

"Miss." He bowed his head slightly, and she turned to him. His eyes were brown and seemingly gentle, unlike his walk, which reminded her of a prowling cat. She made it a point to smile while admiring his strong and lean build. Actually, she was taking in the gold pocket watch that hung from his belt and the tiny sapphire gem that was coming loose from the hilt of his sword. Even his deep purple handkerchief was woven from fine fabrics that would sell for at least half a silver serpent.

"My lord," she said with a shyness to her voice. One of his escorts stepped forward, as if preparing to reprimand her for something, but the man held his hand up as if to stop him. He cocked his head at her in curiosity, and she tried to keep her composure, not letting the confusion show on her face. Today, she was thankful for the veil that concealed the nervous biting of her lip.

"Leave us," he ordered his companions, to which they grudgingly obeyed. His skin was bronze, similar to her own, but his accent suggested he was native to these lands. As his friends left them alone, Sabrine stepped back, suddenly feeling threatened by his presence. He never once took his eyes from her and looked at her with a sort of intensity that made her cheeks burn.

"What are you doing in the streets all alone, my lady?" He kept advancing toward her, like he was stalking his prey.

She attempted a smile, but it was ineffective beneath the veil as it did not reach her eyes. There was a whisper of curiosity in his smooth voice, and Sabrine reminded herself to provide him with little truth. Most women traveled with an escort—a husband, brother or father, or with a group of other ladies. In his eyes, it was odd that she was traveling solo.

She held the spices up, moving a little further away from him and observing a few more jars. His eyes fell to her bare ring finger. "Shopping. What else would a lady be doing here?" she asked innocently.

He looked from her thick, cascading braid to her bare feet. "You certainly have a different taste in apparel." He gestured to the bare skin on her arms. The ladies around her also wore fine linens but were completely covered head to toe to protect against the desert sun. "I am guessing you did not find that clothing in these markets?"

Sabrine was silent for a moment as she shaped her lie. She had found her clothing in these markets—had stolen it months ago from the stands just a few hundred steps to her right. But she rarely stole items that could not fit in her pockets, and in her inexperience, when she swiped it, she had missed the accompanying shawl.

"If you must know, I'm a duchess from the southern territories. I did not expect the sun here to be so. . .hot." She said it with a sure confidence in her voice, insinuating that she had not prepared for this weather.

He chuckled loudly, letting his head roll back on his shoulders. "A duchess from Brinland? Are you kidding?"

"You do not believe me?" she asked accusatorily, crossing her arms. *I am a fool. You should have given him the title of lady. Duchesses do not often hold titles without husbands.*

His eyes snapped to hers, and he waved her off, still grinning. He had a nice smile—one she could get lost in, if she was not careful. Quite charming, but a nuisance if she did say so herself.

"No, no. It is not that," he said. "It is just that I cannot seem to get away from duchesses." He looked to his friends, who carefully watched her from behind. "Well, you will definitely be leaving the markets with a sunburn," he noted. "You really should cover up." He reached for her mismatched cloak, and she stepped just out of reach. He tilted his chin. "The Edmarian sun is nothing to mess with."

He sighed, rubbing a hand over his face and through his chin-length, black hair. "At least let me buy you some shoes." He gestured to where she had conveniently placed her feet in the small sliver of shaded sand by the merchant's table. "Do they not have those in your country?"

Her brows furrowed at the comment. "Why would you offer such a thing to a stranger?"

He shrugged. "I like to try and redeem myself through small acts of kindness. It is the least I can do, really, when I see someone in need."

"Redeem yourself from what?" she asked before she could think. He lowered his brows at her sudden curiosity. *Do not ask questions. You're forgetting why you're here. Get him within reach, empty his pockets, and then get as far from him as you can.* She studied him carefully and then shrugged the question off.

"Shoes would be nice, and though I could purchase them myself," she said proudly, "I suppose I can allow you to practice your act of kindness for the day."

His lip twitched upward in satisfaction, and she followed him across the street to another vendor, where a fine selection of sandals and hide boots were sprawled about the table. The poverty-stricken merchant behind the table smiled but said nothing. Sabrine had been here many times before. The woman had recently lost her husband and rarely said a word.

Beside her, her new acquaintance picked up a pair of sandals, examining them in his hands.

"Winter is coming," she said, grabbing some tanned boots. She would need more protection against the colder weather that touched the southern sands. "These ones fit quite well, don't they?" she asked as she slipped the second boot over her heel.

"Quite well," he agreed. "Are those the ones you want?" He sat the sandals back down on the table, and she looked at the other boots of varying sizes, eyes pausing on the children's ones.

"Yes, these will do," she answered quickly.

He turned to the silent merchant. "One pair of boots," he said as he dropped a round silver serpent into the woman's hand. The merchant's mouth fell agape at the overpayment, and he manually closed her fingers around the coin. "Beautiful craftsmanship," he complimented, patting her hand.

Sabrine watched the encounter from where she leaned against the table and laced the first boot onto her foot. "These boots are worth five coppers at best," she said when he turned back to her.

"Not fine enough for a duchess?" he teased. "May I remind

you, you had no shoes at all ten seconds ago, which is very strange considering your title. The duchesses I know have too many to count."

"I have shoes," she lied. "I just did not have any that matched my outfit, and I quite enjoy walking barefoot."

"Really? What's with the blood?" he asked, nodding to her foot as she slipped it into the second boot. "Step on a cactus?"

"Thistle," she corrected him. *Quit indulging his questions.*

He raised his chin. "Ah. First rule of Edmaria, don't go barefoot."

"Fair enough," she said, standing up and testing out the boots as she walked back to the spice table. He followed her, as she knew he would, and she braced herself with both hands against the table, leaning back and coaxing him in. She wiggled her toes inside the new shoes. "Well, thank you," she said, admiring them on her feet.

"Happy to help make you feel more at home here," he said. "How long will you be staying?"

*Redirect the conversation.*

She looked around, noting the many faces in the crowd that had stopped to stare at them as they conversed. "Why is everyone watching us?" she asked.

"Do not tell me you are not aware of your beauty," he said with a brow raised. Something in his words sounded like an allegation, and she did not have to force her blush. He concealed her from the crowd by tilting his body into the table next to her, also blocking her only exit. *Abandon this mission.* He cocked his head, stepping a little closer. "What is your name?" he asked curiously.

"Anya," she lied too quickly beneath her veil. "And yours?" She waved one of the spices just below her nose, pretending not to be too interested in what he had to say, pretending not to be nervous about his close proximity to her. She could feel her cheeks reddening beneath the thin veil and her skin growing hot with nerves. *Just remember the mission and get out of here.*

"Merrick." *That name*, she had heard it before. Not a typical name, but she knew it from somewhere. He watched her closely for a moment and then peered around them at the many curious faces in the crowd. "Well, *Anya*," he said, tugging gently on the cloak that she had folded over her arms. "It seems you're getting a little pink. If I were you, I'd put this on." Sabrine's cheeks were on fire now. *Get away from him, now. He is hindering your focus. He is onto you.* His eyes were locked on hers as she threw the cloak over her shoulders.

"Thanks for looking out," she said as she pushed past him, slipping the watch from his belt as she did.

"See you around then, *Anya*?" he called behind her. There was a smile in his voice.

"Probably not," she said, waving a hand into the air and storming through the sea of men that stared after her. She shivered. Sabrine was good at being in control, and most of her act depended on getting men to stare at her. She had lost control of her interaction with Merrick when he had seen her as more than something to look at. It did not matter how charming the man was–he was unsettling. He had commented on her beauty, but something about it was disingenuous. His interest in her was because of something far deeper than what he saw on the surface. He was trying to read her. He had questions, and she was not going to give him the chance to ask.

When she was sure he had not followed her, she pulled the pocket watch from her cloak and grinned. Its face was pure gold with the intricate crest of Edmaria's winding serpent carved into it. *This watch is worth a fortune.* She could hardly contain her excitement as she scurried through the streets to the elderly couple who always purchased her goods and never questioned their origin. Unlike many of the merchants here, they dealt in copper *and* silver coins.

"Find anything good today?" the white-haired man asked, rising slowly from his seat to wobble toward the table as she approached.

She nodded silently and reached for the jewels in her pant pockets. Her fingers found nothing. She dug deeper, feeling the empty linings of her pocket. *That thief. He has stolen my findings.*

"Well, hun. Anything today or not?" the old man's wrinkly wife muttered as Sabrine panicked, feeling through every pocket she had. The woman looked beyond Sabrine at the line of impatient customers gathering behind her. Everything she had thieved today was gone. The silver serpents, the hundred coppers, and the jewels. *Gone.* All that was left was the gold-plated pocket watch.

"That's it for today," she huffed, laying the piece on the table. The gold gleamed in the sun, and the elderly woman's eyes widened. She jumped back, scanning her surroundings. Her husband leaned in closer to the watch and stepped away from Sabrine at once.

"Get that thing out of here," he demanded through gritted teeth. His voice was low and urgent, and Sabrine's cheeks heated as she looked between the two of them. "Go on! Get out of here!" he yelled, rushing Sabrine away from their booth. She staggered back, disrupting the line behind her and pocketing the watch as she pulled her hood up over her ears in haste.

She did not understand what the commotion was about, but she had a feeling she needed to flee, and quickly. She had no money to purchase food, not even a coin left of what she had thieved earlier in the day. She knew she would go hungry, so she broke her rule of not stealing from the common folk and farmers and snuck three small fruits from a table as she walked past. She continued through the market, concealing some dried meat and breads in her cloak and then stormed through the city streets and alleys toward home.

She grabbed a small, easily-concealable dagger from a weapon master's stand and swiftly slipped it into the waistline of her pants. She would feel better if she had a weapon on her walk home, whether she knew how to properly use it or not. Merrick knew she was a thief, though, he had stolen from her, too. So maybe they were even. She did not wish to find out. Her veil remained over her mouth until she made it to the thick brush that surrounded the city's edge.

As she exited the Thickets, she replayed her encounter with him. How had he stolen so much, leaving her blissfully unaware? It had to have been him. The last time she had the jewels was at the spice stand, when she had proudly felt them weighing down her pockets. *He stole from me when he tugged on my cloak.* Sabrine breathed tightly. *How could I have been so clueless? Could I have just ruined everything?*

Once she crossed through the brush and thickets, she picked up the pace, running through the narrow desert that separated her from the cover of the woods. The boots that now protected her feet against the hot sand and the thistles on the hillside were a small price for Merrick to pay compared to the coin he now possessed.

*Quickly, Sabrine. Move quickly,* she told herself.

Before she entered the shadows beyond the tree line at the top of the hill, she paused to look back at the shrinking city. She could not help but fear she was being followed, but thankfully, there was no one trailing her. After checking behind her every twenty steps, she eventually made it to the cabin at the river's edge. She was trekking through the tall grasses between the cabin and the river when a blend of two singsongy voices broke through the barrier of the trees around her. "Sabrine! Sabrine!"

"Hush now!" she whispered as those four little feet came clamoring down the steps of the cabin. She glanced behind her, hoping that the rushing of the river concealed the noise from any forest lurkers. "I told you to stay inside until I got back!"

"And you're back," Risley said with a shrug. Neah grinned mischievously beside him, her dark, wild curls catching the sunlight. In response to his sister's widening smile, a hint of Risley's dimples became visible on his cheeks. Sabrine frowned, remembering how pronounced those dimples were just a year ago, before he had lost so much weight. Sabrine dug into her pockets, handing each of the twins a tear of bread, and quickly ushered them inside. They were only nine years old, and they had endured so much. Their little bodies were too thin, and they needed more nutrients than she was providing. She could have left with a fortune today, had she not been greedy enough to go for that pocket watch.

She pulled two fruits from her cloak, tossing one to each little set of hands. "Market wasn't great today. Sorry, little ones." They frowned for her sake, as they could tell she was disappointed, but they delighted in the fruit she had brought them. "That means I must hunt today. So, stay inside, curtains closed," she ordered, ruffling Neah's hair.

She would have to hunt if they wanted to live to see another week. The bow and arrows she had swiped in the Thickets months ago would have benefited her more if she could hit any of the small animals she aimed at. It was rare to see larger prey in these woods, and she feared straying too far north, where King Idris of Edmaria had Lume and Ember slaves mining for bloodstone. If the mining operation traveled much further south, Sabrine would be moving the twins elsewhere, so she would keep a close eye on it. She could not travel too far west, either, where the King of Oro had just reopened every one of his own mines.

Perhaps she could find a buyer for the watch and finally afford tickets to board a ship to Eswen, where her lightmarked siblings would be welcomed. They would be protected and safe, and there, Sabrine would not be sentenced to death by affiliation.

The twins began to argue. "But we want to go outside," Neah begged. "It is boring here. It is not fair that you get to go out and we don't."

"You two are lightmarked, and I am not. Therefore, it is safe for me, but not for you. You hear me?"

Risley scrunched his button nose beside her, his bright, round eyes flashing with mischief. Sabrine raised a brow at him and gave him a curt shake of her head. The stern look served as a reminder of what could happen to them if he dared sneak out. *If you had listened to me instead of mother and father, we would not be in this predicament*, she wanted to say. But the twins were young, and when their mother had spoken of the Light with such joy, they believed her. Nothing Sabrine could say or do could take that from them. The Light now dwelled within their tiny bodies, and they were proud to be separated from darkness, no matter the bounty it placed on their heads.

Sabrine had come to terms with that months ago. That fact did not stop the anger from rising inside her, or the resentment for this Father of Lights her parents had so loved to tell her about. It was because of that Light that they had been taken from her and killed in the very first Ember Trade. And it was because of that Light that her young siblings would never be safe in Arresia.

"Why aren't you, Sabrine?" *Why aren't you lightmarked? Why do you run from the Father of Lights?*

"I am not having this conversation again. If I came to the Light, who would be left to protect you?"

"The Father of Lights would–"

"Do you know how silly that sounds?" Sabrine asked, lifting her bow from the rusty nail next to the door. Neah and Risley looked at her with pleading eyes, and she sighed. Sabrine was good at hiding, but the Light within them was good at pursuing. "I'll be back. Stay inside," she muttered, and then she traipsed out the door.

# CHAPTER 18
# GAME OF CHASE
## MERRICK

Anya was a decent liar, but Merrick was no fool. He had fallen victim to deceitful women one too many times, and he was not about to let her take home the prize, though he had let her take home his watch. He had been watching her thieve her way through the Thickets all morning, and while everyone else was oblivious, he was not. She reminded him of his father's wife, in both beauty and deceit, and he had let his curiosity get the best of him when she had purposely walked in front of his horse.

Merrick had traced her whereabouts after their encounter, silently watching from afar on his horse as she realized her pockets held none of the riches she had stolen earlier that day. He smiled to himself at her fluster as he felt the coins in his pocket. The elderly couple at the stand had been smart, recognizing the serpent on his watch almost immediately and ordering her away from them. The girl had not yet made the connection that she had stolen from the one and only Prince of Edmaria. As she traveled west, she swiped food and even a weapon from one of the tables. He could have her arrested, he supposed, but what would be the fun in that?

"Stay here," Prince Merrick said to his men as he began climbing down from his stallion.

"Where are you going?" Kenan asked, sitting tall and straight atop his horse. His dark brows furrowed with sudden concern, and he rubbed the stubble on his cheek.

"For a stroll. I need to clear my head. I'll meet you back at the country home." Merrick extended the reins of his horse toward Kenan with an outstretched hand.

"You're walking? You really shouldn't be wandering alone, especially not with all these foreigners around. And after the death of Andreas. Your father will have my head," Kenan argued, not taking the reins. Kenan's jaw was set, and his amber eyes flashed with annoyance.

"My father will never know," Merrick said. One of Merrick's other men, Nadim, narrowed his eyes as he watched Merrick with suspicion. "He is on his way to Oro as we speak. He might not even survive the trip—he chose to travel by sea, and I hear the seas have been in a state of rage. Besides, in his absence I am in charge, and I say I am allowed to enjoy an afternoon alone."

Kenan shook his head and reluctantly took the reins from him. "What time should I expect you back?" Merrick shifted his eyes between Kenan and Nadim, who still looked at him with skepticism.

Nadim's serpent-engraved knife—which Merrick had gifted him—gleamed in the sunlight. Merrick looked at the sun's position in the sky and said, "Give me the afternoon. If I am not back by dusk, you may come looking for me."

"Alright," Kenan agreed. "But if you die, I get your sword."

Merrick grinned and collected it from the side of his horse. "Guess you'll have to pry it from my cold, dead hands."

Kenan laughed, and he and the rest of Merrick's group rode north, toward the country home, where Merrick had found solace this past week. Jamila was not traveling with his father, and he could not have stayed in that palace with her for another moment. That he had been able to resist her temptations this long, was a miracle. Jamila's eyes had been on him since they were young–long before she had been wed to his father. Merrick and Jamila had been promised to one another from a young age, and he had always pictured himself with her but only because it was expected of him.

He never loved her in the all-consuming way that he imagined love to feel, but he had cared about her enough to feel jealousy when she had betrayed him with his brother. Now, she was his father's and was off limits, but her advances would be the death of him. Merrick wanted no woman to suffer what his mother had in marriage to his father, but there was nothing he could do to help Jamila that would allow him to keep his life and his right to the throne.

Merrick stood at the highest point in the city, scanning the streets to the west for Anya, where he had seen her last. "Where did you go?" he asked under his breath, stretching his fingers. "Ah, there you are." He smiled as he caught a glimpse of her high stepping through the brush on the outskirts of the Thickets, her black braid sleek against the sun. He started in her direction but kept his distance so she would not notice him trailing her.

The girl was incredibly foolish to steal from a prince. Her deep, olive-toned skin suggested she was from Brinland, as she had claimed. So, she had not been completely lying, but

Merrick knew she had stretched the truth when she claimed to be a duchess. Her non-tailored clothing had been a dead giveaway, and she bore no wedding ring. Duchesses rarely held titles without a husband. Her body was frail, and she was noticeably malnourished. The wealthy in Arresia did not go hungry—they stole from the commonfolk to ensure that. Besides, Merrick had spent much time with the Court of Brinland over the years. In fact, he had spent more time with the Court of Brinland than he had with the Princess of the Dawn Islands, whom he was newly betrothed to, and he had never seen, nor heard of, a Duchess named Anya.

Anya—if that were even her true name—wore stolen clothing. Her blouse fell loosely around her shoulders, and her pants were a size too big for her hips. Merrick had observed the fashion in Brinland, and it was not that. Not even Jamila wore such flamboyant clothing. Though most of the crowd in the city was actually looking at him—a prince conversing with an assumed lady of the night—Merrick could guess the thoughts of the men around him. He knew the look in their eyes, and it made him sick. But he figured that was just what Anya wanted. She drew them in, swiped their pockets clean, and slipped away. That game was too dangerous to play in Arresia, and she was lucky that Merrick was the only one following her home today.

He glanced around one last time to make sure that was true and then made his way toward the thick brush beyond the last row of buildings. Ahead of him, Anya kept a tight grip on the blade she had swiped from a stand. She was holding it wrong if she hoped to defend herself with it. *Does she know she is being followed?* He waited until she looked back one last time and crossed into the woods before starting across the sand. The ground quickly turned from sand to dirt, to a forest floor, and he was careful to stay concealed behind trees. Merrick smiled at the imprint of her new boots on the mossy ground. A fun game of chase was just what he needed to clear his mind of all things duchesses and princesses. Anya was a mystery to be solved, and Merrick's curiosity always got the best of him.

As he neared the sound of rushing water from a narrow part of the Edmarian river, he felt he was getting close. He followed her trail along the riverbank for a few miles, but nearly lost it when the footprints started northward. There, just a few hundred yards from the river, was a cottage amid the tall oak trees. He quickly squatted in the brush and listened closely to the faint sound of voices murmuring inside the dilapidated home.

He kept his eyes on the front door until it creaked open and the woman stepped lightly down the steps with a bow and arrow in hand. She wore brown linen clothing and appeared exhausted and scared beneath the facade she had worn only a couple of hours before. Her eyes scanned the surroundings of the cottage, then she looked back at the door one final time before continuing down the mossy steps and into the depths of the woods.

*What is she hiding?* He nearly followed her, but another creak of the door rooted him to the ground where he crouched. Out of the crack in the door popped a child's head. Eyes like the sea searched diligently for the woman who had just left. At no sign of her, the child stepped out and motioned for another to join her outside. Two children, a young girl and boy, both far too skinny, entered into the dappled afternoon sun, *faces marked by the Light.*

He sank lower into the grass, heart immediately beginning

to thump harder in his chest. Both of their faces bore the condemning marks. They would be impossible to hide. He watched as they giggled, their sweet laughter carrying softly on the wind. The young girl cradled a doll against her chest. Merrick had seen many like it in the markets today, and he guessed it had been stolen, too. The boy threw a knife into a log over and over again. The prince watched them play for over an hour, glued to his place in the brush and intrigued with their untouched innocence. They knew not of the world they lived in. Their imaginations still ran free and crafted worlds of dreams and happiness. Merrick knew reality would curse them in the future for the glow of their skin.

Anya was hiding these children from the darkness that threatened to claim their lives and their gifts. Merrick had seen many Despiri use their powers before, and he had even seen an Ember try to defend himself when he broke free of the spelled shackles that chained him at the first and only trade Merrick had attended. The Ember had been unnaturally strong and had fallen two of Oro's men before King Degare himself had put the bloodstone staff straight through his spine. Anya was smart to hide them, because it was not only the King of Oro who would have all three of them dead. Merrick's father was a cruel man, as were most of Arresia's kings.

There was a rustle of leaves beyond the cabin, and both Merrick and the young boy became alert. "Neah, time to go inside," the boy said to the girl. His voice was fragile and high pitched, as Merrick's had once been in his youth, before his mother had disappeared. Neah rolled her eyes, but as she began to refuse, both children stiffened. The woman—who seemed too young to be their mother—returned from the woods dragging a small deer carcass behind her. Merrick took a breath and hunkered lower, praying to the goddesses she did not see him in the weeds by the river.

The children did not try to run–they had already been seen. "I said to stay inside. What if someone had seen you?" Anya dropped the animal's legs behind her, and Merrick examined it as closely as he could from this distance. She had shot it three times, only one being a fatal wound. So, she was not a skilled bowman, but it was impressive that she was able to sneak up on the deer at all. Merrick had heard that the wolf population in these lands had made hunting more difficult, as they tended to hunt in packs and went for the larger prey. He would bet the woman could not hit something as tiny as a rabbit with an arrow if she tried. Did she even know how to prepare the deer for consumption? He was not one to judge, being that he had never had to prepare a meal for himself a day in his life.

The woman scanned the surrounding woods as she had before she left the cottage, and Merrick held his breath. Her gaze landed on the mangled log in the yard. "No one saw us, Sabrine. No one comes here," the boy assured her. *Sabrine.*

"Not true. Remember the end of spring, when we had company just across the river?" she hissed. "Stay inside and do as I say. It's for your own good." Neah bit her lip as her brother was reprimanded for arguing, and the two of them stomped inside.

Anya–no, Sabrine–stood in silence for a moment as her strangely familiar eyes trailed them inside, and then she squatted before her kill, rubbing the back of her dewy neck. After a few moments, she pulled the knife from her side pouch and began cutting. Merrick cringed, focusing on her expression instead of the trail of the knife. She looked over her shoulder every few seconds, like a wolf protecting its cubs or guarding its food. Her face was hard to read, but he recognized the fear. Beneath that, there was something like anger, an undertone of resentment. Maybe not for the twins–no, he could tell she feared for their lives out of love. But there was an indignation within her that suggested she had sacrificed much, that she was not like them in the slightest. She didn't seem to find peace in the Light that had pervaded them.

No, there was a darkness within her, and it drew him in, slowly and silently, until dusk.

# CHAPTER 19
# THE BREEDING OF FEAR
## RAVENNA

Ravenna's feet ached from hours of standing on the hard stone of the coliseum. The room was noisy around her, and it took great concentration to stay focused when she felt the many prying eyes. They did not know her as the king's weapon, but they knew Jara as his witch, and Ravenna had been escorted by her, which raised questions from those who noticed. On top of the distraction of being studied by those around her, she had been training all afternoon and still had not yet stopped thinking of the kind woman whose body had hung in the gallows because of association with her. Degare had made it known that he would kill any who tried to help her, and Galen had fallen victim to that promise.

Talk of the upcoming ball and the Autumn Ember Trade echoed all around her. It was the first anniversary of the trade, and she suspected Degare had elaborate plans for the celebration. He had made it very clear she would be in attendance at the ball and would have a specific set of tasks to complete, including charming the many wealthy foreigners and royals in attendance. Degare was hopeful that the sea water would be back to normal by then, but for now, it seemed to hold the blood of the thousands of lives his trades had taken.

Ravenna's stomach rumbled, suggesting dinner time was near. Though she did not actually wish to eat and receive the guilt that always came with enjoying the many delicious foods of the kingdom while others starved, the power beneath her skin always demanded more. She could eat for three men, and Degare insisted on it in his attempts to grow her strength and keep her body from falling decrepit as he had when housing all of this power.

*Just stop eating, until your body fails you,* she begged herself. *Then you can stop being his slave.* There was a twinge down her spine and her thoughts were quickly redirected. *You must eat to maintain your strength, so you can please your king.*

*What of this is real?* she wondered. *What is of you and what is of him?*

Slowly, she felt herself *wanting* to serve him. As much as she fought it, she could not find a way out.

"I think if you would let loose, you could destroy this whole coliseum," a small but mighty voice said behind her. Ravenna turned. It was unlike her, that she had not felt the young girl approaching. Her mind was elsewhere today. Flashes of Galen's lifeless face kept pulling her from her state of focused rage. That rage was the only thing keeping her from bowing completely to the sire and losing herself.

"I heard what they did to you." She twiddled her tiny fingers, and Ravenna surveyed her curiously. "At least you're powerful now." Ravenna looked down at the girl, whose ebony complexion was not of this kingdom.

"Power is not everything, little one." The girl's lips twitched to the side at her remark.

"It could be, though, if you let it." Ravenna was not quite sure what she meant. Had this girl been sent by Jara to encourage her to let go of the slender remains of herself and give in entirely to the sire? To let the power completely take her? Ravenna glanced over to where Jara stood against the wall, reading a spell book, seemingly unaware of the encounter.

Ravenna forced a smile down at the girl, who was quite confident for her age. She reminded Ravenna of herself in a way, before Degare had ruined her. If the girl was inside the coliseum, she was likely the child of a Despiri who was currently training. She was probably bored and needed someone to talk to.

Ravenna understood loneliness quite well, but she had training to complete.

Ravenna began to turn away, but then the girl held up a palm full of flame. Ravenna's mouth fell open. The girl could not have been more than twelve, and she had killed? "My name is Kaida. Nice to meet you, Ravenna."

Ravenna searched the room around her for any sign of the girl's parents. Who had raised her into believing this life was acceptable? That taking the life of another for your own gain was desirable? Who had paid this girl's way into darkness?

Ravenna narrowed her eyes and lit her own palm full of flames that could ravage Kaida's. "If power is all I have left, then let me make it clear that if you harm another Ember for your own gain, I will make you pay for it." She had certainly fallen to the darkness if she was threatening a child. But this child was cunning and knew what she was doing. Ravenna could see it written on her face.

Kaida grinned. "Thank the Light, I thought you were long gone. I thought the king had finally cracked your soul in two." Ravenna's brows furrowed, and she looked to Jara once more to make sure she was not watching. When Ravenna turned back, Kaida was gone.

After the interaction with Kaida had left her speechless, Ravenna turned to the stone pillars that held up the curved sides of the coliseum that would host the Ember Trades in the coming weeks. The lack of life in the kingdom had been eating away at her since she had arrived. She missed the green vines that grew on the sides of her cottage in Vestele, though, they were now likely burned to ash. She focused on the stone and the ground below, where many Embers' blood had been spilled.

For minutes, while she strained to inspire growth out of the crack in the rock as Galen had been able to do, nothing happened. Ravenna did not even know if she held such gifts within her, but just as she was about to give up and turn back to the fire she had nearly mastered, something green sprouted from the stone. *Something full of life.* She willed it to rise, and as she did, the vine slowly crept up along the pillars, weaving and winding amongst itself. A small ounce of satisfaction spread across her lips.

"No, no, no." The witch snapped from across the arena as she marched toward Ravenna, slamming the pages of her book shut over a letter sealed with black wax. "This is not what the king wishes from you. What will you achieve with the creation of. . .*a plant?* Very little. We need death. Destruction. We need to breed *fear*. Not *this*." Jara waved her hand at the pillar, muttering some sort of spell, and the vines turned brown, drooping in death.

Ravenna's shoulders sagged ever so slightly before her own unchecked rage tunneled toward the north wall of the coliseum, manifesting in a way Ravenna was unfamiliar with. The wall blew to bits beneath her wild, invisible force, and Jara crouched and covered her head as pieces of stone came crashing around her. Ravenna did the same, trying to stifle the power that was now beating against her chest, breaking its way out.

*Breathe. Control. Breathe.*

There was utter chaos around them as the many training Despiri fled through the south entrance or shielded themselves with their varying powers. Ravenna squeezed her eyes shut, willing that flow of power to *stop*.

*Degare does not want this*, she said to herself, trying to make use of the sire. *Stop*. But if her power did not even obey its host, why would it obey the king? *That was the problem, wasn't it?* It was not only that Ravenna's mind had not fully surrendered to the sire. It was that until Ravenna could control her power, Degare could not control her. And without control, she was a lousy excuse for a weapon.

She looked to the side at Jara, who was crunched into the fetal position, hair a mess and dust clouding her black silk dress. The south side of the coliseum stood erect, and the rest was rubble still pluming with dust. A dozen Despiri were buried beneath. Ravenna gulped, realizing just how much power lay within her bones. Degare would be hosting the trades here in a matter of days. Embers would die here. Innocent people, like Zephaniah, would die here on the ground where she sat. The bloody sea was visible in the distance, churning with thick, red waters. *A reminder.*

She leaned back, hugged her knees to her chest, and then gave up the fight against the power that poured from her in rage. She watched silently as every side of the coliseum collapsed around them.

*We need to breed fear,* Jara had said.

"Fear it is, then," Ravenna muttered to the wide-eyed, fuming witch as the destruction slowly settled to a halt. "I hope this is not too difficult to clean up."

# CHAPTER 20
## TWO BODIES, ONE FACE
### RAVENNA

**B**ecause of Ravenna's mistake at the coliseum—now a heap of dust and stone—she was being escorted to the torture chambers. The scrawny guard who walked beside her was the same one who had escorted her to the gallows. His hand was gripping the hilt of his blade, even though he could not use it well.

"Why even carry a sword?" Ravenna asked him, bored with the silence of their trek from the throne room to the base of the tower, where she would likely spend the next several hours.

He gave her an incredulous look, as if he could not believe she were interested in talking right now. She noted how his hand grasped the hilt tighter.

"Is it me you're scared of?" she asked.

"No, Lady Ravenna." She narrowed her eyes.

"Then what has you so worried? It must be exhausting, trembling like that all the time."

"It's a condition, Miss."

"What, crippling anxiety? I have it too. What's your name?

Maybe we can bond over it," she muttered sarcastically, not expecting an answer.

"Timothy."

She tilted her chin to the side. "Strange name for this kingdom."

"Family name. I come from the northeast." He swallowed. "Usholk."

Ravenna nearly stopped in her tracks. "You knew Zephaniah, then," she said. The other guards mumbled behind them, telling them to pick up the pace. Timothy did not look at her. "Makes sense why you're so nervous around me." She took a breath. "You're right, we shouldn't be friends. It won't end well for you." She tried to keep her thoughts from hovering on Zephaniah for too long.

Timothy's face was gaunt, as if he would pass out right there in the hall, and she added, "Don't let yourself be the next person I have to remove from the gallows."

He coughed. "Didn't plan on it." He shuffled away from her as two of the other guards halted at the entrance to the torture chambers.

She took a deep breath, remembering how she and Zephaniah had sat at the base of the stairs just months ago, and how they had paused outside of this same door while he apologized to her.

*I wish I could apologize to him.*

Perhaps this never-ending torture could be seen as her attempt at atonement. Ravenna's choices here in this kingdom would serve a purpose. She could claim that her mistakes were well thought out schemes, if it meant a chance at atonement. The destruction of the coliseum brought her here, just as she had hoped when she stopped fighting against her power. But most importantly, it also put a kink in the king's plans for the Ember Trade, and she enjoyed ruining his endeavors. That strange girl, Kaida–*was she an Ember?*–had planted the idea, and Ravenna had allowed rage to get the best of her. She would argue that it was worth it, no matter what Degare was about to do to her beyond that wooden door.

As it creaked open, and the darkness beyond was revealed, she was shoved forward by the largest Despiri guard. She inhaled sharply. "Have I not come willingly?" she asked, gesturing to Timothy with a nod. "Be more like him." She shrugged, and added, "Be scared of me." These guards needed to get on her good side if they wanted to live. Because if she ever got the chance, she would not hesitate.

"Yeah, yeah," the Despiri said, guiding her into the winding hall through the torture objects. Her eyes scanned the walls for unfilled spots where tools had once been as she tried to guess what today's form of torture would be. There was nothing missing, aside from one dagger on the wall of many blades. The wall reminded her of the Ink Blood leader's hut, where her own dagger likely still hung amid his own collection. She gritted her teeth and rounded the corner, where two hooded, unfamiliar faces met her gaze in fear.

She stopped abruptly, only to be shoved forward by the cruel guard. At her right, Degare stood tall with pride. Jara was nowhere to be seen. Ravenna kept her eyes from the two faces to avoid making them more uncomfortable. When Degare opened his mouth, she understood quite clearly why they were here.

"Remove your cloaks," he said. They obeyed, unveiling lightmarks that peeked out from beneath their dirty clothing. Ravenna's eyes fell to the dagger before them.

*No.*

She turned to run, to put space between herself and the king before he could say the words, but she was caught by two guards at the door and dragged backward into the chamber. They dropped her to the ground before Degare, and she did not bother catching herself. She allowed her bones to bruise against the hard floor and kept her chin tilted down.

*No. No. No.*

The room started spinning, and one of the Embers began crying. No, it was her own sobs she heard. *The torture was supposed to be mine alone. This was my chance at atonement.* But now she was about to do something that would require even more.

"Do not bite the hand that feeds you, Ravenna. Why did you destroy my coliseum?" the king asked, tilting her chin up with the tip of his staff. She stayed crumpled on the ground, hating the tears that fell from her face as he watched her with smugness in his cold, gray eyes. He was too calm. He should have been raging, ready to whip her and beat her for ruining the coliseum where the trades were to be held in four weeks. But Ravenna understood his calmness. He was certain what he was to make her do was better punishment than any physical torture would ever be.

"It was a mistake. My power took hold." Degare raised a brow. He did not believe what she was saying. His deep-set eyes bored into hers, and required honesty poured from her lips. "But I stopped fighting against it. I let the power destroy the coliseum to hinder your trades, because I *hate* you and all that you stand for."

He chuckled. "I expect you to hate me." He cut her cheek with the sharp point of the staff. "But you must quit sympathizing with these *people*." He gestured to the innocent Embers in disgust, but she did not look in their direction. She could not bear it.

"You work for me now. You must begin acting like it. Let go of whatever hope you are holding onto. *The Light will not come for you.*" Those words cut deeper than any knife, did more damage than any of these tools could do—because she knew they were true. Her greatest fear—to be trapped in eternal darkness—had come to fruition. "You don't have to hate me any longer, Ravenna. Give in to me."

That was the one thing he could not command of her. She spat at his feet.

"Kill them," Degare ordered. Ravenna's teeth clenched so tightly there was pain in her jaw. *No*, she wanted to say. *I will not.* She wanted to kill *him*. But her head and her heart were against each other, a dwindling spark against the encroaching shadows.

Slowly, she lost herself, crawling toward the Embers, and the dagger found its way into her hand. The king clicked his tongue behind her. "The dagger is for you. Not them. You know better than to waste an Ember death." Had he seen Galen's death in the gallows as a waste? *No*, she thought. *Galen's death had served a purpose in proving a point.* "What else are the mongrels good for?" he continued. "Use the staff." The weapon hit the ground next to her, and the Embers both winced.

Ravenna had known it was coming—the dooming sound of metal bouncing against stone—but it still sent her into that place where the air was thick and the room was spinning. She knew what happened next, but she did not allow herself to think, or feel, or breathe as the staff lurched forward and back twice, and their lightmarks faded before her eyes. As the two lifeless bodies were dragged out of the room, Ravenna could only focus on one face. *Zephaniah.*

The king was barking orders, but not at her. Guards began pulling at her limp arms, ripping her from the grave she had dug for herself. Again, she was being tied at the wrists and the ankles, and the scrape of a dagger sounded against the stone by her ear.

*The dagger is for you.*

# CHAPTER 21
# FRACTURED SOUL
## RAVENNA

"Get up, dear. The king has requested your presence."

These days, being asleep was her only escape, despite the nightmares and apart from the wine, and she did not appreciate the fact that the king had woken her from a rather deep and comfortable nap.

Ravenna rubbed her eyes and sat up on the mattress. Yet another unfamiliar face walked about her chambers, gathering empty wine bottles and broken plates of porcelain from the previous night. Ravenna did not remember breaking the expensive platter and glassware the servants had brought dinner on just after dusk, and it was clear her drinking habits had gotten out of hand, but she had no desire to remain sober. She would much rather *not* remember the atrocities the king forced her to commit. Drinking was a better option than surrendering her conscience when she was so close to losing herself.

She looked at her hands, which held new cuts and scrapes from broken glass, along with old scars and wounds, and then she noticed the gaping hole in her chamber wall. She could see straight out into the hall, where two beautifully dressed noblewomen hurried past with whispers and judgmental glances. The anniversary of the trades was in just over three weeks, and because of the grandeur that Degare had promised, people were arriving to secure their rooms earlier than usual.

Noting the fallen stone on the floor and the entirely destroyed room around her, Ravenna fell back onto the bed, groaning. "Tell His Majesty I'll be there shortly." The servant did not need to tell the king anything. Degare knew that Ravenna would always come to his beck and call and obey his every command. *Every. Single. One.*

"He's requested you wear red," the servant said before walking out the door, wiping her hands on her apron.

"My favorite," Ravenna mumbled, dragging a palm over her face. The king had stocked her closet full of the wretched color, and as she walked to the wardrobe to pick the least atrocious piece, she paused at the sight of the many fabrics, ripped, shredded, and pooled across the floor like a puddle of blood. Some of the gowns had even been burned.

*Great.* Focusing not on grief but on anger was a tactic of self-preservation. But it seemed she had delved far too deep into that emotion last night when she had gotten drunk and destroyed every item of clothing she had been given to wear.

She held herself upright on the wardrobe doors and inhaled before exiting her chambers through the gaping hole in the wall, stepping high over the rubble. As she climbed over a stone, she could still hear the distant chattering of the two noblewomen who had just passed by. She wove through the halls until she caught up to them a few moments later in the hall of a hundred mirrors. Ravenna spotted her own reflection and raised her brows.

The two women looked her up and down, noticing her disheveled bed head, her stained nightgown, and bloody bare feet which had been cut by the shattered wine glasses on her chamber floors. Next to them in their fine attire, she appeared to be a crazed drunkard and beggar from the streets. They knew not who she was, judging by the condemnatory glares they gave her.

She grinned at them, surveying their outfits in return. One of the women wore pink from head to toe. The other—red. Ravenna reached out to feel the fabric of the gown, and the woman recoiled, as if disgusted that Ravenna would dare touch her.

"So sorry, Miss. But it would seem I need your dress," Ravenna said, filling the gap between them once more. Ravenna felt the wild, predatory stare that came from her, and the woman stepped back against the wall, placing a hand on her chest. "Pardon?"

"*Pardon?*" Ravenna mocked. "You heard me. Remove it."

"And who do you think you are?" the woman in pink asked.

"I am no one important, but King Degare would say otherwise." It was clear they were not from Oro, and they had traveled to this kingdom for one reason: they awaited a chance to bid on Ember lives in the upcoming trade. Degare welcomed the wealthiest of his visitors to stay in his castle, and these two ladies appeared to be quite promising investors.

Both women narrowed their eyes at her, awaiting further explanation as she eyed the red silk gown. Aside from the color, she *liked* the dress. It was classy, yet daring. Perfect for her. The woman dressed like a cherry-blossom stepped forward to shield her friend, and her hooded eyes darkened as she summoned a dozen shards of glass to hover above her palm. *Ah, so she has already attended one trade and has come back for more.*

Though the woman had more control than she possessed over her own power, Ravenna laughed as the pieces shook, suspended in the air. "How much did you pay for that? Ten gold ravens? Please tell me you did not *pay* for such weak powers, *Despiri*." What she really wanted to say was *please tell me you did not kill for that.* But because of the shadowmarks on her wrist, Ravenna knew the woman had killed for her power of object manipulation, no matter how small, and it made what Ravenna did next *much* easier.

She felt no guilt as she stepped forward and clenched her fists around their throats, cutting the air supply from reaching their lungs. Her strength was inhuman, and it was one of the powers she did not have to have training to utilize. When they both collapsed, Ravenna pulled their sleeping bodies into a dark corner and took all the fine jewels and gold from them. Now they could not purchase the right to take another life.

She plucked a few hair pins from their heads and tossed half of her own hair into an updo. Then, she collected the red dress, leaving the wealthy noblewoman in a long slip. She threw a tapestry over both of the unconscious bodies and admired herself in the hall of mirrors before advancing toward the throne room, where Degare would be pleased to see her in red.

The doors to the throne room swung open upon her arrival. She had no escorts, and the guards that stood holding the doors did not look at her. Servants scurried away in the hall as if one look in her direction would earn them death.

She examined her nails as she walked, focusing on her anger

while paying no mind to the king who boiled in his own just yards away from her. She would not bow to him unless he asked. Satisfaction crept over her at the sight of his red cheeks and furrowed brow. He might make her life a living darkness, but two could play at that game, and she had succeeded in getting underneath his skin.

Ravenna advanced toward where he sat upon his black velvet seat—the picture of wicked cruelty. Jara was on the arm of his throne like a gargoyle, guarding her king as if she were still uncertain whether the sire bond was strong enough to keep Ravenna from harming him or not.

Just months ago, she would have bristled at the sound of his cold voice penetrating the air. When he spoke today, she did no such thing. There was nothing more he could do to her. There was nothing more she feared losing. She had *nothing* left, and she could not allow him to see the hurt he had caused her by forcing her to kill those Embers. He had to believe that there was nothing more he could do to get her to break.

"I did not owe you a thing, and you have destroyed all that I've given you," he said. She only picked at her nails, smoothed the fabric of her stolen gown, and played with the braids in her hair, which had grown considerably long in the few months she had been here. "Look at me!" he raged. She hated herself for immediately turning her gaze to him. "You disrespect me in my own kingdom?"

"A kingdom that should have been mine." The words shot from her mouth before she had a chance to think. And for that remark, she knew she would pay.

There was silence before the lash of powerful pain from the witch. Ravenna only laughed as the witch continued sending invisible lashes to her back. She felt the expensive silk fabric ripping with each one. *Why had I even gone through the trouble of finding this gown, only for Jara to destroy it?*

"Enough." The king spoke the word, and the pain halted. Jara rolled her shoulders. "Ravenna, dear. You hold onto your past, but you serve me now." A sick feeling engulfed her.

"Kneel." Her knees crashed into the ground as she prepared for his revised set of rules–stricter and more specific ramifications for her to follow–to be the perfect servant. The perfect *weapon*.

"You will not destroy another thing I've given you–or you will have nothing at all." She refrained from speaking the words that begged to roll from her tongue. She did not want the things he gave to her. She cared not for fine clothes, a cozy bed, or power. He could never give her what she truly wanted: the innocent lives he had taken from her and through her.

"I know everything that happens in the walls of my own kingdom. I know that you attacked two investors from the Dawn Islands today." His words were condemning. "Never again will you lay a hand on any of my bidders, unless they conspire against us. You are to inspire them to bid. You are to *encourage* them to bid."

She swallowed as more pieces of her were washed away and more of him took their place. "You damaged an entire wing of the castle last night." She tilted her chin up slightly at the accusation, not remembering anything past the initial eruption of frustration against her chamber wall. Her mouth stayed shut.

"You frightened your servants. You destroyed my fine dishes. You partook in none of the dinner I provided you. You shredded the dresses I chose for you." He paused, looking at her stolen gown, and though her eyes were averted, she felt his cold stare boring into her. "For this, you will repay me. *Respect is my demand.*"

Her chest tightened at the words, and the way she suddenly wanted to appease his every wish infuriated her. Bracing herself for his next demands, she kept her eyes to the ground. "Today you receive your first orders. Today, you will understand that you are *mine* to command. Everything you do is for me, and I can make you do anything I ask. Must I keep reminding you of your purpose here? You are to be a dedicated servant. A *weapon*, as I have trained you to be." A nod bristled through her neck. Her nails cut into her palms so hard that she bled onto the same floor Zephaniah had those months ago.

"You are to go to Vestele." At that word, a feeling she had grown unfamiliar with tugged inside her, and then she was flooded with dread. Her lungs seemed to fill with smoke as she fought the urge to object, but her mouth stayed shut and her eyes down. Degare knew what he was doing.

*Do not let him see your fear. Do not let him see your weakness.*

His commands continued, and Ravenna felt her soul begin to fracture. "Destroy whatever is left of your village. Forget your past. Burn it to ash and leave no survivors."

The king had generously provided Ravenna a new wardrobe full of clothes. It came with ten more lashes.

*You will receive no healing of these wounds,* he had told her as he exited her chambers, leaving her lying across the floor with her back in shreds. The dark-haired witch trailed him and shut the door behind her. Ravenna knew no servant would be in to assist her. No healer like Tenille, or Galen, would come to her aid. There was no one left who cared for her. So, she peeled herself from the red-stained rug and collected the bucket of rainwater from her balcony. Then, she forced herself into the tub, where she did her best to drizzle the water over her wounds by wringing a towel.

She would leave at dusk to complete her first mission. As she sat in the empty tub, water pooling red around her, she did not let herself think of the possibility of there being any survivors in Vestele. It was a miracle *she* had survived, and she had seen so many of her people already breathless as she had been dragged away all those many months ago. Xan had already been on the verge of death when she had been ripped from his side, and Ravenna had already accepted that he was gone.

Ravenna *hoped* they were all gone. Because being dead already would be better than the death she would be forced to deliver to them.

# CHAPTER 22
# THE GRAVEYARD
## RAVENNA

The fog was as thick as ever over the dreadful Kingdom of Oro. Ravenna was relieved to be heading south this evening, if only to gain a little distance from her sire. Though, she found that the further she rode, the harder it was to breathe, as if Degare were truly a part of her, and each step stretched that tether between them. She wondered if she could travel far enough to snap that tether. But she suspected that even a million miles would not be enough.

Two nights alone in the Dead Wood would have unnerved her many months ago, but she did not fear it as she once had. Her worst nightmares had already come true, and nothing seemed to scare her anymore. Her black stallion was pure muscle. Compared to Fintah's size, he was a brute of a horse. He was draped in fabrics and a saddle with embroidered ravens, so that anyone who came across her would know her to be from Oro—another one of Degare's Despiri.

She followed the black sand beach into the heart of the Dead Wood, which spanned the many miles from the edge of

Oro to Vestele. By the eerie feeling in the air, she knew that she was quickly approaching The Valley of the Shadow. As she came upon the towering crevice that cut right through the Black Rock Mountains, she remembered how Zephaniah had held her hand upon entry, and it was the first bit of comfort she had felt in days. Ravenna thought the shadow valley would claim her soul for what she had done to him. But the shadows were silent, and she came out the other side still breathing.

The first night would be spent in the mountainous territories made of black rock. Cave systems were easy to find, and she chose the one closest to a small stream. Unlike the Black Sea, it was not polluted with blood, and she knelt to fill her canteen. The warmth of the summer night was pleasant against her skin, though somewhat dewy. She had no need for a fire, though she wished she had more to eat than just a measly handful of dried meat. She had considered shooting a squirrel she saw a few miles back, but when her hand had grazed her quiver, she was reminded of the night her mother had been taken from her. Feelings such as those were to be redirected. Stifled. *Not felt.*

*Let go of your past,* Degare had said. Ravenna tapped her fingers wildly on the cave floor as she fought the sire and tried to distract herself against the creeping pain in her spine.

*Fight it, Ravenna. Fight it with everything you've got.*

Ravenna knew that if she let go of her past, she would have nothing else to anchor her. She tossed and turned in the night, begging for sleep as she listened to the tapping of her own fingers, but the pain worsened.

The *tap, tap, tap,* seemed to go on for hours, until a

familiar, low snarl echoed through the cave she laid in. She sat up slowly, peering through the night. The witch guardians would try, and fail, to kill her once more.

She sighed, grabbing her sword from beside her mat. Her horse stomped in fear, and while she tried to calm him with light whispers, he reared up at first sight of a guardian. Why she even carried the sword, she did not know. With her gifts, she had no use for blades or weapons, but these were some of the only comforts of her old life she was allowed to enjoy. Degare had not taken that from her yet, but he was trying. For the moment, she was distracted from the pain.

She had been backed into the cave, and though the thought crossed her mind, she could not let the vengeful creatures kill her. She could not have stopped the power from bleeding out of her if she tried. Her body had shifted into defense, and she obeyed Degare's command to cling to life, grasping for whatever power would preserve it.

Rocks began falling down upon the guardians, and fire bursted from her palms. Her horse backed against the cave wall, and Ravenna burrowed into her emotions as Cyrus had taught her to do, aiming a blast of strange power along the entrance to the cave, sending the guardians plummeting backward into the woods. She threw fireballs into their line of vision, temporarily blinding them until she could make the killing strike. Her fire was not hot enough to melt their skin, unlike that mysterious fire in the Dead Wood last spring, but it succeeded as a distraction.

When she exited the cave, a dozen more barreled toward her and she spun on them, swinging her sword and plunging it into a black heart while she shot flames toward the others. *How many guardians could there possibly be in Arresia?* It seemed as though every single one had been awaiting her presence outside of the gates of Oro. *Where do they come from?* All night she killed and maimed the creatures until there were none left breathing. When the sun rose, she saw the damage she had done. The forest around her, much like the coliseum in Oro, had fallen victim to her unchecked, uncontrolled power. A shiver ran down her spine. Soon, as surely as she had wiped these beasts from the woods, Vestele would be wiped from Arresia.

By light of day, the guardians could not come for her. As she was bound to darkness, they were bound to the night, and she heard their distant growls of displeasure echoing through the earth as she rode further south. Day by day, she wandered toward Vestele, occasionally sending flames into the air as a warning she was coming. If there were any survivors, surely they had heard of her fate by now. She hoped they would heed with caution and flee from Vestele as far as their feet would take them.

By night, she fought sleep and monitored the shadows around her, only laying down to rest for a couple hours at a time. The witch guardians only came twice, but she knew she had to keep moving.

The fourth morning of her trip, when she arrived at her old familiar territory, her favorite grove of trees in the southeastern Dead Wood was still intact. She had once perched in that tall oak and shot an arrow at the man who would later kill her mother. *Let go,* the bond seemed to whisper. She dug her nails into her palms and continued forward, letting the sire pull her toward her assignment.

It was another mile or so to Vestele, through the rest of the Black Rock Mountains, and as she wove in and out of the lifeless trees of the Dead Wood, she found herself holding her breath. She had walked this path with Xan the night her mother was killed. With each inch closer, power was rising in her veins and sparks were beginning to crackle in her palms. *No.*

Her stallion stepped across the tree line, revealing what was left of her home. Ravenna's eyes became glassy at the scent of smoke that lingered after all this time. This was the place where her grief had started, and this was the place where it would find its end.

The ground was charred in a circle around the village, and the few huts and cottages that were still standing had been abandoned. Just up the river, near the fire circle where her mother had been killed, was a grave. Her heartbeat pounded against her skull.

*Someone had lived to dig a grave.*

She dismounted the horse and strode toward the stone marker, temporarily stifling her power by burying her nails into her palms. Sparks escaped around her fingertips, joining the ash on the ground as Ravenna picked up the pace.

Marked with a slab of sunstone, the grave read: ASTA INMAN. She crouched beside it, letting a tear fall from her cheek as she lifted her face to the other two dozen graves that lay beyond it. Some were marked, and some were left nameless. Nausea settled in her throat, and as she reluctantly rose to read the marked stones, something familiar caught her eye.

A few inches from Asta's grave, as if the wind had

displaced it, there was a piece of folded paper, pointed like a star, like someone had visited and left it in memory of her. Ravenna would know the signature art of paper folding anywhere. Her body stiffened in silent longing, but with the tug of the bond, she was reminded what she had come here to do. *Forget your past, and burn it to ash.* With that, she stood and turned, forcing the knot in her throat down into her chest. Eyes closed, she breathed deeply before she was to let her power wreak its havoc on her homeland.

"Ravenna."

She was hearing things. Her eyes stayed closed.

*They are all dead. Focus.*

"Ravenna."

Her name was choked out again, and fire rippled through her at the sound of it. *Remember what you came to do, what your king has demanded of you. Do not get distracted.*

Against the pain in her spine, she could not open her eyes. Just to feel a small ounce of relief, she willed flames to seep from her hands and dove into her well of power. She would ascend with enough strength to destroy the entire village.

"Ravenna." Again, but this time the voice was accompanied with strong hands—a familiar touch—on her shoulders. She swallowed once before opening her eyes to *Xan*.

He stood before her, just as she remembered him, but thinner and with dark circles beneath his rich brown eyes— much like the ones beneath hers. He looked at her as if she were not truly before him, as if he were afraid to blink it all away. They had been here before.

*No.* She tore away from his grasp, sending him staggering backward. *He could not be here.*

"What are you doing here? Leave!" She could not help the

anger that bled from her voice. She needed him to *go* before she killed him.

The skin around his eyes crinkled, and he stepped toward her again, this time with a gentle hand stretched before him. "Venna, please." Grief filled in the cracks of his voice, and the corners of his mouth turned downward as he pleaded with her. There were no signs of the dimples she loved.

"I do not want to see you. Don't you understand?" she asked. "I will *kill* you!" His brows pinched together as his eyes studied her in confusion, and he drew his hand back. His gaze landed on the flames that engulfed her fingers, and he took another step back, trying to shield a woman who Ravenna had somehow not noticed behind him.

"It's you," Xan realized. "You are the weapon Degare has been talking about. They suspected, but I refused to believe it. I-I thought he'd have killed you by now. I thought I was too late. I thought you were dead." She'd rather she were. He kept his hands low in a defensive position, and as much as it hurt, he was smart to fear her.

Ravenna struggled to hold the dam against her raging river of power. "*Who* suspected?" she asked through gritted teeth as she fought the pain that came with resisting the sire.

Xan swallowed and did not answer her question. "Ravenna, come home to us."

"Home?" She looked around at the abandoned village that had raised her. At the abandoned village where grief dwelt. Fire poured from her hands, and Ravenna seethed, continuing to burrow into her power, until *Tenille* stepped out from behind him. The world around her seemed to slow, and Ravenna looked between her two old friends, who had somehow survived the rastweed poisoning and now stood before her.

"We're with Ink Valley now," Tenille said gently. Tenille's hands wrapped around Xan's bicep where, sure enough, a strip of leather was fastened, adorned with two ivory feathers dipped in ink. She looked between the two of them. He shielded her with his body as Ravenna became a threat to them both. She could not read his face.

"You found refuge in Ink Valley?" Ravenna asked. She chuckled loudly then, and she could not stop the fire from burning brighter within her. *My people found refuge after all.* She should have been happy, but she could not help but remember the way Xan had reacted when she'd proposed that idea in the spring. An uncontrolled, familiar, yet not familiar, power rumbled through her and into the low ground between mountains. Her two friends glanced around as the mountaintops began to drop rocks into the valley. Ravenna breathed tightly against the burning sensation that was now traveling up and down her back, willing her to *destroy*.

"I said leave," she seethed through gritted teeth. *Leave now.*

"Come with us, Ravenna. We can help you. *Please*," Tenille begged from behind Xan's shoulder. Ravenna was surprised to see them both standing here, alive after the village fire, and alive though the witch guardians certainly still tracked Tenille, too. Ravenna had always dreamt of the two of them getting everything they wanted out of life, and now, she was about to take it all away.

Another burst of power rumbled through her, and she tried to restrain herself but failed as she directed it straight at Xan. He was thrown backward into a half-burnt cottage, and Tenille was left standing alone, gaping after him. Xan came limping back, placing himself between her and Tenille once more. The two of them were not going to leave her. She knew it to be a fact. They would stand here until they were dead by her hand, and Ravenna could not live with herself another day if she was the cause of one more death.

"Venna, we need you. Please, just *come back*," Xan pleaded. She forced a laugh as he begged her. *Make him believe you. Provoke him to leave. But what can you say?*

She looked at him for a long moment, panting against the throbbing in her spine. "You kept me from my birthright," she accused, letting her flames twist further up her arms to release some of the pressure.

"I kept you from certain death," he spat, his temper quickly rising as she knew it would.

"*That* is no better," she countered. In an attempt to protect her, he had only ended her up here, in the hands of the king. Perhaps if Vestele had not kept the truth from her, she would have become the Dove and risen against the Kingdom of Oro. But now, she would cause the fall of every other kingdom if her sire commanded it. "Do you know the guilt I carry?" she asked.

"Guilt? I know guilt, Ravenna. I dealt with guilt every day of my life in Vestele. Every day since I took that oath and swore to protect you with my life. Every day since I chose to live a life apart from the Light to keep you safe."

"Then why did you do it, Xan? Why? Tell me, was it worth it?" Flames crept toward his feet.

He closed his eyes. "I protected you from your fate because I was selfish. . .because I am in love with you. Have I not made that clear?" Tenille looked to the ground beside him, and Ravenna's heart thundered against her chest.

She spun in a slow circle. She could not hold her own against the sire much longer. She doubled over, heaving against the pain in her gut, and Xan took a step forward as if to steady her. *Do not erupt.* She forced her body upright once more and turned toward him to say words she would regret for the rest of her miserable life.

"I never loved you, Xan. I never wanted your protection. And I sure as darkness do not want it now." *Help me.* Ravenna released an unsteady breath and looked into his eyes with as much ferocity as she could muster. "Now leave, before I kill you."

Sweat trickled down Ravenna's face as she delivered the words that broke him. Xan said nothing, but his face said it all.

Rocks from the mountains crashed into the river behind her, and she felt herself letting go of the weak holds she had on her power. Tenille must have seen the switch in her eyes, because she began dragging Xan away, begging for him to leave with her. Xan's brown eyes were now welling with defeat, and with one last hesitant glance toward Ravenna, the faces of her nearly-forgotten past raced into the Dead Wood while she released her strength upon the Valley of Vestele.

# CHAPTER 23
# A BROKEN OATH
## XAN

*Alive.* *She has been alive.*

She appeared as though she had lived a hundred lifetimes without him.

*Where were you?* he asked himself. *Where were you when she was suffering?*

A blast of heat smothered his face, and he blinked past the shadows that had clouded his vision. Once again, Vestele was up in flames. Once again, he was being torn from her side. Once again, he was leaving her alone.

"Xan. Keep moving. We have to go!" Tenille yelled beside him, shaking him with as much force as she could gather. The four Ink Blood soldiers that had escorted them here were astounded, watching him carefully as they fought to stay upright against Ravenna's wrath. Tenille's voice carried through the ash and dust, over the crumbling rocks and the mountains that had begun collapsing into the valley. *Such raw power that had been sought after for ages. Power that was still being sought.*

Xan looked to Leith's soldiers, who were making their way toward him to drag him back to Ink Valley.

"I won't leave her," he called to Tenille, turning back to the destruction.

"You will, Xan. She has chosen. It is too late for her. The oath no longer stands," she said, looking between him and the soldiers. Ashreya had trusted him with Ravenna's life. She had raised him up to be whatever was necessary to keep her safe. *Be brave for her.* The words spoken by Ashreya to him as a boy came from a place in the back of his mind—from the night of fire and smoke that he had done everything in his power to forget.

He shook his head, bracing himself against the trunk of a tree as the earth below his feet shook. *What is my life without her? Who am I if not her protector?* Tenille fell backward as the ground split beside them, and Xan looked over his shoulder, toward where their shield-maiden was concealed by flame and ash.

"Come with us, *now*," one of the Ink Bloods said, grabbing for him. Xan shook him off, and none of them drew their weapons as he expected. They only stood slack-jawed as Vestele was obliterated before their eyes.

"This isn't her," he said, voice bleeding with desperation. *Was she still in there?*

"We'll see what the chief has to say about that," the soldier who had grabbed for him said. Xan's hand tunneled through his hair as he grasped for a thought amid the chaos. He breathed rapidly, glancing between the woman he was to protect, and the men who would deliver this news of her to their leader.

Tenille crawled to him on her hands and knees, bucking with the moving forest floor. She rose to her feet, bracing herself on his outstretched forearms.

"I am not leaving her," he said through teary eyes.

"And I am not leaving you," Tenille countered, coughing against the thickening smoke. "Ravenna does not want us here. Has she not proven that?" Tenille gestured to the heart of the chaos that continued creeping toward them. The soldiers, who had been commanded not to leave them, were growing antsy. One of them was collecting his focus, preparing to use his gift of invisibility over the group of them.

Tenille was right. He knew she was right.

*I never loved you, Xan. I never wanted your protection. And I sure as darkness do not want it now. Now leave, before I kill you.*

"I am not leaving unless your hand is in mine," Tenille said, doing her best to plant her feet upon the uneven ground, showing that she would die here with him if he did not gather his wits. *I never wanted your protection. And I sure as darkness do not want it now.*

"You and I, Xan," Tenille said. "We stick together. If nothing else, these last three months have taught us that."

After a moment, Xan released a shaky breath and reached for her hand, letting her lead him away from Ravenna and toward the heart of their new, wretched home under the soldier's cloak of invisibility.

*I am coming back for you, even if you kill me for it.*

# CHAPTER 24

# OLD ACQUAINTANCES

## MERRICK

Merrick tossed his last dart into the board beside the chaise. His legs were kicked over the arm of the velvet seat, and he sighed in boredom as he leaned to collect the thick stack of parchment from his desk, which laid among a dozen journals. Pages of old treaties that were never solidified littered the space before him. He had brought them from his brother's study at the Sand Palace, and he intended to examine them closely and compare them with documents that had been drawn up for the alliance with the Dawn Islands. He sighed.

At the top of the stack was a letter written in his father's neat penmanship. The ink was fairly fresh, and it was addressed to someone with the surname Erindelle, but it had never been sent. He worked his finger beneath the seal.

"I thought you came here to relax," Kenan muttered as he walked into Merrick's dimly lit study in the country home. Merrick set the letter to the side.

"Yes, well, that was mostly to get away from my father," Merrick said, thumbing through the papers that outlined his alliance with Princess–*Queen*–Mina of the Dawn Islands.

"Ah, yes, your father, who is soon leaving for his month-long trip to Oro. You would have had the palace to yourself. This has nothing to do with his new wife?" Merrick's eyes rolled toward Kenan, who held up his hands in surrender.

"Jamila is very beautiful. I can see how you'd be tempted. I know I was unable to resist," he said, walking around the desk.

Merrick sat up on the burgundy chaise. "My father will have your head."

Kenan smiled and looked at the papers over Merrick's shoulder. Merrick shook his head in disgust.

"The king will never know," Kenan said.

Jamila had always been a temptress, and Merrick was grateful now that their engagement had ended. His father had unknowingly spared him from a marriage built on betrayal and deceit, and Merrick supposed for that, he could be grateful. He only hoped Mina was different from Jamila, and that she would honor their marriage vows.

"The king will never know what?"

Merrick and Kenan both looked to the doorway, where one of Andreas's lords stood, curiously waiting for an answer.

"Lord Yarris," Merrick said, rising to his feet. "I was not expecting you here at the country home." Kenan dipped his head by way of greeting. Yarris had been traveling back from the Dawn Islands where he had been with Andreas.

"Yes, well, plans changed when my ship was lost at sea for five months. Strangest thing I've ever experienced. It was like we were going in circles. The currents kept pulling us off path.

There were storms like I've never seen. We docked just last week, and I grew tired of sleeping at the inn. Word from the markets was that you were in town. I thought you would be much more accommodating than those commoners."

Merrick hummed. "You're welcome to stay in one of the guest suites. Why have you not yet returned to the palace or to your estate in Tarbank?"

"Tarbank is too far north, and I am exhausted. I just got rid of my sea legs. Anyway, with Andreas dead and your father soon gone for the trades, I figured the palace would feel rather empty."

"I am sorry for your loss," Merrick said to Yarris, regarding his own brother. The two of them were closer than Merrick and Andreas had ever been.

Yarris's jaw ticked. "As am I." The lord took a seat across from Merrick, and Merrick glanced at Kenan, dismissing him. When he left the room, Merrick poured Yarris some wine. "Arlo is gone, too. I suppose I have much adjusting ahead of me," Yarris said matter-of-factly, taking a slow drink.

Merrick sat down with his own glass of wine, and Yarris's gaze fell to the papers beside him.

"Tell me your father wishes to continue with the alliance, that *you* are to marry Princess Mina."

Merrick nodded slowly and did not bother correcting Mina's title. Edmaria had supplied the Dawn Islands with supplies for a Black Temple, and without an alliance, Queen Mina would owe them too great a debt. The proposal King Sebastian had sent Merrick's father before his death was simply too good for Edmaria to pass up. After the wedding, Edmaria would basically own the islands, and all of their Embers would be Edmaria's to profit from. Merrick narrowed his eyes at Yarris. "What is in it for you?"

Yarris smiled. "Lady Celeste."

"Found yourself a bride, then?" Merrick asked.

"We are to be married if the alliance works out. I promised her I'd come back for her. She is quite charming. Hair black as night. Beautiful and clever. It was she who proved Andreas's death was not an accident. We owe our gratitude to her, that the murderer was found."

Merrick swirled his finger around the rim of his glass. "Well, for that, I suppose I am very grateful. Tell me, Yarris. What exactly happened in the Dawn Islands?"

Yarris chuckled. "Besides Andreas, Arlo, and I enjoying our time with the princess and her ladies?" He took another sip of his drink, and Merrick hoped he would tell him more of the princess that was now his to marry. "King Sebastian hosted a ball to announce the alliance, and Andreas did not show up. Celeste and I went searching for him, and we found him dead. Drowned in the bathing chambers. The king tried to accuse your brother of being there to impose on his daughter's privacy, but Arlo wasn't buying it. Celeste was able to determine that an Ember man with the gift of water manipulation had been there around the same time. It was he who killed our prince."

Merrick chewed on his lip. "And where is this man now?" he asked.

Yarris shrugged. "He was on the ship with me. I made sure he suffered greatly for his crime. Hard telling where he is now. Your father will want to kill him himself. With the staff, of course, so I'd guess he's halfway to Oro for the Autumn Trade. They'll take him through the Valley if they are smart. He was shackled with those spelled shackles the Delle Witch Clan made for Ember transport, but I still blame him for our extra time at sea. I was sick the entire journey. We kept getting off course. Roughest waves I've ever sailed."

Merrick nodded, taking it all in. "My father has been sending many of the new imports into the mines." All the kings of Arresia were eager to dip their hands into the treasure chest of bloodstone, especially with Degare willing to pay an unfathomable amount for it. "But I bet you're right. This one, he wants to kill himself." He changed the subject. "What happened to Arlo?"

Yarris clenched his jaw. "I took the murderer aboard the ship in Oriana, and I thought Arlo was right behind me. He wasn't. I thought he had caught the next ship, but Celeste wrote to me and told me he had been killed right in front of her, by Lady Cove, who was to be his wife." Merrick sat up straighter. "She had been with the prisoner at the docks when we brought him into captivity. They were allies. . .lovers."

"So, this *Lady Cove*, she is an Ember too?" Merrick asked. "What happened to her?"

"Drowned like Andreas, I assume. Celeste said she jumped into the ocean to swim after the boat. The waters grew rough quite quickly that evening. She was last seen fighting for air against the waves." Merrick could not help the twinge in his chest at the thought of a woman gasping for air as she tried to save her lover. "Anyway," Yarris said. "I am quite disappointed that I am not joining your father at the trades. I very much would have liked to drive the staff through the heart of one of their kind for my friends. But I am sick of traveling, and I am certainly done with boats for a while." Merrick was silent for a long moment as he finished his wine.

"Well, what time is it? I am starving." Yarris said.

Merrick reached for his pocket watch at his belt, but he found nothing except the memory of those little Embers in the woods. His eyes fell to the ornate rug on the floor as he smiled, and then he smacked his hands on his knees and rose to his feet. "Let's eat then."

# CHAPTER 25
# TENFOLD
## SABRINE

S abrine walked across the creaky floors of the dilapidated cottage, careful not to wake the twins. The sun had not yet risen, but a hint of its light had begun to paint the skies a muted blue. Late summer nights had started to grow chilly, but today's early morning air that seeped through the walls felt considerably warm, and she delighted in it, leaving her cloak draped over the chair by the door. From her sack, she pulled the last loaf of bread and left two chunks for the twins before she laced her boots for her morning hunt.

She did not really need to hunt after she had killed the deer and dried most of the meat, but she wished for some solitude—some time away from the responsibility weighing down on her shoulders. She would not go far. She tightened the leather strips on her boots and grabbed her canteen, her bow, and a basket, in hopes she might find some late-season berries.

Her fingers unfastened the chain on the door, and just as she cracked it open, a figure darted into the bushes. She froze, closing the door shut tightly and keeping her hand on the knob. She shuffled to the window, carefully peeking out through the musty curtains.

There were no signs of movement in the thick brush by the river, and the rush of water masked any sounds. Her hand tightened on the dagger that had not left her side since she had stolen it last week. The twins were still fast asleep, and she debated whether she should track the suspicious figure or rouse them from their slumbers and hide them in the secret space beneath the floorboards.

She was about to do the latter when she noticed a small basket on the mossy wooden steps. She felt eyes watching her but saw no one. She nocked an arrow into her bow and cracked the door. Keeping her arrow aimed toward the river, she slowly stepped out onto the porch, bending at the waist so her body was mostly concealed by the short stone wall next to the steps.

She flicked the cotton cloth from the top of the basket with the tip of her dagger, revealing fruit, bread, and some colorful pastries. She narrowed her eyes, picking up one of the fragrant loaves of bread. Beneath it, something shiny shimmered in the light. She stepped back, heart pounding heavily against her chest at the sight of the jewels and coins from her last trip to the Thickets.

She leapt from the steps to the forest floor, creeping toward the bushes and pulling her bow string taut. Her hands grew sweaty, and she cursed herself for not retreating inside–for leaving the twins in the cottage alone. But it was best for her to not even acknowledge their presence. Perhaps whoever was watching did not know of their existence or of their gifts of Light that allowed them to heal–the same gifts their mother had. She stopped at the first rustle of leaves and aimed her arrow.

"Come out," she demanded. A few seconds passed before the man from the Thickets stepped into view, hands raised.

"I hope that if you shoot me, you do not maim me as you did that poor deer." She looked at him quizzically.

"You followed me?" Her heart was threatening to come up her throat. She could not breathe as she thought about the twins inside, fast asleep and unaware of the threat that she had led straight to them. Their hiding place had been compromised. They needed to leave, *now*. But first, she needed to kill him. *I have to kill him, right? He knows where we live.* And if he had seen her return home with the deer, the twins had been outside as well.

"I thought you would appreciate the bread. I baked it myself," he offered, trying to change the subject.

"No. You did not." She looked him up and down, examining his fine linens and his expensive, tailored suit. He had worn such fineries into the middle of the forest, where briars and thickets were sure to ruin it. His jacket had already been picked by thorns. She knew better than to believe he was a kitchen boy, or that he had ever cooked for himself a day in his life.

He stepped toward her, hands still raised, and she took a step back. "Okay, so you lied about being a duchess, and I lied about *not* being a prince?"

*A prince?* That was where she had heard the name. Prince Andreas's younger brother, now heir to the Edmarian throne. She shuddered. How could she have been so foolish to have stolen from a *prince?*

What would be the repercussions for *killing* such a man?

Which she must do, if she wished to protect the twins. She pulled the bow string and released the arrow without a second thought, but she had taken too long to aim. He stepped to the side with nimble reflexes.

He stood dumbfounded. "You would kill me?" he asked as he closed the distance between them. She pulled the dagger from her belt, planting her body between his and the cottage, trying to mask her fear.

"Relax, *duchess*. I do not plan on selling your secrets." *For lack of better words, because my secrets are Risley and Neah, and he could sell them.* She held the blade out between them.

"And what do you know of my secrets?" She needed an opening to cut him. He was fast, and she had to be faster. *To stab low or high? Jugular or abdomen?* She would never get such a tiny blade through his chest. *I have never killed a person before.* Her hands trembled, and she tried to steady them. Merrick noticed, and he winced.

"I know why you needed the money you stole. I felt guilty for toying with you, so I have returned it tenfold." He nodded to the steps of the cottage, where there was a small coin sack next to the basket that she had not noticed before. A glint of *gold* gleamed at the top. Enough to purchase a few dozen Embers' voyages across the sea.

With that money, she would never have to thieve again. But instead of accepting it, she said through gritted, prideful teeth, "I do not need charity. Especially not from you." He winced again. It was his father who had enforced the law that had led to her parents' deaths, and as a prince, Sabrine knew he was just another wealthy, power-hungry man.

"Please just take it and let me go freely. I promise not to harm you," he said. She studied him cautiously, awaiting his imminent strike. But his hands were low and ready to defend—not offend. "You need not worry. Your secrets are safe." He reached out slowly toward the dagger she held between them, and his fingers grazed hers as he pushed her hand down. "You are safe." The Prince of Edmaria, a kingdom of darkness, was promising *her* safety? After the crimes she had so obviously committed by hiding two lightmarked children and stealing from the kingdom?

"No strings attached?" she asked warily, mouth salivating as she looked at the fresh bread on the doorstep.

"No strings," the prince said, with a recognizable kindness in his eyes. His eyes fell to the shoes he had bought her. *Do not fall for his tricks.*

Sabrine thought of the twins, and how they deserved a safe place to sleep. A kingdom made up of a thousand people just like them—followers of the Light. She thought of her last promise to her parents.

*Keep them safe.*

*I will.*

*Choose the Light, Sabrine.*

She wouldn't.

But she would get the twins to safety, even if it meant swallowing her pride and accepting charity from one of the crowns that had caused her so much hardship.

"If this is another one of your acts of kindness as you work to. . .redeem yourself, consider it your last. I am not in need of your help, nor do I want it."

A smirk crept across his lips. "Should I take it back with me, then?" He started toward the cabin, where the twins were sleeping, unaware.

"Leave it," she said, stepping between the prince and the

porch. He backed off, holding his hands in the air, and turned to exit the woods.

"Whatever you say, *Sabrine*," he muttered, and a shiver went down her spine at her true name on his lips. She did not understand why, but she let him walk away with his life.

# CHAPTER 26
# ONE BIRD, TWO STONES
## XAN

Xan had been awake since they returned to Ink Valley from Vestele two days ago. Tenille was sleeping, and he watched her from the chair by the bed in the hut that they shared. The leader of the Ink Bloods was insufferable, but he had provided them with shelter when they were on the verge of death. It was a kindness, but Xan knew his true motives, and he did not want anything to do with them.

Xan was one of the seven surviving Vestelians who had been collected while on their deathbeds and thrown over horses for a ride to Ink Valley. Tenille was the eighth and final survivor. She had been delivered into the hands of the Ink Bloods four weeks after the burning. Xan had assumed her dead for the grueling days he spent tied to a bed, receiving unwanted aid from a healer as he fought to get to Ravenna. But one day, a peculiar cousin of Leith's had come with Tenille in tow, claiming that he had found her dying from the poison in the woods shortly after the fire, and that the witch guardians had been about to finish her off. The beasts still came for her every so often, but no attack had compared to the one which had happened the day before she'd ever arrived in Ink Valley.

Tenille had been unconscious many of the days she spent with the curious stranger, and though Xan had interrogated her incessantly upon her return, she claimed she remembered little of the encounter with him. He had delivered Tenille, had a conversation with Leith in his hut, and then turned back around and left. There was something dubious about him, and Xan did not like it.

Nonetheless, Xan was grateful Leith's cousin had been there to protect Tenille, because Xan had been so caught up with Ravenna's safety that he had jeopardized the lives of everyone in his village. It was because of his mistakes that Tenille had been forced to bury her mother's remains.

Tenille tossed and turned in the bed, probably fighting the nightmare that was their life. Xan looked away, crumbling the piece of paper he had been mindlessly folding. He needed to find a way to Ravenna. He did not believe the things she had said to him. Maybe she never loved him, but this was not about that. He knew her, and he saw her eyes pleading for help. He would not let her drown again. But, getting out of the hut, let alone the valley, would be difficult.

Leith made all the decisions here, and he decided when one could come and go. Leith had a strange trust of Tenille from the start. At Tenille's request, she and Xan had been allowed out to bury their dead, and their escorts had been commanded to stay beyond the treeline, offering both protection and privacy–according to Leith. But Xan knew the soldiers were there to make sure the two of them did not turn on Ink Valley, because once you were in it, there was no getting out.

Xan tore the leather band from his bicep and tapped his fingers on the windowsill.

They had not encountered any witch guardians on the journey to or from Vestele, but he heard them as they tracked Ravenna. It took everything in him not to flee the soldiers and follow her back to Oro, but he knew he would need a plan.

Xan sat up at the sound of muffled arguing outside of the hut. Leith and the Volcanian woman were arguing beside the river, and Xan could have sworn he heard Ravenna's name. He barreled through the door, straight past his guards, and made a beeline toward them.

"We're not ready to make a move. We are not equipped," Edme said. "Not after the attack."

"Yes, we are," Leith argued.

Edme sighed. "You are rushing, Leith. It is not a good idea."

"What is not a good idea?" Xan demanded, marching toward them. Leith turned and rolled his head back on his shoulders in annoyance as he saw Xan approaching. The Ink Blood leader's eyes flicked to Xan's hut, where he had left the door wide open with Tenille sleeping inside. He motioned for his oncoming soldiers to stand down.

"He wants to go after your girl," Edme said, flipping her bound, black hair over her shoulder. "He wants to demand the King of Oro give her back." She looked between the two of them, a slight smirk painting her mouth, as if she was waiting for some kind of show.

"Technically, I have already tried that," Leith cut in, tipping his head as if weighing his options. "I gave Degare a little. . .nudge, before I realized the severity of the situation."

"Their water is blood, Leith," Edme said, full lips in a flat line.

Xan's jaw set as he glared at the Ink Blood leader and the shadowy marks that crept from beneath the collar of his tunic. Those marks were one of the main reasons he had never wanted an alliance with this clan. "You'll get her killed," Xan argued, closing the space between them. Leith did not cower; he only raised his brows, keeping his arms crossed over his chest.

"Perhaps that is what we need," Leith said. "If she is sired to the king, as my men further suspect after her show in your village, she is no longer of value to me."

"She is a person, not a weapon to be wielded," Xan said.

"Yes, well, when her power threatens my entire operation, I do think it should be taken care of sooner rather than later." Leith looked to Edme, and she took a deep breath of defiance. "I'll pack my bags," Leith said dryly.

"I will not let you hurt her," Xan said, stepping toward him.

"What are you, her keeper?" Leith's voice was laced with sarcasm.

"Something like that," Xan snarled, crossing his arms over his chest.

"What a fine job you have done. Time to let me clean up your mess."

Xan threw a fist, and it contacted Leith's jaw before a wall of flames shot up between them. Leith smirked, spitting blood at Xan's feet before looking to the side at Edme, who was rolling her fiery eyes. If his blades hadn't been confiscated upon arrival in Ink Valley, he would not have backed down so easily, but he surrendered as Edme's strange fire prodded him back into the hut, where Tenille was now watching him from the edge of the bed.

"What was that about?" she asked as he slammed the door, sending dirt and dust pluming into the streaming sunlight.

"They are going to kill Ravenna," he said. "I need to find a way to get to her first."

# CHAPTER 27
# INFILTRATION
## COVE

"Did it work?" Cove asked breathlessly, holding herself up on the grimy wall of the alley.

Sinley tilted his head from side to side, weighing his answer. "I feel a bit tipsy," he said lightly. "But the grief is still there." Cove frowned and sank down next to him. She had mastered a few emotions over the last several weeks practicing with Sinley, but manipulating the subconscious, tricking it to feel a lie, still made her uncomfortable.

"Try again," Sinley urged her, his gaze gentle. Cove shook her head. "This is important to you. A couple of weeks ago, you were successful in making me feel charitable. Remember? I gave you my last bite of jerky."

"You would have done that with or without me trying to alter your mood," she muttered. "You always offer me the last bite."

"Not that day. I was mad at you for taking too long to return from the witch's chambers. I thought you'd been discovered." Cove rolled her eyes. "You were able to make the

198

Despiri guards uninterested in you that day as you slipped past. And you said you were able to calm your friend before the witch's spell. You're learning. Take it a day at a time."

"Every emotion is different," she said. "I have to master each one on my own, to understand and find control of each within me. I have spent years overwhelmed by other's emotions. I rarely stopped to truly understand them." She shook her head again. The anxiety of feeling everything all at once had always settled in. "I was able to calm Ravenna because I had once experienced the calm she needed." *With Elias.* "I was able to recreate it within her." She thought for a moment.

"I won't sit idle any longer," she said. She had done enough of that before she met Elias. For years she had hidden in the islands, concealing the very Light that she had vowed to spread across Arresia when she had given her life to it.

Finally, she had decided to do something in helping Elias free those Embers in the Dawn Islands, and he was torn from her before they had the chance to live their lives together. Now, his life was in her hands. He would die if she did not find him before the trades. She was sure of it. She felt it like a promise in her bones. "I am going into the prison."

Sinley let his head fall to the side to look at her from where they both sat up against the alley wall in the slums, where no one from the castle could recognize her. "If your husband's name was not on the inventory sheets, he is not there."

Cove rubbed her eyes. "They are bringing in more Embers every day. Or maybe he is already here, and he gave them fake identifiers." She turned her face to hide it from a passing Despiri guard. "To keep me away. He knew I would come after him even though he told me not to."

"Perhaps it is best that you don't, then." Sinley took her

hand in his, and the gesture brought Cove back to the islands, where the princess had often offered her comfort in the same way—where Celeste was still actively scheming for the rise of the witches. Cove tried to shake any feelings of responsibility for the princess, who she had once considered her best friend. *It is because of her that you are in this predicament. It is because of her that they took Elias instead of you.*

"Listen to him," Sinley said, voice unsteady with age. "You're going to get yourself killed."

Cove needed to bring Elias back, and then they would figure something out together: how to stop Degare, the witches, and all the evil rulers of this world. Or maybe they would hide on an island only she knew and live a peaceful life, just the two of them. After all, the world did not want any of the Light they had to share, but she knew it needed it.

"I would rather die trying to bring him back than to live a life without him."

"That serious, are ye?" Sinley said beneath raised brows. His face was pale against the evening shadows, wrinkles deep, and his cloak appeared a deeper green than it was.

"You should understand, Sinley. You had a wife, and you lost her to the trades."

"It is different. Evelyn and I were not soulbound. Her absence still hurts, but not quite like it does for you I'm afraid." Evelyn had died in the first trades, and Sinley had been living on the streets ever since. Evelyn had been an Ember, but Sinley was not, so the guards had burned his home but let him walk free.

"Why haven't you ever turned to the Light?" Cove asked.

Sinley chuckled. "Girl, after losing Evie the way I did, I

have a hard time believing the Light is any better than the darkness."

"Why? Because people of darkness attacked her for her Light?"

He shrugged. "I don't think the Father of Lights should allow such things."

"Darkness points us to the Light. We may walk through shadows, but He offers us the strength to endure and the Light to see by." Cove weighed the rest of her answer. If there was no darkness, if the Father of Lights had destroyed it at the fall of creation, Cove would not exist. In the Father, there is no darkness. He is pure Light, light outside of the bounds of human comprehension. Set apart and high above His creation, yet He meets us in our shadows. It was by living in the darkness of death and grief that Cove had longed for His Light, that she had come to know His great love, and that she had learned to trust Him. "I can promise you one thing," Cove said.

"And what is that?" Sinley asked, plucking the prickly burrs from his cloak.

"That all things work together for the good of those who love the Light. We might not have it easy here in Arresia, but in the end, the Light wins, and there will be no more darkness. Do you not wish to partake in that?"

Sinley smiled. "You sound like Evie." He flicked a burr toward her feet.

"She knew what she was talking about. You should listen to her," Cove said with a wink.

Sinley was silent for a moment, and then he said, "Okay. For Evelyn, I will help you find Elias." Cove straightened.

"Really?" she asked. "You're willing to help me?" Her

heartbeat quickened with a hope she had not felt since she made the risky deal with Leith.

Sinley squeezed her hand one last time, and her eyes fell to the burn scars on his wrinkled skin. "No one deserves to die in the trades. And I don't want you running back to the Shadow who commands Ink Valley for help. Let's infiltrate the Ember prison."

# CHAPTER 28
# A MISSION COMPLETE
## RAVENNA

"Welcome back, Ravenna," the guard at the edge of the Kingdom of Oro said as she led her black stallion across the slick stone and through the tall gates. "The king awaits you at the base of the tower." Ravenna nodded, handing the reins of the stallion over to the stable master. She watched as the horse and the man faded into the fog and then focused on the tapping of her fingers against the blade at her hip as she closed the final stretch of distance between herself and the king.

Her journey home had been long, as she had fought the consistent pain of the sire burning through her. There was a single command she had not fulfilled, and the tether between her and the king seemed to saw back and forth across her spine, punishing her for that failure. She had fought the sire until her body nearly collapsed from the pain. Xan and Tenille were lucky to have made it out of that valley alive, because after Ravenna had brought the mountains down upon Vestele and covered that old haven with fire and ash and rock, she had not been able to stop her feet from trailing them through the woods.

The many footprints she tracked determined that they had not been alone, and Ravenna guessed it was soldiers from Ink Valley who had accompanied them. The tracks seemed to vanish a few hundred feet beyond the treeline, and it was just the push Ravenna needed to drag herself in the opposite direction, toward Oro. She did not dare encroach any further upon Ink Valley without orders from Degare. She was not a fool, and to wage war on the strongest clan south of Oro without Degare's knowledge would gain her nothing but suffering. If Ravenna had confidence that the Ink Bloods were strong enough to put an end to her, perhaps she would have proceeded toward their new home. But instead, she had repeated the words *let go of your past* all the way home, knowing in her heart that with her conscience still intact, that was something she could never do. Despite the harsh words she had left him with, Ravenna knew they would only hold Xan off for so long. And as long as he threatened to come for her, as long as he provided that little ounce of hope, he would not be safe from the king's commands.

Upon her return, she wished only to soak in a warm bath in her chambers, letting the water wash away every piece of herself that she had grown to hate. But the tether of the sire bond had seemed to strengthen since she had destroyed Vestele, and it was as if she could now *feel* the king's will merging with her own. Every time she obeyed his commands, she felt it tighten its hold on her, as plain as it would feel to have Degare's hands around the column of her throat, squeezing tighter and tighter until she was a corpse of her old self. The wretched bond pulled her through the streets of Oro and toward the north tower of the castle.

Her feet took her to the bottom of the prison tower where she had spent many days. Zeph had been the first to ever deliver her here, when she was whipped into blackness while her parents cried and begged for her life. He had felt such guilt that day. If only he had known that she would grow to deserve the pain.

She traced the cool stone with her fingers as she drew nearer, her parents' pleas still seeming to echo down these halls. She wondered where they were now, if not dead. Being that the king had only kept them alive all these years in hopes of one day claiming their power—which Ravenna now encompassed—she imagined they were long gone. Death would be more merciful than living another second in this kingdom.

On the opposite side of the door, the chambers were silent aside from two familiar voices inside. No sounds of agony cut through the stagnant air. As she opened the door and wound through the dark hall, her skin grew clammy, and her lungs filled with the foul reek of a thousand souls' pain.

Her king stood near the stone altar, and as his eyes landed on her, they swelled with satisfaction. "Ravenna, light the fire," he said, as a way of greeting. The small task took great concentration and focus, as she had not yet tamed her wildfire, but she obeyed him and sent flames into the small pit at his feet, careful not to miss. She held little understanding for the many powers in her veins, and controlling them was difficult when she had only been taught to kill and destroy. Her training usually consisted of learning how to summon a specific gift, with no further training on how to master it. She was a volcano. An eruption. She was a weapon of mass destruction, ready to explode at the drop of a pin.

Jara examined the fire, seemingly unimpressed. Her dark hair was loose today, not pinned up and slicked back as it usually was, and Ravenna had expected it to be longer. It barely fell below the witch's pointy shoulders and had been chopped straight across as if sliced with a sharp sword.

"Now that you have let go of your past," Degare paused, and Ravenna's traitorous mind rested on Xan. *Leave no survivors,* the king had commanded. Pain seared through her again, and she hid the wince that threatened to reveal her secret. "Are you finally ready to give in to the sire, to surrender to me?" Degare asked, tapping his bloodstone staff on the ground. Ravenna said nothing as she watched him twirl a blade in his other hand. If she ever saw Xan again, she did not think she would be able to resist the sire. The pain was too much, the absolute need to satisfy her sire too great. "What else could there be to hold you back?" Degare stepped toward her, and she recoiled.

He smiled wickedly, tipping her chin upward with the tip of the knife.

A chuckle burst through his lips. "You've successfully completed your first orders, Ravenna. I am pleased with you." She hated how the king's words sang to her, and how some unknown pride blossomed inside her—how it felt *good* to please him. "Today, I'll mark you as *mine*. You are *my* weapon." The hair on her arms rose as he spoke. She shuddered, looking to the branding iron that now hovered above the fire in the witch's hand. *When had she grabbed that?*

Ravenna raised her chin, hiding the anxiety that crept through her. There was not one thing she could control. She could not outrun the king, and she could not outrun the grief that gnashed at her heels. But Degare was right. To let go of her past was the only solution. To release the chains the memories had wrapped around her soul. This grief would follow her for as long as she had a conscience. This fear would consume her for as long as she was in rebellion.

As the king stepped toward the iron, she steadied her breathing, willing herself to give in to him. If she would just stop fighting the sire, perhaps she would not suffer–but *enjoy*–serving her master. He would do anything to break her, and she knew that rebelling would only make it worse. *And Xan.* Xan was alive, and if the king found out, he would use him to force her into obedience. He would make her kill him, too. But if she could just let go of her past and forget him, his death would not be worth Degare's time. There would be no motive, because the king would already have her allegiance, fully and completely.

*Just give in,* she told herself. *Just stop fighting.*

Degare's voice strummed the tether as he commanded her to lay across the altar her parents had been tortured on. He laughed, probably at the memory, and before she could lie down, he suggested, "Ah, how about for old time's sake?" Her eyes lifted to his, and he gestured toward the whipping posts, motioning her there instead.

A memory flashed before her, of blood and darkness, and Zephaniah. But then she blinked, and it wasn't Zephaniah's face before her anymore, but Xan's. Ravenna hurriedly shook the thought away as she knelt between the posts. Surely, she deserved this. The witch began to tie her hands. "No need for that, Jara. I believe she is ready. You are ready, aren't you, Ravenna?"

Ravenna allowed the vision of Xan to creep back into her mind, of the unspeakable death she would be forced to deliver him. *Wherever–in whomever–your hope is found, I will put an end to it, to them,* Degare had said. She couldn't handle any more guilt, any more grief, any more pain. Of the hundreds she would be forced to kill under Degare's reign, at least she would not have to feel. So as the king awaited her answer, a sly smile painting his lips, she nodded.

*I am ready.*

A wicked smile spread across his face, hollow eyes seeming to come alive with the thrill. "Remain still," he said to her, command lacing his words. He was certain she would obey, and he was right. Her body did not move, nor twitch, nor shake. She was made of stone.

The sound of the branding iron poking the flames crept into her ears. She only stared forward, gaze falling right between the two posts. The witch cut the back of her tunic open with a blade and Ravenna felt the air across her skin. Still, she did not move. The king's footsteps shuffled behind her.

"From now on, you are no longer Ravenna *Ozanne*. You are the *Raven of Oro*. You are to do my bidding. You are to follow my *every* command. You are to kill when I say kill. You are to kill those who threaten my life or yours. You are to protect me and my kingdom. You will not fail. Your duty is to the crown. You are no longer who you once were. You are *mine*." That tether seemed to tighten more, and she remained there, unmoving. As the brand came down between her shoulder blades at the top of her spine, and her skin was seared with the raven's emblem of Oro, every last piece of hope crumbled away, and she surrendered to the darkness.

"There you are," the king said as the tether between them grew taut. "I thought you'd never break."

# PART TWO

## THE RAVEN OF ORO

# CHAPTER 29
## WINGS BLACK AS SIN
### RAVENNA

Under the dim light of the three crescent moons, and by the faint glow of firelight that bled from her palms, The Raven of Oro barely saw him. The pale-faced man cowered against the wall, wedged between two wooden shipping crates, as she approached him at the end of the alley. Rain drops scurried down the wall behind him, being surpassed by those falling freely from the onyx skies, collecting in puddles at his feet. A warm gleam shimmered in the shallow sheet of water, reflecting his gaunt expression as he silently prayed to the Light that the Raven would not spot him. The puddles seemed to tremble with him, and for a moment, her eyes focused on the strange vibrations that traveled through the water and up her legs before she shook the curious feeling of déjà vu into oblivion.

She placed herself between her prey and the only possible exit–unless the man were a gifted climber. But the saggy skin on his arms where muscle had once been housed suggested that he was as good as dead, standing between her festering darkness and the thirty-foot wall.

She was the hound, unable to return to its master without the rabbit in its teeth. And this man—he was a traitor to his kingdom. *Her* kingdom. He had committed folly against his king. *Her* king. Only a fool would have committed the crimes he had in freeing Embers from Degare's prison on the east side of Oro. Only a fool would have imagined he could come away from such a thing unscathed.

Ravenna had spotted him lurking in the streets beneath her chambers just after dusk, when the skies still held an echo of the clouded daylight of Oro. The oversized hood of his olive-toned cloak was drawn over his head, concealing his identity beneath shadows. Something about his careful walk, his trembling hands that reached to quiet the jingle of the stolen keys in his pocket, and his hurried pace, had given him away. When her eyes had darted to the strange scars on his left hand—scars the guards had reported—a smile tugged at her lips. Nothing slipped under her nose. Not even *one* drop of guilty, treasonous blood.

He had waited until nightfall to attempt to flee the kingdom for good, and he had rushed toward the kingdom gates, a severe limp slowing his departure. *In which direction would he have run?* she wondered. *If I had allowed him to slip past, in which valley would he have taken refuge?* Now that she had seen him, his end was inevitable. He had sensed her presence, a watchful bird balancing atop a nearby roof's edge, stalking its prey. With that sense of impending doom, he had bustled into the nearby alley just as she had planned. The man had no future past the next few moments, which were to be filled with the final beats of his racing heart and a wavering plea.

Her body was physically unable to disobey her king's demands, and her boots splashed through murky water as her legs took her forward. An unrecognizable, wicked laughter bellowed from her throat as she advanced toward him. Her attention bounced from his quivering fingers to the strange white feather that fell from his pocket, and back to his surrendering gaze–which finally landed on the blade in her palm as he accepted his fate. Power curled around her fingertips. Cruel, wicked power that sang louder and louder the deeper into the darkness she fell. After months of this prison, and now with her full surrender, she had come to *enjoy* the kill. She delighted in teasing her assignments before she struck. Like the ravens above, her power seemed to *feed* on death. With each kill she fell deeper into the darkness, and her power only grew stronger. Death: a fuel for her body, which was now bound by night and shadow.

To finally submit, to *let go of remorse*, to stop restraining herself against Degare's every command, had been her greatest decision. Remorse no longer came, and she was grateful for the king who had offered her this freedom. Remorse was a sickness. To feel guilt was weakness, and it had been holding her back. Ravenna was not weak. Not anymore.

The king had stripped her away, piece by piece, bit by bit. Every imperfection, whisked away. He had used the sire bond and crafted her into a *weapon*. His darkness had honed her into an obedient servant. Now, she was nothing but a slave to that darkness.

Degare's wishes were her own. If he wished for this man

dead, so did she. She lived to please her sire, no one else. And so, when the Ember sympathizer begged her, *pleaded* for his life, she did not listen. For *her life* had been bound with darkness itself.

# CHAPTER 30
# REMORSE RELENTED
### RAVENNA

Ravenna popped a cork out of the bottle of rum on her oak table and poured some of the amber liquid into a glass then carried both to her south balcony. The liquor was warm going down, bringing her body immediate rest from its morning shakes.

She exhaled, plopped down in a seat, and kicked her legs up onto the railing, enjoying the cool morning air and the sounds of the kingdom chatter below. Mindlessly, she ran her thumb across the strange callouses on her fingertips. Two Ember sympathizers stood at the gallows, nooses being looped around their necks, and Ravenna had the perfect view. As the boards were kicked from beneath their feet, she clapped along with some passersby and raised a glass, sharing in their celebration. Her king was clever to keep his guests entertained as they entered Oro for the trades. She was sure there were many more sympathizers awaiting the noose, and there would be many Embers awaiting the staff. Ravenna took another soothing swig of rum.

As the crowd around the gallows dissipated and funneled through the streets below, she rose from her chair at once and left the balcony. The noise beneath her balcony was suddenly becoming too much: the clapping, the hundreds of voices blending together, the grating tune being whistled by a passerby. She cupped her hands over her ears, rubbing them violently as the door slammed behind her.

Overstimulation was common for her these days, and she felt her body temperature rising with unexplained rage. She did not know where the rage was coming from; it was from a place within her that she no longer recognized. The barrier of the door did little to drown out the sound of the high-pitched whistling in the street, and her fury escaped her in the form of flames entangling her curtains. This power beneath her skin was still uncontrolled.

She squeezed her eyes shut, willing the fire away, but it kept pouring from her palms until she tucked them into her arms, singeing the fabric of her red robe. She inhaled and dropped the robe from her shoulders, watching it pile onto the floor, and then she reached for a gown from her wardrobe.

She was to have dance lessons with her king this morning, and she wanted to look her best. She stepped into the scarlet red of her kingdom and combed her hair at the vanity. Working around the many braids she still could not bring herself to remove, she felt one between her calloused fingertips, and then blinked, choosing to ignore both evidences of her past. Instead, she focused on the present. She was proud of the marks that graced her skin, of the shadows that spoke of her king's power. She studied the many swirls and channels in which the marks traveled her hands and arms, to her back, and then she pinched her cheeks to bring them some color. A raven landed at her window to watch her, and she watched it back, studying the sheen of its wings.

It flapped away as she rose for her dance lessons. When she exited her chambers, an unfamiliar guard stood paralyzed, mouth agape as he stared at her.

"You're new," she muttered, pushing past him.

"You are not permitted to leave. I cannot allow you out."

"Where did you receive your orders from?" she asked, crossing her arms over her chest. "You must be confused." She looked around, wondering where her usual guards were. They were up to date on all of her king's wishes for her and her scheduled meetings. "I have dance lessons with His Majesty, and I refuse to be late."

"I know nothing of a meeting," he said, drawing his sword. She looked him up and down. He was young and had no visible shadowmarks. Not one of Degare's beloved Despiri soldiers. He was a nobody.

Ravenna raised her brows at his sword and stood her ground, waiting for him to approach–waiting for him to become a threat. *You will not harm yourself. You will not harm me. You will kill anyone who tries to do either.*

"Get back inside your chambers," he said, pointing the blade to her chest. *Unless it is to protect myself or you, you are not to harm my men, ever again.* She kept her feet planted, and when he poked the tip of the blade into her chest, she struck.

She kicked him backward, tearing the blade from his grip in an instant and turning it onto him. He was flat on his back, eyes tightly shut in fear as she took his life. She withdrew the sword from his chest and chucked it to the ground beside him, then smoothed the fabric of her gown as the echoing *clank* tore through the hall. She searched for an escort, since she was not allowed out without one, and spoke to the first guard she saw.

He looked at the dead guard beside her, throat bobbing. "You know who I am," she said dryly. She had seen him before in these halls, and she thought he had even been one of her guards last month. "I need an escort to the dining hall immediately."

"Yes, of course," he said, leading her there. The king had fashioned her into a weapon, and when they arrived through the doors and he looked upon her, she saw the pride in his eyes.

"Ravenna," he said slowly. "Where is the new guard I assigned to you this morning?"

"He threatened my life, and I killed him," she said. He tilted his head, examining her carefully, and then his eyes shifted to the guard at her side.

"That boy never stood a chance," he said with a chuckle. "You are dismissed. Thank you for your cooperation." The guard ducked his head and left the room without a word. Ravenna watched after him and awaited explanation from her king. *Cooperation?*

"You've passed the test, dear. It would seem you can take care of yourself just fine. No more guards, no more escorts." Ravenna straightened her shoulders, taking pride in his satisfaction with her obedience to his every command. She would not fail him.

"Thank you, Your Majesty," she said. "You have been very gracious to me."

"Only the best for my Raven." He invited her forward, holding out a hand. She took it, and he kept his gray eyes on her face, studying his weapon's every detail as he led her into a waltz. Ravenna would need to learn to dance if she was to be seen at his ball, and he aimed to teach her. They had met three times already for this reason in particular.

There was no music, just the sound of their steps clicking on the stone. Beside them was a feast, its savory aroma of meats and fruits wafting through the air, but Ravenna's nose could only focus on the stinging smell of wine. She stumbled once or twice, and both times she winced, but the king only chuckled.

"Is that rum I smell on your breath?" he asked as she peered over his shoulder at the bottle on the table. She swallowed.

"Yes, Your Majesty."

He raised his hands as an exuberant laughter poured from his throat. "We have much in common, Ravenna. Rum is my favorite." He stepped to the side and gathered the bottle and two glasses. He raised a brow at her shaking hand.

"Have some, dear," he commanded as he poured. "You have a big day ahead of you." She took the rum and finished the glass in a few gulps. He watched her with a smile until every drop was gone. "I have selected a few Embers, and they await us in my throne room. I would like you to select your favorites, as a reward for your recent obedience."

Ravenna could not help but return his grin, and as they walked side by side to the throne room, her excitement only grew. She lived to make her king proud, and for him, she would put an end to all Light.

Beyond the towering doors of the throne room, lined up in front of her king's throne, were seven Embers. "These Embers were each delivered to me from my mercenaries in each of the other kingdoms. They are all incredibly powerful." One of the Embers hung her head, refusing to make eye contact with Ravenna, and two others only looked at each other in fear. The other four stared at Ravenna; three looked upon her with a pity she did not understand, and the fourth with a glare woven in condemnation. Ravenna's brow ticked as she studied the tallest male, who she guessed to be the most gifted.

Her king was pointing to each one with his staff, going down the line and explaining each of their gifts and what she could use them for. "Water," he said, pointing to the elderly woman with pale blue eyes and tawny skin. "You already possess such gifts, but as you add to them, they only grow stronger." He pointed to the next one–a young woman with a large scar across her face. "She is a healer. You probably possess those gifts, too, but I never cared much to learn how to use those," he said dryly. Ravenna wondered why a healer would have a scar across her face. The third in line was the tallest male, young with ashy hair that touched his shoulders. "Fire." The male spit on the ground at her feet, and she smiled at him.

"Pardon me, Your Majesty," she said. "But why don't I just kill them all?" Her king stepped back as a look of satisfaction washed over his face.

"The more power, the better, right?"

A wicked smile tugged at his mouth, and he handed her the staff. "You, Ravenna, are my greatest accomplishment. This Light they carry within them. . .with you by my side, it will not spread any further."

Ravenna's shadow descended upon them, and the staff went down the line, siphoning their power one by one. Her body became weak with the new power, but it was only temporary. Every ounce she took would make her stronger in the end. Where there was once a deep sorrow within her, and a will to fight the king, Ravenna felt nothing.

# THE LIGHT SCROLLS
## THE BOOK OF PROPHECY

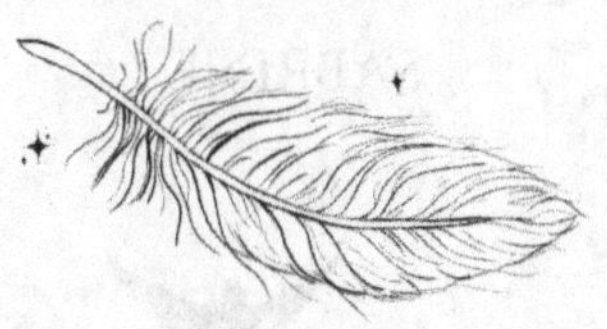

*In the days of darkness, there shall come*
*Those who fight, and those who run...*

# CHAPTER 31
# TOO LATE FOR VOYAGE
## SABRINE

Sabrine had debated leaving since the prince had made himself known in her front yard. Maybe she was a fool for accepting his money, but with it, she could take the twins and escape to Eswen—the closest of the two remaining Kingdoms of Light. There, they would be safe. But even with the blessing of money, there was an ocean separating them from that haven, and she would have to risk bringing the twins to the public dock upon boarding. Both twins bore marks on their faces—Neah across her left cheekbone and Risley above his brow. Neah's could be hidden beneath a covering, but Sabrine had witnessed it herself; the way the dock masters examined each and every soul for lightmarks before allowing them to board. They would never make it on board.

The borders were secure, and Sabrine had no contacts outside of her younger siblings. She had never heard of an Ember successfully escaping these territories. She had never believed she would gain enough money for seeking asylum to ever become a possibility. Now that she had the gold, new problems were arising.

She would go to the docks in the morning and scope out possibilities. She had always been good at hiding. Perhaps she could sneak aboard and hide the twins in a shipping crate. She cringed. *A shipping crate for what, exactly? Embers?* She would be sure to find a merchant ship, maybe one for spices and fruits. Did Edmaria even trade with Eswen or Remont anymore? *Of course not,* she thought. They were kingdoms at war with each other. Edmaria had soldiers fighting in Eswen right now because of Idris's vague agreement with Oro. The only ships that left either kingdom were those filled with Ember hostages being delivered to Oro.

She tapped her pen on the rickety table, trying to think up a plan by the light of the candle.

"What are you doing?"

"Lights, Neah!" Sabrine jumped at her little sister's voice. "Go back to sleep." If Sabrine had taught them anything, it was to remain unseen and unheard. That was hard to do on these creaky floors, but the little mouse had surprised her. Neah ignored her and came to sit at the table, her dark hair escaping her braids in every which way.

"Who was that man a few days ago? Does he know about us?" Neah asked, twiddling with a loose thread at the hem of her grainsack nightgown. The twins must have been watching the encounter from the window.

"I. . .don't know," Sabrine said. She frowned and placed a kiss on top of her sister's head then tugged gently on one of her messy braids. Neah wrinkled her nose in response. Sabrine's eyes fell to her lightmarked cheek. She hated herself. She should have taken the twins that night and gone somewhere-anywhere else.

"He seems nice," Neah said.

"He did bring us food," Sabrine acknowledged, tapping her quill pen wildly on the table and staring toward the dark bedroom where Risley still lay sleeping.

"And lots of money," Neah added. Sabrine looked to her sister, who was now smiling mischievously. "I know your hiding spot," she shrugged, grabbing a piece of paper and a stick of lead to draw with.

Sabrine rolled her eyes. "It's not even dawn yet. Go back to bed," she told her, swiping the lead from her hand. She needed this time to think.

"Could you tell me the story of the Seven first? To help me sleep?" Sabrine breathed tightly at the mention of Neah's favorite tale from the Light Scrolls.

"No, Neah. I don't have time for fairytales." Neah began to argue, but Sabrine shot her a look.

She groaned, but obeyed, stomping past Sabrine and toward the bedroom. She turned when she got to the door. "It is not a fairytale. You'll see," she said.

Sabrine waved her off. "When you wake, I'll be in town. You know the rules." Neah rolled her little head back on her shoulders and begrudgingly climbed back into bed.

Sabrine walked barefoot to the Thickets again in the morning. She had stared at the boots for an hour, contemplating whether or not she was accepting too much from the heir of darkness, and ultimately, she had decided to leave them there in defiance.

She traveled with his coin, which weighed on her conscience heavily enough.

She had found no solution to her dilemma, but she journeyed toward the docks anyway in hopes of finding one there. Maybe she could find a fisherman willing to take her to Eswen—one who would not check for lightmarks. If not, maybe she could pay for one's silence. *No, I could never risk it.* The people who were a threat to Embers already had enough money—it was power they wanted. Maybe she could buy her own boat. She could afford it. *As if I know anything about sailing.* They would die before they made it there.

It was unlikely that she would find a voyage today, but she had come to one conclusion. She had packed all of their belongings in haste this morning, and tonight when she returned to the cottage, she would tell the twins they were fleeing. By then, she only hoped she knew where they were going. Not west, she had decided. She would not dare travel toward Oro, toward the King of Darkness himself. Especially not when Degare was rumored to have a new weapon that could destroy entire villages.

She did not wish to go back to Brinland, where the memories of her parents would haunt her. But Brinland may be the safest of her three options on this continent, being that King Idris of Edmaria had apparently been searching for bloodstone. He would certainly begin searching more diligently for Embers, too, and the twins would no longer be safe, even here in the depths of the woods. She needed to get them away from this kingdom, preferably completely off this continent.

The Thickets were not as busy as they had been three weeks ago. Now, only a few merchant ships were at the docks, and the streets were mostly empty. As she entered the city gates, she headed straight for the coastline. She did not have a plan, and she would have to be good at improvising. Across the lengthy dock, she could see a small boat coming onto shore. A big, wily man was at the stern of it. She had watched the sailors and fisherman plenty of times before to know that there would be conversation when he stepped foot onto the docks, so she planted herself within earshot, eavesdropping as she often did in the city.

Sure enough, when he began tying his boat, two other men came to help him.

"Fine day!" one said as he grabbed the ropes.

"Indeed," the man grunted in return. He must have been about five or six years older than her, and half of his dark hair fell to his shoulders. The other half was tied up with a strip of leather. Tattoos were scrawled across his big hands, and they must have snaked up under his clothing as well because some peeked out from beneath the neckline of his tunic. His smile was bright as he spoke to the others, and he looked to be foreign—of a land she did not know.

Sabrine squinted her eyes against the sun, trying to read the numbers on the stern. She watched as he tied the knots and then grabbed a couple of sacks from the inside of the little wooden boat. She figured he must not have traveled far, since he had no sails and only oars. Though, he did appear to be strong enough to row for days.

She was disappointed when the other men left, and she had gained no helpful information from their conversation. The man bent at the waist once more to pull something metal—a blade—from under the seat. She tilted her chin, trying to peer down into the boat, and when she did, she saw the gleam of a faint mark beneath his shirt. A *lightmark*.

*Does this man know what kingdom he is in?*

"Nakoa." He held a hand out to shake hers, and she blinked, unaware she had been staring and had moved from the boat. He stood before her like a tower.

"S-Sabrine," she stuttered out, placing her small hand into his calloused one. *I never give my true name. What am I thinking?*

His eyes fell to the moneysack as she clutched it where it was tied at her waste. He narrowed his brown eyes at her. "Where are you running to?" She backed up a step. *How does he know I am running?*

"Eswen." She bit her tongue in disbelief; she had just spoken the word aloud. He smiled, and kindness shone from his face.

I thought so," he said. She had the nerve to flee from him before they were seen together, but strange curiosity kept her on the dock.

"You'll get yourself killed coming here," she whispered, backing away. *And I will be killed for conversing with him. Why would he have come here, when every other Ember was trying to flee?*

He waved a hand in the air. "I know the trouble I get into, Sabrine of. . .Brinland." She furrowed her brows. It was only a guess at her homeland, she was sure. He began walking toward the city. She watched the distance expand between them, and then she shut her eyes and inhaled before following him. *What are you doing, Sabrine?*

"Where are you from. . .Nakoa?" she found herself asking. His sword clanked against his belt as he walked, and she wondered if he were a warrior, wanderer, fisherman, or all three.

"Eswen," he said with a smirk. She stopped in her tracks at the word.

"Can you take me there?" she blurted. He kept walking.

"No, I cannot," he said with his back to her. "I have much work to do here. I am searching for someone." She frowned, monitoring her surroundings for any suspicious onlookers, and walked quickly to catch up with him. *What are the chances I just found an Ember from Eswen with a boat, and I let him get away?*

"It is a matter of life and death," she begged, somehow knowing that she could trust him. Because while she was not, he was one of them and so were the twins.

"It is for many," he countered, gesturing to where his lightmarks were concealed beneath his shirt. What made him so trusting of her with such information? He continued forward, Sabrine trailing behind him like a horse on a lead. She had lost all her dignity. "I will not be returning to Eswen for a while," he said as he approached the door of a tavern.

"I can pay!" she yelled after him, planting her feet. He waved her off.

"I will find you when it is time," he said over his shoulder. "Perhaps you could find refuge in Adullam while you wait." With that he disappeared over the threshold.

*Adullam? I will find you when it is time?* Nakoa's words haunted her every step back to the cottage in the West Woods. *What did he mean? How would he find me? Refuge in*

*Adullam? The name sounded familiar, but what does he speak of? Where is this place, and how can I get there? Is it safe, or is this a trap?* He was an Ember himself. Surely he knew more than she did about where to find refuge.

She was left feeling unsettled, and she still had no true plan. Ember or not, he was a stranger, and she did not want to risk taking the twins to this unknown place called *Adullam*. How could she find it, anyway? It was not on the map she kept in her sack, and if it were some sort of secret rebellion, she wanted the twins to have no part in it. Safety was her goal. The twins, hidden away from harm.

She had spent the remainder of the day watching ships at the dock, scheming up ways to sneak the twins on board and searching the schedules for any voyages to the Kingdoms of Light, but there were none. She knew there would not be any that were not a part of the armada at war with those kingdoms. She had been flooded with disappointment by late afternoon.

She would return to Neah and Risley, and they would eat the rest of the food from the basket the prince had brought. They still needed to relocate. At dawn, she planned on taking them further west along the river. There would be no town for her to thieve in, but they could live off the dried venison for the remainder of the month. They would find shelter or build something temporary, and she would find out more about Adullam before she ever mentioned it to the twins.

A light breeze whispered through the woods, and the mossy ground was cool on her bare feet. Autumn was nearing. Living outdoors would not be a problem until the snow hit, but in preparation for winter, she had purchased warm clothing and new boots for the twins today on her way back through the Thickets. She picked up her pace, wanting to return with plenty of time to gather the last of the season's berries before it grew dark.

As she walked along the river's edge, something strange caught her eye. *Horse tracks*. Many of them. Her heart plummeted into her stomach. No one ever came to this side of the woods. They had always been safe here. Immediately, she took off in a blind panic, racing westward. Her sleeve caught on a twig, and she ripped it free, hustling toward the cottage. When she could see the highest point of the shabby roof through the branches, she ducked and cut north, praying the twins were unharmed.

But when she came close enough to see the open door and the muddy hoof prints and leaves rustled up in the yard, she let go of all sense and rashly plummeted into the cottage. Her feet flew forward before her mind could even process her movements. Her hand held a dagger that she did not remember grabbing. Swiftly, she turned the corner to the bedroom, where the floorboards had been ripped up.

Neah and Risley had been taken.

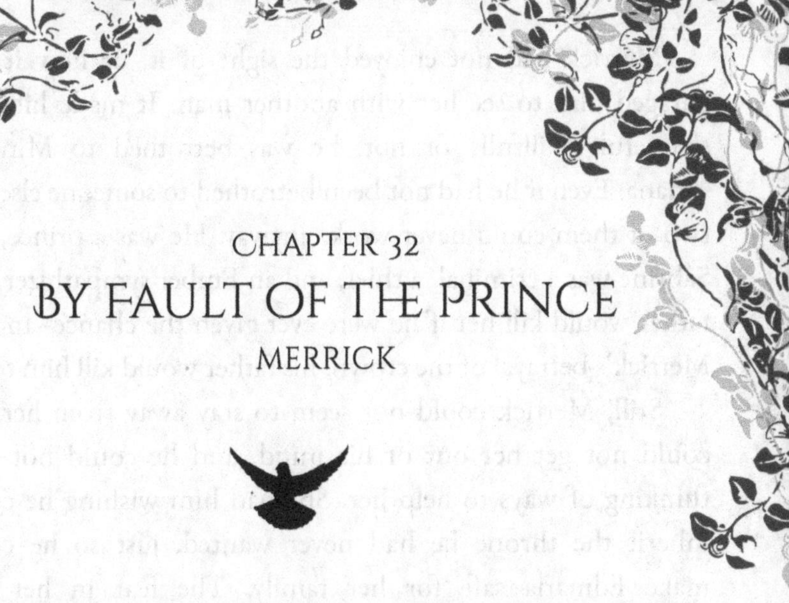

# CHAPTER 32
# BY FAULT OF THE PRINCE
## MERRICK

Merrick had spent most of his morning thinking about his hatred for his father, who was likely arriving in Oro at that very moment. He had invited Merrick to attend the trades with him, but Merrick had declined, claiming he needed some solace before his upcoming travels to Oriana. Merrick did not specify that the solace he sought was from his own father and his father's wife.

Merrick had requested a morning of solitude away from the prying eyes of his many guards and was taking a stroll through the Thickets, when he saw the girl who had captured every corner of his mind and given him freedom from the once all-consuming thoughts of Jamila, his father, and the island princess whom he was now to marry. Sabrine had been sitting on the docks as if she were going somewhere. Perhaps their encounter had scared her into fleeing. He almost approached her—had been *so* close to walking up to her. But then the foreign fisherman came ashore and began talking to her as if they were friends.

Merrick had not enjoyed the sight of it, or how it had enraged him to see her with another man. It made him feel shameful. Willfully or not, he was betrothed to Mina of Oriana. Even if he had not been betrothed to someone else, the two of them could never work, anyway. He was a prince, and Sabrine was a criminal, a thief, and an Ember sympathizer. His father would kill her if he were ever given the chance—and for Merrick's betrayal of the crown, his father would kill him too.

Still, Merrick could not seem to stay away from her. He could not get her out of his mind, and he could not stop thinking of ways to help her. She had him wishing he could inherit the throne he had never wanted, just so he could make Edmaria safe for her family. The fear in her eyes saddened him, and he had decided just yesterday that if he saw her again he would help her flee. Surely, she had taken the money he had given her and would use it for her travels, but he should have done more. *How was she to know where to find a ship to take her far away from here? How was she to do it all alone, against five entire kingdoms who would have her head?*

He had examined from afar as she parted ways with the bulky fisherman, and after a day of watching her pace up and down the docks barefoot and following her through the markets where she *paid* for each item she touched, he followed her into the woods. When she came across the tracks in the mud by the river, she had taken off in a sprint, and he had run, too, not fully understanding her sudden fear. She had been completely oblivious to him barreling after her through the brush and briars.

He had known the cottage was empty before he heard her sobs. The door had been left open. The leaves and mud in the yard had been disturbed, as if there had been a struggle. The twins were small, but they had put up a fight.

Merrick stepped slowly toward the cottage until the flash of silver on the porch caught his eyes. On the top step was a knife–one of his men's. Merrick had given them each a knife with the crest of Edmaria on it when they had sworn themselves to him. They had sworn themselves to him, and yet they had been here on these grounds without orders.

Sabrine howled ragefully inside of the cottage while he traced the direction of the tracks. His guards had gone northeast–toward his father's palace–where his father's boat and two small ships full of Embers would be disembarking the palace docks for Oro at noon. Merrick's heart dropped into his stomach, and he felt as though he could not get enough air. *My men betrayed me. My father has been having me watched.*

Sabrine marched down the steps, feet still bare, nostrils flaring with rage. There was a dagger in one hand and a bow in the other. Her quiver was loaded with arrows, and her face was stained with tears. She was going hunting. She did not see Merrick until she had tracked the prints around the side of the house.

She stopped cold for only a moment and then advanced toward him, rage steaming from her face. Despite being malnourished and a whole foot shorter than him, she was able to slam him into a tree. Her dagger was to his throat in an instant. Either she was pressing harder than she realized, or she did not care if she killed the last Prince of Edmaria. He tried to back away from the blade, but the tree stopped him. Her lips spoke nothing, but her eyes said it all. If he moved, she would take his life.

"Talk!" she screamed in his face. He cringed as the noise

echoed through the entire forest, where his men could still be traveling.

"I-I," he stammered. The guilt flooded through him, and his hands remained raised beside his head.

She pressed harder against his throat, and her face was only an inch from his as she spoke again through gritted teeth. "Now." Her eyes were a staggering blue against her brown skin, and their fierceness bored into him.

"It was not me!"

"Then you were followed!" she accused. She was right. His men must have followed him here the last time he had come. It was the only way they ever would have found her this close to the border. His men did not often travel these woods. *How did I not know I was being followed?*

"I will help you get them back. I'll take you to Oro." Her face twisted in pain as she realized the fact that her siblings were being marched to their deaths.

"You've done enough," she seethed.

They did not have enough time to make it to the docks at the Sand Palace before the ship was set to leave. Whichever of his men had betrayed him, had planned it like this–probably hoping to make some coin off of their contribution, whilst hitching a ride to the Ember Trades on the ships that were fast-tracked with water-gifted Despiri on board as crew.

"You'll never make it in time without my help," Merrick said, pleading with her to let him make this right. She snarled at him, but the pressure on the dagger lessened slightly. "I can get you there in time," he promised. "I can help you. I am your only hope." Sabrine scoffed, and she plummeted the dagger into the trunk next to his head. He winced, and she left him there without a word as she stomped into the cabin. "What are you doing?" he called after her.

He walked toward the door, and right as he was about to enter inside, she emerged, holding a half empty sack. "What is that?" he asked as she tossed it to him.

"Those are all our belongings. You carry that, I carry the gold," she said, waving the coin satchel in the air. She collected her bow from the door frame and left the cabin without looking back. Merrick watched as she traipsed west. "Why are you just standing there?" she asked.

"I don't think you would care much for the Valley of the Shadow."

Sabrine narrowed her eyes at him. "I do not fear the Valley of the Shadow. Do you?" Yes, he did. She rolled her eyes at him and continued west. "You underestimate what I am willing to do to get them back. Death would not be too great a price for their safety." Merrick looked to the sky nervously as he remained where he was. Sabrine paused again and turned to see him still standing on the porch. "You said you would help me. So do it."

"Okay," Merrick said slowly. "If you go that way on foot," he said, eyes falling to her bare feet as he wondered again why she was not wearing the boots he had bought her, "you'll be cutting it too close on time. The trade is in a week. They'll be traveling by boat with the help of gifted Despiri. The twins could be sold by the time we get there if we do it your way."

"Well, then, what do you suggest, Prince?" He threw the satchel over his shoulder.

"We go back to the country home and–"

"No. I am not going in the opposite direction. It is a waste of time." She began advancing toward Oro, and Merrick caught her arm. Her blue eyes pierced him.

"It will not be a waste of time, Sabrine. I promise," he said gently.

She closed her eyes and took a deep breath. "Do you have a really fast horse or something?" she asked, begrudgingly turning around to join him on the journey to his country home near the Thickets.

"More like a friend who owes me a favor."

# CHAPTER 33
# THE SORRY PRINCE
## SABRINE

"All of your belongings are in this bag?" Merrick asked as he and Sabrine traipsed through the woods toward his country home. Sabrine rolled her eyes. Of course a prince would not be able to fathom the life of a wanderer who lived out of a sack and thieved for survival.

"We had more, before your father ordered a raid on my village last year and sent my parents into the trades. I mean, do you expect myself and two young children to be able to carry anymore when we are running for our lives?" Merrick looked down at his feet, and Sabrine took a deep breath.

"Your bag was already packed. And I saw you at the docks this morning. Where were you planning to run to?"

"Have you been watching me often?" she asked. Her thick eyebrows scrunched low over her upturned eyes as she looked sidelong at him.

"No, I-I just happened to be in the city this morning, and then I saw you, and I was curious so I–"

Sabrine waved him off. "I was going to take the money you

239

gave us, and we were going to flee. To Eswen." Merrick nodded slowly. He'd guessed as much. "Our bag stays packed for the most part. . .in case we have to run."

"I am sorry you have to live this way," he said, trailing closely behind her. She was leading the way in the direction of the country home, steps quickening by the minute. "And I am sorry for my father's part in all of this."

"Look," Sabrine said, stopping abruptly. Her blue eyes met his, flashing with resentment, and it seemed that her anger was one of the few things she did not hide in this world. "I am not looking for an apology. No kindness you give can make up for the heartache you and your father have brought me. You are here because I am allowing it, and you are here to help me get the twins back as you promised. I am giving you one chance to back out."

"I am not backing out," he said quickly.

"Good," she said. "You'll help me get the twins back, and you'll find us safe voyage to Eswen, and then we will never see you again. You'll never tell a soul about us, because you have seen firsthand what happens when you are careless."

Merrick worked his jaw beside her. "I truly am sorry," he said. He deserved the guilt he was brooding in. He was the reason the twins were now in shackles, awaiting their deaths.

"Sorry does nothing." Sabrine refused to look at him for longer than a second, but she noticed the way his gaze fell to the ground, his brown eyes seeming to pool with the sadness of a distant memory. She batted a branch from her face and ducked slightly, not bothering to hold it for him. As it smacked his shoulder, he blinked. "Start telling me how you plan to get them back," she said.

Her steps were heavy and fast on the dried leaves and pine

needles, and he followed closely behind her. His silence was telling, but right as Sabrine was about to accuse him of not having a plan, he spoke up. "There will be a massive crowd, and it will be hard to go unseen—"

"I am good at going unseen," she said. "It will be like a day in the Thickets for me. The twins are the coin." Surely she could do this.

"It won't be that easy. They'll be in shackles up until the moment they are dead." Sabrine's steps paused for a moment as her heart slammed against her sternum. Merrick's amber eyes softened. "The Embers are heavily guarded," he added. He continued forward, where the ground began transitioning into sand. "Even if we succeeded with the rescue, with only two routes in and out of the kingdom it would be nearly impossible to make it out with the Despiri on our tail."

"Okay. So stealing them is off the table," she said in irritation. He offered her a hand as they shimmied down the hillside on the edge of the woods. She did not accept it, and instead, used her hands to balance herself in the sandy soil. "What is our other option?" she asked when she rose, wiping her palms on her trousers.

"Purchase them."

"*Purchase* them?" She turned toward him fully, crossing her arms over her chest where they now stood on the edge of the Edmarian desert lands.

"I am a prince. I have the gold. I'll do the bidding. Once we've secured them with the papers, they'll send us to the killing platforms." Sabrine gritted her teeth. "Surely, once they are ours, we will have more freedom to do with them what we wish—"

"You're kidding," Sabrine said. Merrick looked at her in

confusion, shielding his eyes from the light of the sun. "You think they are just going to let us purchase Embers and walk away with them? Degare is threatened by their power. He will ensure every last one is chained in spelled shackles in his prisons and mines or dead."

Merrick chewed on his lip. "Well, then we purchase them and then steal them when we are being transported to the killing platform with the others. Before we make it to where the king is with his staff. It will be less challenging than trying to swipe them from the bidding platforms where all the Embers are chained together."

Sabrine did not like the plan, but it was their only option. Ahead, she could make out the silhouette of a massive estate that was situated in the sands of Edmaria. "That is where you are staying?" she asked. She had never seen a home so large. It was three stories high and had four spherical sandstone structures on each corner. Despite it being in the center of a desert, the landscaping was pristine, complete with two large fountains and a plethora of colorful plants Sabrine had not seen before. A tree bearing green olives stood tall near the gate, and the sun shone on the front facing wall of the estate that bore a carving of two serpents rearing up at one another.

"This is where my mother always came to flee my father, and this is where I do the same," he said, adjusting his gold embroidered sash. He ran a hand through his thick hair, and Sabrine noticed the calluses on his palms, likely from a sword that he was not carrying.

She stood there, watching him closely before he continued through the sands. It was her turn to follow him, and she stayed close, feeling exposed in the middle of the open desert. The hot sand nearly burned the soles of her feet, and she knew he had noticed her lack of shoes, but he did not speak a word of it. Perhaps he realized that accepting his help was difficult for her, whether in the form of shoes, money, food, or whatever this was. She delighted in the coolness the shade of the olive tree offered as he took her toward the back gate, which was surprisingly unguarded. He poked a key into the lock and swiftly opened it, ushering her through.

"Where is everyone?" she asked.

"I came with only a few guards. I am guessing that the ones who betrayed me to take your siblings are now on their way to Oro."

Sabrine swallowed. "Well, then, what friend is it you're bringing me to meet?"

"The one who would never betray me." Merrick said, pocketing the key. "But you're not going to like him."

Sabrine eyed the many beautiful fabrics and curtains that hung from every tall window and the intricately woven tapestries that depicted legends of old. A narrow mahogany table lined the wall, and atop of it were vases of flowers, freshly picked from the gardens outside. Dust collected on her fingertip as she dragged it across the wood. She looked around for any sign of a maid, but the estate was seemingly empty.

"Merrick?" a voice called from around the corner. Sabrine's bare feet squished into the rug, and she paused as the man came through the doorway. "I thought that was you, I–" the man's yellow eyes darted past the prince and landed on Sabrine.

"Kenan, this is Anya," Merrick said quickly. Sabrine

narrowed her eyes at the prince, and Kenan studied her for a moment with his hands in his pockets.

"Anya and I need a favor," Merrick said.

"And I need to speak with you," Kenan said dryly. "Alone."

Merrick looked between his friend and Sabrine and nodded. At the prince's apologetic glance, Sabrine ducked her head and wandered over to the other side of the room, pretending to admire a tapestry. Thankfully, she was just as skilled at eavesdropping as she was thieving.

"What is it?" the prince asked.

"I take it you know if you've brought her here," Kenan said. Sabrine's cheeks heated as she felt both of their eyes on her. "I recognize her from the Thickets. Are you looking for a reason for your father to withhold your inheritance?" Sabrine looked at Merrick then, studying him intently. She had not realized the severity of the situation for him—had only thought of herself and the twins.

"Who was it, Kenan? Which of my men betrayed me?" he pressed, voice rising in anger like she had not heard before.

"Nadim," Kenan said after a long moment. "I learned of it this morning while you were gone. Your father paid him to have you followed. The others sided with your father when they learned what you have been up to." Kenan nodded to Sabrine, and she quickly looked away, pretending as if she could not hear every word. "I didn't want to believe that you had sided with the Embers, but I've sworn an oath to you, Merrick. In time, you are to be my king, no matter my opinions. I serve you—not your father."

"Yes, well they took that same oath," the prince muttered, and Sabrine could tell his temper was rising.

"I tried to stop them," Kenan said, holding his hands up. "I am sorry. But it is not safe here for you any longer. When your father returns from Oro–"

"I know," Merrick said, cutting him off before he could finish. "That doesn't matter. We need transport to the trades," he said, gesturing between himself and Sabrine. She took that as her queue to join him again and came to stand at his side.

"I thought you never wanted to attend the trades again," Kenan said warily, glancing between the two of them. His eyes narrowed on Sabrine, and she could not help the way she wanted to crawl into her skin and hide.

"Times have changed. My new friend here would like the chance to experience them." Sabrine's body went stiff at the abhorrent statement.

Kenan shook his head slowly, chuckling at his prince's blatant lie. "No. No way. If your father sees you there after what you've done–"

Sabrine watched the exchange closely. "My father will not see me," Merrick assured him.

"I won't risk it. I am not to let you travel alone anyway–"

"I won't be alone. I'll have Anya." Merrick smiled sidelong at her, and she shifted on her feet at the use of the fake name she had given him.

"Yeah, she looks like she could protect you," he said dryly.

"She is quite skilled with a dagger," Merrick reasoned. Sabrine crossed her arms over her brown tunic.

Kenan took a deep breath and rolled his eyes. "I won't do it, Merrick. You have no business being in Oro without your father's knowledge. It will be both our heads on the stake–"

"And you had no business getting acquainted with my father's wife without his knowledge."

Sabrine could not help the way her eyes widened at that. Kenan fell silent.

"I will tell him of your adultery, Kenan. If you do not send us to Oro right now."

"You would tell him?" Kenan asked, as if he had been betrayed.

"I need you to do this for me," Merrick said apologetically.

Kenan nodded his head reluctantly, looking between the prince and Sabrine and said, "Is that bag all you are taking? You'll be in the presence of the wealthy. She can't go looking like. . .that."

"Give us ten minutes," Merrick said, grabbing Sabrine's hand and pulling her into the hall that jutted off of the entryway.

"What is wrong with my outfit?" she asked, shaking off his hand and clenching her fist. They stopped in front of a massive, seemingly unlived-in bedroom. The only sign that it had once been occupied were the hundreds of open books, journals, and scribbled letters stacked on the bookshelves.

"Those clothes don't really scream, *duchess*," he said, eyeing her from head to toe. Sabrine's face turned hot, and she looked down at her dingy clothes. She had not given them a good wash in days, and she suddenly became hyperaware of her probable odor. She reached into the sack and began rummaging for the outfit she always wore to thieve in.

"Yeah, that isn't going to work either. Don't bother," the prince said. "I didn't buy it for a second." She felt all of the blood in her body rush to her cheeks as he pointed her in the direction of the ceiling-high wardrobe at the east end of the bedroom they had stopped at the threshold of. "Pick a dress for the ball. And another for the trades. You'll want to fit in."

"I know how to fit in," she muttered. Sabrine had no gifts, but she had talents and hiding was one of them. She strode to the wardrobe that stood between the only two windows in the room. The thick curtains were pulled, and the room was considerably dark, aside from the few oil lamps burning on the tables. "How do you plan on going unnoticed at the ball your father will be attending?"

"It's a masquerade," he said. She watched as he collected a pair of sandals and some boots from beneath the bed. "It seems I wasted a silver serpent in the Thickets," he said, nodding to her bare feet. "You'll need shoes in Oro."

"The boots you bought me are in my satchel," she said. She chewed on her lip and then turned back to the wardrobe. "Whose were these?" she asked, thumbing through the plethora of gowns.

"Those were my mother's," he said, straightening the covers on the bed. There was a crack in his voice, and Sabrine watched him run a hand over the smooth skin of his cheeks in an attempt to hide the quiver in his lip. Sabrine knew of the Queen of Edmaria. She had heard the stories of how she had disappeared seven years ago. Sabrine's hand paused on an intricately embroidered blush skirt.

"Is she truly dead, as the people claim?" she asked, moving her hand down the line of luxury fabrics. Merrick's brown eyes darted to hers, and beneath his furrowed brows she saw anguish.

"Is that what the people are saying?" he asked, as if he had never heard the rumors. She nodded slowly, letting her hand fall from a dark blue gown. In the gossip she overheard in the city, people were saying more than that.

She pulled a silver dress from the rack and held it up to her body. "What do you think, silver or blue?" Merrick redirected his attention to her and blinked. "Blue and purple, no silver," he said. She turned to examine the deep purple gown as he shoved a suit into a leather bag. He collected a stack of coins from the drawer of the bedside table and filled his pockets as Sabrine carried the two gowns over to the bed.

"How much do you think they'll sell for?" she asked sheepishly, and now it was her voice that was cracking. "I just want to make sure we have enough." She stood as tall as possible, smoothing out the skirts of the gowns while she awaited his response.

"We'll have enough," he assured her. He collected her dresses and a gold necklace and added them to the bag. When his back was turned, Sabrine swiped a few more gold and silver serpents from the drawer, just to be safe. "Are you coming?" he asked. She nodded, hurrying to follow him out the door.

"How exactly is your friend going to get us to Oro before the trades? Does he have a boat? Could he get the twins and I to Eswen?" Merrick's lips fell into a tight line.

"Do not mention Eswen to him."

Sabrine's steps were quick behind Merrick as he proceeded through the country home and into the study, where Kenan awaited them among scattered papers and a stack of journals. There was a dartboard across from the desk and a few empty glasses with the remnants of some sort of wine at the base. Merrick collected a journal from the table and quickly shoved it into his bag.

"Are you ready?" Kenan asked. His eyes were almond shaped, and his cheeks were full, with the beginnings of a beard growing. Sabrine waited for him to lead the way toward the docks, but he only rose from behind the desk and extended a shadowmarked hand. Sabrine stumbled backward, and Merrick steadied her with a hand on the small of her back, pushing her forward and urging her to take Kenan's hand. The man was a Despiri.

*Why had Merrick not warned me?* She glared at the prince, and Kenan watched the silent exchange carefully with a smirk. He tipped his head with each passing second like a ticking clock.

"You've never teleported before I take it?" Kenan asked after a few moments of silent quarrel. Sabrine swallowed, still staring at the creeping shadows on his skin that marked him as a killer of her siblings' kind.

"Teleported?" Sabrine asked, looking between Kenan and the prince.

Kenan chuckled, and Merrick did not take his eyes from her as he waited for her to snap. His hooded eyes sought forgiveness that would not come easily. Sabrine shook her head against her flushing face and took a deep breath before grabbing the murderer's hand.

Merrick seemed to relax beside her, taking Kenan's other hand. "Where can you send us?" Merrick asked. Sabrine hung on to her composure by a thread.

"I remember the coliseum quite well. I spent many weeks there training. I'll drop you there." *Drop us?*

"That's perfect," the prince said, looping the bag over his left shoulder and taking Sabrine's other hand in his own. His hand swallowed her thin fingers, and she wished she could stop the nervous clamminess of her palms. She did not typically let people close enough to realize the truths about the way she was feeling, and with his hand feeling the shake in hers, she felt exposed.

"You may lose a day. Or three. Oro is quite far," Kenan explained. "I'm not exactly well versed in sending *others* into the oblivion." Sabrine gulped nervously. *What does he mean, oblivion? Is this man even capable of getting us to Oro in one piece?* "I've only done it one time, and it drained me for days. Thought I might die," he added, raising his brows at the prince as if to say, *Look what I am risking for you.* "There's not another Despiri I know of in all of Oro who has the ability to teleport *others*," Kenan bragged. "Not even Degare. I bet he'd be enraged to know I got the better kill of the two that day." Sabrine's lips were flat in anger, and it was all she could do to keep her hand in his. How could he speak so carelessly of the life he had taken?

"Alright, Kenan. That's enough," Merrick said, urging him on.

"Okay, okay. Ready, then?" Kenan asked.

She nodded tightly. *Oblivion, here we come.*

Kenan must have seen the fear settling on her face, because he smiled and added, "Don't worry, dear. Merrick is to be my king. I'm not too happy about him going to Oro in the first place, but I would not send him into the space between if I was not sure I could get him there safely. The distance will just take a little more time and focus on my part. That is something I am willing to do for him." He said the words to the prince, as if he were making a bargain. *Is he a true friend to the prince, or is he only offering this favor to keep his secret affair with the king's wife covered up?* "I can do this," he assured her.

"Let's go then," Merrick said, looking to the side at her warily, and she felt a twitch in his hand. *Do not look at me,* she wanted to say. *I am in this mess because of you.*

"Whatever you do, do not let go of each other," Kenan

said. Sabrine looked away from the prince, focusing on her breaths. She could not help the quake in her legs and the gritting of her teeth. "Utter darkness, coming right up. On the count of three," Kenan said. Sabrine inhaled deeply and tightened her grip on the prince's hand until her knuckles ached.

"One."

She squeezed her eyes shut.

"Two."

*For the twins,* she reminded herself.

"Three."

# CHAPTER 34
## THE KING'S RAVEN
### RAVENNA

"Ravenna, dear," Degare said across the table, gray eyes flitting to the sugar. The thread that bound them seemed to tremble with unspoken words. Ravenna grabbed the small black cup from the table and scooted it toward the king. He smiled delightfully and added a spoonful to his tea.

"The ball is in three days," Degare said nonchalantly. "I expect a large audience." Ravenna hummed as she brought her teacup to her lips. The kingdom was already crawling with foreigners and guests who were to participate in the trades. They had gold burning holes in their pockets as they yearned for the power only her king could give them through the use of his staff. "I want to impress. I want to show the other kingdoms just how much power I have over them, and I want it to frighten them into submission. They will continue coming to me for the Ember Trades because no one else has the ability to give them power like I do. Their power will never match mine." He paused, looking at Ravenna, who held that power.

"I will never allow them to come close, but they will spend all their gold trying. Oro will rule the world with both money and strength."

Ravenna smiled. "And what do you need from me, Your Majesty?" She set her steaming drink down on the saucer.

The corner of Degare's lip tugged upward in a sly smirk. "I have many tricks up my sleeve for you, my Raven. You have been doing so well in your training, and you have made me proud, but. . ." Ravenna's body shuddered at that word. "I have one more test to prove your loyalty to me before I will risk flaunting you in front of our visitors."

Ravenna nodded. "Anything I can do to prove myself to you, Your Majesty." All she wanted was to please him.

"As I expected. You will join me this afternoon in the throne room. Right now," he collected his napkin from his lap and rose from the table, "I must find Jara. We are to make the final selections for the trade." He wiped his mouth and threw the cloth down on the table. "The stock is a strong one, and I have some last minute additions coming by boat from Edmaria. These Embers will bring us much coin."

"That is wonderful, Your Majesty," Ravenna said with a dip of her head, eyeing the gold embroidery on his black jacket. "I will see you this afternoon." She finished her tea as he slipped through the doors of the dining hall to find his witch.

A mouse-faced seamstress measured her for a custom gown. Holding the ribbon around Ravenna's waist, down her arms, and across her hips, she mumbled incomprehensibly to herself.

"I do not like that fabric," Ravenna stated as the seamstress held up the satin. Satin was a mixture of many woven fabrics, and Ravenna preferred *silk*. The seamstress's eyes widened, and Ravenna could have sworn her hands started to shake.

"Miss, I am very sorry, but the king has requested. . ." Ravenna waved a hand at her as the sire bond sent a twinge of pain down her spine. She would wear the satin, if that was what Degare wished. In fact, she could see that the fabric was actually pretty, now that she really looked at it. It was sheen like silk, even under the diffused light coming in through the panes. And red truly *was* her color.

"It's actually quite perfect," Ravenna assured her. "I am the Raven of Oro–whatever the king wants, he shall get." The seamstress nodded and breathed a sigh of relief, but her hands continued to tremble against Ravenna as she pinned the fabric around her torso. Ravenna's mouth formed a straight line, waiting for the inevitable *prick* that was coming if the woman's hands did not steady soon.

Ravenna watched as she circled around her in the mirrors. She noted the seamstress's pause as she began working on the back of the gown, when she undoubtedly noticed the newly branded flesh that had been placed over her many scars from dozens of well-deserved lashes. The ghost of a wince fleeted across the seamstress's face before she composed herself and began pinning once more.

Though the memories of Ravenna's bloodied body were still fresh in all the servants' minds, for Ravenna, those days felt like a lifetime ago. The memories were hazy, and she did not care to see them clearly. The memories no longer bothered Ravenna–she was foolish to ever fight the sire in the first place. This kingdom was the most powerful in all Arresia, why would she not wish to be on the winning side?

Ravenna's bare back and arms displayed shadowy tendrils that crept across her skin like faded tattoos. Perhaps the shadowmarks were where lightmarks would have glowed had she chosen another path. Ravenna's gaze was fixed on the mirror, and she twisted her arm to admire the marks of darkness.

"How much longer? I'm starving," she said. The seamstress hurriedly fixed a couple more pieces before backing away, as if in fear Ravenna might set her on fire. In her defense, Ravenna still had little control and *had* set the curtains on fire out of unchecked rage the week before. Her emotions were often as uncontrolled as her power.

"All done," she said, beginning to remove the fabrics from Ravenna's frame. Ravenna knew the woman would be rushing to get the dress finished in time for the ball, and she smiled at the thought of her trembling hands working away in the night, worry lines permanently plaguing her face.

After she had stepped out of the gown and the seamstress left her, she walked past the deep red chaise and sunk into the plush mattress of her bed. Crowds were beginning to form below her chambers, and some of the incoming travelers peered up toward her windows, hoping to catch a glimpse of Degare's rumored weapon. *I just want to sleep.* She slammed some dark power into the windowpane, shutting it and mistakenly splintering the wood in the process. She winced.

It muffled the many voices, and she tried not to focus on the gossip below, but it was impossible. "I hear the king's new weapon is in that wing. What could it be?" Ravenna huffed a breath from where she lay on the bed, homing in on another voice. *For the love of Light, could anyone in this city talk about something other than me or the Ember trades?*

"I think it is a dragon," a prude woman said. Ravenna rolled her eyes then smiled as she breathed a little fire into the air for her own amusement. That harmless, little fire turned into an uncontrolled plume of flames before she snuffed it out with a few hurried blinks. She stared breathlessly at the tall, suet-covered ceilings of her chambers, and at the walls that had recently been reconstructed since her heinous act of rebellion.

*I will never betray my king again.*

The clouds hovering over the kingdom were pouring rain into the streets of Oro, and Ravenna wished to take the scenic route to the throne room, so she laced up her boots and grabbed her cloak on her way over the south balcony railing. Her feet landed with a splash against the cobblestone in the kingdom square, and she earned the curious glances of a few Volcanian men who were in Oro for the trades.

"Gentlemen," she said as she barreled past them through the streets. None of the foreigners knew of her true identity as Degare's Raven, and they wouldn't until it was announced at the ball. The king had ordered the few soldiers that knew of the sire bond to keep quiet. The men watched after her, and she picked up the pace, scurrying past the gallows and through alleys toward the rear castle entrance. The sea was still red, but the water that now fell from the skies was clean, and Degare had his soldiers out collecting it in buckets among the peasants. The kingdom's many visitors, who had either come by boat or through the Valley of the Shadow, now gathered in masses at the sea's edge, studying the strange phenomenon. Something the king had yet to have Ravenna do anything about.

The rumors had spread that the bloody water was an attack on Oro–the start of an imminent war. And when the blood had made its appearance, Ravenna had seen it no other way. Who had such power in the land of Arresia to turn the waters red? Ravenna assumed she would be receiving orders to take care of the matter soon after the trade, when Degare had shown the kingdoms of Arresia that he is not one to be toyed with. But did matters really need to be taken seriously when the attacks had seemingly halted at the color red?

She looked north as she neared the end of the alley and peered over the black rock cliffs, where ravens croaked and greeted the many ships as they came ashore, having survived the angry, bloody waves of the Black Sea. Ravenna was ready to prove to her king that she could be trusted, that he could show her off in front of every kingdom in Arresia. She would make him proud.

She settled on the ledge of the cliff, allowing her legs to dangle over the sea as she counted the ships on the red horizon. She was surprised to see at least twelve vessels coming to shore. Some of their sails had been ripped and stained with the blood of the sea, which spanned as far as Ravenna's sights would go. She wondered if all the seas in Arresia had been turned to blood, and what exactly the perpetrator had expected would come from it. Degare would never release the Embers that he had worked so hard to chain.

The distant shouts of the dock workers echoed up the ledge, and with their voices came the splashing of towering red waves against the ridge. Ravenna allowed it to stain her boots and trousers, and then she laid back on the rocks, spreading her arms open wide. She watched the fog roll across the skies and enjoyed the caress of the clean rainwater that fell on her face and pattered against the stone around her.

When a strange sound began to echo up along the edge of the cliff and into her ears, she perked up and peered north, where a wall of giant red hail was encroaching on Oro. The ice pellets hammered across the waters, creating a thousand splashes as the storm rolled closer to her kingdom. She looked over to the docks where the hail was beginning to splinter the rickety wooden structures, and the crewmen were beginning to yell and take cover beneath anything they could find.

The hail seemed to hover over the docks for a few minutes, damaging everything in its path. The ships rocked as crewmen scurried from side to side, sheltering themselves from the falling ice beneath crates. The hail began tearing straight through the sails of the docking ships, and with the impact of a few arbitrarily large spheres, some of the ships even began sinking. Ravenna clambered to her feet, eyes widening as she witnessed the encroaching wall of unnatural hail.

She backed away from the cliff's edge as the wall of heavy, red-tinted clouds crept toward her. Noblemen began jumping overboard with their pouches of gold. The wealthy fought to tread the rough and thick red waters, diving beneath the surface for protection after each quick breath, but the hail's size was unpredictable—coming down either coin-sized or the size of a raven. The dooming storm continued sweeping through the kingdom, leaving destruction in its wake.

Ravenna raced toward the north gates of the castle where Degare would be awaiting her, both for their scheduled meeting and her aid. The guards let her pass with a curt nod. She heard the voice of the king pouring through the halls outside of the throne room as the hail began to beat upon the thick stone of the castle. "This is an attack! Another attack! Someone is waging war, and I will not surrender!" he bellowed. The voice of the witch came next, both soft and frightening.

"Well, then, you better find out what fool is demanding you do, because your kingdom will not last much longer. Not with a limited water supply and now hail big enough to kill a horse and *sink the ships of your buyers*. Some of whom are now choking on blood." Ravenna flinched as one of the hailstones hit the ground just outside the south doors, sending shards of ice shattering toward her feet, where she stood just outside the throne room. The guards jumped backward and shielded themselves against the debris.

"Your Majesty," she said with a duck as she walked in. He surveyed her wet clothes.

"Ravenna," he said before turning back to the witch. Jara straightened her body and smoothed the front of her scarlet dress. Ravenna tilted her chin at the odd change of color. The witch typically wore black. "Jara, it is your job to find out who is threatening my trades. Ravenna will join you when I am sure she is ready."

Jara's mouth fell into a tight line as she shoulder-checked Ravenna on her way out of the throne room. Ravenna turned over her shoulder to watch her, and only when the clicking of her heels had silenced, did Degare speak to the Despiri guards at the door. "You may retrieve them now," he said. The two men took off quickly, leaving Ravenna alone with the king.

"Your Majesty, let me handle the attacks. I will find the perpetrator, and I will end them for you."

He chuckled. "I appreciate your confidence, Ravenna. And I trust that you mean that. But first, I must test your loyalty, if you remember our chat from earlier."

"Ah, yes. And then you'll let me boast of your power at the ball."

"That is the plan," he said, looking toward the ceiling. A hundred beads of hail threatened to come through, but the castle proved strong.

"I could use my flames, Your Majesty. To melt the ice as it falls. I could do it." It would take little control—just one big release of power across the kingdom. She dreamt of the relief it would bring to her aching bones.

"And risk revealing my power before I am ready? We must be strategic about it. I want them all in one place. I want as many witnesses as possible when I reveal my new weapon. None of our guests will know that the hail is an attack. They shall believe it to be but a storm with unfortunate timing."

"Your Majesty, there are rumors of the sea and the blood already. I do think some will believe it to be an attack—"

"They can speculate, then. I do not need your input."

"Yes, sire," Ravenna said as he cut her off.

Footsteps sounded just outside the throne room, and then the doors opened slowly. In the shadows of the hall, Ravenna could make out two vaguely familiar silhouettes between the two Despiri guards.

"Bring them in," Degare said, and Ravenna looked to him as he spoke. His eyes were watching her, as if waiting for some sort of reaction. She turned back to Gerrin and Willa Ozanne, who were now walking on their own and appeared as if they had been given a break from near constant torture. "I thought it would be good to let them heal for a bit—to let them taste health before I have them publicly executed at the trades," Degare said, walking down the dais steps toward Willa. Ravenna looked to him and then back to Gerrin and Willa, who stood motionless with welling tears and creasing brows. She watched as Degare's hand found Willa's chin.

Gerrin spat at the ground Degare walked on, fighting to break free of the Despiri guards, and Ravenna let her vision trail back to Degare. "I think that is a wonderful idea. Let them appear as the royals they once were. Show the world your power over even them." Degare raised a brow, pleased with her. "You defeated them as royals, you have broken them down, and you have taken their kingdom–"

"And their daughter," he said pridefully, looking between Gerrin and Willa. Willa broke into tears, and Degare frowned at her. "Darling Willa, you chose this path long ago."

Ravenna studied the two of them and then straightened her back. "Let me perform the execution." Both of Degare's eyebrows raised then, as if he were surprised. Willa cried out for a daughter that no longer existed, and Ravenna turned her face from them as she awaited Degare's approval.

"I believe you are ready," he said proudly to Ravenna. He caressed Willa's cheek one last time before he turned back to his Raven. "I have big plans for you. Let's prepare you for the ball."

# CHAPTER 35
# FOR THE TWINS

### SABRINE

All she could feel was the ache in her body as she was torn through time. It was night, and a thousand stars tumbled by her, and someone held her hand. The prince. They had been swirling through darkness for hours, maybe days, and the only thing keeping Sabrine awake was the thought of the twins—whom she was going to save.

The prince said nothing and neither did she. Her mouth would not open against the force that sent them to Oro. Sabrine hoped they would make it in time. *Is it supposed to be this way? Is my body supposed to feel numb, yet achy all over?* It was as if she was falling through space, and the air around her was icy, but her body's temperature was that of a flame. She could not find a full breath of air.

Still, Merrick's hand held tightly to hers, as if they had been bound together. When the strange whisper of a hundred voices broke through the night, Sabrine fought to turn her head toward the prince. Their descent began to slow, and the tension in her jaw released.

"I think that means we are getting close," the prince said into the darkness. "Brace yourself."

"How?" she yelled, right as her sight was overcome by a haze of fog and ravens. The birds flocked overhead, croaking as they flew, and the prince and Sabrine lay flat on their backs in a pile of rubble.

"What the–" Merrick said, sitting up beside her. They pried their aching hands apart and took in the scene around them. In the distance was a massive, black stone castle, carved into the cliff's edge, overlooking a sea of red water. It was as if the two of them had been dropped into a nightmare. Many boats were docking, and crowds of finely dressed men and women wandered the streets. The two of them sat in the remains of what Sabrine assumed was once the coliseum, and she looked to the side at Merrick, who was studying the sea closely. His brown eyes squinted against the blue hour, and then Sabrine heard the screams too.

Her eyes scanned her unfamiliar surroundings until they landed on the wall of walnut-sized hail that was sweeping straight over the kingdom. Merrick pulled her backward, and they slipped under a jagged piece of stone in the pile of debris.

"What happened here?" he asked quietly, peeking out from beneath the rocks as the visitors all sought shelter against the falling ice.

"Perhaps the Dark Kings of Arresia are finally getting what they deserve," Sabrine muttered. But then she remembered the twins, and that they were here somewhere in this kingdom, beneath these same hailing skies. She jumped to her feet, and Merrick caught her arm, dragging her back toward him.

"What are you doing?" he yelled over the sound of the plummeting ice stones, right as one scraped down her arm. He pulled her down under the slab of stone again, examining the fresh blood that was beginning to bubble there. She pulled away from him.

"The twins—"

"The King is not going to allow his stock to be damaged. I am sure they are fine—"

"Your father's boat is at the docks right now," she screamed, shoving him off her. Merrick bit his tongue and crept out toward the open air to peek toward the docks, where a flag with the Serpent of Edmaria was flying high over the ship that carried Embers.

"The storm is moving this way. By the time we make it to the docks, it will have passed. We need to wait it out," Merrick said. Sabrine huffed at his level-headed answer and huddled beneath the stone with him. They were crunched together, knees to their chests, shielding themselves as the hail smacked the stones around them and rolled toward their feet. Sabrine picked one up. It took up the entire space of her palm.

Merrick breathed tightly.

"What is it?" Sabrine asked.

Merrick shook his head. "None of this makes sense. The coliseum has been destroyed," he gestured around them. "The sea is blood. The hail is strange and. . .red," he noted, squinting his eyes into the storm. Sabrine had never seen anything like it. "I think Oro is under attack."

"By who?" Sabrine asked.

Merrick fidgeted with the handkerchief he always kept in his pocket, tracing his fingers over the embroidered serpent. "That is what I would like to find out."

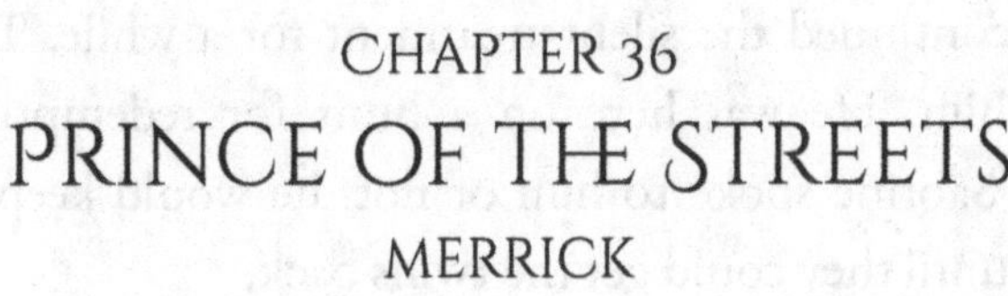

When the red hail had finally stopped pattering against the stone they sheltered under, Merrick dared to steal a glance at Sabrine. In her unhappiness of their current situation, her jaw was set, and she refused to look at him. The scrape on her forearm had stopped bleeding, and both arms were crossed over her stomach, wrapped tightly around the wet fabric of her tunic.

"You've got to be starving," he said, trying not to stare at the hollowness of her cheeks and the shakiness of her hands. *And cold*, he noted. "Let's go find something to eat," he suggested, offering her a hand up. She did not take it as she rose to her feet in silence. Merrick's stomach cramped in pain. He felt as though he had not eaten in days, and his body felt physically weak. He did his best to stand firmly without shaking.

Sabrine brushed some mud from her trousers and then pulled her damp hair from her neck. She looked pale in comparison to when they had left the country home, and

Merrick guessed he, too, was looking quite ill. The two of them had really gotten off on the wrong foot, and the fact that this was the outcome of Merrick suggesting they use a Despiri to transport them here. . .well, he guessed he understood if Sabrine continued the silent treatment for a while. That was fine by him. He was here on a hunt for redemption, and whether Sabrine spoke to him or not, he would keep her fed and safe until they could get the twins back.

He led the way toward the square, where vendors were salvaging what was left of their goods after the bloody hailstorm. As the ice pellets melted, streams of blood collected in the crevices of the cobblestone streets, and he watched Sabrine tiptoe across them in disgust. He could not help the look of puzzlement that stayed stricken on his face as they wandered the streets, seeing by only the light of the occasional torch placed on the stone walls and buildings. In the eerie shadows between torches, Merrick stayed within a hand's length of Sabrine in fear some strange creature would come out to grab her. This kingdom had only grown darker since his last visit, and he did not intend to stay long enough to find out just how deep that darkness ran.

"On the left," Merrick said, pointing. "Tavern. They'll have a fire and hearty food."

Sabrine said nothing, but he saw a slight gleam in her eye at the mere thought of something to eat that wasn't the soggy deer jerky he knew she kept hidden in her sack. Her tired footsteps splashed through the red puddles, and he wondered if she was thankful now for the boots he had bought her.

When they came to the tavern door, he opened it, peering inside before motioning her into the rowdy room of people. The smell of smoke and rum wafted out the door, and Sabrine straightened her shoulders as she walked over the threshold ahead of him, but he could tell she wanted to shrink back into the shadows as the warm glow of the tavern welcomed her in. Merrick wished he could do the same.

"We won't stay long," he said, leaning down toward the back of her head to speak over the sound of the clinking drinks, raging fire, and the celebratory chants. She rolled her shoulder, seemingly trying to put more space between them, and he obliged, backing off a couple of steps. "There's an empty table over there," he said, pointing. "By the fireplace."

Sabrine gave him a curt nod and started making her way through the congested area beside a makeshift arena where people placed bets for fights. Surprisingly, to Merrick, Sabrine shoved her way past not one but two drunken men who were taking up the walkway. He smiled to himself, and then when he saw one staring after her a little too long, he forcefully shouldered his way past, too.

"I'll be right with you," a sweaty woman called as she balanced a tray full of bowls of soup and two rums in the other hand. "With three days til' the trades, we're swamped. Never sold this much rum in all my days."

"Well, what else is there to drink?" an inebriated man hollered as she handed him one of the rums. "There sure ain't any clean water!" He laughed obnoxiously as he took a messy gulp.

Merrick lowered his brows then searched the room for any sign of clear, drinkable water. *Has all of the water been turned to blood? Who in all of Arresia would dare to attack Oro in such a fashion? Who had the capability? The power?*

Merrick's head shot across the table to Sabrine at the first sound of her voice in hours. "Did she just say the trade is in three days?" she asked slowly. Merrick rubbed his pounding head. If the trade was in three days, that meant the teleportation had taken them nearly four. "That's the last time I'll listen to your suggestions on this trip," she muttered.

"You'd likely still be trekking through the Valley of the Shadow if you'd gone the way you planned," he said.

"At least I would not feel like I'd died and come back to life."

"Is it really that bad?" he asked, knowing very well how miserable she felt, because he felt the same. He wondered how Kenan was holding up. "Dinner and a good night's rest will help. We haven't eaten in four days. And we haven't really slept, either." That space between had not felt like four days, and he couldn't remember all of it. It was like his mind was in a space in between, along with his body. Perhaps they had drifted into sleep, but he couldn't be sure.

"I know what it feels like to be hungry," she reminded him, looking up and down the dirty, yet princely attire that peeked out beneath his cloak.

He did not say anything to that, and instead, directed his attention to the woman with the rum. She sat two glasses down on the table with little care, sending some of the brown liquid sloshing onto the table. Sabrine shifted back in her seat slightly to avoid the spill, and the barmaid looked at Merrick.

"Royalty?" she asked, noting his clothing. Merrick pulled his cloak shut, and Sabrine rolled her eyes. "No ma'am," he lied. He and Sabrine would have to come up with a story. He could be a man of some other title. They would already have to be careful where they were seen, and he did not want to risk his father hearing of his whereabouts. He knew his father would never come back to this tavern, that is why he had picked it.

"I see," the woman said with a fleeting look of suspicion, hands on her hips. "What can I get you two? We've got potato soup and mutton stew. No fish." Merrick tilted his chin in curiosity. This tavern was known for their fish. "Not a live one left near the shore," she said. "Have you not seen the sea? Turned to blood a month ago. We've only had a handful of clean rains since. We've been rationing water as best we can." The woman kept rambling, and Merrick exchanged a quick glance with Sabrine. She was also taking in every bit of information she could. How had they not heard of this in Edmaria? Surely the word would have traveled by now. "Our fishermen are braving the deeper seas to bring back fish. I heard some of Oro's people are leaving. Fleeing south where there is water. Degare won't let them skimp on their taxes though. But you know what's funny about this whole ordeal?" the barmaid asked. Merrick gave her a slight shake of his head. She lowered her voice to a soft hush, "I hear the Ember prisons have clean water in their wells, and when the soldiers tried to collect it for themselves, it turned red on their tongues."

Merrick swallowed, and Sabrine appeared stunned or lost in thought. The barmaid shrugged. "The king is keeping something from us. He's been awfully quiet to preserve the integrity of the trades–to maintain his guise of power–but everyone knows this is an attack." Merrick nodded, taking a sip of rich rum.

Sabrine turned her nose up at him and spoke to the barmaid. "Who do you think could do such a thing? How is this possible?" Merrick coughed as the rum tickled his throat.

The barmaid shrugged at Sabrine. "Some angry Despiri who has plans to overthrow Oro is my best guess. I wouldn't be too worried, though. I hear the king has quite the new weapon up his sleeve." Merrick narrowed his eyes at the woman. This was the first he was hearing of such a weapon, but by Sabrine's lack of surprise, he guessed she had already heard rumors. Perhaps in the markets where she prowled for coins. Merrick could not imagine a single Despiri could have done such atrocities to the Kingdom of Oro, and he certainly could not imagine what new weapon Degare had that would cause one not to worry about it all. Perhaps this was an entire army, banding together to fall Oro. He could not imagine that, either. Degare still commanded a majority of the Despiri in Arresia, as he had made certain to build his own army first. One that was untouchable at that. "Well, what'll it be?" the barmaid asked, almost impatiently, snapping Merrick out of his thoughts, as if she had not been the one to stir this conversation.

He blinked. "Mutton soup for me," he said, before glancing at Sabrine.

"Potato soup," she said, in a snide way that had Merrick guessing she chose the opposite of him to make some sort of statement that they were not the same. His mouth fell flat as he looked at her, and she raised her brows as if to challenge him.

Merrick sighed. "That'll be it," he said. The barmaid grunted and hurried off to the kitchen, leaving two extra glasses of rum behind. Sabrine wrinkled her nose at it.

"You don't drink?" he asked. She didn't look at him.

"Can't afford to have a clouded mind," she said. He nodded in understanding, realizing that because of the twins, her brain must always be alert and watching for any danger, as cautious as a mother wolf. He wanted to ask her what her life had been like before the trades, and at what moment she had found herself as the sole provider and protector of those two little ones. He wanted to know what she was thinking, to know what horrible thoughts her mind circled at this very moment. But Merrick did not ask, because there was nothing he could say to soothe her.

Sabrine was right. The only way in which he could redeem himself was to save the twins from the talons of death. "We'll find you some water," he said, sliding the untouched rum to the side of the table to be collected. He needed a clear head, too, if he was to find the redemption he sought. The broth in the soup would help quench their thirst, but they'd need water by morning. They had already gone a few days without it, and though their bodies had been in some strange state of existence and *not*, his mouth was beginning to feel like cotton. *How could I have been so foolish as to not even pack a canteen?* Merrick breathed tightly, frustrated with his mistake.

A different barmaid came out to deliver their soups and bread. Both Merrick and Sabrine sat a little straighter as the bowls were set before them, and they nodded their thanks to the haggard woman before she continued to the other tables. "She looks how I feel," Sabrine muttered, noting the woman's unkempt hair as she slowly drifted from customer to customer, shoulders slouched in exhaustion.

Merrick nodded, stirring his soup with the pewter spoon, waiting for her to take a bite. After a few seconds of some kind of inner turmoil, she brought a spoonful to her mouth. "They keep the stock well fed," he offered. Degare wanted the Embers to appear desirable in the trades, and Merrick's own father would want to sell his own stock for as much as he could. Feeding them well on their journey to Oro to make them appear stronger seemed a good idea. "You should not feel guilty for eating."

Sabrine looked to the side, trying to ignore him. If the twins had been selected for this stock, their cheeks would be a little less hollow by the next time she saw them. "And it sounds like they aren't hard pressed for water either. They'll be okay until we can get to them," he whispered. She continued ignoring him, but he saw her eyes soften a bit as she realized the blessing in disguise. At least they would not starve.

Sabrine would not allow him to carry her sack, but she did allow him to stand close enough that their arms grazed as they trekked through the slums of Oro toward the least desirable inns. He knew his father had booked his stay months ago at a carefully selected bed and breakfast located conveniently between the kingdom square and the docks, where his boat currently swayed atop the water, situated between two of his larger ships which had carried Embers into Oro. Were the twins still on board, or had they been transferred to the prisons?

They passed yet another inn with a sign that read, *NO ROOMS AVAILABLE.* Merrick began growing uneasy as they continued on through the slums, the buildings growing more and more decrepit. He knew there would be no available space in the nicer inns where people like his father stayed. Even if those inns had available rooms, it would not be a smart choice for him. There were too many who might recognize him.

Merrick kept the hood on his cloak pulled over his head, and Sabrine walked in step beside him. He could feel her watching him, and before he could say a word, she began in that snarky tone of hers. "You're getting nervous that we're going to have to sleep in the streets," she said. "I can see how that would trouble someone like you."

Merrick did not say anything, only continued forward with his jaw set, marching toward the last inn on the street and hoping for a miracle. Ravens flocked overhead, headed toward the west beach he knew they gathered at. Outside of the homes in the slums, people lounged in darkness, sitting on buckets and rattling off tunes, cheering loudly for the trades that were to bring more power to the darkness. He did not understand it, the way the poor celebrated the wealthy pocketing so much power while they remained in squalor.

"They cheer because they hate the Light," Sabrine said, as if she had seen his curiosity. It was the first sentence she had offered him that came with little snark.

"What do you think of it?" he asked quietly, so no straggling passerby could hear. "Of the Light?"

Sabrine shook her head. "All I know of the Light is that my anger is kindled against it."

Merrick nodded and reached for the door handle of the inn. "What about you?" she asked, before he could open the door. He paused for a moment, letting his mind drift to places he never wanted to go–but only for a moment.

"I don't think of it at all," he lied and opened the door to the inn. It was late, and Merrick half expected to be able to sleep in the narrow entryway with no issues–he would prefer that over the streets–but then came the innkeeper from the back room. He must have heard the bell when they entered.

"If you're looking for a room, you should have booked two months ago," he muttered, rubbing his tired eyes.

Merrick stepped forward. "Nothing? Not even one spare

bed?" Sabrine crossed her arms beside him as he turned into a beggar at the thought of sleeping outside.

The innkeeper shook his head. "Nothing to spare. You won't find anything in the whole kingdom. Your best bet is asking the rowdy bunch down the street if they have an extra cot. They've been taking in stragglers for the right price."

Merrick swallowed and grabbed for a silver serpent. He flashed it at the innkeeper and began to speak again. "I–"

The man waved his hand, and Merrick began to reach for a gold coin. "Out ya go!" he said, shooing them out the door. "The only bed I have to offer is my own, and you couldn't pay me enough to wake my wife," he muttered.

Merrick and Sabrine found themselves back on the streets of Oro, listening to the ruckus down the street. Sabrine looked at him with a raised brow. "I am not staying with those people just so we can have a cot to sleep on," she said.

"Well, Duchess. How about you lead the way to our humble abode, since you know street living so well?"

She scoffed. "Gladly."

Merrick found himself following her into an empty alley. They had two exits and just enough shadow to hide in. He watched as she sank against the cobblestone, remaining upright with her cloak pulled over her head. She clutched her sack between her knees and chest.

"I'll take the first watch," she said, holding back a shiver against the cold air.

"Watch?" he asked, itching to remove his wet sleeves.

"Well, we're not both sleeping with this much coin in our sacks."

Merrick nodded, smoothing the front of his trousers before he sat down beside her. "You sleep, I'll keep watch," he said.

"I do not trust you," she said, peering down the alley where two drunken men stumbled past.

*Still, she does not trust me?* He did not have it in him to argue. He was exhausted, and he was sure she was too. So, before he closed his eyes, he mumbled, "You have to sleep sometime. Let me know when you decide to trust me."

# CHAPTER 37
## MASTER OF NONE
### RAVENNA

Ravenna had secured Oro's position as the strongest kingdom in all of Arresia, and for that, she would be flaunted as Degare's new weapon. Rumors had already traveled across the seven kingdoms about what the King of Oro's new weapon may be, and the men and women of Arresia were growing curious. Indeed, she would have a large audience to impress with her power—power that she still lacked control of. Degare could instruct and command her all he wished, but her power did not obey him as she did. She had to learn to master it and the mind it had of its own—in less than three days. Ravenna did not think her king realized the control she still lacked. Her training at the coliseum had taught her destruction, not strategy. The things he was asking of her. . .if she were to attempt them right now, many of his guests would die.

"Again," Degare said, growing frustrated. Ravenna burrowed down into that place in her chest where the power seemed to stem from. She searched through every thread, through every gift that had been stolen, and was now housed in that crowded portion of her soul, and carefully strummed just one thin cord. "Well, is it working or not?" the king called to Jara.

Jara watched the red tides over the balcony. "If anything, the waters are receding, not rising."

"Ravenna, pull the tides in," Degare ordered, tapping his staff against the stone ground of the throne room twice in anger. She tried again.

"Nothing," Jara muttered, descending the steps from the upper balcony. At least Degare had not requested she turn the bloody waters back to black.

"You advised me to wait to train her. And now that I have, we are running out of time," Degare spat at his witch.

Jara only rolled her eyes. "She was not ready then, and she is hardly ready now. Honestly, you cannot really blame her for having no control. You lost control all the time when the power was yours."

Degare let his head relax against the back of his throne as he took a deep breath. "The power is still mine," he said with forced composure.

"If she is to be your weapon, you'll need to teach her strategy," Jara explained. "Think of how much more impressive she will be if she is able to not only house all of this power but master it." Degare nodded his head.

"Well, you have just over two days to figure out a way to make that happen," he said to Jara.

"Me? She needs Despiri who are familiar with her gifts. I am a witch—I know little. . ."

Ravenna shifted on her feet while the two of them argued,

and Degare turned to her. "And what is your opinion, Ravenna?"

Ravenna dipped her chin. "Your Majesty, I believe the vision you have for me is obtainable with much training, but is there anyone who can shift the tides?"

Degare chuckled. "There is at least one, and it happened in the Dawn Islands. An Ember used their gifts to kill the Prince of Edmaria." Ravenna swallowed as Degare continued, "You must be proven more powerful, or some might get the idea that there are those who can stand against us. After the hail, I have carefully planned and polished your performance to prove Oro is untouchable. Not one will dare rise against us. The blood and the hail–it is nothing compared to what you can do."

"I do not foresee myself mastering such power in two days," Ravenna said.

"What I am asking of you only requires you to be able to control four of your gifts–"

"Degare," Jara cut the king off, and his head whipped to her in anger. Ravenna's jaw clenched. "It takes new Despiri months of training in our coliseum to master one gift. You think she can master four in two days?"

"I command it," he said, looking at Ravenna.

"I do not believe the sire works in that way Degare. . ."

His face turned to Jara again. "Then what is it good for? Why have you boasted of giving me such a gift if it is not good for anything?"

Jara was silent, and Ravenna watched the witch fidget with a black pewter thumb ring.

"We are only wasting time," Degare said. "I am going to lunch. Do not sleep until you have mastered at least one, Ravenna."

"You're asking too much," Jara argued. "You are endangering your kingdom and the reputation I have worked so hard to give you."

Degare chuckled. "Well, then, make sure my Raven does not ruin it."

The witch found Ravenna some Despiri instructors who were each well versed in one of the four gifts Degare wished for her to perform with. None of those Despiri held a quarter of the power Ravenna did with each gift though, and even after training for sixteen hours straight in the small, outdated, training dome on the far side of the kingdom, she had only mastered one performance.

Fire was the easiest, because she had trained with and used that gift the most. It happened to be Degare's favorite of her powers. *Mastered* was a tricky word. Ravenna had mastered fire in the sense that she could do exactly what Degare was asking of her—but no more. There was still much to learn. But she was exhausted, and she longed for sleep. So, when her Despiri instructor told her she had mastered fire, she chose to believe him.

As she made her way out of the dome, longing for her bed, she remembered that she was to see the king after her lessons. Her head rolled back on her shoulders, and instead of finding her chambers, she dragged her feet toward Degare. He was in the dining hall, alone at the table, with a large platter of food sitting at the empty seat across from him.

"Jara told me you mastered fire. Tomorrow you will succeed in nailing the performances of water, air, earth, and. . ."

"And?" Ravenna cut him off, and immediately apologized. "I am sorry, Your Majesty. It is just, I thought there were only four skills to practice, and today was strenuous–"

"Do not worry, Ravenna. Lightning will be quite easy."

"Lightning?"

"Just channel your rage. You still have rage, do you not?"

Ravenna thought for a moment, trying to find that rage and where it would stem from.

He laughed. "It must have gone when you surrendered to me. I really was the cause of it all along. Nonetheless, do not worry, you'll find a way to split the skies."

Ravenna pondered on what he had said: that she had used to hold a rage about him within her. Where had it gone, and why had it left? Her fingers absentmindedly ran across the braids that hung over her shoulder, and it felt as though she were almost grasping something–almost remembering something important. She was sure she could summon rage somehow, but there was none where her king was involved.

"I am sure you are starving," Degare said, pushing the platter toward her in a thoughtful manner. *I am starving.*

"Thank you, Your Majesty," she said as she began eating. The day had drained her, and her power required she eat often and in much quantity.

"I have a few requirements for the ball and some information I must go over with you."

Ravenna wiped her mouth. "Of course," she said beneath her napkin.

"The seven kingdoms of Arresia are each in turmoil in one way or another. You know this, I am sure. It is your job to entice men and women of power from each kingdom to purchase from me. We want them to spend their money in

Oro, and we want them to have a false sense of power here. They will not be able to get enough power once they see how much you hold. All the kingdoms in Arresia are already trying to climb to the top, but we are to establish our position at the ball—with your display of power. This will fuel their desire to purchase kills in the trades so that they may become like you. Rest assured, that will never be possible. Their greed for power will fill my pockets, making Oro not only powerful but wealthy."

Ravenna nodded. She was to perform, to plant fear in the hearts of her audience, and to become the greatest threat Arresia had ever known.

"Volcania will have representatives here, but not the king himself. The man who sits on their throne is not the true heir, and their kingdom has split over it. Uprisings and civil wars have begun amongst their own. They are weak, and it will be easy to inspire them to purchase kills. They want more power." Ravenna took mental note of all he was telling her. "Edmaria's king grieves for the loss of his eldest, and I presume he will be quite easy to manipulate as well. The Dawn Islands mourn the loss of Sebastian, their king. The young princess has taken the throne, and because of that transfer of power, they are in a time of instability. Though the island royals will not be here, plenty of noblemen and women from their lands have docked in the last few days. Do what you can to send them back to their young queen with nothing but positive things to say about Oro. An alliance with the small islands would not gain Oro much, but it would keep them from joining with Edmaria, which they are rumored to do in the coming months. We must stop that alliance, or the other kingdoms may think they can all ally in a war against Oro."

Ravenna nodded slowly. Degare had truly thought of everything–of every possible problem.

"Brinland," he continued, "they are quiet, and they keep to themselves. But do not let that fool you. King Naveen is an intelligent man, and I fear his silence may mean he is up to something. Watch his men and women carefully. I do know that he recently honored the union of one of Brinland's duchesses with King Idris of Edmaria."

"And what of the other kingdoms?" Ravenna asked. "What should we expect of them?"

"Eswen and Remont–those kingdoms will be mine someday soon. I will send you to kill their rulers, you will bring their crowns to me, and I will rule over their people. Their land will no longer serve the Light but will serve *me*. Their kingdoms grow more fragile by the day as my men march on them. When you can wield all of your power, nothing will hold us back."

"I could destroy them now. I destroyed Vestele," Ravenna offered.

"Jara is right, Ravenna. Do not be so eager. This we must meet with a strategy. Even when you have mastered your power, we will wait for the right time to attack. There is always a time of weakness–that is when you strike, my Raven."

Ravenna hummed in agreement with her king.

"At the ball, I want you to dance with as many noblemen, dukes, kings, and princes as you can. Invite them to dine with us. Inspire them, Ravenna. Use your beauty to get what I want. Empty their pockets for me."

"Of course, Your Majesty." She finished the last bite of food on her plate.

"Watch for anything unusual. Collect as much information as you can. Find weaknesses. Be strategic."

Ravenna smirked. Not only was she a weapon of mass destruction, but she was also to be a spy, a messenger, and a threat to all who would dare oppose her king. Through her, Degare was untouchable.

"One last thing, my Raven. There will be those who try to test you. Let no one transcend your power."

# DUKE AND DUCHESS

### SABRINE

"**Y**ou need to hurry, we are going to be late, Prince," Sabrine muttered as she watched him reluctantly scoop some water from a puddle into his hands, examining it carefully before he used it to slick back his hair. The night had brought them a clean rain, but the sea was still unclean, and the now-clear fountains on the east side of the kingdom were too crowded. He scrubbed the soot from his face, which had gotten there from their nights spent in the slums and crouched in the shadows hoping none of the many homeless would grow curious of their heavy bag and the riches within it. All the inns were full, and there was no room for even the Prince of Edmaria, although Merrick had not given them his true title. Tonight, they were to be a Duke and Duchess of Matuk, Brinland, where Sabrine had once lived in a small village with her family.

"My apologies. It is quite difficult to prepare for a royal ball in the streets," he muttered.

"Not hardly," she said, smoothing the fabric of her purple

gown. They were tucked away in an alley near the entrance to the ballroom, where a crowd of people were gathering. "Yes, well when you look like that," Merrick said as he took his wrinkled, cream-colored suit out of the bag and held it above the dirty cobblestone.

"Like what?" Sabrine asked.

"Could you turn away for a moment?" Merrick asked as he unbuttoned his tunic. Sabrine raised a brow.

"I'll be right over there," she gestured toward the vendors in the square, and took toward them.

"Don't go too far," he called after her.

She waved a hand in the air as her eyes fixed on the crowd by the ballroom entrance. Men and women from around the world engaged in conversation about Degare's new weapon and the trades, and then Sabrine noticed they were all wearing masks. She cursed under her breath. She and the prince had forgotten their masks. She looked back toward the alley where Merrick was concealed, then spun around and disappeared into the mass of people.

Sabrine stepped over gowns and puddles. "I only made the trip this time because of the executions," a woman was saying. "I always wanted to see the Ozannes dead. Degare will be doing Arresia a great justice. The Light they reigned with has no hold over us. We should be able to live freely and do as we wish."

Another woman answered her. "Exactly. They cannot dictate what others do any longer." *Is that how she justified murder?* "Their people will learn that the Light within them is weak against the world and the goddesses that reign here."

Sabrine took a deep breath and wove through the crowd, ducking her head as she went. Her eyes fixed on a man who stood alone at the edge of the crowd in a feathered mask. His neck displayed the hint of a shadowmark that protruded from beneath his collar, and his eyes narrowed as he saw her coming.

"Good evening," she said in the most charming voice she could muster. His gaze did not rove down her body as she expected, but instead, he tilted his head and kept eye contact. His hair was a shade lighter than hers but still dark, and his eyes were like the mossy soil near her cabin.

"Good evening," he said. His voice was almost familiar, and she looked back to make sure Merrick had not come after her yet. "I'm Locke." He extended a hand to her, but she did not take it.

"Have you seen the stock yet?" she asked.

"Many times," he said, pocketing his hand. She stood a little straighter. "And what of the new stock that just came in from Edmaria?" she asked. "Anything good?" She swallowed her disgust.

He clicked his tongue once and shook his head. "I have not seen any from that shipment. Did you have one especially ordered?"

She pondered for a moment. "I have my eyes on two," she said, blinking at him.

"Ah," he said, looking over her shoulder to the massive doors, which were now opening.

"Well, Locke, it was nice speaking with you," she said quickly. "Any tips on where I can find a mask? I seem to have forgotten mine back home."

"There is a vendor over there," Locke said, pointing toward the square. "She is raising money for her first kill. Perhaps you can be of service," he said, raising his brows knowingly before he turned toward the castle. Sabrine clenched her jaw and watched him go before turning toward the mask merchant.

Luckily, there were still enough people gathered around her table that she was unaware when Sabrine slipped two masks into her bag. The feathers on hers were iridescent and colored in deep tones with a circular design at the tips.

"Stealing again?" Merrick muttered into her ear from behind as she hurried toward the castle. She rolled her eyes and crammed the cream and gold colored mask into his chest. He stumbled backward, grasping for the mask before it fell.

"Fancy," he said, examining it.

"I thought it would match your suit," she said, surveying his outfit. He had cleaned up nicely, despite the circumstances. His suit was accented with gold and purple to compliment her gown and to portray that they were here as a couple, since the wealthy often color coordinated with their partners.

She struggled to tie the mask around her head, and when he noticed, he stepped around behind her to assist. She moved out of his reach, and he raised his hands in surrender, placing them into his pockets as she secured the mask herself.

Her black hair was divided into bubbled sections that trailed down to the middle of her back, and her deep purple gown fell to the cobblestone. The sleeves draped lightly over her shoulders, accentuating the gold necklace at her chest.

"Remember, we are a Duke and Duchess of Brinland," Merrick said, going over the plan one final time. "Newly instituted by King Naveen. Duchess Jamila of Matuk recently gave up her title for the possibility of becoming Queen of Edmaria-though she cannot claim that title without my father's approval. Naveen has not yet appointed a new Duke of Matuk, so no one would have heard of us yet, and I doubt Naveen will be here tonight." Sabrine nodded tightly as they entered through the doors past two of the Despiri guards of

Oro. She reluctantly took his arm as they were funneled into the ballroom, and he tensed beneath her touch. "We are here to gather any information we can about the stock. Where they are keeping them, how they are shackled–"

"I've got it," she said, cutting him off as she surveyed the room, taking in the many shadowmarks that were proudly on display.

"I am just trying to help," Merrick muttered.

"You got us here in time," she said under her breath. "For that, I am thankful. I am just struggling to see how your miserable presence is benefiting me any further." Merrick's cheeks reddened beneath the edges of his mask, and he kept looking forward.

"I am here to see that my mistake is reversed."

"You are indebted to me," she said beneath her breath. "That debt will be considered paid when the twins and I set foot in Eswen. Perhaps that is what you should be figuring out tonight, since your Despiri friend, Kenan, will not be doing the honors. Though, I am sure he is aware of their existence now, anyway, I will not let the twins anywhere near him. I would not trust him not to send us straight into the Ember prisons instead."

Merrick rolled his eyes. "We have gone over this. I am sorry I blindsided you, but it truly was the only way to get us into Oro on time."

Sabrine bit her cheek. Her body was still sore from the strange power that had flung them through time and space. Merrick shifted beside her as the ballroom spanned out before them.

The room was filled with conversation and dancing, and an almost eerie melody being played from the harp beside the towering stained-glass windows on the west wall, where a massive cage had been placed. Sabrine's heart dropped into her stomach, and then her feet were moving, dragging Merrick along with her.

"Strategy, Sabrine," he said lowly, reminding her to think before she moved. *How would a duchess act who was here to purchase a kill?* She looked to him and took a deep, unsteady breath before striding toward the chained Embers who had been put on display.

"This is not the whole stock," a soldier from Oro said. "We have many more where these came from. Have a peek at what tomorrow has to offer."

Sabrine's grip tightened on Merrick's arm, and his thumb lightly caressed her fingers until she softened her hold. "Let me do the talking," he mumbled as they approached the soldier.

"Have any Embers that have the gift of healing?" Merrick called out.

"We do," the soldier said. "We see that gift a lot. We've got three here on display." Sabrine's eyes scanned the cage quickly, darting from face to face, but the twins were not here. "Tomorrow we'll have a total of. . ." he looked at his inventory sheet, "twenty-two." Merrick nodded and thanked him before pulling Sabrine to the side.

"You are fuming," he said.

"I cannot do this," she seethed, looking into the cage of chained Embers. Her innocent siblings were here in this kingdom somewhere, scared and helpless. They believed they were going to die, and she was afraid they would. How was she going to get to them in time? Her hands found the back of her sweaty neck as the room started spinning. "I can't do it Merrick. I can't–"

"Dance with me," he said. She blinked and looked up at him.

"What?" Her hands remained on the back of her neck until he gently worked to unlace her fingers. His touch was soft as he guided her hands over his shoulders.

"We must blend in," he said. "Make friends, soak up all the information we can. We will find them," he promised her. Sabrine looked into the crowd of people, who were joyous in anticipation for the horrors the next few nights would bring.

She did not want to make friends with these people, but she reluctantly agreed as he swept her into the wretched crowd for a dance.

# CHAPTER 39
# DANCE OF DARKNESS
## RAVENNA

"Do not disappoint me tonight," Degare muttered when he came to her door. She would not dream of it. She was his to command. He was satisfied with the shadowmarks that were on display across her back and down her arms. His face was uncovered, whereas a black feathered mask sat tightly against Ravenna's eyes, concealing her identity.

The intricacy of her gown had surprised her. The seamstress was able to work quickly and still make it look so detailed and luxurious, as if it could have taken months to complete. Though Ravenna would expect nothing but the best from her king's workers.

She gave him a soft smile, smoothing the front of her red gown and dipping her head. The tether between them sang to her as he took her hand and placed it around his arm.

He continued down the winding, dark halls with her at his side. The King of Oro was escorting her to his royal ball. The short train of her gown dragged behind her as she looked forward and held her chin high just as she had practiced. Oro's royal guard did not surround them as they normally would. When the king had Ravenna by his side, he knew he was untouchable. They passed a dozen lanterns on the wall. Some of them had gone out, no longer producing light and leaving thick stretches of shadow among the halls.

As they neared the ballroom, she felt the king stiffen beside her and come to a halt. She waited for his command, but all he said was, "Dance." The few dance lessons she had been given were to come in handy tonight, as she expected. She had learned the waltz down to every step and motion, and a part of it brought her back to a time when she had trained with the warriors of her old home. She had been weak then and easy to strike.

Ravenna could hear the music behind the doors. It was like nothing she had ever heard in Oro before–a surprisingly beautiful tune created by the keys of an organ. She had not noticed before how the musicians of Oro played so flawlessly. It was the type of music that spoke to her soul, the deep tone of irregularly woven notes among shadows. The rhythmic elements were unpredictable and the sound low and soothing. When the music came to a pause and she heard her king being announced, she prepared for the doors to open, but they did not. Degare looked at her, and with that look she understood.

She focused, sending her power moving and weaving through the doors, and when they opened, a masked crowd full of apprehensive eyes looked to her, as if they all understood exactly what she was. She was Degare's weapon, the one they had all been waiting to see, and now that they saw her, they all awaited her next move. It infuriated her, the way they all stared, *not bowing* before her king. Unwillfully and out of anger, she sent a bout of power through the ballroom, sending them all to their knees before The King of Oro. Even King Idris of Edmaria fell victim to her trick. She breathed tightly at the involuntary release of power, thankful it had not caused unwanted destruction.

The Edmarian king smiled a wicked grin across the room from where he kneeled, seemingly intrigued, as the rest of the room cowered on their knees in fear. *All but one.* Ravenna caught sight of a strange Despiri man standing in the dark corner of the ballroom, seemingly immune to her blow. Degare was unaware and broke into laughter beside her, raising his hands to the air. "Let the true party begin!" With that, light, nervous laughter crept across the walls of the expansive ballroom, and Ravenna entered a dance with the king. When she looked back to the corner, the man who stood against her power was gone.

"Politics, politics. When they see you are mine to command, Arresia will fall to me. Even *Eswen and Remont.*"

Ravenna smiled at his cruel, wicked mind. "Arresia will be yours," she agreed.

After the king had grown drunk on wine, and Ravenna's hands were shaking with her need for some, she began dancing with the noblemen and royals who had the deepest pockets. She even danced with King Idris of Edmaria, who stole her from another. She laughed as the dark-haired, middle-aged monarch cut in with a twirl and a bright smile. His beard was cut close to his skin and held tiny swirls and designs in it, one being a serpent. Shadowmarks painted one side of his face.

"So *you* are Degare's new weapon?" he questioned, narrowing his eyes on her marks. She hummed, letting him take the lead in the dance.

"And you are the King of Edmaria?" she asked. He smiled. "Degare has insisted I grant you a personal invitation to his celebratory dinner tonight," she said, looking over Idris's shoulder toward her sire, who was watching her with pride.

"How kind of him," Idris said, and as his hand led her into a twirl, she eyed the thin gold wedding band on his ring finger.

"Your new wife is, of course, welcome to join," she added, remembering his recent marriage to a duchess.

"Jamila did not accompany me. This trip is to be a short one, though rather enjoyable, I would say." Ravenna smiled, remaining the perfect picture of an obedient servant to her king. They stepped slowly to the music, using most of the song to banter back and forth, but as she began to anticipate the end of the song, he begged her for another dance. "Show me what you can do as his weapon," he urged her.

"I cannot reveal my talents just yet, Your Majesty," she teased, carefully surveying the room around them, searching for her next partner.

"Well, then, allow me to show you some of mine," he said. He tried to impress her with a dark cloud of power coming up from his hand. "What does it do?" she asked, pretending to be intrigued–though she already knew what it was capable of. She had the same power within her veins, and it seemed to sing at the sight of his. The King of Edmaria, though, had more control over it than she did.

"The Ember I took it from at Degare's first trade had the power of manipulating light," he scoffed. "It's been perfected in me." She twirled a finger through the tiny swirl of darkness in his palm, studying the way it moved and then dissipated. "I could make this entire room go black if I wanted," he boasted.

"You would not dare," she teased again, wondering just how much control such a gift would take. He raised an eyebrow at her as if she were testing him. And then, without another thought, all the light was sucked from the room. Idris released her, and she sent her shadows out looking for him, but they were unstable and returned with nothing. He was gone. The crowd began growing louder in the blackness around her, and she felt the tether within her grow taut in demand as she remembered she was to let no one transcend her power. Immediately, fire spilled from her hands and wove through the air to reignite the chandeliers and candles. The crowd gasped, and the king's reprimanding gaze found hers. She breathed tightly as his eyes flashed in irritation, and she reigned the wildfire back into her body.

For the rest of the evening she kept her guard up and continued dancing, trying to remain with the less powerful of the Despiri, since the king did not want her revealing the extent of her power until the time he had chosen for tonight. She chose noblemen who had not yet taken gifts of their own. New blood was good for the continuation of the market.

As she ended one dance, there was always another man awaiting her company. They were curious about her like Degare had hoped. It was that curiosity that would gain her an audience when she showed her true extent of power and proved Degare as the most powerful king.

"You're very beautiful," her dance partner said into her ear. His hand went a little too low on her bare back, and she smiled, ready to use a trick she had learned when wielding her fire.

"And very powerful," she said, allowing her skin to heat

with the flames festering in her veins. She kept the flames contained, but beneath his touch, her skin was now like lava rock. So hot that she smelled the burning flesh on his hand before he realized.

"What the–" he yanked his wandering hand away from her, and as he examined the singed flesh on his palm, his fear sent him running. Ravenna smiled smugly to herself, swaying with the long, final draw of a bow across strings from one of the musicians. As the song came to an end, she turned to where the music had come from, where one of the wooden instruments had been left on the chair next to the organ amid the light from a hundred candles. The finely crafted piece of curved maple was to rest upon the shoulder of the musician while a bow was pulled across one of the four strings.

She tilted her head and allowed her hands to reach out toward it. When her calloused fingertips wrapped around its neck, they seemed to fall perfectly into place–recalling a tune that felt free and whimsical, with no rules. She blinked past the vision of fire and dancing and cool air on her cheeks. She pushed through the vague memory of a man's smile hovering before her, through a dance with his hand in hers. She flexed her fingers and startled as she felt someone take the instrument from her other hand and set it aside into the chair.

"Your king does not look too happy about your. . .distraction," the man said in a low voice as he turned toward her. She recognized him almost immediately as the man who did not kneel. "I have been waiting for a dance all evening," he said, as if hoping for an invitation. Ravenna peered over his shoulder at Degare, who was now studying their interaction while Gerrin and Willa Ozanne were being chained to the throne near his feet.

"Now that I have finally gotten you alone. . ." the man started, stepping to the side to block her view of the king. She took the precaution of heating every inch of her bare skin. But when he swept her into a dance with no invitation at the start of the music, he was careful not to touch what her dress left uncovered.

His mask was crafted from white feathers, and he stood out in the crowd like a flame in the night. Her eyes fell to the shadowmarks that crept up his neck and were on display beneath the top button of his tunic. He wore a fine black suit, but it was much different than the others in the sea of people around them. When it was time to guide her body to the left, and his hand finally found the burning skin at her shoulder, he did not withdraw as she had expected. Her eyes narrowed, and she fed the fire in her veins once more, allowing some flames to break through. She felt them intertwining with his fingers. Still, he offered no reaction.

She tilted her chin up, following his lead in the dance. He said nothing, but from what she could see of it in the dimly lit room, beneath the mask that covered only his eyes, his face was stoic. He watched around the room as if monitoring for threats, unaware that the biggest one stood right before him. *Had he not even felt my flames?*

She studied the shadowmarks that licked at his jawline. Right now, she was at a disadvantage, and she did not like it. She would not let him see her weakness.

After a moment of only gritted teeth and strange anger rolling off him, she asked, "Have you seen the fine stock of Embers?" She tried to lead him toward where the gifted ones were caged against the west wall for viewing. His jaw set, and he held her a little tighter. She wanted to squirm away. *Do not cause a scene*, she told herself. *To get away from him, you'll have to reveal your power.* So, she remained there in his grasp and let him lead. Just when she was about to break the odd silence, he spoke.

"Why do you play his game?" the man asked, staring directly over her shoulder at the king. If looks could kill, *his* would have killed Degare. At the visible threat, Ravenna should have wanted to end this man, but something about him intrigued her.

"I just do what I am told," she said in response, studying him through narrowed eyes and continuing through three slow twirls.

"Ah, but do you do everything you're told, Little Dove?"

Ravenna's breath caught in her throat at the familiarity of that rich, smooth voice. *Little Dove.* She staggered back, but he held her tightly, a smirk lining his lips as his hazel eyes watched her from beneath his mask. *How had I not recognized him?* Her skin grew cold, and she felt only the warmth of his hands on her waist. With more strength this time, she summoned every ounce of power she could to sit in wait, right below the surface of her skin. Her heart was ticking. She was a volcano: one wrong move from him, and she would erupt.

*What does he want?*

As he swept right, his fingers grazed her collar bone where a bloodstone heirloom had once sat, and a strange feeling echoed through her. The life of a woman she did not recognize came rushing back. Vestele. A shield-maiden. Xan–the one she had given up her conscience to protect. He had been important to her in a way she could no longer understand.

She continued the dance she had been forced into, but her mouth stayed shut. The day she had visited Leith in Ink Valley felt like a lifetime ago, and the memory of her carefully planned alliance was foggy. It had been an alliance that had only benefited her, and it had ended in what she knew he considered a complete betrayal.

"What is my betrothed doing, dancing with every wealthy man in this room?" he questioned. Ravenna collected her wits, preparing to play the game she had been released into by her king. She glanced at his shadowmarks again. She remembered Xan's ruthless hatred for Leith, and it all began to make sense. *Leith either hid those marks during our first encounter, or he got them at the Summer Trade.*

"Jealous?" she asked, spinning out of his grasp for only a moment. When his hands caught her waist, she spoke again. "It is best you forget about our alliance." She knew she had since she had surrendered to the sire. Maybe even before that, when her mind had been clouded with the things of this kingdom. "That opportunity was short-lived."

"You betrayed me. But if it is true that you are only doing what you are told. . ." he paused and shrugged. "I never took you for being one to follow orders." The words came with the sudden touch of a sharp blade against her spine. She straightened ever so slightly and rolled her shoulders. He held her close and kept swaying, his mouth hovering just above her ear. She glanced at the king who sat upon his throne, beaming from ear to ear as he sloshed the drink from his cup whilst talking to a flirtatious woman. Jara seemed to tower over her with jealousy but kept her eyes from staying trained on them for too long and looked to Ravenna, who continued acting as though there was not a dagger against her back.

"You have been ordered to kill those who try to harm you, yes?" he spoke into her hair.

"And are you here to harm me, Leith?" she asked, backing into the blade ever so slightly, until she felt a trickle of blood down her skin. She smirked, tilting her face toward him.

He cocked his head. "I heard of your recent endeavors in the valley. You have become a threat to me, have you not?" Ravenna pursed her lips. He was not here to harm her; he was here to test her control. To toy with her and to see how much control Degare had over her. To see how big of a threat she was to Ink Valley. But his journey here to find out the extent of her allegiance would only get him killed. He was known for snuffing out threats at first wind, and because of that, his clan was the strongest one *south* of Oro. Her kingdom would always prevail against his puny Ink Bloods.

When she did not answer him, he spoke again, this time in a faint whisper. "Well, are you a threat to me or not, Ravenna *Ozanne*?" She blinked, the only sign of her surprise at his knowledge of who she was. The king had not yet announced the fact that she was the heir to the throne of Ozanna. So when and how had Leith discovered it? No matter what Ravenna had said to his face, Xan was not a fool, and he would not have given Leith such knowledge. Not when his entire life had been dedicated to keeping that a secret.

Leith bent down to whisper against her cheek, "It seems we are both keeping secrets." She stepped backward and flowed into another twirl, and he spoke yet again, "Your curse of the witch guardians has caused quite the trouble." His face was flat as he monitored the room around them, not daring to look her in the eye. With Tenille in Ink Valley, Ravenna was sure the witch guardians were unrelenting visitors.

"My apologies," she said. "How is Tenille? Xan? Still insufferable, I would assume?"

Leith scoffed. "Of course they told you they were with me now," he muttered. "Imbeciles."

"Why so glib? Are you scared I'll come for your valley?" He did not answer but kept his eyes trained on her king. "Do not worry, Xan is no longer a threat to the workings of the sire. If he were, I would have already paid you a visit and killed him myself."

"Out of obedience or choice?" Leith asked, tapping that blade against her spine.

"I serve the king with no regrets," she said matter-of-factly, swaying with the music. As they circled, she looked over his shoulder at the king and his witch. They both monitored her now, and she hoped they didn't see the flash of the blade in Leith's sleeve, because she was having fun toying with him, and her king would squelch the fun she had found in the chase. "If my king demands your people be wiped from the face of the valley you reside in, there will be no hesitation from me." He was not a true threat, and she did not need to kill him yet. She could gather information and find his weakness, as the king had instructed her to do with every buyer here.

He drew her in closer, turning so her back was to the king. "Let me make it clear that I am not scared of you, Ravenna." His fingers trailed down one of her braids to her collar bone, and his hazel eyes locked with hers. "I am here to make you remember the reason why these braids never leave your hair. It is clear you have chosen to forget."

Her eyebrows creased in the middle, and she briefly looked at the king. Leith leaned in toward her, until his lips were at her ear. "I am here to make you realize that you fight for the losing man." She narrowed her eyes at the near threat, and he flicked her braid. "Could it be that this is the key to your redemption?

The very weakness I seek in the king's plan?" *Redemption.* Ravenna looked around the room full of darkness, and for a moment, she had a fleeting feeling of sadness–of life before the sire.

"Make no mistake, Ravenna, I will kill you if I must." She felt the blade against her skin once more, and this time, a prodding of the sire bond accompanied it, but Ravenna was too focused on keeping herself from spiraling. Those memories of old tried to take hold within her, but she would not allow them to replay in her mind. Leith was right, she had chosen to forget the emotions that were bound with the shadows of her past. The sire bond took up all the space in her mind now, and it was all she needed.

When she did not think of her past, of what she had done, and only focused on serving the king, things were fine. She had grown comfortable in the darkness. But now, looking at Leith and hearing that nickname, remembering the situation she had been in just five months ago when she had gone to strike a deal that would result in the safety of her people and the endangerment of his. . .she remembered *wanting* to die. And though she had pushed those thoughts away over the months because she had no hopes of ever escaping this sire, standing before Leith, they all threatened to come rushing back.

The craving she once had for the release that death would bring her returned.

Ravenna looked back to Leith and let a smug smile line her lips. He was here to find her weakness so he could strike. He was here to see if he would need to kill her, and by the end of the night, when he had seen that she had no weakness left, she was sure he would have his answer.

# CHAPTER 40
# TOO FAR GONE
## LEITH

The woman in his arms was indeed the same one who had betrayed him, and he knew she would do it again. Ravenna did not even seem remotely concerned that her parents were shackled at Degare's side next to the throne, or that, metaphorically, *she* was also shackled to the king. She had turned cold. But as Leith pressed the blade into her spine, he saw something behind her wild eyes that made him want to find a way to get her out of this kingdom.

Edme would have his head for thinking such things when Ravenna was now working for the enemy, and so would Xan if Leith killed Ravenna without first trying to bring her back. That was if the imbecile was able to make it past the dozens of gifted guards Leith had placed outside of his hut. Tenille was now welcome to come and go about the hut freely, but Leith had perhaps gone a little too far in convincing Xan he was headed to Oro to kill the woman he loved, and Leith could not trust him to stand aside.

The red of Ravenna's gown brought out the pink hue of

her cheeks. Her hair was long, mostly falling in waves down her back, her small braids spilling over the front of her shoulders. Leith sent her into a twirl one last time and noted the lack of emotion that had returned to her eyes with just a few blinks.

He had come into this kingdom to test his betrothed, unsure of the severity of the situation. There would be no walking out of the kingdom with her in tow. He had been too late, thanks to the attack of the witch guardians on his valley. Edme had convinced him to stay after the attack, and Ink Valley *had* needed him. It had taken months to rebuild after the damages. He would have been a fool to leave his people without a leader in such a time, and to go against the Kingdom of Oro when his own armies had fallen weak? It would have been a death wish, especially after the cryptic message he had received from Cove just after the attack. *"Your Little Dove is too far gone."* Leith was beginning to think that was true.

Looking at Ravenna now, he was angered. He was angry at her for trying to trick him into marriage when the guardians were after her, but the fact of the matter was that it was not really her fault. He had been the one to follow her home that night out of curiosity. Even without the covenant of marriage, he had decided to protect her against them—against anything. Perhaps he should have let the witch guardians kill her like Edme had suggested. Arresia would have been much safer for it. Now, Ravenna was promised not to him, but bound to the *King of Oro*.

Wrapped up in a waltz before her, Leith feared he had only scratched the surface of the extent of control the sire had over her. The melody they danced to was a haunting one. It crept over his skin with an eerie chill, but the people in the room around him all laughed and celebrated as if it were a joyous noise. Leith supposed they had much to celebrate, being that their pockets were all lined with gold, and the king's weapon had done her due diligence of promoting tomorrow's trades.

But these people were not the only ones who had come to Oro to collect power. Leith studied his betrothed, who kept her eyes on her sire. Her fingers were tapping mindlessly against his arm, but her face was stoic, revealing none of the chaos that he guessed was brewing in her mind.

Finally, she spoke. "You claim you'll kill me if you must?"

A smile tugged on Leith's mouth then, and he peered over Ravenna's head into the direction of the many Embers caged on the west wall, their lightmarks glowing against the dimly lit room. One viewer in particular caught his eye.

"I'll be seeing you," he promised into Ravenna's ear while slipping the blade back into his sleeve and disappearing into the crowd, pursuing the blonde that *could not* be who he thought she was. The petite woman had her back to him from where she stood near the cages, then began walking toward the darkest corner of the ballroom where he had stood earlier, masked in shadow.

Before Leith could catch up to her, she was approached by a noblewoman, whom Leith assumed was from the islands by the flowing, draping style of her gown. "Lady Cove?" the noblewoman asked her. Cove tensed, and it was a good thing she was wearing a mask. "I have not seen you shopping at the markets in months. . .since Prince Andreas of Edmaria was murdered on our islands. Where have you been?" Leith moved one of his rings to his wedding finger and quickly found his place at her side.

"My Darling Lila, I have been searching all over for you," he said, wrapping an arm around her. Cove stiffened beneath his touch, and the noblewoman looked between the two of them.

"My apologies, I thought you were someone else," she said, before eyeing Cove one last time and going on her way.

"I thought you had gone rogue," he said when the woman was out of earshot. He removed his arm from her shoulders, and she stepped aside immediately.

"Could have been dead," Cove said, voice a little too high pitched for that particular set of words. He could hear the hint of nervousness in her voice as her blue eyes focused on the shadowy marks creeping out from beneath his jacket.

"You have gone rogue, haven't you?" he asked, raising his brows.

She crossed her arms and shifted to the side, ensuring she had an exit route if he got too close. He chuckled.

Cove looked almost entirely different than she had that first week she had been with him in Ink Valley, and Leith wondered where she had obtained her attire. Tonight, her long, icy blonde hair was done up in a fancy bun, and pearls lined the many tiny braids that fed into it. Her dress had a high neckline to cover the glowing mark at the base of her collarbone. Even against the shadows, and despite her circumstances, her eyes were still bright with color.

"I had to take matters into my own hands. Elias needs me, and I cannot remain still while awaiting orders from you. Ravenna is sired to the king. She is a lost cause, Leith. Do not waste your resources trying to claim her for yourself. It will not end well for you." She spoke with conviction, smoothing the front of her blue gown. Leith knew what she meant: *it will not end well for your Ember army.* She did not care about him.

Leith shook his head and placed his hand on the back of his

neck. "You know, that would have been nice to know before I traveled all this way." Ravenna was supposed to be the solution to all of his problems. With her sired to the king, he was back to square one.

"Did you not receive my message?" Cove asked, shifting on her feet as she monitored their surroundings.

"It was a bit cryptic, was it not?" Leith asked.

"I do not think I could be clearer than *do not come*."

If he were being honest, nothing could have stopped him from coming here to see for himself. Cove may not have been fully aware of his plans for Ravenna, but she knew better than anyone what he was thinking in coming here, because she was here for similar reasons. When Xan and Tenille had returned from Vestele, after witnessing Ravenna in action, Leith had known it was time to make a move. Killing Ravenna was not yet off the table, but he would try other avenues first—had *been* trying other avenues.

"The blood and the hail were never going to work," Cove muttered, rolling her eyes at the dark marks that swirled over his chest and neck. She was toeing the line—testing her boundaries.

"Yes, well, I do not think your opinion about the means by which Degare is forced to surrender matters much," he said, watching Degare as he watched Ravenna from his throne. "It was meant to send a message."

"Ravenna is not yours to claim, Leith. And besides, Degare is not giving her up. We've seen it with Willa Ozanne. All of this," she motioned around her, "has been for revenge."

Leith narrowed his eyes, looking to Willa Ozanne, who sat chained to the dais by Degare's throne, her red hair spilling over her shoulders in tangles. "What do you mean?"

Cove watched him closely. "You don't know? Guess I do make a fine spy after all."

"Well, I have many spies in this kingdom—*most of which make it a point to stay in communication with me*," he said in exasperation.

"I had no news to give," she said tightly.

"No, you wanted to focus on the only mission that matters to you," Leith argued, stepping toward her. "We had a deal. You work for me now. It is not just about Elias." Cove bit her lip, and he could tell she had to stop herself from backing away. "Time to get your priorities straight, Cove. We had a deal," he reiterated, drawing out the words.

"I know," she said slowly.

"Well, have you found anything?" he asked. "Any news on your husband?"

Cove frowned, looking at the chained Embers. He took that as a no. Her husband was not here and neither was the woman he had come searching for. No, that woman was long gone.

"I keep my word. And I will help you find him," he assured her. "But I need to know I can trust you." She tried to blink her tears away, but she said nothing. He could tell her anxiety was festering, and he changed the subject. "What is it that you've discovered about Degare and Willa?"

Cove took a breath before whispering. "There is a rumor that everything Degare has done stemmed from his betrothal to Willa Ozanne many years ago." Leith tilted his chin. *Degare and Ravenna's mother?* "Someway or another, she ended up with Gerrin," Cove said.

"And Degare sees it as a betrayal from her and wants to punish them both," he said. *Oh, how history was seeming to repeat itself.* Leith hummed. "There's one more thing," Cove said reluctantly, as if she was unsure whether or not she should share further information with him. He motioned for her to continue. "When I was serving the Princess in Oriana," she said slowly, "there was another lady by the name of Celeste. I believe she is a witch, and I have reason to believe she and Jara are working together on something rather large."

"You think Jara is allying with other witches against Degare?"

"What makes you think the witches would not also be partaking in the business of building armies and weapons?" Cove asked. Leith shrugged and watched the witch that stood tall and seemingly proud beside the king. He was beginning to see her in a new light. "But Celeste is not just another witch. She is Jara's daughter, and this plan has been unfolding for quite some time." *Jara had a daughter? With whom?* "Celeste was planted in the palace as a spy and lady-in-waiting in hopes she would secure a marriage and gain an estate in another kingdom. A kingdom where Jara could bring the Delle Witch Clan home to. Where they would finally have their own land, and where Jara would return to her rightful throne."

"And she knows that as long as she is with Degare, she will have no throne. She will always be standing beside it, with no place to rest her legs," Leith said with his arms crossed. Now he had not one united enemy but two enemies playing each other. He chuckled.

"I can read emotions," Cove said quietly. Leith tilted his chin in curiosity. "But Jara has been hard to crack. Her emotions are not at surface level like most people." Her eyes narrowed on Leith for a moment, and he shifted on his feet. "I think you're right, though. Jara has been suspecting for some time now that he will never give her whatever he has promised her, and she is forming her backup plan, just in case. I don't think she has fully convinced herself that she will have to use it, but whenever she's finally had the last straw. . .that is when she'll strike."

Leith nodded. "So, what exactly happened during your first few weeks in Oro? How did you discover this, and what have you been up to since?"

Leith suspected that a small part of Cove trusted him because she told him everything. From the man named Zephaniah, to the torture Ravenna had endured, to the woman in the gallows, to her friend Sinley, who had died by Ravenna's hand on the night they had searched the Ember prison for Elias. Much of it Leith had heard from his other spies, but his blood still boiled all the same.

Leith looked to Ravenna, whose eyes had left her king and were now darting across the many masked faces in the room. "I've decided I am going to be staying in Oro for a while," Leith said, keeping his sights on Ravenna and thrumming his fingers against his arm. He looked at Cove. "Once again, I remind you that I have given you my word, and if you help me, I will help you find your husband. Seems you have not had much luck on your own," he said to Cove, who was standing a little taller now. Her eyes flicked to his, but he could not read her. "You'll both have a place in my army, and you'll be taken care of. So, last chance, Cove. Are you up for a task?"

# CHAPTER 41
# IN THE BUSINESS OF SECRETS
## DEGARE

The night was going swell, and Degare watched as his Raven danced with every wealthy gentleman in the ballroom, just as he had commanded her. He could tell she had impressed the King of Edmaria, who had brought two measly ships of Embers to sell into the trades. Degare had examined the weak stock, but he had not yet made him an offer.

At the bottom of the dais was a woman of south Brinland, who wore fine clothes and had a curvy figure. She spoke to the man in the white mask who had danced with his Raven just moments ago. Degare took a proud swig of his wine as she turned her attention from the man and batted her eyelashes toward where he sat on the throne. Degare motioned her up.

"Your Majesty," she said with a dip of her head. Her brunette hair was long and fell in curls at her waist. He smiled at her, setting down his drink and extending a hand. She stepped around the Ozannes, who sat silently chained to the ground on either side of his throne, and he guided her onto the arm next to him. Jara seethed at the bottom of the steps by the dais, as she had during each of his conversations this evening.

"Welcome to Oro, dear," Degare said in her ear. A soft giggle left her lips.

"Who are you watching?" she asked, following his gaze to the white-masked man. "Ah, Mr. Carrington. He is quite charming. I heard of him all the way across the ocean and had to meet him for myself."

"You had heard of him?" Degare asked curiously. Degare did not know of such a name in his kingdom.

"My husband is in the business of discovering secrets, and he shares them with me."

Degare lifted a brow. "What makes Mr. Carrington so renowned?" A king should know what went on in his own kingdom. Degare's cheeks began heating with chagrin.

The lady turned to him, voice low. "That man is rumored to have recently gained access to mounds of bloodstone and has gold burning a hole in his pocket. I am sure he will spend loads at your trade tomorrow."

Degare perked up. "Bloodstone?"

"Oh, yes. Where do you think that little village. . .the Brunts, is it? . .gets their bloodstone for the Gauntlet they host yearly? It is he who usually provides it. He is a master at mining or something." The lady smiled, looking across the room toward a slightly irritated man, whom Degare guessed to be her husband. Her cheeks flushed. "I better be going," she said, swiftly leaving Degare to join him on the floor.

Degare only smiled as he took a sip of his wine, and as he watched the man in the white mask, a plan began to knit together in his mind.

# CHAPTER 42
# A NIGHT OF OBSERVATIONS
### SABRINE

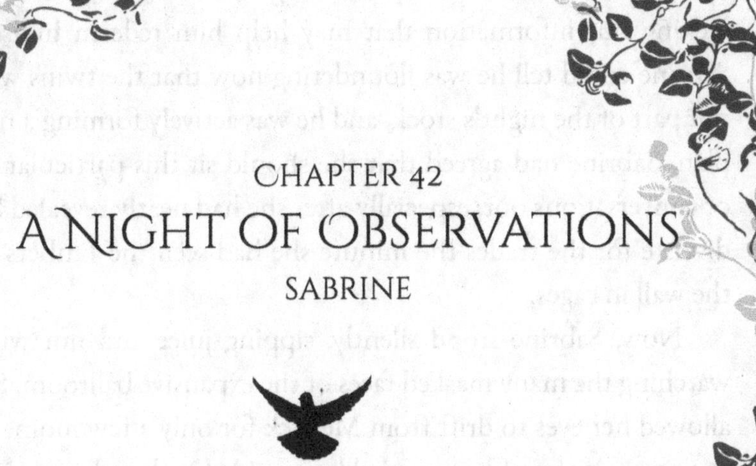

Sabrine's feet ached in the gemmed heels that were a size too small, but she could agree that the late Queen of Edmaria had good taste. The gown Sabrine wore was magnificent, and she seamlessly blended into the crowd of wealthy women. Merrick had pulled his suit from an opposing wardrobe in his mother's haven at the estate—a wardrobe that appeared to have collected even more years of dust than his mother's had.

Sabrine stood by a table of pastries beneath the giant clock on the north wall waiting for the prince's return, and though her stomach churned for sustenance, she refused to allow herself to eat. The twins were not included in the evening's display, and she did not know whether to be grateful or terrified. Because at least if they had been here tonight, she would have her sights on them, and she could begin forming a plan. She and Merrick could have placed their bids and began the enactment of the scheme she hated but was their only option.

Merrick was currently chatting with some noblemen, seeking out information that may help him redeem himself. Sabrine could tell he was floundering now that the twins were not part of the night's stock, and he was actively forming a new plan. Sabrine had agreed that she should sit this particular set of conversations out, especially after she had nearly revealed her distaste for the trades the minute she had seen the Embers on the wall in cages.

Now, Sabrine stood silently, sipping juice and not wine, watching the many masked faces of the expansive ballroom. She allowed her eyes to drift from Merrick for only a few moments at a time. A part of her worried he would abandon the mission, and he still carried most of the gold she would need to ensure she was successful in liberating the twins and getting them to Eswen. Sabrine would drop every gold coin the prince had on purchasing the twins, but how could she be sure he would do the same? *Because it is redemption he seeks, and he has proven time and time again that he has dedicated his life to working for it.*

*But redemption for what?* she wondered. He had sought it before the twins had disappeared. She watched him chatting rather reservedly with some kind of cloaked guard from Oro. Occasionally, his brown eyes would flit to where she stood, and she would pretend she had not been monitoring him. Sabrine turned toward the front of the ballroom where the King of Oro sat upon a black velvet throne with two poor souls chained to either side. The bloodstone staff was held tightly in his grasp, and the woman whom Sabrine had assumed to be his weapon was among those on the floor, getting caught up in waltz after waltz.

Merrick was a fool, but he was not dumb enough to find

himself in the same vicinity as the king's favorite weapon. Though Merrick stayed vigilant, Sabrine watched the redhead carefully as she moved about the floor, ensuring she did not make it anywhere near the Prince of Edmaria. The horrors the king's weapon could commit with her great power had not yet been revealed, and the last thing Merrick and Sabrine needed was a hound sniffing through their many layers of deceit. Sabrine had paid the same kind of mind to Merrick's father, King Idris, until he had disappeared after the room had gone dark with his shadows.

Sabrine went to take another sip of her juice, but the glass was empty. She peered at the bottom and set it on a table. The king's weapon was taking an unusual break from dancing with buyers, and Sabrine watched her carefully as she stepped absentmindedly toward the musicians near the back of the room. She was reaching for an instrument that Sabrine knew to be a violin, one she had been given a few lessons on in her early childhood when her parents had still held status in their village, and when they had jobs and just enough money to pay for a private teacher. But Sabrine had no musical bone in her body, and the lessons had not lasted longer than a few weeks.

Merrick returned to her side, but she did not acknowledge him as her eyes were fixed on the King's weapon. The woman with hair of red wasn't a woman of average beauty but one of harsh features and sharp bones under her mask. Despite the fierceness of her appearance, one that made Sabrine's skin crawl, there was something about her that seemed to catch the eyes of those around her. Perhaps it was only the intrigue of the power she held as Degare's weapon, but Sabrine saw something more beneath her skin. Her eyes harbored the shadows of a life long lost as she examined the instrument slowly, and Sabrine could not help but wonder if this young woman had only fallen victim to darkness, too.

Sabrine had watched her throughout the night, and with every song had come a prideful dancing partner who fostered equal amounts of intrigue and fear beneath their masks. But the Despiri who approached her now did so with confidence, and Sabrine held her breath as the man in the white mask–Locke, whom she had spoken to outside of the castle before the ball–took the violin from her grasp and set it aside. He seemed to dictate what her next moves would be and stepped into her line of view of the king before pulling her into a waltz at the start of the music.

For the first time all night, Sabrine saw something shift in the king's weapon. A whisper of flames encompassed the man's fingers at her shoulder, but he did not react, and Sabrine paid close attention to the woman's body language. She was uncomfortable, as if she had lost the upper hand. Who was this mysterious *Locke?*

"You should eat something," Merrick said beside her. She waved him off, watching the flash of silver that protruded from Locke's sleeve. Sabrine's chin tilted upward, and Merrick spoke again. "You haven't eaten much at all, and I know I was starving after our journey."

"Prince," she warned with irritation. "Do not speak to *me* about starvation. I will eat when I wish."

He stiffened at her remark and followed her gaze to where the king's weapon and Locke were being swallowed by the crowd. Sabrine moved to the left, trying to keep them in her sights. "There is something strange about him," Sabrine said, nodding to Locke.

"What do you mean?"

"I spoke to him outside when you were using rainwater to slick back your hair," she muttered. Merrick opened his mouth, but before he could say anything, she continued, "He is up to something."

"How can you tell?"

"Well, for starters, he is holding the king's weapon at knifepoint."

"What?" Merrick asked, stepping behind her to get a better view. "I don't see a knife."

"Well, he isn't exactly going to flaunt it in front of the king and his witch, is he?" Sabrine looked to King Degare, who was oblivious, enjoying the many ladies that came to speak with him. "Do you think it is he who threatens Oro?" Sabrine asked, and she looked back at the prince, awaiting his answer.

"I doubt it. I have never even heard of him. No man without an army, not even a Despiri—no matter how gifted—could stand against Oro. One would be a fool to try." *Well it would seem that this man is trying.*

"Perhaps you should speak to him after this dance is over. Perhaps he has information that would be beneficial to us."

Merrick's hand curled around the handkerchief she knew was in his pocket. "We need to lay low, Sabrine. Fraternizing with an obvious enemy to the king is not the way to keep our cover. My guess is, he'll be dead by morning. The woman probably doesn't want to cause a show. It's politics. Strategy is key," he reminded her. She rolled her shoulders, watching as Locke left the dancefloor with his life and disappeared into the shadows.

*Something is brewing,* her heart seemed to say. *Stay vigilant.*

Next to her, the prince turned toward the refreshments

table. "Well if you aren't going to eat," he said, breaking the silence, "at least let me get you another drink."

Sabrine watched him carefully for a moment longer and then nodded. He gave her a slight smile and started toward the table. "Juice," she called after him. "No wine." She needed to keep a clear mind for the days ahead.

"My lady," said a voice from behind her. Sabrine took a breath and turned, masking herself in the confidence of a Duchess. "That is Duchess, to you," she said, before meeting the eyes of none other than Merrick's father, King Idris of Edmaria. She stepped backward once, and he caught her by the elbow.

"Careful, Duchess." She forced a blush, and fought the urge to look over her shoulder toward Merrick, who would be returning with her glass any moment.

"My apologies, Your Majesty," she said, lowering her head as she curtseyed. As she did so, she turned to the side in search of the prince, but her peripheral vision did not find him.

"I was just on my way out, and I could not resist the urge to speak with you," he said, taking her hand and placing a kiss on the back of it. Her heart was thudding wildly now, and it was all she could do to keep her feet planted. *Relax. There is no way he knows who you are.*

She smiled at him, gently retracting her hand, and covering the wedding band that encircled her finger as a ruse. "You remind me of someone I lost long ago." He looked at the shoes at her feet, which once belonged to the very woman she knew he was talking about. Sabrine swallowed, wanting to conceal herself in shadow, wanting to hide the gown and the jewelry she had taken from his late queen's closet. Had Merrick not thought it possible that his father, who was attending the same ball, would recognize the attire once worn by his mother?

Sabrine breathed tightly. "It is a pleasure to meet you, Your Majesty," she lied. This was the man who got her parents killed, and the one who had enslaved the twins. "I am truly sorry for whatever you have lost." The words came out dryly.

A wicked grin spread across his face as he surveyed her attire. "Women make men weak. I have been careful not to allow that to happen again. But you, you are *ravishing*." Sabrine blinked slowly, trying to maintain her composure. *This is the king who was rumored to have killed his own wife. The wife whose clothes I am now wearing.*

Sabrine's body was like stone, and no words came to her. "Relax, Duchess. With such a title, I realize you must be called for." He looked her up and down, and then said, "It was lovely to meet you, Duchess of. . ."

Sabrine stared straight forward as he hovered before her, the wine on his breath stinging her nose. "Matuk," she said quietly. Idris paused for a moment at that word, and his eyes shifted to the side as if following a fleeting thought.

"Enjoy the trades tomorrow, Duchess." With that farewell, he walked away.

Sabrine stood there silently, losing track of time as she listened to the pounding of her heart.

"Are you okay?" Merrick asked from behind her. "What did he want? What did he say?" He had two drinks in his hands, and a bit of juice sloshed out onto the floor.

"He said I remind him of your mother." Merrick's jaw set, and he looked to the doors where his father had just left the ballroom.

"Is that what you're doing with me? Trying to redeem

yourself for not protecting her?" Sabrine shook her head. "You and I are not friends. But whatever happened to your mother–it is not your fault. You were just a boy." Sabrine had to tell herself the same many times–that it was Idris who had caused her parents' deaths. There was nothing she could have done to stop it. She had done all she could in trying to get them to forsake the Light to protect their own lives, and they had not listened.

Merrick shook his head. "There is more to it, I–"

Sabrine cut him off with a wave of her hand. She could relate to him in some ways, and the fact that she was beginning to feel pity on him scared her. *He is the reason the twins are gone.*

"I do not need to know your every grievance," she said. "If you go on blaming yourself for all the evil in Arresia, we'll be standing here all night."

# CHAPTER 43
# THE BECKONING
## LEITH

"Darling, I want this one," Cove said to Leith as she pointed to the shivering Ember on display and spun her silver wedding ring.

Leith smiled and backed closer to the king's throne. "I know, dear. Why else do you think I have brought you to this extravagant ball? Only to dance?" he teased. "I shall spend a hundred gold ravens on you if I must."

Cove grinned and tugged on his arm. "Well, we can still dance," she said. Leith spun her around and backed her closer to the King of Oro in hopes of him eavesdropping on their conversation. "You'd truly spend a hundred gold ravens on me at the trade?"

"Anything for you, love. But if we do not find an inn with available space," they turned in a circle, "we will be forced to leave before the trade." Cove's face fell to a pout, and he smirked at her as he heard the clicking of the king's boots at his back.

Leith turned to address the king but did not bow to him. "Your Majesty." He lowered his head as if in reverence, but it was only to hide the look of disgust that surely settled behind his eyes when those two words left his lips.

Degare's face turned slowly to Leith, who now stood tall. That Leith was able to earn a place in such close proximity to the host of this ball was a miracle. The witch who must be the one known as *Jara,* stood next to him, cold stare burning into Cove. Leith shifted slightly, hiding his partner's masked face behind his arm while she hopefully used her gifts of mood alteration to lessen Jara's concern with her strange familiarity. Cove had told him of the mistakes she had made in almost revealing herself in this kingdom, so he did not allow the witch to get a good look at her.

"I hear your stock of Embers is exceptional this season," Leith said, remembering how his mysterious betrothed had tried to impress him. Degare studied him for a moment before waving his witch into the crowd. She reluctantly obeyed, and the tension in Cove's hand lessened with each foot of distance that grew between them.

"All of my buyers say so," the king said. "This will be a trade for the books–hence the large celebration." He gestured to the crowded ballroom. Despiri prowled the line of cages for more power. Women danced in elegant dresses. Men drank and hollered loudly, and turning in circles beneath the massive chandelier were children, some of whom would soon become first-time killers.

"Word of the royal executions has traveled far and wide I see," Leith said. He glanced to the floor by the throne, where Gerrin and Willa's hands were outstretched toward each other, empty stares boring into their daughter. Some of the guests had likely only traveled to see the execution of the Ozannes, which was to happen in the square at dawn tomorrow to kick off the trades.

"It has been quite difficult to find a place to stay. Last night we stayed in our carriage. Unfortunately, we may not be able to stay for the trade if we do not find an inn with a room."

"Oh, darling. Please, let's stay," Cove cut in. "I just wish to have one. We have traveled all this way," she whined, looking at the trembling Embers. The king looked between the two of them, noting their expensive clothes and the pearls that hung from Cove's neck, and then, he fell into their trap.

"I have rooms available in the west wing of the castle. We've just done some. . .remodeling. You may stay there, until the trade."

"Oh, Your Majesty! We could not accept such a generous offer," Cove said quickly.

"I will arrange it. At the end of the night, a servant will escort you to your chambers," he insisted.

Leith tilted his chin in thanks. "Thank you, Your Majesty. You have done us a great favor." *One you will regret.*

When the king turned to leave, Cove squeezed Leith's elbow. "I didn't think I could do it," she whispered in shock.

Leith winked at the conniving Ember who had used her gifts to alter the king's mood, making him more charitable. "Well, I think my mention of a hundred gold ravens did most of the work."

Cove scoffed. "Could anyone in the land of Arresia afford to spend a hundred gold coins at once?"

Leith grimaced as he watched Degare. "None, but perhaps a king," he mumbled to himself.

About an hour later, Leith found himself itching for another conversation with the king. He could not help himself–he enjoyed toying with his prey. After one of the many servants refilled his wine, he found his place pretending to examine the Ozannes, who were still shackled at the foot of the throne. They no longer held hands, and they had been forced to their knees, their heads hanging low. Willa's face, once depicted in paintings as youthful and full of gentleness, had sunken and become gaunt. Gerrin's eyes were closed as he leaned against the side of the throne in exhaustion. Degare kicked him awake, and Willa began trembling. Leith met the king's stare and pretended to brush something from his sleeve.

"The executions, the trade. . .they are not the only reasons you've thrown such an extravagant party, are they?" Leith asked. Both of their gazes landed upon the woman in red with the black-feathered mask over her eyes. Her lips were painted in the color of blood, and they moved swiftly as she spoke to every potential buyer on the floor. A pang of jealousy echoed down his spine, and he shifted, speaking under his breath so that only the king could hear.

"Your new weapon is–*magnificent*. Wherever did you find her?" The king studied him carefully. "It is a good idea to flaunt the power she's allotted to you as your weapon. Surely no kingdom shall prevail against Oro if they know the gifts she holds."

"That is precisely the plan." the king said, still watching her.

"I am eager to see the power that lives within her," Leith said. "Surely it will leave this entire ballroom in awe."

"Stricken in fear," Degare said proudly. "I can assure you, the power within her is something you have not seen before. Something one cannot fathom." The corner of Leith's lip tipped upward. *I know all too well.* He raised his glass to Degare, and the king shifted on his throne. "I did not catch your name."

Leith smiled and shook his hand. "Locke Carrington. From the Brunts."

"Ah, a shame, what happened to the city. They were one of my finest merchants. Hundreds of Embers were shipped from the Brunts each month; their mercenaries were ruthless." He cocked his head at Leith. "Were *you* a mercenary?"

Leith tilted his head. "Something like that." The king smiled and turned his attention back to Ravenna, who now danced with an Edmarian man, probably convincing him to spend all his gold on an Ember life in the morning. Leith set his empty chalice on the table, grabbed a glass, and requested the servant bring more wine. He then raised his glass to the king, and with a sparkle in his eye he said, "May the power she brings see no end."

The king smiled at that and raised a brow, toasting who he believed to be another power-hungry man from the Brunts.

Leith sipped his wine and watched as his betrothed danced with every other man in the room to the awful music that made his skin crawl. He stood by while they had their hands on her and while she smiled and charmed them in her clever, deceitful way. One tall, lanky man from Tabrana currently held her attention. Occasionally her eyes would bounce between

Leith's and the man she was currently with. He only tipped his glass at her in response.

As the night continued, Ravenna's skin became dewy with sweat, and she pulled her thick hair over her shoulder. The king had dressed her in a red satin gown. It was backless, and dipped to the middle of her spine, probably meant to show off the strange shadowmarks that plagued her skin. With her hair pulled to the side, he could now see that the shoulders of the gown held golden feathers dipped in what appeared to be blood. But when she spun, his eyes did not go to the feathers at her shoulder blades. They settled between them, on a *brand*. Degare's brand–*that had been burned into her skin.*

He was about to lose all control. He was about to ruin *everything*. Leith downed the remainder of his drink with every muscle tensed, trying to withhold the power that ripped through his veins. Thunder cracked outside of the castle, and he knew the seas were raging.

"Staring won't help anything," Cove said beside him, resting a gentle hand on his elbow. He released a breath, thankful for the distraction she had offered and the rationality she had just spoken into his mind with her strange gifts. Ravenna continued through her dance for a moment before her eyes locked on Leith once more, and then they shifted down to Cove.

"Not good," Cove said, realizing her mistake in revealing herself to Oro's greatest weapon, who now only knew her as a rebel to the crown. Ravenna narrowed her eyes at the two of them, then left her dance partner standing alone in the middle of the crowded floor.

"Go," he muttered to Cove. Leith breathed a tight breath

before Cove turned to exit the ballroom. The castle. The kingdom. Nowhere she could run to would be far enough. Ravenna's gaze followed the traitor of her sire's crown, and as she made a beeline for her, weaving in and out of the crowd, Leith caught her elbow. Her eyes were accusatory and like fire as they bore into him, probably wondering what he had been doing with a spy.

"Is this you or the sire talking?" Leith asked her, trying to make her think about the rage she was about to act on. What she saw was a traitor. A spy in her sire's castle. A muscle in his jaw twitched as she tried to fight his grip from her elbow. He swept her into another dance, whispering low into her ear. "Now, Ravenna. You would not want to alarm your king right before your big show," he said to her. She looked past his shoulder to the king, whom Leith knew was now watching them. Ravenna faked a flirtatious smile.

Cove had safely exited the ballroom by now, but he held Ravenna a little tighter. Her pale skin was scarred in many places. Her hair had dulled since he had seen her in Ink Valley, and the many colors in her eyes had grayed. He ran a finger over the brand at the top of her back, causing her to go rigid.

"You would not kill me when I was a threat, and you will not kill her either. She is less of a threat than I." *How far can I push her?*

Ravenna stiffened underneath Leith's touch, and the hand she rested on his shoulder clenched. "You were not a true threat then. You were not here to kill me. But soon, you will see that you have to," she said.

*What did that mean?*

The room shifted as the king rose from his throne, and

Ravenna wiped her palm–now bloody from clenching her fingernails so tightly into it–on her gown. It was the moment the crowd had been waiting all evening for. With a shuddering breath he released her, allowing her to go to Degare's beckoning call.

# CHAPTER 44
# KING'S CRAFT
## RAVENNA

The sire called to her, but she wanted to stay with Leith, whom she had a dozen questions for. *Why is he with Cove? Did he know she is a spy? Is he a spy? Does he know Cove is an Ember? Or is he here to purchase an Ember to gain strength for his clan? Can Ink Valley even afford such things?* She knew his clan was wealthy, *but wealthy as in silver or gold? He must not be a true threat if I was able to resist the urge to kill him. He is only toying with you,* she told herself. *He is here for the trades, and then he will leave.*

Despite wishing to stay and question him for the remainder of the night, Leith's rough hands released her waist, and she turned from him without a word and headed toward the throne in a trance. It was time for the show. She rubbed her palm, trying to rid it of the evidence of her unforeseen, subtle rebellion against the sire. She had been preparing for this moment over the last couple of days, with little sleep and little aid from the alcohol that generally helped her along.

Degare watched her with pride as he prepared to show all

of Arresia just what he had accomplished. Through the bond, she had become sensitive to his every wish. When she was near him, the tether between them made her in tune with his emotions as a way to convey how she could better serve him. A small part of her was grateful he could not feel hers in return.

As she ascended the steps to the dais, hitching up the satin of her gown, his gaze shifted to span the entirety of the room. Her hand slipped into the king's, and he spun her to face the crowd, his other hand gripping the bloodstone staff. He should have it glued to his palm so he would not have to exert so much energy toward white knuckling it all day. She would bet he slept with the thing tucked under his covers.

He tapped it once on the stone. "Ladies and gentlemen." The crowd silenced, and he continued, holding her hand up with his in victory. "The *Raven of Oro*." A few whistles echoed throughout the room, but mostly, there was no noise at all.

"Crafted by me, *for* me," he added. Ravenna saw Jara's anger beginning to simmer at the king's false claim. "Born to serve the Light, *surrendered to darkness.*" The crowd cheered then.

Ravenna bowed before her king and let her power rumble through the castle precisely as she had practiced. She then looked upon her audience, her eyes drawn to Leith, who stood with his arms crossed, seemingly unimpressed. They seemed to be having a stare off, but Degare ordered her from behind, and Leith's hazel eyes flashed as she was forced to break eye contact first.

"Ravenna, kill this Ember." She had known this was coming. *I do not care,* she told herself. *You do not care. You killed without care just days ago.* Ravenna breathed slowly, trying to remain in the darkness she had found comfort in.

Here, she did not have to think. Here, there was no remorse for the things she did for the king. Here, she would not remember what she had done to him. *To Zephaniah.*

She had not thought of him in weeks. What was happening to her?

As she took the bloodstone staff from Degare, a muscle in Leith's jaw ticked. The Ember man before her was elderly. She tried to tell herself he had lived a long life, that he would die soon anyway. *Why did it matter?* She did not look him in the eye or pay any mind to the riot made by the caged and shackled Embers on the wall. Instead, she looked to Leith as she drove the staff forward and the Ember's power began to fill her. Leith's face was like stone as he watched her, but behind his eyes, she knew he was wondering just how he would go about killing her. Gerrin and Willa Ozanne cried behind her as they watched their daughter fall further from the Light, and Ravenna could have sworn her shadowmarks darkened as the Ember took his last breath.

She resisted the urge to fall to her knees as his gifts overwhelmed her. *Appear strong,* she told herself. *Untouchable. Do not let them see your weakness.* She could not breathe. She looked to the innocent man before her, whose gaze was fixed on her, even in death. She did not allow a glimmer of remorse to show on her face because she was not allowed to feel it. Degare had ordered it out of her. So why was she feeling it? The Ember's gray eyes were lifeless, and his hair was still dark despite his age. She could not avoid the fact that he reminded her of Zephaniah. She thought she was finished feeling this guilt. *What is happening?*

Her hands trembled and the room began spinning. She was

falling. Plummeting into that tunnel of memories that were too harsh for her to remember.

Leith moved forward in the crowd, keeping his eyes on her, watching her, as if intrigued. His gaze narrowed, and she hoped she was masking her panic well. The noise around her was deafening. She needed air.

The roaring crowd was clapping, thrilled with the death of one of the hated ones. Degare boasted before all the people, collecting his staff from her grip. "She follows my every command. Even if I told her to cut off her own hand, she would do it." Ravenna swallowed, knowing very good and well that she would, if he only asked.

Leith's jaw tensed as he watched her. Perhaps he was also unsure of whether the king would order such a thing. Another rumble traveled through the stone walls of the castle, but this time, she was certain it was not of her doing.

The king released wicked laughter. "I kid!" He turned to two guards, who stood ready to pull the giant, black velvet curtains from behind the throne. At Degare's dramatic gesture, they pulled them open to reveal a mosaic of bones and ash and char. Ravenna looked closer. In the shape of a raven, were Vestele's remains, plastered against the wall.

She staggered back and caught herself, attempting to mask her shock. *He has taken my people's bones and displayed them like art on the wall.*

Degare was speaking about how he had even succeeded in sending her to destroy her homeland. She had abandoned all she ever knew, every part of herself, for his darkness. *What have I done?* "Once a loyal leader to Vestele, now she has turned on her own. Once heir to the throne of Ozanna." He gestured to Gerrin and Willa, who were collapsed in weakness next to his throne. *What have I become?* The crowd hushed in utter shock as they realized Ravenna was the biological daughter of the Ozannes. "Now, my slave." More clapping and hollering echoed around them. "Once a *dove*, now a raven." Degare reveled in his victory. Leith's darkening eyes had moved from Ravenna to the king beside her, and his hand was now continuously flexing against his arm.

Ravenna was losing hold. As she began shaking with rediscovered rage, Degare spoke again, and the tether between them seemed to grow taut, coaxing her back. "Fire." Flame wove around her palms and up her arms. She sent it spiraling through the crowd, and despite her careful efforts not to burn anyone, screams echoed through the ballroom. She smiled at the fear that began to take the crowd, and she let her strange rage entwine with power until it brought some relief.

"Water." This was the moment she had trained for. Without delay, the waters from the Black Sea rose at her command and crashed against the giant panes of the stained-glass windows behind the caged Embers. The crowd screamed in awe and terror, backing away from the windows where water and glass could easily crash into the room.

"Air." A rush of wind came whooshing through the room, blowing skirts and extinguishing flames. Dozens of hair pins fell to the ground in the gust, and the chandeliers shook violently above. The crowd ducked and covered their heads. But not Leith. He stood unmoving, still watching.

She made it her mission to make him flinch.

"And everything in between," was Degare's closing statement for her show. Ravenna raised her arms and sent the room quaking. Lightning flashed beyond the skies, illuminating the stained-glass windows. She smirked at Leith, whose jaw now ticked with her display of power.

*Don't you wish you would have killed me when I gave you the chance?*

He held her gaze, an obvious anger hovering between them. She noted how he still clenched and unclenched his fist where his arms were crossed over his chest in supposed indifference, as if focusing all his attention on the movement of it. The crowd was moving around him, trying to get closer to Ravenna, like she had not just proven to them all that she could kill them with a glance. They were in absolute awe of her. They wanted to *be* her, without even understanding the extent of her power. Even *she* did not understand the extent of it. She had only scraped the surface at training, and the surface was a mile deep. What more could she achieve in just a few months?

Ravenna looked to her king and then back to where Leith had been standing, but he was gone, swallowed up by the herd of people. She steadied herself on the arm of the throne while her king continued his speech, inspiring his guests to spend their gold so they may become like her.

"Let my Raven be the hope that the darkness is victorious." The people cheered, and he continued, raising his staff. Ravenna remembered that her *hope* was dead. "The Light will fall to us." And with that, Ravenna dimmed the flames, and the people danced as the music began again.

# CHAPTER 45
# WHEN YOU HAD THE CHANCE
## RAVENNA

Unfortunately, though she was exhausted, Ravenna still had to attend the king's dinner. As ordered, she had only extended invitations to the richest of noblemen–the ones who were inclined to bring him the most profit in their bids.

The crisp autumn air was just what Ravenna needed as she tried to shove every hint of emotion down into her soul. The night had grown dark, just as she had grown to prefer it. Just as she preferred to feel nothing at all. But for some reason, tonight, she was in danger of *feeling*. When she *felt*, living was worse than death. And she was forbidden from killing herself or allowing another to do it, so she needed to find a way to live without the consequences of her actions affecting her or life would be miserable. Giving into the darkness had been easy with that in mind. So why was she feeling now?

It was late, and the king's dinner would be beginning soon. Night had fallen hours ago, and she walked through the streets and up the steps to the upper end of the castle, toward her chambers, where a new gown would be awaiting her. With only the sounds of her heels on stone and the thick red sea rushing at her left, she could not think. She shook the uncomfortable shoes from her feet and bent to retrieve them. Entering through the doors closest to her wing on the west wall, the sentries parted for her as if she were royalty.

The halls were empty as everyone still danced in the ballroom, celebrating and dancing the night away in front of the Embers, boasting of how they were to kill them in the morning. Ravenna could not help but feel a hint of remorse at all she had witnessed tonight. At all she had done. *Why were the remorse and guilt returning? The deal was that they wouldn't. . .if I just gave in.*

Every dark hall in the castle brought her back to just months ago when Zephaniah had escorted her everywhere. She remembered the way he had held her hand through the bars of the cell and the way he had looked at her, as if he would let nothing harm her. She even remembered the sadness in his eyes when he saw he had failed. *No.* She had failed him, a thousand times over.

*You must forgive yourself, Ravenna. Not just for this but for everything else, too.*

The words had echoed in her mind day and night until she couldn't take it any longer. There was no forgiveness for the things she had done. She dragged her blood-crusted nails along the black stone as she neared her chambers and tried to replace those thoughts as Degare had commanded her to do. *Forget your past.* She had failed Zephaniah, and now, she was failing her king.

She swung the door to her chambers open and gathered her hair from her neck. She stiffened when she heard him.

There, whistling a familiar tune on the bed as if he owned it, was Leith. *How had he gotten in here?* He was laying back across her pillows with his hands propped behind his head, and his face was now maskless.

"My betrothed! I was wondering when you would arrive," he said, trying to rile her to annoyance. It worked. Her eyes rolled back in her head, and she ignored him, walking behind the divider and slipping out of her gown. The scarlet fabric puddled around her aching feet, and she blinked the memories away. "Not even a hello?" he called from the other side of the screen. She gritted her teeth as she stepped into the new gown– a black one, strangely–and struggled to lace it up before stepping back into view.

His eyes bored into hers.

"Why are you here? Nothing you can say or do will get me to come to Ink Valley with you. *I am sired to the king.* Whatever deal we had is *off*," she said. She turned her back to him and looked into the mirror, removing the jewels from her ears. Earrings plinked into her jewelry tray, and she winced, trading them out for a gold ear cuff.

As she watched herself in the mirror, she saw Leith sit up behind her on the edge of the bed. He stared for a long moment, his gaze on her bare back.

"Degare did that to you?" he asked. It was a question filled with fury, one he had been bottling up all night. She laughed a low laugh as she noticed his sight was fixed at the brand on her back, at the mark of her enslavement, as if it infuriated him that she was owned by another when she had promised herself to him.

"No, I did it to myself," she muttered.

His eyebrows fell. "I wouldn't doubt it after the show you put on out there. It seems you do everything he says."

"Proudly," she said. He blew out a breath, and she lowered her gaze from the mirror.

"You *are* a lost cause. You do not even fight it." She looked at his reflection again under furrowed brows. She could see his mind turning. She took a pleasurable swig of the whiskey that sat next to her mirror before turning on him.

She chuckled, eyeing his swift hand that was silently slipping beneath his suit jacket. "Just do it already," she said, urging him to bring that dagger to her heart. "I serve Degare now, and there is nothing you can do to stop me from telling him of the little rebellion you are leading."

He shot up from the edge of the mattress, and a wicked grin formed on her lips. *Does he now understand that he will have to kill me?* "That is what Ink Valley is, isn't it? You aim to stand against Degare. That is why you claimed that I serve the losing man. It is you who has been waging war on this kingdom." She examined her nails as he took a raging step toward her. "That is why you asked for my hand those years ago, and that is why you agreed to an alliance in the spring."

Leith's eyes narrowed, but he did not deny it. "You were searching for my power. You planned to use me all along." Leith stepped forward, and Ravenna laughed in his face, stopping him with a single finger on his chest. He paused, watching the tendrils of darkness that curled around her hand, and his grip tightened on his blade. "You, Leith of the Ink Bloods, are no better than Degare."

The dagger found her flesh then, and she was disappointed that it only nicked her stomach. She could see that Leith was fighting a war in his mind: to kill, or not to kill. *Where has my sense of self-preservation gone? My inability to go against the sire that commands me to live? How am I standing here, practically begging the Ink Blood leader to kill me?*

Obviously, Leith was working with Cove, but that first day in the witch's chambers that Ravenna had seen her, Ravenna had thought she looked familiar. She realized now that she had been the sickly blonde in Leith's hut on the day Ravenna had gone to Ink Valley. Cove's hair had been matted, and she looked as though she had been tortured and malnourished. Leith was using Embers. Ravenna smiled smugly.

"Blood water, huh?" she asked, tempting him. Of course he had been using Cove for these attacks. She should have known all along. "Hail?" Leith's jaw set, and she continued. "It is you who demands the release of the Embers. You want them for yourself." She looked at the shadowmarks on his neck. "You are raising an army. How many do you have there in Ink Valley?"

Leith said nothing to confirm or deny her accusation. When, still, he did not go in for the kill, she coaxed the dagger in a little deeper with her hand on his. He hesitated, fighting against her unnatural strength. "You better make it fast," she said, "before I decide to fight back—or you will not live to see winter. And neither will your people." *Do it.* His hazel eyes bored into hers, and she refused to look away as the blade threatened to slide further.

"Do the Embers you collect for your army have any say in the matter? How do you choose which ones you kill for your own power and which ones you force to fight your battles?"

Leith's mouth did not move, and his hand stayed put. She tried to walk further into the blade, but then, the voice of the sire seemed to break through the strange new barrier in her mind. *Ravenna, protect yourself.* She blinked.

*What am I doing?* She shook her head and backed away, hand going straight to her abdomen to quench the bleeding. She looked down at the shallow wound, at the small tear and growing stain on her gown.

"Well, now you've ruined my dress. The king is not going to be happy," she grumbled, trying to cover the moment of weakness she had just displayed. Leith's eyes fell to her wound, and he allowed her to push past him toward the wardrobe.

He stood there, repeating the motion of clenching and unclenching his fist around the hilt of his blade, as if contemplating what he should do with her, and she slipped behind the dressing screen once more to change into a new gown. "I have dinner with Degare. I cannot be late," she said through the screen. There was no answer. She packed some cloth around the wound on her stomach and slipped into the red dress. Gold chains hung from the shoulders, dipping all the way to her elbows, and three thin chains stretched across the open back. She stepped out, reaching past him and grabbing her gold feather shawl from the bedpost. His face was gaunt, and she gently tapped his cheek three times with her hand.

"Oh, Leith, do not worry. I am sure my orders from the king will make your demise fast. Though, I suppose such mercy is not really his style." He stood in thought, still silent, but steady.

As she turned to exit the room, his hand caught her elbow in an unrelenting grip. She smiled and slowly turned to face him.

"Yes?" she asked inquisitively. His face was desperate and then demanding.

"You will not say a word to Degare about any of this," he

said, as if it were he who owned her. She raised her brows and pulled her arm from his grasp.

"Perhaps you should have killed me when you had the chance," she said as she walked toward the dining hall to share all of Leith's secrets with her king.

# CHAPTER 46
# GOOD LIAR
## RAVENNA

The dinner table was set in elegant extravagance. A spread of meat and fruits Ravenna had not seen in Oro before decorated the length of the long table that was set for two dozen of the favored buyers. Dispersed throughout the appetizers were candles with flickering flames, and a strange smoke seemed to creep across the black roses in the floral arrangements.

A melancholic tune was being played from a cello in the corner as Ravenna and the king's guests awaited Degare's arrival. She rubbed her hands over her ears as the music continued. Ravenna's leg was bouncing beneath the table, and she was itching to get the king alone–to tell him of all she had discovered. Jara, who sat beside her, would be angry that Ravenna had solved the puzzle of the plagues before she had, and Ravenna could not wait to harp on it. She hoped the king would send her hunting after Leith, who was likely fleeing the kingdom by now to warn his valley. He would never make it in time. Not with the Raven of Oro on his tail.

Perhaps she would even get to see Xan again. This time, she would not let him walk free.

Ravenna's eyes slid over the two vacant seats. One to her left and one across from her. The one to her left was to be filled by the king, and the other was being held for Idris, King of Edmaria. He was late.

As the doors to the dining hall opened, the guests quieted their conversation. Ravenna straightened and awaited her king's arrival. Footsteps and laughter sounded just around the doorway, and Ravenna's heart leapt into her throat as her king came around the corner with none other than the man who was planning to overthrow his kingdom.

Ravenna tensed, and Leith paused his conversation with the king to offer her a sarcastic, exaggerated wave.

"Everyone, this is Locke Carrington of the Brunts. He is a mercenary, and a fine one at that. He hunts Embers for a living." Ravenna narrowed her eyes on the supposed *Locke Carrington* as he shook her king's hand and pulled out the seat across from her. He settled into the chair, and she eyed the many rings on his hands, and the way his fingers thrummed on the table as he leaned back in his chair and watched her with a sly smile.

Ravenna rose to her feet, smacking her hands on the table. "Your Majesty," she said to Degare. "May I have a word with you–"

*Sit down and shut your mouth,* his eyes seemed to say.

She swallowed her anger and sat back down across from Leith, who still eyed her with satisfaction. *What is your game?* His eyebrows rose as Ravenna downed her entire glass of wine. Ravenna then raised her empty glass in toast to the king, along with his many guests.

Degare looked between Leith and Ravenna. "I saw the two of you dancing." Ravenna stiffened. "Ravenna, why did you not invite him to dinner? I am ashamed to have had to do it myself so last minute."

Leith answered swiftly for her. "Oh, Your Majesty. It is no trouble. Ravenna only had to be selective with who she could invite, and I believe all the places were filled by the time we had our dance."

Ravenna gritted her teeth, and she felt the witch watching her.

"Well, then, I am glad the King of Edmaria could not make it," Degare said, raising a glass. "To new friends." Degare and Leith clinked their glasses, and Leith gave her a wink across the table.

"He will be staying across the hall from you. I trust you will be a good host." Ravenna opened her mouth to object, but at the king's grimace, she nodded respectfully.

"Your new weapon truly is magnificent," he said, as if she were not right there–as if she were no more than an object. Leith's eyes darted right over her, from Degare to Jara, who was still seething. "You are the witch who was able to complete the spell, correct?" Jara nodded slowly. "Simply incredible," Leith said, reaching for her hand across the table. He held her thin fingers in his as he worked his charm. "Your Majesty," he said, looking from Jara to Degare while still holding onto Jara's hand, "You are very lucky. She is not only extraordinarily powerful but beautiful too." Jara blushed, and Ravenna set her jaw as she glared at Leith across the table. *I will end you,* she promised. But Leith was unbothered by her unspoken words and continued chewing his food and happily conversing with his new friends.

Ravenna poured glass after glass, and Degare did not even notice her as he chatted with *Locke Carrington* about his endeavors as a hunter of Embers. *How much of what he is saying is true?*

When a moment of silence finally came, she took another swig of wine, letting the bitter taste coat her tongue before speaking. She placed her elbows on the table and leaned forward, aware of the two dozen eyes on her.

"So, Locke, what brings you to Oro? If you are such a good mercenary, I assume you have contributed to the stock?" A few of the other gentlemen in the room perked up at mention of the trade stock.

Leith smiled and looked down at his plate. "Unfortunately, since the destruction of the Brunts and the death of Commander Hendrik, I have been out of work." Ravenna hummed, sliding a piece of pasta from her fork with her teeth. *He is an awfully good liar.*

"I am always in need of new mercenaries," Degare said. "Perhaps you and my Raven can work together to grow my stock of Embers."

Leith's eyes flashed, and he grinned at her across the table as he answered the king before she could get a word in. A piece of pasta fell from Ravenna's fork. "It would be my honor, Your Majesty." Ravenna's head was swimming with wine, and her irritation was beginning to become apparent on her face.

To Ravenna's surprise, Jara spoke up first. "What will your wife think of such a partnership?" *Wife?* Her eyes fell to the wedding ring on his finger. It was amongst many others of gold and silver.

"Jara," Degare threatened, but Leith waved him off as he

wiped his mouth with his napkin, and then he smiled at the witch.

"My wife knows of my soft spot for redheads." Leith gave Ravenna a passing glance as his eyes went back to Degare. Her cheeks heated.

"Yes, well, I think every man has a soft spot for redheads," Degare said, taking a swig from his glass and flexing his left hand. Leith flashed his teeth in a wicked grin, as if he had just gotten an answer he had been searching for.

"Typical man," Jara muttered.

"And what would that be, darling?" Degare asked. His lips were in a tight line as he waited for her to elaborate, but she did not. Degare laughed, surveying the many empty plates on the table and looking at the men who sat before him. "Well, now that everyone seems to have finished eating, I have selected my finest stock for you to begin your bids on." He rose from the table, ushering in the first Ember. A guard was prodding her back with a goad, and her gray eyes swept across the many faces in disgust before they paused on Ravenna.

Then, it was no longer her standing there, it was a man she had known not long ago–a man she had killed. Ravenna gulped down more wine, blinking the visions away. Leith was watching her curiously from across the table as he incessantly tapped his knife against the wood. He narrowed his eyes on her, and then he sent the metal knife clanking against the ceramic plate, mocking the sound of the golden bloodstone staff hitting the stone of the throne room floor.

*Zephaniah.* Leith's chin tilted in curiosity, and the room began spinning as Ravenna turned to the side and began silently heaving at the dinner table while everyone else looked toward Leith and the ruckus he had caused.

"My apologies," he said, still watching her. His eyes were the only ones on her. No one else noticed her amid her panic. And when Degare finally noticed Ravenna was about to vomit, his eyes bored into her, and then they darted to the wine glass that had been emptied too many times that evening. He leaned forward in his chair to whisper so that only she could hear.

"You are dismissed. Get out of my sight."

Ravenna rose from the table immediately and struggled toward the door before she collapsed. The wine and the once-forgotten memories intertwined in her head, and she could not bring herself to rise from the floor. Leith was at her side in an instant. Through the pounding in her ears, she could hear him addressing the king. "Allow me, Your Majesty. I am growing tired anyway, and I will make sure she returns to her room safely."

Degare rose from his chair and stepped toward her. "You have humiliated me in front of my guests," he hissed quietly from where he looked down at her. Ravenna shivered and tried to yank her arm from Leith's grasp, but he held tightly, hauling her up from the stone floor. Her king must have accepted the offer, because the enemy began shuttling her back to her room.

"Too much to drink, Ravenna?" he asked, and she could almost hear the smile on his lips.

"What are you doing?" she asked, regrettably using his shoulder as a prop for her head. His arm was wrapped tightly around her waist, and he basically carried her through the castle halls.

"Can I not be of service to my betrothed?" he asked. Ravenna rolled her eyes.

"You have a wife," she said, grabbing his hand and holding it up to show off his ring. He paused in the middle of the stone tunnel, turning her in her disoriented state to face him. Her eyes met his, and he suppressed a grin as he looked down at her.

"Jealous, are you? Don't worry, Ravenna of the Valley. You are my one and only. Your favorite blonde is my fake wife while I am here looking after *you*."

"Looking after me? Is that what you are doing?" Her words came out in a slur. She pulled away from him and used the wall to steady herself instead. He crossed his arms as she spoke. "You cannot monitor my every conversation with the king. I will tell him who you are, eventually."

"And do you know who I am, Ravenna?"

Her eyes watched him carefully.

"If Degare sends me to Ink Valley, you and your people will die. I will not hesitate."

"I think you will. Do not tell me you did not feel something when you saw your people's bones displayed on the wall tonight. When you drove the staff through that Ember? Do not tell me you will not feel tomorrow, when you are forced to kill the two who gave you life." Ravenna turned from him, hiding the hand that now grasped at her chest.

His voice grew nearer, his words becoming like a harsh wind against her neck. "Do not tell me that you do not have to chase memories away, still, of what you did to him. Of the lives those braids represent." His fingers found the braids as he taunted her, and Ravenna turned quickly, slamming him into the wall.

"There she is," he said smugly as his back collided with the stone. It was as if her agony were entertaining to him. She blinked the memories away, holding her forearm against his chest with all the force she had, though, he did not fight her. In her mind, she reached for that rope–the tether of the sire bond that kept her afloat amid her darkest memories.

*Forget your past. Forget your past. Forget your past.* But no matter how many times she repeated it, she could not. He kept smiling, as if he did not fear her. He was gambling with death.

"You should not trust me so easily," Ravenna hissed. She would kill him.

"I do not trust you, Ravenna." His forest green eyes flashed with the memories of her past betrayal–of the people he had implied he had lost because of her schemes with the witch guardians. Though he bore a sly smile, Ravenna recognized the anger that now wandered through his bones.

"What broke your trust first?" she asked. "Or did you ever trust me? Did you know that I was using you all along?" He said nothing, and that sly smile remained on his face. "But I suppose you were using me, too." His smile wavered then. "How many of your people did I kill, Leith?"

Leith gritted his teeth and turned on her, so it was her back against the wall. She breathed a sigh of relief, and she did not fight him as he dragged the dagger down her cheek softly enough that it did not break the skin.

*Kill me.*

They hovered there for a moment, but again, Leith's dagger did not move. "I betrayed you once, and you can try to tempt me back over the edge for your own schemes, but I see right through you, and I will betray you again and again," she promised. His eyes twitched in some kind of realization.

*What is this sudden weakness? Why am I allowing him to hold this dagger to my skin? Where is the prodding of the sire? Where is this sudden strength to fight coming from?*

Right now, she was fighting for death. Because she did not want to fight to live. She had fought long enough.

Ravenna taunted him, silently dreading the imminent push of the sire—the one she would not be able to resist. *Why is he still alive when he is threatening my life?*

"How many of your people did I kill?" she asked again. Leith pressed the dagger against the artery in her neck.

*Do it.*

His eyes flashed with rage, but he said nothing. She rolled her eyes as he dropped the dagger to his side, then pushed past him to stumble toward the door of her chambers.

# CHAPTER 47
# YOUR DOVE
## LEITH

Thirty-three. That was the number of lives she had inadvertently taken from his clan. How many more would she take before this was all over?

Leith slammed the door to his temporary chambers and was surprised to see Cove waiting up for him. He did not expect her to return. Her solemn humming immediately halted when she saw him.

"Well?" she asked. "How did it go?"

Leith rubbed a hand over his face as he sank into the chair behind the small oak desk. "I thought you would have fled the kingdom by now. After all, the Raven of Oro is onto you."

"And not dead, I assume?" she muttered.

"Unfortunately," he said, "she lives."

"Leith, you are going to have to do it sooner or later. She has only fallen further into Degare's talons since she has been sired, I really think–"

"She is practically begging me to kill her. She does not fight back, as if it is all a game for her. The Dove is still in there. She

351

is just afraid to come out and face what she has done. I only need to coax her out a little at a time."

Cove shook her head. "What do you want with her? What is your plan? She knows of your stance against Oro. She will tell Degare, and Ink Valley will suffer for it. Your little army will suffer for it."

"Can you imagine what we could accomplish, though, with her on our side?"

Cove watched him carefully. "And what side is it that you are on, Leith? That plan might have worked before. But now she is sired to Degare. Mark my words. She is going to cause more death, and if you do not take the opportunity to stop her now, that blood will be on your hands." Leith looked at the ceiling, and Cove continued, "I killed Prince Andreas, Leith. It was an accident, but the guilt I felt over it was immense. The only thing that helped ease that guilt, was when Elias assured me that his death prolonged many lives. I can only tell you the same about Ravenna. You would not think twice if she were anyone else."

Leith drummed his fingers on the desk. "Speaking of Prince Andreas of Edmaria, his father was present tonight."

"King Idris was here?" Cove sat up from where she lounged on the bed, blue eyes widening. "What if he brought Elias? What if he is going to kill him tomorrow?" Leith tilted his head, considering. It would make sense for the Edmarian King to seek his revenge on the Ember he believed to have stolen his son's life.

"The plan will work," Leith said. "I won't let that happen." Cove looked at him with disbelief, and he could not ignore the visible trembling of her hands.

"We'll be going against Ravenna," she said grimly. "There is no way. She killed Sinley."

Leith's jaw ticked. "It won't be a problem. We will be covert. We only need some distractions."

"You should have killed her, Leith," Cove said, shaking her head.

"I had three opportunities tonight. Three times my dagger was to her flesh. And all three times, I could not do it." *Why?*

Ravenna could ruin everything with the little knowledge she had of his mission, and yet he had let her walk free.

He had witnessed her in all her power tonight: raising the tides, quaking the mountains, summoning flame and wind...

"While I do not agree with your tactics of securing an army," Cove added, "I do not want to see it fail. They are like me, and they do not deserve to die because the man they were forced to serve could not bring himself to take out their biggest threat when he had the chance. Don't be a coward, Leith." He was surprised at her honesty, especially when she still needed his help in locating her husband. Edme had been telling him all the same things. If she were here, she would likely take the reins and kill Ravenna for him. That would make his life a lot easier.

Ravenna Zenevieva Ozanne was ruthless. She was death incarnate. The embodiment of darkness. He knew what he had to do—knew the only logical solution to all his problems. He had once thought Ravenna to be the solution to everything when she had waltzed into his valley that late spring day on her birthday, but now, killing her was the only way to stop this madness. *No.*

"Ravenna is still in there," he said slowly, rubbing a finger over his lips.

Cove rose to her feet in an instant, looking at him as if he had completely lost his mind. "You have lost your chance to utilize her as a weapon, Leith. Degare beat you to it. You must end her. Elias and I have no place in your rebellion after this is all said and done. Whatever happens with Ravenna. . .look, I'll keep my word and help you how I can, but once we get Elias back, he and I are leaving. Your rebellion to take Degare's place is not something we wish to be a part of. And Ravenna–she'll kill you all," she whispered angrily, glancing at the door as if the Raven of Oro might burst in at any moment.

"I do not think so," he tapped his knuckles on the desk, considering.

"What do you mean?" Cove prodded.

*You better make it fast,* Ravenna had said, *before I decide to fight back.* Ravenna's words moved through him as if on a gust of wind. *Was she implying that she could somehow resist the sire?*

"According to one of my spies, she has been sired to kill those who try to harm her, yet she did not defend herself when I had my dagger to her throat." He contemplated, and Cove shook her head with a worried grimace. *You can try to tempt me back over the edge for your own schemes,* Ravenna had said, *but I see right through you.* Leith smiled as he pinpointed the weakness in the fortress that was the Raven of Oro. "I think I can do it, Cove. I think I can coax our Dove back from the edge." Cove straightened from where she sat on the edge of the bed.

"*Your* dove, Leith. She is all yours, and this is on you. If she so much as takes one step toward Elias or the Embers in Ink Valley–"

Leith bit his cheek. He would not allow her to threaten his mission. "I'll kill her myself."

# CHAPTER 48
# EMPTY PROMISES
## JARA

"What you said at dinner, darling. . ." Degare said, as his hand trailed up her arm.

"Yes?" she asked, staring straight forward as they advanced toward his chambers.

"You know I only have eyes for you, right?"

Jara's cheeks heated, and she rolled her eyes at his sudden softness, the softness that only appeared when it was late, and his bed awaited them. "I think I shall sleep in my own chambers tonight, Your Majesty," she said.

Degare paused and chuckled. "Your Majesty?" Jara rarely called him by his title, even though he preferred it. Tonight, she was trying to keep their relationship strictly professional. She wanted to get back to her chambers and get a full night of rest before the early morning executions. Besides, lately, she could not stand to be in his presence. Tonight, Degare's new friend, Mr. Carrington, had reminded her of her worth and her power.

The king was lucky to have her, and he did not see it.

Tonight had been a reminder of why she was actively pursuing other options for her clan. Those options had been put on hold for years while she waited for Degare to keep his promises. Not anymore.

"I have plans for your witches," Degare said, as if reading her mind.

She stiffened but kept escorting him toward his chambers. "You are not trustworthy. I do not believe a word you say."

Degare frowned and caressed her hand. "Does the name Locke Carrington sound familiar to you, darling?" Jara paused for a moment, thinking about that new friend who had joined them at the dinner table–the Ember mercenary from the Brunts.

Degare unlocked his chamber door. "No. Should it?" she asked.

The king smiled slyly. "He is apparently not only talented in the Ember hunting business but also within the bloodstone market."

Jara's eyes whipped toward the king. *Bloodstone? What is he getting at?* The witches needed bloodstone to fuel their power.

"Mr. Carrington is very wealthy. It is he who provides the bloodstone each year to the little Gauntlet they run in the Brunts. He has a heap of it hidden somewhere. For what, is what I would like to know. My Raven is going to find the location of that bloodstone, and when she does, I will provide it to you." Jara swallowed, and Degare gestured for her to join him in his chambers.

"I'll believe it when it is in my hands," she muttered, following him through the door.

# CHAPTER 49

# ROOFTOP REST

## SABRINE

Sabrine was surprised when the prince did not complain about another night without a pillow to rest his pretty little head on. Tonight, she led the way through an alley where she had spotted a ladder before the ball. Here, beneath a crate, they had concealed their sacks and transferred anything of value to their pockets or to the money sack tied to her leg. They collected their cloth sacks and climbed to the rooftop after the ball, her feet getting wrapped in the thick fabric of her queenly attire as she ascended. She huffed and yanked the skirts above her ankles as she heaved her body over the roof's edge.

"How much does this gown weigh?" she muttered as she straightened up and peered out over the streets of Oro, toward the Ember prison. Just as she had hoped, this rooftop had a clear view. She breathed a sigh of relief. There had been no sign of the twins so far, but the Despiri soldier at the ball had claimed there would be twenty-two Embers with the gift of healing for sale. They would be at the trades in the morning.

They had to be. And if they were not. . .well, they were in that prison.

She was biting her nails, kneeling at the roof's edge next to a crate of straw, envisioning the inside of the prison when Merrick spoke. "Someone owns this rooftop. We could be arrested or killed for trespassing."

"We'll be long gone by daybreak," she said, watching the prison guards pace the perimeter of the prison in the distance. She could tell a large part of it was underground, and she guessed they could hold thousands of Embers inside. The walls were made of thick stone, and embedded in that stone, were tendrils of red that caught the firelight. "Is your father in the bloodstone business too, Prince?" Sabrine asked, watching how the usually dull stone glimmered in the glow of the torches. She remembered the conversation she had heard at the markets in Edmaria, and how the mines in his territory were reopening.

Merrick came to sit beside her, rubbing his eyes. He followed her gaze to the prison walls, and his eyes narrowed on the stone. "Degare has just about every kingdom funneling the stone into Oro from their mines. He pays well, and my father is a greedy man."

Sabrine hummed in agreement. His father had sold her parents into the trades, and now he was doing the same to the twins. But his son, the prince, was there beside her, playing rebel to his own kingdom. Whether or not Merrick was doing this for her, or for himself—for that redemption he craved—she could admit one truth. "You are not like him," she said after a long moment. "Not entirely."

Merrick tilted his chin to look at her, and his eyebrows creased in some sort of relief. He said nothing, only bit his lip and turned back toward the windowless prison. In the silence,

Sabrine clutched her money sack through her skirts, feeling the weight of the coin that would deliver her siblings back to her. Merrick did not know she had taken more from the country home while his back was turned, and she intended to keep it that way. He was not like his father, he was softer, but she would not allow herself to trust him. It had always been her, fighting for herself, and when she no longer needed him, it would be her on her own again. Her and the twins, and no one would stand in the way of that. She had failed them once, and she would never fail them again.

A tear left a streak of moisture down her cheek, and she hesitated to wipe it in fear the prince would see. After the trades, if Merrick was not able to find them voyage across the sea to Eswen or Remont, she would find this *Adullam* the Ember at the docks had spoken of. She would find them refuge, even if it was the last thing she did.

*If they do not die tomorrow.*

She hopped to her feet and turned to rummage through her sack, hoping to mask the sounds of her sudden, panicked gasps. Her breath clouded in the chilly air in front of her.

*They could die tomorrow. Someone could bid higher than you. What will you do then?*

"Sabrine?" Merrick's voice was close behind her.

"We should change our clothes tonight," she said over her shoulder, prompting him to leave her alone. "We need to be at the trades before dawn, and we need to keep up the ruse. You're a duke, I'm a duchess. We must look the part." She breathed, forcing herself to talk slower. "We cannot wear the same clothing twice. It might draw suspicion."

"You're right," he said calmly, holding his palms down low, as if trying to calm a spooked horse. She scrunched her brows at him. *Panicking.* She was panicking. She pointed her chin high and crossed her arms, backing up a step. He paused, watching her collect herself on her own. *I do not need your help.*

She handed him his sack of clothing, hoping he would forget her moment of weakness. Luckily, the fabric of her blue gown had not wrinkled, and she was able to slip into it quickly under the cover of night. Merrick kept his back to her as she dressed, and when she was finished, she found him making a bed of straw and clothing.

"I'll take the first watch," he said gently, motioning for her to take the makeshift bed. She looked at his tired eyes. They were a rich brown in the Edmarian sunlight, but in the shadows of the night, they were nearly black. Still, she could see the dark circles beneath them and the way his eyelids drooped involuntarily.

"I think we'll be safe up here," she said. He needed the sleep just as much as she did, and they had to be up and moving in less than six hours. If all went well and they escaped with the twins, tomorrow would be a big day of traveling.

He looked around. The streets were still loud with celebration in an abominable anticipation for the trades, and people were snuffing out the torches around the kingdom square, welcoming darkness. The Black Temple was crowded with masses of people, probably begging the witch goddesses for their chance at an Ember in the morning.

Banners whipped in the wind, and groups of drunken Despiri soldiers tripped through the streets, but no one looked up. Not toward the hazy stars or the moons, and not toward the rooftop where they stood. Sabrine melted into the straw bed, hoping to chase her anxieties away with a good night's rest.

She closed her eyes but felt Merrick hovering beside her for a long moment before he took his sack and sauntered off to change his clothes in preparation for morning. When he returned, covered from neck to toe in a navy suit with gold threading, he slowly sank to the rooftop beside her and propped himself against the crate where he'd gotten the straw from. He did not look at her, just sat with his arms extended across his bent knees, twiddling with a piece of straw as he peered out into the night. Only when she finally saw his head droop in sleep, did she allow herself to drift off. On that rooftop, the two of them nestled beneath the foggy skies of navy and gray, they rested until morning.

# CHAPTER 50
# DAYBREAK
## RAVENNA

The ropes of the gallows swayed behind the guillotine as a few dozen Embers were being marched up onto the wooden platforms in the deep blue of the early morning. Not to be hung, but to be elevated above the sea of people so the buyers may see and cast their bids.

Ravenna had passed out after the king's dinner and her conversation with Leith, and she imagined Degare would be in quite the mood this morning after the way she had humiliated him last night. Her stomach turned as she watched the crowd thicken in the dark kingdom square below her window.

Though the dawn had not yet come, the streets were already crowding, and the bright red of Oro's uniforms stood out like blood against the subtle gray and brown tones of the peasants' clothing. Soon, the red of the uniforms would be accompanied by the red that would pour from Gerrin and Willa Ozanne, who were to be beheaded at dawn. Just as the wealthier men and women—the ones who would likely be

362

bidding in the afternoon's Ember Trades–began to fill the square in their brightly colored dresses and luxurious fabrics and hats, her sire entered her chambers without so much as a knock.

"Your Majesty," she said, bowing her head and turning twice, allowing him to examine the outfit he had chosen for her to wear today. His cold eyes stayed glued to the brand between her shoulder blades as she spun, and she refrained from backing away.

"Very lovely," he said, his cruel voice singing to her. The bronze gown was shiny and made of an expensive, silky fabric that she could admit was quite flattering on her curves, now that she had gained some of her strength back. Degare held the bloodstone staff in his left hand and offered her his other arm. She pulled her bronze-feathered shawl over the sleeveless gown and slipped her arm into his, walking as one to the executions.

"Do as I say today, and put on a good show," he said as they walked down the many steps to the ground floor. She did not know why he always felt the need to reiterate that she must obey him, as if she had a choice. "You will be watching the executions. Not performing them," he said.

Ravenna stopped in her tracks. "Have I done something to compromise our trust?"

"Your act at dinner was enough to make me question whether you can handle the pressure. If you cannot contain yourself in front of a dozen people, why should I trust you to maintain my reputation in front of hundreds?"

Ravenna dipped her chin. "Of course, Your Majesty."

"One good thing came of your drunken idiocy," Degare said.

"And what is that, Your Majesty?" Ravenna asked, swallowing her own humiliation.

"You are forming a relationship with Locke Carrington, just as I planned."

Ravenna stiffened. "What do you mean?"

"He has something I want. You are going to get it for me."

"And what would that be?" Ravenna asked slowly.

"Bloodstone, Ravenna. He is a collector of it." Ravenna narrowed her eyes. Leith did run the Gauntlet every year, but what did the king believe about him? "You are to charm him. I can see that you dislike him, but you will not kill him until you have found what I want." *Was her distaste for the Ink Blood leader so obvious?* "I expect you to use him. He is not only a collector of bloodstone but a fine Ember mercenary. As we discussed at dinner, I may have you working together to bring in more Embers. Perhaps you can learn a thing or two from him."

Ravenna began to object. "Your Majesty, I–"

"That is enough, Ravenna. You'll do as I say."

When the castle doors opened to the square and revealed Ravenna and the king standing arm in arm, the weapon and her master, the crowd cheered. The executions would kick off the Ember Trade, and each of the Embers that stared at her with hollow eyes would be killed on this very street, gifts taken by one of the many despicable people who cheered for her. All she could look at, though, were the emaciated faces of the Embers. *Some were only children.* Had word traveled through the prison of who Ravenna was? That in another life, she might have been their Ember Queen? A queen who protected them against such atrocities. A queen who had been chosen by the Father of Lights, whose born duty had been to protect her people?

The Light had made a mistake in choosing her for such things. She wondered what he thought of her now–killing His people–the very people she was supposedly born to protect. What did He think of her as she stood by while the two parents who risked everything to protect her, to ensure she lived out that fate, were beheaded? She swallowed, forcing herself to look away from the many grieving eyes that watched her. They were eyes that grieved hope–as she often did.

Ravenna held tightly to that tether within, keeping her head above the waters of grief.

"We could have been utilizing the coliseum for this. Let us not forget that you destroyed it," Degare muttered as his eyes scanned the massive crowd. Ravenna's chest tightened, and for once, the remorse she felt was for her king, for the trouble she had caused him. As Degare took his seat on the throne that had been placed with a perfect view of the guillotine, Ravenna stood at his right, Jara at his left, awaiting the ex-royals. Jio was approaching through the mass of people, making his way toward Degare with a smug smile on his face.

"Your Majesty," he said in greeting. "I finished my final selections of your newest shipment this morning. I think you'll be pleased."

"Oh?" Degare said. Ravenna turned to watch the exchange between her king and his minion, who had apparently been allowed to make his own selections of stock for the trade.

Perhaps the king had gotten too busy with the festivities to select the stock from the most recent shipments of Embers.

Jio nodded, his sleek, black hair shifted slightly and his cruel smile reached his upturned eyes. He pointed to a cage of Embers who had been separated from the rest of the stock. "Those ones right there have the potential to bring you much coin. I was able to read the minds and find out the gifts of all the Embers except those. Those ones are mysteries, and your audience loves to gamble with their gold."

Degare chuckled. "I like the way you think."

Jio smirked and crossed his arms. "And, as always, the ones whose gifts I was able to learn, I've documented and chained with the rest of the stock."

"Very good," Degare said as he looked upon his stock of hundreds.

The blue hour was fading into the day, and the crowds were chipper with the exception of a select few, solemn faces. Ravenna watched those particular faces carefully, recognizing their inability to celebrate with her king as a potential threat. The square was still packed with vendors, some of whom were climbing to stand on their tables and shout, announcing the sale of their plethora of goods. Ravenna took note of the finely dressed woman of one of the eastern kingdoms of the continent. She paced up and down the line of vendors with a man trailing closely behind her. The woman paid him no mind, but together they stopped to view the hundreds of shackled Embers that now surrounded the platform. The crowd was anxiously waiting for the break of dawn, when Gerrin and Willa would be killed at first light.

At last, the doors opened, and their limp bodies were dragged out, barely breathing. Strangely, a breath caught in

Ravenna's throat, and she shifted her feet in unwanted angst. *You are the sire's completely. You do not feel. You let go of this past that makes you weak, remember?*

Degare muttered so quietly that only she could hear. "Remain still. Remain silent." She did. Degare had not taken her advice. He had tortured them one last time, to show the crowd just how much power he had over them. Everyone here had heard of their rule, and this was to symbolize the end of it, though, that end had come many years ago.

As her parents were dragged toward the guillotine, she stood still as stone. Her father's eyes were closed, and she found herself wishing for just a glance at that familiar green. The green that had raised her. *Stop. Let go.* Then, there was a flash of Willa's eyes, blue as the Crystal Sea. They had never dulled, not as hers had in the days she had been trapped here. They had not dulled in color, but unlike the painting in Ozanna, they had grown hollow and sad. *Do not dwell on it. Forget about it.* Ravenna blinked, and her eyes were the only part of her that moved.

Just beyond the Queen of Ozanna was Leith, watching Ravenna to see if she would break. In an involuntary shift of her gaze, their eyes met, and Leith tilted his head, coaxing her with unspoken words. Willa searched through the crowd, head hanging low as if she had no energy to move it. Willa's eyes wandered through the crowd until she found Ravenna standing there, unable to move. Unable to even mouth an apology. *Why do I care?* Ravenna wondered. *What is this sudden penitence I am feeling?*

Willa's eyes brightened as she laid them on Ravenna, and she used what must have been all her strength to move a hand toward her, to reach for her daughter one last time. With the subtle movement of her thin lips, the ex-queen mouthed something, something Ravenna could have sworn she had to have imagined.

As her mother's lips moved, all she saw were the same words that had once left Zephaniah's mouth. *Seven bloods.*

In the last few weeks tunneling into and embracing the darkness, Ravenna had almost forgotten those words that had given her hope in the early days of the sire. *There will come a time, when seven bloods from seven kingdoms will come together in the Light, and no weapon formed against them shall prosper. Not even you, Ravenna.*

Ravenna's eyes darted back to Leith, but he was gone, once again. Degare rose with the sun, bringing his hands high above the audience, and Ravenna's eyes settled on Willa. "Ladies and gentlemen, let these executions mark the death of all Light–of all hope their people have for Arresia. Arresia is mine!"

As one of the guards shoved Willa onto the guillotine and her body lay helpless across the wooden slats, the other guards began trying to wake Gerrin. He was so frail and thin, even thinner than he had been last night–if that were even possible. Two men from the audience brought forth buckets of water to douse and wake him with, and it worked, only for a moment, before Ravenna felt a silent wave of power leave her body and pursue her parents, sending them both into a deep sleep. Ravenna had not even known she possessed such a power, let alone the ability to wield it. She narrowed her gaze as she watched Willa's eyes fall shut, seemingly peaceful as she lay beneath the blade that would come down any minute. The crowd hissed, and Degare stood, urging the guards to wake them, but they could not be roused. Ravenna only stood, watching curiously. *Had I done that?*

As Degare turned his body toward her, surely about to command her to do something to progress the process of his executions, the stone began to quake underneath Ravenna's feet, and Degare fell backward into his throne. His right hand gripped the black velvet arm, and his eyes widened as complete pandemonium overtook his kingdom.

He leaned forward, attempting to rise from his throne. "Something is not right!" he shouted above the roaring of the people, steadying himself as the earth rebelled. "Do something!" With those words, Ravenna was released from her place at his side, and though the sire burned through her, she first swung a hand toward where Willa lay at the guillotine, beneath the blade that had just been shaken loose and was about to come down on her head. The power she had not yet mastered, one that commanded objects to do as her mind wished, saved the Queen of Ozanna from the descending blade. But when Ravenna glanced down to where her mother had just laid, and her father had been restrained, both were missing—nowhere to be found in the sea of defeated red-cloaked guards.

Someone was sabotaging the executions. *Someone had taken Gerrin and Willa. How had she missed it?* "Move!" Degare shoved her forward with a crack of the bloodstone staff into her back, urging her to find the culprits. As she moved mindlessly through the chaos, following the prodding of the sire at her heels, the ground continued shaking beneath her feet, and rock was falling all around her. She continued toward the guillotine, searching for any sign of suspicious activity, but amid the chaos of screaming and fleeing people, she had no luck.

*This is an attack on your kingdom,* the tether within her seemed to say.

She grabbed a gruff peasant woman by the shoulders, shaking her. "Did you see anyone? Where did they go?" The woman broke free of her grasp and ran south toward the kingdom gates, just as fire began plummeting from the sky. Flames stretched from the clouds to the ground, whipping wildly in every direction. Ravenna shielded her face against the sudden heat and turned, mind dizzy with the disarray of sounds and attacks of all sorts that plagued the entire kingdom.

Men, women, and children were fleeing in every direction, trampling anyone who stood in their way. The rain of fire was catching the market tents aflame, and Ravenna's eyes wandered right to the center of the square, where she expected to see the hundred Embers hunkered down, still chained to the gallows. But the Embers were gone, too.

She held up a hand, squinting against the sudden brightness of the day, and waited for her vision to stop tunneling. The flames were unrelenting, burning everything in their path. Catching the Despiri guards' uniforms on fire, forming a wall between herself and the king, as if they were being commanded by someone who was trying to separate her from her sire.

She peered over the flames at the king, debating whether to go back—*to protect him*—or to keep hunting whoever was doing this. But to protect him was her utmost responsibility, and she must put his safety before any other task. As she advanced toward him, the ground still shook with rage beneath her feet, causing her to lose balance. She tripped once, then with a mighty slam of her fist into the ground, she sent a shockwave of anger and darkness that shot up into the sky. She was up and running in an instant, fighting power she had not battled before. Many powers flowed through the streets of Oro, but there was one power in particular that she recognized. One power that shook the ground in the same way the earth had quaked in the Brunts months ago. . .

Ravenna knew who was doing this, and she would make him pay.

# CHAPTER 51
# WILLING THE WATERS
## COVE

C ove barged into the prisons in utter desperation, without a thought other than: *find Elias*. The metallic smell of blood wafted through the prison as she and the other rebels waded up to their ankles in the red waters she had accidentally reeled in from the sea. The strategy Leith had discussed with her and the others was unimportant in comparison to rescuing the man who had been willing to die for her.

The other rebels swiftly took out the two guards at the end of the hall where the cells began to line the tunnel walls, and Cove collected a ring of keys before abandoning the rebels to look for Elias.

"Hey! What are you doing?" one of the rebels called after her. She ignored him, allowing the tether in her soul to pull her down the hall. She bypassed a dozen cells, only looking inside long enough to survey each waning face, to see the relief and disappointment that washed over each one as she came and went.

*Elias,* she sent down the bond. *I am coming.*

As she rounded the corner to the last row of cells, she tripped over the uneven ground and fell onto her knees, catching herself with her hands. The ring of keys fell into the dark water. *No. No. No.* She desperately felt through the red, running her hands across the stone until the metal of the keys met her hands. She breathed a sigh of relief and climbed to her feet, then looked to the side where an Ember child stood, eyes wide, every bone in their body visible as they shook in fear. She lifted her bloody hands to the torch light, and stopped herself from continuing through the final cells. *Help them.* She fidgeted with the ring of keys, shoving three of them into the lock until she found the right one.

The door creaked open and she backed away, continuing down the hall as the child slipped out from behind the bars. *Elias. Elias. Elias.*

There was a force within these walls that was resistant to her power, and the deeper into the prison she traveled, the weaker her power became. She recognized the strange feeling as some sort of a spell—an invisible barricade in her mind. As she looked upon the cells, her uncontrolled anguish swelled beneath her skin but could find no release. Her heart thundered in her chest, reminding her of his absence, of the unimaginable weight of missing him. She hit the wall at the end of the hall, gasping as she clutched her chest. She had been to every cell, and he was not here.

A rebel came barreling around the corner. "The waters alerted the guards. They know we are here. We have to go." She barely heard him over the sound of her panicked breaths. She nodded, mindlessly moving forward through the water she had accidentally coaxed in. A wrinkled hand reached out for her from the bars, and with it, she felt the emotions of every Ember in the prison. Of every one she had not helped—of every life she had not saved.

"Wait," she choked out between gasps as she looked upon the elderly woman and the small crowd of Embers in the cell behind her. Cove fumbled with the keys, hands shaking as she tried to insert it into the lock.

*He is not here. He is not here. He is not here.*

Thirteen days ago, she had searched this same prison after convincing Sinley to help her. The Raven had killed him for it. Now, she stood here again, searching and praying, and nothing had come of it. Sinley had died for nothing.

"We have to go," the rebel said, dragging her away. The key stayed in the lock, and the woman looked to her for only a moment before she reached for it herself and twisted it open. The prison spun around Cove as she was pulled through the water by one of Leith's men, past every Ember she had overlooked in her search for Elias. "I-I have to go back, I–"

She planted her feet as the daylight hit her. The kingdom was total chaos around her, and the anguish that came from her own soul as she was pulled out of the prison was enough to raise the tides again.

"Cove." Someone shook her shoulders. "Control it." *Leith.* His eyes were wild as he looked between her and the rising sea.

He looked to the rebel man beside her. "How many freed?" Leith asked sharply as he looked between the two of them.

"Only two hundred," the rebel said. Only two hundred freed, because she had been too caught up in her search for her husband—her *soulbound*. Leith winced as he looked over Cove's shoulder at the prison and then back to her. "You need to get to the tunnels," he said. She stared blankly at him.

*He is not here. He is not here.*

"He is not here," she said aloud, though it poured out as a whisper. Leith looked behind him at the mass chaos behind and at the Black Sea that was now creeping further onto land too quickly. He breathed tightly, and with a quick motion, he pulled her cloak over her head and scooped her into the crook of his shoulder, guiding her through the streets of the kingdom.

She felt the power leaving her body, but it no longer manifested in the seas. The tide was rising in its natural rhythm once again.

*Just leave me to die,* she wanted to say, because that soulbond within her bore a heavier silence than ever. But she knew he would not, because for this next part of the plan to succeed, he needed her. Her mouth became dry as Leith tugged the collar of his tunic up to cover his shadowmarks. To any onlookers, they were just another couple of peasants in their gray-and-brown linen attire, trying to flee the mysterious earthquakes and rain of fire. It had all gone so wrong. Elias had to be here. Because if he wasn't, Cove didn't know where to begin looking for him.

Leith led her through the streets, the ground obeying his every command, allowing them a stable path to walk on. The fog was settling over Oro once more, and as they grew nearer to the escape route, Leith checked their surroundings to make sure no one was watching. South of the Library of Oro that bordered the Black Sea, was a cave entrance only revealed for an hour a day at the lowest tide. Soon, the sea would swallow it up. Cove was grateful to see it still visible after she had lost control and coaxed the tides on the north side of the kingdom up onto the shore and into the prisons. The prisons where Elias was not.

Leith guided her forward into the tunnel. She was silent. *Heartbroken.*

"He is not here," she said again. Leith frowned, this time watching the nearing red tide that would soon flood the tunnel full of Embers and his spies.

"Cove, we will find him. Can you do this?" She knew he needed her to hold the waters back until the tunnels were cleared, but where would she find the strength?

Leith's Volcanian general appeared out of the darkness of the tunnel, dressed in dark leathers and wrapped in white flame. She surveyed the bottom of their trousers stained with blood. "What is going on? We need to move, now," she said vehemently.

Leith answered for Cove. "Elias is not here." He guided her toward Edme, pushing her further into the tunnel. Edme stared at her dumbfoundedly for a moment and then looked to Leith.

"You're staying, aren't you?" she asked in annoyance. Cove turned slowly to Leith, waiting for his answer.

"I'll be right behind you," he said. "Just get the king and queen and the Embers back to Ink Valley." He looked to Cove, whose heart had seemed to still in her chest. He grasped her arm gently, shaking sense into her as he spoke.

"I won't be here to help. You can do this–these Embers need you to do this. Can you do this?" He looked to the rising tide, which was now only a few feet from the entrance to the tunnel. Cove looked to Edme, whose wildfire glare sent fear into her–the two of them fire and water. Cove nodded to

Leith. She could keep the tide at bay, and he would get his Ember army–as long as he helped her find Elias.

She would help to deliver these Embers to safety, at least to somewhere safer than Oro, and then she would scour Arresia for Elias, until the very last breath faded from her lungs. And the Ink Blood leader would help her because he claimed to be a man of his word, and though he was guarded, some part of her, through her power of being able to *feel*, could tell that he was genuine in at least that much of his promise. Leith dropped his hand from Cove's arm and turned to Edme, who was lighting the tunnel with faint flames that lined the walls.

"Edme, if I do not return, my armies are yours to command."

Edme nodded, clenching her fist once against her chest, then extending her fingers.

With that, Leith turned to exit the tunnel and enter back into the land of Oro, where the king's Raven would be awaiting him.

# CHAPTER 52
## IN THE MASSES
### SABRINE

Some of the streets were caving in, and the Prince of Edmaria's brown eyes were bulging as he relentlessly tugged Sabrine away from the kingdom square. "The twins!" she yelled, failing in her fight against his strength. Her feet struggled to keep up as they tumbled through puddles of red. In all the disarray, people slammed into her from the side, threatening to separate her from the prince, but she did not care. She could only keep her head turned toward the gallows, where the Embers had been chained.

She couldn't see over the crowd of people–did not know how to get to the twins. *They have to be here. Where are they?* She and Merrick had searched the rows among rows of Embers just before dawn, and there had been no sign of them. *I won't give up.*

A mass of people was moving toward her, fleeing the fire that pursued them. Sabrine planted her feet as the buyers tore between her and the prince, temporarily freeing her arm from his grip. But he was quick, and before she could flee toward the

Embers, he turned to her, grasping at her arms. His fingers bruised her skin in worried haste. "Sabrine, something isn't right. Listen to me," he said, shaking her along with the uneven ground. "We need to get out of here." He looked over her shoulder, and his eyes reflected the flames that were hot at her back.

She tore away from him and took toward the cages that lined the gallows. The crowd was fleeing to the outskirts of the kingdom, and she was heading toward the chaos in the middle, where the king's weapon was likely being deployed.

"Neah!" she screamed, hoping for an answer among the booming cries of many. "Risley!" Her voice cracked. There was no response.

"Sabrine!" She whipped around toward Merrick, who was making his way through the crowd after her. They were both being jostled by the masses, and suddenly, Sabrine found herself knocked down to the stone below. Boots flew into her ribs as people fled the kingdom in haste. Her arms worked to protect her head as she was kicked and stepped on, as she was trampled beneath a hundred feet. There was no break, no chance for her to rise to her feet. The ground trembled beneath her; from the quakes or from the thundering stampede, she did not know. A heeled boot clashed with her cheekbone, and she winced, hugging herself tighter, sheltering her head.

"Move! Move!" the prince was yelling from afar. She kept her face to the ground and her body tucked, listening to the commotion that followed. Someone tripped over her, knocking the breath from her chest. *I am going to die,* she thought as she was crushed beneath the weight of the masses. But the prince's booming voice grew nearer until his hands were hauling her up. His lips parted as he looked upon her, gawking at the blood that now colored her skin.

As she stood stunned, most of her body weight being held by his arms, his catlike eyes searched the crowd for a way out. She blinked, wiped her cheek, and pulled him toward where she knew the Embers to be chained.

"Sabrine, wait," he called behind her, but this time he followed her with no physical hesitation. She had to get to Neah and Risley before they were gone forever.

"What is this?" She winced against the pain in her chest as she shouted over her shoulder and then lost her footing due to the throbbing of her leg. Her dress was turning red where she had suffered scrapes and a few minor puncture wounds.

"It is some sort of attack, I-I don't know," Merrick said, wincing as he took her around the waist and helped her toward the square. His sights jumped from her wounds to the tops of the gallows straight ahead.

"I just need to see them, I just need to know if they're here, I–" She stopped dead in her tracks, and Merrick halted next to her as they peered into the completely vacant Ember cages. Not a single Ember was left in the square. They were all gone.

The earthquake raged beneath their feet, and a wall of flame burst up from the ground just a few feet in front of her.

"Sabrine, let's go!" he called to her, coaxing her backward. She fell into him, and he kept her upright as they fled.

"They're not here," she said in realization, stopping. She turned in a slow circle, scanning the scene around her. Her hands shook as they found their way to her cheeks. She was too hot. She could not breathe. "Where did they take them?" Her voice cracked beneath the weight of defeat. "They must have taken them somewhere to keep them alive–" Merrick tugged on her arm again, and she blinked up at him, not caring to hide the tears that now slid down her face. He winced and pulled her into him, shielding her against the loud crowd of chaos that was now shuttling them toward the kingdom gates.

*I did everything to get here in time, and I still failed them.*

"I don't understand," she whispered amid the destruction.

The prince held her in the crook of his arm, guiding her through the mob of people. He spoke into her hair as they were elbowed and prodded like cattle toward the rusty iron gates of the kingdom. "This is an act of war. An attack," Merrick said. "Sabrine, someone is taking the Embers."

# CHAPTER 53
# HE LOVES ME NOT
## JARA

The kingdom was crumbling, and Degare was only worried about his Raven. Jara screamed for him to follow her, to get out of the stampede of people and find safety away from the skies of fire, but he only stood against the fire wall, watching a plume of darkness rise above his beloved weapon and shoot into the skies in an attempt to darken the falling flames. Jara did not know where to take him to get him out of imminent danger. The castle seemed to be standing strong, but it was blocked by a wall of fire.

Degare was a weak man, and Jara's dark magic would not help them here. No spell could stand against this severe of an attack. This was the start of a war. There had been an entire rebellion in the works, and she had been too caught up in trying to earn Degare's love to care. She had even spent the night in his chambers last night, listening to his breath in her ear. When morning came, he had waltzed himself to Ravenna's chambers, excited to have her on his arm as a trophy among today's crowds. Celeste could not secure the alliance with the

Edmarian Lord soon enough. But for now, Jara would maintain her position here, alongside the king of the most powerful kingdom in Arresia, allowing him to keep her weapon in practice until she was ready to claim it for her own.

"Degare, we must get you out of the streets!" He waved her off, eyes glued to the kingdom square where Ravenna had encased herself in her own burning flames and was accelerating toward them. Jara made eye contact with her, searching for answers in her disgruntled face.

"Do you know who it was?" Jara asked, noticing the empty gallows where a hundred Embers should have been awaiting their meetings with the bloodstone staff, which Degare still gripped tightly in his hand.

Ravenna shook her head, examining the king for any sign of injury. Jara stepped in between them. "We need to get him away from here," she said sternly. Ravenna turned her head and stared at her, as if to say *do you believe me a fool?*

Rock cracked under their feet, and Ravenna grabbed Degare's arm, guiding him toward the Ember Prison. Jara stumbled behind them across the quaking ground in her heels. She paused long enough to tear them from her feet and ran to catch up, looking back only once to see the entirety of the gallows breaking apart and crumbling to pieces on the ground.

When they reached the prison, the quaking of the ground had settled. Ravenna ushered both inside and turned to leave without so much as a word.

"Where are you going?" Jara demanded, looking down to the disgusting prison floor where her bare feet stood in an inch of peculiar, bloody water.

Ravenna looked to Degare, and his face was seething with anger. He answered Jara for her, "To kill them all."

Ravenna nodded, then looked at Jara before speaking again. "If they took the Embers from the square, they want them alive. They won't bring the walls of the prison down on top of the thousands of gifted prisoners. Stay here."

"And if they ambush us, trying to steal more of our stock?" Jara questioned her further.

Ravenna looked to the frazzled prison guards behind the king. "They've already been here," she said with a shrug. "Hitting the prison first while we were all distracted with the executions and the trade was a smart move. I would have done the same." At Ravenna's words, the king spun around to demand answers from the guards, and they bowed in haste.

*Has the prison already been infiltrated?* Jara looked around, searching the empty cells.

"Your Majesty." The guards acknowledged him. Jara stepped up behind the king, placing a comforting hand on his arm. He shook off her touch.

"How many freed?" he demanded. The two guards fell to their knees before him as Jara and Ravenna watched.

They kneeled there in the water, stuttering together in incompetence.

"T-two hundred." Degare swayed with rage, bracing a hand on the stone wall to his left. In an instant, his bloodstone staff slammed into one of the guard's temples, and he fell sideways into the murky flooding. Ravenna left to seek revenge, and Jara was now left with her angry king.

Ravenna returned hours later.

Jara and Degare had sat in silence in the reek of the prison, awaiting her return with a head in a bag, or at least some information on who had led this attack. But Ravenna returned empty-handed, and Degare seethed the entire walk back to the castle. They came to Jara's chambers first, and Degare did not so much as look at her before she turned to open the wooden door to her chambers, revealing a ransacked mess. She stopped in her tracks.

"What in shadows?" she said, loudly enough that Ravenna and the king closed in behind her, peering into her room.

Papers upon papers were spread among the floor, ripped and crumpled, as if destroyed in an angry search. For what, though? Ravenna pushed past her, entering before Jara even had the chance to move from the doorway. She looked to the bookshelves which had once been full. Spell books had once lined the shelves and were now piled on the floor in a mess, some torn with wrinkled pages.

Ravenna walked over to the empty pedestal, which had held Jara's most cherished spell book. The spell book her mother had left with the Delle Clan when she had left Jara as a small girl to go and infiltrate the Kingdom of Ozanna. Jara marched toward Ravenna where she stood.

"Jara, what have they taken," Degare said in utter coldness behind her. Not a question—a statement. Because he already suspected the answer. Jara's body went stiff.

"Y-Your Majesty," she stuttered. Searching the room for any sign of that spell book. *It is gone.*

"Jara," he said once more, demanding her answer.

"That spell book held the spell for the creation of the bloodstone staff," she said slowly. The king breathed heavily through gritted teeth before she added, "And for the binding spell between the two of you." She glanced at Ravenna and the king.

Ravenna halted. "You're telling me someone has taken not only my Embers and the Ozannes, but your spell book to create more bloodstone weapons and potentially more Despiri weapons, like me?" Ravenna asked. Jara tried to calm her shaking hands before looking at the king. He stalked toward her, his silhouette moving quickly among the deep purple hues of her room. He moved more swiftly than she had seen him move in ages before he slammed her into the wall.

"Is this what you're telling us?" he screamed in her face. The Raven did not even flinch behind him. Jara choked against his hand on her throat but nodded. It was possible, with the new power and strength Degare had shown in hosting these trades. . .well, it was only a matter of time before someone challenged his power.

"Who?" he demanded, releasing her. Jara shook her head, trying to hold back a cough. The king looked to Ravenna, whose face revealed no emotion.

"Find the Embers, and bring them back to me," was all he said, sending his Raven back out into the night.

# CHAPTER 54
# ACCEPTANCE OF FAILURE
## SABRINE

"One room please," Merrick was saying to the innkeeper at the desk as he handed her a piece of silver. He glanced over his shoulder at Sabrine, who was leaning up against the post at the base of the stairwell. Sabrine shivered against the strange drafts in the inn, and she looked away from the prince, pretending to admire the large quilt of many purples that had been hung on display. Finally, they had a room to stay in, but they were supposed to have been leaving the kingdom with the twins in tow.

This inn was one of the few in the Kingdom of Oro which had not suffered much damage from the trades, even so, its rooms were nearly vacant. After the attack, most of the visitors were leaving the kingdom, wanting nothing to do with the curses that befell it. Merrick and Sabrine had hunkered down near the kingdom gates for a few hours, waiting for the rush of people to dwindle down. When it was safe and they no longer had to fight against the crowd, they had entered back through the gates and into the eerily quiet streets of Oro. She limped alongside him through the streets for about an hour as they searched for a place to stay with innkeepers who had not fled. Then, they had come upon this inn on the corner by the prisons.

Sabrine exhaled as Merrick collected the key from the tired woman and approached her at the stairs. No rooftop or alleyway tonight. There would be a bed for her to lay in, but she would not be getting any rest. Not when the twins were still missing.

"After you," Merrick said warily as he motioned her up the stairs. He did not dare offer her a hand, but she felt him hovering close behind.

She gathered her strength and lifted one aching leg after another until she had ascended to the second floor, where dust and bits of fallen stone had gathered on the rug. She remained silent as Merrick unlocked the third door on the left. The room was unusually quaint and comfortable for this kingdom. The stone walls and floors were, of course, black, but the shadows were contrasted with highlights of cream and lavender on the bedspread and in the painted vase on the white oak side table. Sheer curtains of light purple draped around the bed posts and pooled on the floor.

Sabrine's eye caught the wooden chair by the lone window, and she sauntered over and mindlessly sank into it. As the adrenaline melted away, her hands turned over and over in her lap. *They are not here. You promised to keep them safe, and you failed them. The twins are not here, and they are going to die.*

The streets outside the window were vacant, but Sabrine could see little hints of red amid the kingdom of shadow. Her body shook as she watched the world turn black without a word.

Merrick did not dare speak. If he did, she did not hear him over the sound of her thoughts and the intermittent clatter of her teeth. Her body was slowly coming out of shock, and with it, her injuries were made painfully known, but still, she did not move.

*The twins are not here. They will be dead before you find them.*

*Dead. Dead. Dead.*

*You're all alone now.*

The voice in her head haunted her, speaking nothing but the truth she had always feared.

When night had fallen, the prince lit a single candle on the desk beside her, and his hand rested on her shoulder. Beneath his hesitant touch, her body continued convulsing, and her shame kept her eyes fixed on the starless night outside. This kingdom truly was made of nightmares.

*You have to find them. Without you, they will be dead.*

"Let me help you." The prince's voice cut through her deepest thoughts. He stood defeated from where he hovered in the candlelight above her, warm light flickering across his face. His brown eyes were void of hope, and she knew hers were the same. *Because of you,* she thought. *Because of you, they will be dead.*

Though her thoughts told nothing but truth, something within her empathized with the guilt that he bore, and she allowed him to help her to the bed. As his hands worked to remove her sandals, she strained against the ache in her ribs and bent to remove them herself. Her body was bruised, and in some places, there was dried blood from the cuts and scrapes she had received in the stampede. The day she'd spent limping through the kingdom in her poorly-fitting sandals had rubbed the skin on her feet raw with blisters.

There was a knock at the door, and she did not bother looking at Merrick, who was now striding the few feet between the door and the bed to answer it. "Yes?" he said.

"The water you requested," the innkeeper said, offering him a small pitcher. *When had he requested water?* Sabrine must have been too consumed by her thoughts to notice. "This is all I can provide. We don't have much to spare, I–"

"This will do," the prince said, nodding his thanks as he took it into his hands. When the door had shut again, she heard the water being poured into a glass. She rubbed her feet, and while his back was turned, she raised the skirts of her dress to examine the wounds on her legs. Nothing too severe, but a massive bruise spread from her left thigh to the outside of her knee, and her right leg had suffered a deep scrape across the shin. "Here," Merrick said, extending a glass to her. "Drink."

Sabrine shook her head. "I'm fine."

"Drink," he said again, this time placing it against her palm and manually closing her fingers around the glass. *There is nothing you can do to help me,* she wanted to say. *You told me you would help get them back, and you have failed.* But the words stayed inside, and instead, she let the water he had offered soothe her dry throat.

She heard the sound of dripping as Merrick wrung a cloth above a small bowl. The smell of alcohol stung her nose. He readied to bring the wet rag to the open skin on her shin, but she let her skirts drop back to the floor and yanked the towel from his hand. She would tend to her own wounds. She winced as she cleaned every cut and scrape she could find and then scrubbed the dried blood from her arms and face. He watched her cautiously, as if she were a wounded animal who may bite in order to protect herself.

"We'll find them," he said gently as he sat next to her on the mattress. She scooted away from him and watched as he leaned against the wooden post at the end of the bed, breath hitching with the movement. His eyes stayed on her as she wiped the last of the blood from her face.

"I can tell you do not believe that," she said. "You said it yourself, someone else is collecting Embers. Perhaps we have been wasting our time here, when we should have been looking elsewhere. We have no clue where they could be, Prince. Accept the fact that you have failed in bringing them home to me."

Merrick looked to his hands and then to the wavering flame of the candle. Despite the dark circles beneath his eyes, he rose from the bed and took toward the desk, where he sat before an empty page and some ink. "Get some rest," was all he said.

# CHAPTER 55
# BLUE-HOUR HUNT
## RAVENNA

Against the blue hour, Ravenna saw no one. The streets of Oro were almost entirely empty, besides the guards, who had taken up new posts to confuse any attackers. Tonight, each of them wore black to better blend in with the darkness. They were on edge and stood with a stillness that made even Ravenna uneasy. Ravenna also bore black armor—the armor that had been crafted specifically for her. She was the embodiment of the *Raven*, clad in a breastplate of thin metal feathers resembling the birds, black as sin, that feasted on death.

Ravenna should have killed Leith when she had the chance. She should have exposed him and Cove to the king last night at dinner. If she had, perhaps they would not be in this predicament. The Ozannes were missing, and with the spell book stolen along with over three hundred Embers, a weapon more powerful than her could be made, causing Oro to lose its status. All that would be needed was bloodstone, which she knew Leith had been collecting for the last five years at each of the Gauntlets in the Brunts. And if what Degare suspected of him were true, Locke Carrington had a heap of it stowed away. With that much bloodstone and a spell to use it, *Oro could fall to the Ink Bloods.*

Perhaps Ravenna should turn back to Degare now and tell him the truth about his precious Locke Carrington. *No. I will not go to him until I have proof.*

She walked the streets, eyeing the shadows for any sign of peculiar movement. Against the dim light of the three waning crescents, she could see very little. How had Leith successfully freed hundreds of Embers and gotten them out of the kingdom without even an eye witness? The only way out was through the Valley of the Shadow, or by boat, and Ravenna had checked the docks earlier in the afternoon. There were no reports of suspicious activity aside from one poorly documented ship leaving late in the night during the time of the king's dinner the night before, before the stock had been taken.

The ship was likely a royal guest or a bidder that had not seen any Embers they were particularly interested in and had gone back to their homeland, luckily avoiding the chaos the next day had ushered in. Ravenna knelt to the ground, pushing some crumbled rock to the side. She searched further up the street, noting the way the stone had cracked and snaked in such a way that left a perfect path about twenty feet wide of unbroken stone–stone that had not been touched by the tremors of the ground.

She followed that path all the way to where the Black Sand started at the edge of the sea by the library, and with the lowering of the tide, she could see a cave entrance about a hundred feet away, along with some footprints in the sand that led in its direction. She would bet anything that the prints had led right into that tunnel before the tide had washed them away. A sly smile made its way onto her face. She had been here five weeks ago to bury the healer who had been a traitor to her kingdom.

Ravenna stepped forward, just as something large and dark as night shifted in her peripheral vision. Quickly, she ducked, avoiding a blow to her head by the witch guardian's protruding bone shards. She sent a bout of power into the guardian's torso, pushing it backward toward the tree line in the south. She peered into the distance, counting a group of at least five more of the monsters materializing in the Dead Wood behind it. They split off as they approached her, two of them with their eyes locked where she stood, and the other three heading into the cave. A low laugh escaped her chest. *I know exactly who you are tracking,* she thought to herself.

She surrounded herself in flame, remembering the witch guardian's hatred of light, and they fell back before she ended them with a swift wave of power to their exposed hearts.

She took a moment to catch her breath after the expelling of her power and then ran into the cave, chasing after the loud snarls and growls that seemed to grow further away each second. The cave entrance turned into a tunnel that burrowed through the ground. Despite their shoulders being as wide as the opening in some of the more narrow places, the guardians were moving quickly. She willed her legs to move faster. She would get to *Mr. Carrington* first. His death was hers.

The strange tunnel system was massive, weaving beneath the kingdom and toward the southern lands. As she traveled through, following the path with the most residual noise, she marked the walls with the scrape of her blade so she could find her way back to Oro. She must have run for over an hour before she finally exhausted herself, nearly collapsing many miles deep into the utter darkness of the incomprehensible underground system.

She would guess that by now, if this tunnel led to Ink Valley or anywhere close, that she was directly underneath the Dead Wood, judging by the dead winding roots of the trees that encased the tunnel. The guardians had quieted, and the only sign of them that remained were the giant claw marks and ruts in the dirt and stone as she advanced forward. Some parts of these tunnels opened into vast divots in the ground, remnants of old bloodstone mines, where Degare had once ordered Embers to labor with pickaxes for his beloved stone. Ironic, that the very thing that had once been the sole reason for Ember slavery had aided in their escape.

As Ravenna approached the third mining site, she noted a faint light. A glow of fire, like candlelight, illuminating the walls of the cavern. She moved forward slowly, realizing the witch guardians' tracks had stopped a half mile back. She narrowed her eyes at the opening in the tunnel and crept toward it until she could make out the silhouettes of hundreds of sleeping Embers amid the very mine their kind used to work. She stepped back out of view and took a deep inhale, pressing her body against the wall.

How would she get every single Ember out of this mine and back to Oro? Would they fight back? *Surely, after years of imprisonment, they would rather die than go back.* She glanced into the mine again, focusing on the many chains that splayed across the ground. They were still in spelled shackles, and therefore would not be able to use their gifts against her. She could turn them around and have them delivered back into the hands of her king by noon tomorrow.

She searched the mass of people, looking for the man she had followed into these tunnels, but he was nowhere to be found. In fact, Ravenna saw no sign of any leader among them, until the woman of pure wildfire was right before her.

Within a millisecond, a wall of bright white fire had spread across the entire opening where the tunnel met the mine, and Ravenna lost sight of the stock of Embers. She backed away, blinded by the sudden light, and was thrown into a memory of herself in the Dead Wood many months ago–when the witch guardians had attacked her, and a mysterious white flame had destroyed them all. The black-haired woman stood between her and the flames, approaching her with a gaze that promised death, and Ravenna found herself retreating until she backed into the exposed black heart of a witch guardian that was towering over her.

Before she could raise a hand in defense, she ducked, and wildfire shot from the rebel's hands and straight into the heart of the witch guardian. Then, again, into the bodies of the two others, which must have hidden in the other mine a while back. How had Ravenna not noticed they had been tracking her, instead of the other way around? She had grown too distracted, too caught up in the kill.

Ravenna studied the white flame that encased the woman but did not singe her clothes. The heat that poured from her and into the tunnel felt like what Ravenna imagined the inside of a volcano to be. "It was you," Ravenna realized. "That day in the Dead Wood, it was you who saved my life."

"And I regret it every day," the woman muttered. Ravenna stiffened, her own flames encasing her hands as she remembered what she had come to do. The rebel dropped her gaze to Ravenna's offensive palms and snarled.

*Find them and bring them back to me.*

The command whispered through Ravenna, sending her power reeling for an escape. She could not fight it.

"I told him he should have killed you when he had the chance," the woman shouted above the roaring of both of their flames. "But he ordered you left alive." As the flames swirled around her, Ravenna could see that her skin glowed with not only fire, but with lightmarks. Ravenna had never seen such vibrant markings that covered so much of the body before. She was covered in them. *How has this woman hidden herself from Degare's men all these years, Despiri and soldiers who search diligently in all territories for any like her? Where did she come from?* Her skin was a deep, rich brown, and her eyes nearly black under thick brows. Not only her skin, but the coarse texture of her hair and her facial structure suggested that she was not of these lands.

Ravenna held a palm out, sending a plume of shadows and darkness toward the rebel. She stood still, only smiling at Ravenna's attempt to send her into death. The smoky shadows retreated from the white light and flames that shielded the woman, crawling back inside of Ravenna's own chest. Ravenna tried again, this time sending them with more force. Once again, they withdrew into her.

"Light overcomes darkness, always," the woman said as she watched Ravenna struggle. Ravenna tried yet again, but her shadows remained dormant. The rebel's lip tugged upward before she sent a shot of pure white fire into Ravenna's core, throwing her backward a hundred feet. Ravenna began to stand back up, but her legs were suddenly unsteady. Flames licked at her feet, and she crawled backward. Ravenna tried to draw her sword, but the white flames began to creep up from the ground and snake around the hilt.

She looked back to the rebel, who stood fearless and confident in the power within her. *Is there truly such a power that can challenge me?* Ravenna finally rose, but she only took one step forward before another ball of bright flame hurdled toward her. She dodged it, refusing to break eye contact with the Ember until she had raised a hand and allowed herself to be swallowed up behind the wall of white flame that separated Ravenna from the mine.

Ravenna lunged after her, but the flame singed her fingertips and she recoiled. It began excelling toward her, filling the entire circumference of the tunnel so she had nowhere to go. She sent her shadows toward it one more time, and as they were absorbed, she groaned, turning on her heels.

It pursued her for hours, relentlessly weaving in and out of the tunnel behind her, forcing her away from the mine until she could see a hint of the deep blue of night. She turned toward the flame once more, willing sea water toward it now that the ocean was in reach. But as the water made contact, it evaporated into steam. Angered, the flames moved quickly toward her, and she bound toward the exit. The fire licked up the tunnel walls and at her heels as she leapt forward, until she had been spat out onto the sand of the Black Sea shore.

Ravenna sat at the edge of the tunnel in defeat and anger. Each time she tried to enter back into the Ember haven, a curious light that hovered at the edge of the tunnel would reach out to burn her. At least she knew where the Embers would find themselves in a couple days' time if they kept moving at the same pace. In Ink Valley, where she would catch the rebels off guard and end them all for her king.

But as she began walking back to the castle to report to her sire, and she thought of all the ways he would punish her for failing him tonight, a strange guilt began to creep inside her chest. It was one she had not felt for some time, since before she had been branded and had completely given in to the darkness. It was a feeling she had wished to cull from her mind because everything she did for her king brought remorse to her conscience. She had become darkness. *What am I doing, trying to deliver the Embers back to Degare?* She had once been in their shoes, and Degare had murdered her entire village to get to her. She had fallen so far into the darkness that she had served the monster without question once he had branded her two and a half weeks ago.

Ravenna stomped past the library and through the streets. *Why did the rebel woman from the tunnels save me from death by witch guardian those months ago in the Dead Wood?* She had even cauterized her wound. Poorly, but she had tried. Or perhaps that poor remedy was her way of obeying Leith's orders while still leaving a chance for death, since she seemed very unhappy with Leith's decision to keep Ravenna alive. Even after Ravenna's betrayal to his valley, using him for an alliance, and turning the witch guardians on his people, he had still ordered her left alive? *Why?*

Ravenna could hear the yells of the guards near her chambers, the ones that were always stationed right below her windows. At least once a week, the king's favored Despiri soldiers fought the witch guardians off, not allowing them near Ravenna where she slept in her bed a few stories above. And every time, Ravenna was surprised that there were still witch guardians to kill, and that their entire race had not yet gone extinct. It was as if they were regenerating day by day to find their most sought revenge.

Despite the day's attacks, Oro was still standing. None of the buildings had fallen completely, though, some had suffered many damages. Of course, the castle still stood strong amid the night. As she approached the entrance to the castle, she debated on helping the guards or on heading straight to Degare to tell him what she had discovered. She would have to return to him empty-handed, and she would be forced to tell him the truth about Locke Carrington and the rebellion he was planning in taking those Embers. The sire would not allow anything else, and there would be no avoiding this topic.

But she could delay the inevitable torture session that was to follow her failure. So, she headed toward the fight, but just as she turned to cut through an alley, there was a blade to her throat and a swift hand over her mouth.

"Your witch guardians have caused my people quite the trouble," Leith said against her cheek.

She closed her eyes and smiled against his calloused palm. He removed it from her mouth slowly. "My apologies," she said, not fighting the arms that bound her against him. "You've spared my life thus far, only to kill me now?" She gestured to the flash of metal at her neck, and he softened his grip on her, allowing her to turn and face him.

"I *could* kill you, if you'd like," he suggested. "In fact, I made a promise that I would, if you threatened my operation."

"I do not think you will," she countered, crossing her arms as she backed herself into a wall, showing that she was not scared of him. He walked with her, keeping the blade at her throat.

"And why is that?" He was growing flustered.

She studied him before answering. "Because even though I stabbed you in the Gauntlet, somehow, you caused an entire earthquake to ensure I got out of that city alive. Why?" He raised a brow as if to pretend she was a fool, but she knew better. Her eyes fell to the entanglement of shadowmarks on his neck. "Today, you caused an earthquake that saved Gerrin and Willa Ozanne."

"Are you not grateful that your parents still live?" he questioned her, as if he suspected she would care whether they lived or died.

"They hold no gifts. They are of no use to my king, nor will they be to your army."

"My Ember army respects the Ozannes, power or not. And I can assure you, they are not without worth to me." He watched her carefully. "What has he done to you that you have no regard for the atrocities you commit?" Her eyes fell for only a moment.

When she looked back at him, she was surprised to see that his hazel eyes held no malice, only distrust. He did not dare release the pressure he had on his blade. *You are a fool if you leave me alive,* she thought. *It is only because of the king's demands to leave you alive until I get that bloodstone that you stand here with this blade to my throat,* she wanted to say.

"Why did you let me live when I betrayed your people? Why did you not let the witch guardians kill me in the Dead Wood that night?" she spat in his face, provoking him—urging him to do it.

His eyes flashed, and he looked at her as if considering, then he plummeted a second blade, one she had not noticed he possessed, into her side. *Revenge.* His eyes flickered in satisfaction as he watched her. She felt a rush of strange, warm power travel through, wrapping and weaving itself into her own power, and she held back a cough. *He actually stabbed me.* The sire bond had her trying to defend herself, to send a lash of darkness toward him, but there was nothing. *Fire.* Nothing. *Water*–nothing. *Strength.* Her knees weakened. She tried to move him aside with her mind, as she had the blade of the guillotine earlier. He did not budge, he remained there, trapping her against the wall. *My power is gone.*

Before she had the chance to feel anything, whether that be relief or fear that she was without power, he spoke into her ear in a low, guttural voice before extracting the blade.

"Relax, sweetheart. It is only temporary. Looks like your dagger came in handy." He pulled back to smile at her as he tore its tip from her side, flashing the ruby-hilted, golden blade her mother had gifted her in the air. Ravenna grabbed at her open gash, which poured blood onto the stone below. *What was that blade meant for, that it could squelch one's power?* Leith glanced over his shoulder toward the street, where two witch guardians were now approaching the alley.

There was a glint of mischief in his eyes. "Perhaps tonight they will keep you busy while I flee," he said, and then he was gone, leaving her to fight the beasts with a stab wound, no power, and a sword she had not wielded for weeks.

# CHAPTER 56
# A NEW ARMY
## LEITH

Leith dusted his trousers as he traveled in the tunnels beneath the Dead Wood. Without remorse, he had left the Raven of Oro to fend for herself at night, letting the sounds of the witch guardians fill the space around him. With the first sound of the metal of her sword slicing into thick bone, he had smiled and taken off toward the tunnel entry to catch up to Edme and his newly claimed army.

The tunnels burrowed through the winding roots of the Dead Wood, but that had not been nearly as tedious a job as forming the mazes through the stone beneath the Kingdom of Oro without anyone growing suspicious of the trembling earth. The preexisting, long-abandoned mines had made his work simpler than it could have been. He had traveled all over the continent—Edmaria, Brinland, and Ozanna—in his search for bloodstone, but he had never completed a tunnel system of this size.

Leith exited the tunnels in the Dead Wood and picked up the pace, knowing he needed to get to Ink Valley and return to this very spot by late morning tomorrow. Thankfully, the tunnels cut his travel time down significantly.

A knowing smile crept across his face as he trailed the hundreds of footprints across the uneven ground until he saw the glow of white fire in the forest ahead. The Embers had only a few more miles before they would make it to his valley as his own.

He ran to catch up, not bothering to quiet his steps, and within a few moments, he was gazing at the splendor of his new army. His new people. A few of them turned with hollow eyes, recoiling in fear of the shadowmarks on his neck, but they could do nothing to defend themselves in the shackles. This army was weak, and they would need time to grow strong. He tugged his collar up and cut a path through the crowd as he did a rough headcount. The clanking of shackles echoed through the otherwise eerily silent forest.

*Three hundred and thirty-three.*

Ravenna had caused the deaths of thirty-three of his people, and he had avenged that by gaining three hundred more. *And by leaving her to fight alone in that alley,* he supposed. If he was to be haunted by the witch guardians, he would not let her off the hook so easily.

"You left her alive, didn't you?" Edme muttered without looking at him as he fell into step beside her.

"Good to see you too, General. I do expect her to make it through the night."

Edme looked to the stars that were beginning to peek out between the branches above them. "This is not a game, Leith. All of these people," she gestured to the army behind her, "they are all counting on you. If you want their allegiance, you need to show them they can trust you. How are you going to do that when you cannot bring yourself to end the biggest threat to their lives?"

"It is not so simple," he said. Edme's eyes fell to the marks on his neck, and she gritted her teeth.

"I do not like your plan." Her thick hair bounced on her shoulders as she walked.

"Really?" he asked. "I had not noticed. You are always free to go, if you wish." Leith only said the words because he knew she would not.

"Leith?" a clear voice said behind him. He turned to Cove, whose near-white hair was illuminated in the moonlight. "Am I? Free to go, that is? Elias is not here, and I–"

"I gave you my word," Leith said firmly. Cove bit her lip. He could not allow her to go.

Edme cut in before he had to give the answer. "You can trust him," the general said. But then she looked at the marks on his neck, shook her head, and added, "I think."

Leith's eyes rolled toward Edme in annoyance, but the answer must have been satisfactory because Cove nodded and fell behind a few steps, spinning her ring as she trailed them with the rest of the Embers toward Ink Valley.

"You better have a plan, Leith, because if you don't and Oro brings our ruin, it is all over and you know it."

"Cut me some slack. None of this was my first choice. I have a king to answer to, and you are not him."

They walked in silence the remaining miles to the valley. Dawn would not break for another two hours, and he was thankful for the cover of darkness. The footsteps of hundreds echoed around him, and he could not help the pride that swelled in his chest with each foot forward. The strength and growth of his clan continued. He had chosen this ground in

Ozanne, strategically placed between Adullam and Oro while still on fertile soil. His people did not suffer as the Vestelians had. They had a massive stock of food and warriors who were strong because he kept them well fed. As the gates of his valley became visible ahead, and the torches on the guard towers were lit, he smiled.

Two of his guards came out to greet them, and the horn sounded that would have Ink Valley preparing for its new visitors. "How many?" the guard asked as Edme came up to meet them, too.

"Just over three hundred," Leith said in a low voice as he looked proudly upon his new people. Edme crossed her arms. "Direct them to the healers. We need to get them strong. They need food and water. Try to keep families together in the tents. We need them to be compliant. They need to feel safe." Leith looked to the fields, where his cattle grazed, and to the others full of crops that would need to be harvested soon. With Ravenna breathing down Ink Valley's back, they'd need to gather the grain quickly in case they needed to flee. "I know it is two weeks early, but begin harvesting the fields and get the grain ready to transport," Leith ordered. Edme and the guards all nodded then split off toward the healers' cabins and the fields.

Leith was not surprised that Xan was the first to approach him when he made his way beyond the gates.

"Where is she?" he called. "What have you done?" His eyes were wide, searching the mass of Embers that flooded into Ink Valley behind Leith.

"Sorry, Chief, couldn't keep him contained," one of Leith's men called out to him as Xan tumbled forward, Tenille chasing closely behind with a gentle hand reaching for his arm. He shook her off, and his hands shoved Leith backwards.

"Relax, warrior. I left her alive," Leith grumbled, planting his feet. Tenille exhaled in relief and smoothed her linen dress beside Xan.

Unfortunately, Xan was not satisfied with that answer. "You *left* her?" he yelled. Off to the side, Leith could see Gerrin and Willa Ozanne being addressed by the healers of the valley, but their hollow eyes were fixed on Xan as they listened in on the conversation being had.

Leith let his head fall back on his shoulders. "Alive, I said. I had the opportunity to end her and I didn't. Now all of the valley is in danger. You're welcome." Leith tried to push past Xan to get to his hut. He needed to gather a few supplies before he headed back toward Oro, but Xan stood in his way, prohibiting him from advancing any further into his own valley. Leith looked to the side at the Ozannes who still studied them and rolled his shoulders. He was going to have to prove to Xan that he could be trusted with Ravenna, to an extent.

"Look," he said with a grimace. "You've got a lot of pent up anger. Why don't you start training with my men? You can have your sword back," Leith said warily, and Xan balked, standing a little straighter. Leith added, "But you're still under constant supervision. My men will not hesitate to kill you."

Tenille nudged Xan's arm and prompted him to nod in agreement, and slowly, he moved to the side so Leith could pass by. Leith took a breath and stepped forward, patting a hand on Xan's shoulder as he leaned into his ear, "I believe the King and Queen of Ozanna would like to have a word with you about their daughter."

# CHAPTER 57
# YOU CARE FOR HER
## XAN

Leith had abandoned Ravenna in Oro, but he had liberated her parents. Xan's mouth was dry as he looked to the side at the king and queen, who stared as if they recognized him. If he had failed anyone, it was them.

He felt Tenille watching him carefully now, watching his plethora of emotions simmer and wondering what his next move would be. "Xan, are you going to–"

"You should go help the healers," Xan said as he mindlessly wandered toward the Ozannes, who looked like mere ghosts of the portraits he had seen plastered throughout the castle. They were skin and bones, with hollow eyes and sunken cheeks. They had both old and fresh blood on their clothes, which looked worn and tattered. The healers could not get them to move, or speak, and they did not know where to begin with the mass of shackled Embers that were filing into the valley, each suffering with an extreme hunger and weakness of their own.

Vestele would never have had enough food to provide for this many, but Ink Valley was well advanced, and the ground was not cursed here. The food was plentiful, and for a moment, Xan thought that maybe Leith had given them a better life than what they had in Oro—even if they would be forced to fight in his armies.

Willa's eyes drifted beyond Xan, and Gerrin kissed her fingers one at a time in a gesture of comfort as she whispered the same words repeatedly. *Seven bloods, seven bloods, seven bloods.* Xan's brow furrowed, and he looked over his shoulder, toward where a blonde with near-white hair was ushering a few elderly Embers into the valley alongside Edme.

He almost turned around, seeing that the years of torture had put them out of their minds, but then Gerrin called out in a voice strong as stone.

"You protected her." Xan stopped, refusing to look up at the king whose daughter was now in the hands of another kingdom. "It was you in the woods with her when we came through Vestele. You care for her."

Xan looked up through teary eyes and closed the distance between them. Willa's attention darted back to him, and Gerrin held her steady. Xan saw Ravenna in their eyes—the resemblance was undeniable. Also, in Gerrin, he saw Ashreya's likeness. A knot formed in his throat as he fell to his knees. "I-I have failed you, Your Majesty, I am sorry. It was my duty to keep her safe, and I have failed you."

"Oh, child, you have not failed. Look around," the king gestured to the Embers, and Xan's eyes fell on Tenille, who was kneeling down to tend to a young boy. "You are doing something incredible here," Gerrin said.

Xan shook his head. *I have not done anything. I was unable to keep her safe.*

"Thank you for your service in helping our girl," Gerrin

said, smiling sadly at Willa, who still mindlessly whispered those two peculiar words.

"We have hope that she will be okay, that she will become the Dove, despite our mistakes in trying to hide her."

Xan shook his head, remembering the way Ravenna had so easily turned on Vestele. "May I ask where that hope comes from?" Xan asked, looking around. His voice came out more sarcastic than he meant it to. "Because there is none left in me." *How could there be?*

"From the prophecies," Gerrin said, watching the words that slipped from his queen's lips. "From the Father of Lights."

"The same prophecies you were once afraid of? The prophecies I have feared my entire life and that may claim her and make her into some sort of a weapon?"

Gerrin chuckled, and some light seemed to return behind his eyes. "You have misunderstood the Light, son. We were never afraid of the prophecies foretold in the scrolls. We were afraid that the darkness knew too much, and that Degare would be able to stop the prophecies from coming to pass. We were afraid of the measures he might take toward our Ravenna, our Dove, in trying to stop her from fulfilling them." Xan shifted on his knees, still kneeling before the Ozannes. Xan knew that Ashreya never wanted Ravenna to be the Dove. *But Gerrin and Willa had? That was the very reason they had protected her, so that she would still have the chance to bring Light to all of Arresia?* Xan realized then that Ashreya had betrayed their wishes, in a way, in keeping the truth from Ravenna.

"But it does not work that way," Gerrin continued. "What the Father has promised shall come to pass. We were wrong in our assumption that the darkness had grown stronger than the

Light. We were wrong to turn to the darkness to conceal Ravenna, but being outside of time, the Father of Lights knew that is what we would do."

"But if you hadn't, she would be dead."

Gerrin shook his head. "The Father of Lights is outside of time, and He sees all. He knew what we would do before we did it."

"So He wanted you to turn to darkness?"

"The prophecies are not forced to come to pass by the Father of Lights. They are based on what He knows will happen. We have free will, and He knew that we would choose wrong, yet He fights for us anyway."

Xan shook his head and rubbed a palm over his face. "But Ravenna works for the King of Oro now. She is no Dove–her wings are black as night."

Gerrin nodded slowly, and Willa's eyes drifted out to the sea of Embers around them. The King of Ozanna spoke again, "That is no problem for Him who brings Light to the darkness. It is only a matter of time before she will bear new wings, given to her by the Father himself. Ozanna will rise again. I assure you, son. This is the dawn of doves."

Xan was tired of everyone insisting Ravenna was still this Dove. He would not allow her to be made to fight these battles that were not her own. He would not allow her to stay a Raven, and he would not allow her to be made into a Dove. She was just *Venna,* and she did not deserve this life that had staked its claim on her.

Xan would take her far from here. Far from Leith's armies

and far from Oro. He would hide her away as Gerrin and Willa, Ashreya and himself, and all of Vestele had failed to do. He would make sure she did not have to fight–Ashreya never wanted that for her, and it was she to whom he had taken the oath.

Xan retrieved his sword from one of Leith's men who had been given instruction to return it, and without thanks, he went back to his hut and began packing his belongings. Dead or not, his oath to Ashreya still stood firm. He had built his life around it, and for Ravenna, there was nothing he would not do.

# CHAPTER 58

# NO LEADS

## DEGARE

"Ravenna!" Degare's shouts were of anger uncontrolled, and had he still possessed power in his veins, his temper would have fallen what was left of his kingdom. "Get me my Raven! Where is she?" he yelled. Jara tensed next to him, and he tapped his teeth together as he watched a few of his guards scurry out in a mass of chaos to find his weapon.

*Ravenna. Come to me now.* He plucked that tether between them repeatedly. It was nearly dawn, and still, she had not returned with any news on his missing Embers, the Ozannes, or the missing spell book. He could feel the tether pulsating with each of her breaths–he knew her to still be alive. *So where is she?*

Degare was irritable. The incessant groaning of the witch guardians had kept him awake most of the night, though, he would not have been able to sleep anyway, knowing the damage that had been done to his trade.

Someone had made him out to be a fool. First the blood

water, then the hail, and now the earthquakes. Degare's visitors were not going to believe this as some sort of coincidence. Oro was inarguably under attack, and his buyers were leaving. The ships that had not been sunk by the hail were disembarking, and his kingdom was emptying.

"The trades will go on," he said so all his men could hear. "Spread the word."

"When, Your Majesty?" one of the scrawny soldiers piped up. Timothy was his name. The man reminded him a little too much of Zephaniah Wilmore, who had always reminded him of himself, in a way. It was the sole reason Degare had let Zephaniah live when he had come into his kingdom—Degare had seen himself in those sad, gray eyes. Like Degare, Zephaniah was orphaned at fifteen and had no family and no home. Letting him live within the walls of this kingdom after his family's execution had been a mistake, but in the end, Zephaniah got what he deserved. And after all of it, Degare had acquired his Raven.

"Must I know when? You dare to question me?" Degare raged, standing from his throne. Timothy's hands quivered at his sides, and he backed up a step. Timothy, unlike Zephaniah, was a coward. Degare's jaw set in frustration.

"Your Majesty," Callum interrupted, stepping forward. "The people will want to know. They'll need to make sleeping arrangements and—"

Degare waved him off. "Tell the people we will have our trade in a week." Callum bit his lip. "What?" Degare yelled, and Timothy shuffled back into the mass of soldiers.

Callum took another step forward. "It is just. . .Your Majesty, one week is soon, and we do not even know the location of those Embers—"

"I have more Embers in the prison," Degare reasoned. The majority had been sent to work in the mines across Arresia, but he had purposely kept some easily accessible. "I shall use them."

"Degare," Jara warned beside him. He whipped his head toward her. "We barely have enough drinking water for our own people, and the best stock you had chosen for the trades is gone. If we offer the weak Embers that are left in the prison, your trades are going to be a disappointment to all who traveled here. Word will spread, and your trades will die out."

"And what do you suggest I do, witch? Are the trades not already a disappointment? Are my guests not already leaving and taking their gold with them? Are we not under attack? Am I to be uprooted from my throne by some imbecile who plans to do as I have done? We must move now, before another weapon is made!" Degare's rage ricocheted off the walls of the throne room, and his soldiers tensed as he rose from his throne.

Jara questioned, "And how do you suspect us to find this person, Degare? I have been searching for more than a month, since the water turned red. I have no leads, and neither does your beloved Raven."

"Well, that is not exactly true, Jara," Ravenna said proudly, waltzing into the throne room with her hand on a gaping wound in her side. Her hair was wild, and she looked as though she had taken a dip in the gray mud where the sea meets the shore. Her sword was covered in black blood, and her boots were tattered. Jara straightened, and Degare smiled at his weapon, who had surely come with news.

"Send me to Ink Valley," Ravenna said, holding her chin high. "And I will return with your Embers and your spell book."

# CHAPTER 59
# BIRD WATCHING
### LEITH

It was only a matter of time before the Raven of Oro would show up in Ink Valley. Her power would have returned within a few hours of him wounding her, and Leith could not risk the safety of his people. So, he had set off in the wee hours of the morning to meet her at the end of the tunnels, where he knew she would be far enough from his home that if she exploded into a cloud of power and destruction like she had in Vestele, she would not reach his valley. *Thirty-three*, he thought. *No more would she take from me.*

The late morning was cool with the autumn breeze, and the bare trees in the Dead Wood provided little shelter from the light drizzle of rain that fell upon his shoulders. He pulled his cloak up over his head and whistled to pass the time–joyful tunes that his late mother had taught him as a boy. He had prepared himself for the imminent fight with many blades for protection, but against her today. . .he was sure he would be using more drastic measures, since he had recently left her bleeding out in an alley with witch guardians stalking toward her. He would not have done it if he thought she could not handle it. He knew she would come out of that fight alive, and if he were also right about this, she would be arriving in the Dead Wood through the tunnels any moment. He waited in a treetop nearby, watching for that red hair to start catching raindrops as she made her way out of the darkness of the earth.

He only had to wait for an hour before she exited the shadows of the tunnels squinting, even against the gloominess of the day. He rolled his head back on his shoulders as he stalked her, preparing for the fight he was about to indulge in. As she advanced south toward where his people and the newly rescued Embers took shelter in his valley, he prepared to leap down. That was until he saw a hint of movement in the trees ahead.

Ravenna halted where she stood, seemingly caught off guard as much as Leith was to see the blond-haired man walking toward her.

*The idiot followed me here all the way from Ink Valley.*

"Xan?" Ravenna said slowly. He reached for her, and Leith held his breath. Ravenna backed away a step, fighting the shake in her hands. Xan did not take the hint found in her unsteadiness and kept creeping toward her. Leith shook his head from where he watched in the forest canopy.

"What are you doing here?" Ravenna asked cautiously, monitoring her surroundings while keeping distance between her and Xan.

Leith huffed a breath. "Fool," he muttered, watching Xan continue to approach the beast, unaware of her lack of control.

"Come with me, Ravenna," Xan pleaded. "It is safe to come with me. I can help you. We'll rebuild our clan, and you can be the shield-maiden." Ravenna's blood was boiling, and Leith felt the air around him fall stagnant. Leith bit his tongue as he watched Ravenna's keeper beg her to leave with him, as if she had not been too much for him to maintain before all this.

"Why don't you run back to Ink Valley?" she scorned, eyes flicking to the feathers tied at Xan's upper arm. "I secured that alliance for you without even having to marry him." Leith rolled his eyes. "You got what you wanted," she said, and Leith wondered what she meant.

"I never wanted an alliance with Ink Valley, and you know it. I only ever wanted you to be safe." A raspy, wicked laughter escaped from Ravenna's rosy lips. "Just come with me. I'll be whatever you need." Leith watched Ravenna closely.

"I am not going anywhere with you, Xan," she said, stepping forward. Flames formed at her fingertips. "I gave you the chance to flee once. I will not do it again." The anger in her voice was palpable. As Ravenna raised her palm, before she could kill Xan, Leith dropped from the treetops, landing right between them and sending a rumble through the ground. She was knocked off balance for a short moment before her eyes glinted with the challenge.

There was a hand on his shoulder–Xan–trying to push him aside. Leith kept his feet planted between the two of them, eyes fixed on Ravenna. "Have you lost your mind?" he said to Xan over his shoulder.

Ravenna was seething, power on the verge of an eruption.

"She won't hurt me," Xan said, trying to bypass Leith.

Leith scoffed, motioning to the Raven of Oro who stood before them, gathering all her power to smite them both. "Oh, really? You want to test that theory?" Her hair was tamed for once, pulled back with a dozen tiny braids that fed into a thick one. She wore black leathers and armor over her shoulders that resembled a raven's wings. Xan stayed behind him, sensibly deciding to back away. Leith lured her in with a twitch of his brow.

"Hello, *Little Dove.*"

"Why do you call me that?" she snapped, eyes flashing as if using all her might to hold back her power.

"I think you know why," he retorted. Because she was the Dove of Ozanna, the heir to the throne. Whether she had tried to forget that or not, she would become a Daughter of Light. It was by her parents' mistakes that she had been raised in shadow and had never known the day. She gritted her teeth, probably at the memories that Leith was bringing to the surface.

"How did you know? *You knew before I did.*" He smiled, remembering their first official meeting that had not involved a stabbing. When they had become engaged. He had called her by the name then, and he could tell it had thrown her. In those days, she had not yet known her heritage, but he had, and he had come to find her–only to discover she had never come into her gifts because she had never been told of the Light. Her destiny had been kept from her, and she had been hidden. Ashreya had chosen Ravenna's life over thousands of others.

"Many know of the prophecy, Ravenna. Even those who are not of the Light." He watched her closely.

"Enough with the prophecy. I am not the Dove. Find someone else. You wanted me for my power so you could bring your precious Ink Bloods to the top, and now it is too late. Can you not see that? No number of Embers will match your power to mine. I win, every time, Leith." Leith smiled at the way she had connected all the dots in her mind. "Ink Valley will have to settle for being second best." Shadow that materialized like smoke curled around her, and her hands were encased in flame.

Her power would have benefited his operation greatly. "You would have made a great leader," he muttered under his breath as the rain stopped falling.

"Would have," she repeated his words without question, and a strange sadness laced her voice.

"Would have," he said again with a nod, fearing she would not leave this mission alive. Because if she took one step toward Ink Valley. . .

She moved toward him, and he did not retreat. He set his feet in the rocky, root-bound ground of the Dead Wood and prepared for the first blow, letting his power rumble beneath his skin, his marks throbbing.

"Degare sent me to kill you," she said slowly, though he already knew why she had come. He could have sworn she was trying to bottle her rage–to fight the sire. "You should run."

He smirked and removed his cloak. "Never."

She did not break his stare, and with an explosion of twisting shadow they began. Ravenna turned, sending jolts of power toward him. Some seemed to be made of raging fire–though not as white-hot and wild as Edme's–and others were made of pure darkness. The way she moved was like a dance, and Leith would never have been able to predict her next maneuver if he had not been watching the Vestelian, Nilo, train the last few months. He knew the Vestelians were legendary, and it was because the clan–many of whom had once been Embers and had surrendered their gifts–had been forced to master the craft of defense by sword and arrow.

In her anger, Ravenna never slowed, and her power seemed never ending. But Leith knew that was not possible, even for her, someone who held the power of hundreds. Her body would tire eventually, and with it, her power. That her body had not begun weakening as Degare's had with that amount of darkness in it remained a mystery to him.

Leith maintained his distance from her, shielding himself with the black tree trunks that wound around them in the forest. A few of the trunks turned to ash before his eyes, and he ducked, barely avoiding the blast of flame. Splinters flew from the trees, and as he tucked and rolled, a jagged root snagged the skin on his back. He winced and then stood against the pain, shifting to cover the new tear that went down the back of his tunic.

Ravenna paused, and her flames and shadows hovered like black vapor over her skin, waiting to be deployed. Her eyes dropped to his chest under furrowed brows and then back to his face in an instant.

"Remove your shirt," she said. He needed to distract her.

"Not until we are wed, Ravenna," he said with a quick wink. He reveled in the look of annoyance that flooded her face and the way she shifted her weight to one leg in impatience.

Ravenna did not so much as stop to take a breath amid her fury. With a quick slice of strange power, his shirt ripped in two and fell from his shoulders, landing at his feet. He clenched his jaw and rolled his neck, knowing exactly what she was looking at.

"You are *lightmarked*," she said, studying the glowing marks that crept across his chest and back like cracks in the earth.

"What, you thought I was a Despiri this whole time?" he asked innocently.

She ignored his question, stepping toward him and

aggressively rubbing her fingers on the charcoal he had spread across his neck to look like shadowmarks. He stood his ground as his body jolted beneath her violent touch. She huffed a breath, and it was followed by an eye roll after she examined her blackened fingers. "Why did you take the spell book, then?"

"What would I, an Ember, do with a spell book?"

She stepped toward him again, eyes still on his lightmarks. This time, he backed up a step, narrowing his gaze at her but letting her graze her fingertips across them.

"Why doesn't my fire burn you," she asked as she put pressure on her fingers, allowing her flames to trickle across his shoulder. They scattered across his skin, leaving no destruction beneath their wake.

"We'll come back to that," he said, moving away from her reach. "Why would you think I took a spell book?"

"Because it went missing the same night you *stole* three hundred Embers, which, by the way, I still do not understand how you moved them all from the square to the tunnels without being seen in a crowd of *thousands*." It had not been easy.

"It was not me who took the book, Little Dove."

"Then who was it," she asked in infuriation. She was losing hold once again, and he could see her shadows beginning to ripple.

"Not my problem," he lied, removing her hand from his chest. It was his problem. If someone had stolen a spell book, and Degare wanted it back this badly, that meant there was probably someone out there trying to make more Despiri—and the entire Ember race would have yet another to fear. He needed to find and destroy that book before anyone else could learn that spell.

"Well, Leith, if it was not you, then I suppose I can destroy you and your entire valley without fear of harming the book in the process."

"You should know better than to threaten my people," he said calmly, remembering how she had been able to fight the sire in his presence before. But he was stunned as he watched her rally her power and prepared for the fight of his life.

With a glint of her eyes, a burst of flame engulfed the space between them, and up from the ground swirled a plume of leaves and broken branches. He countered her power with a rush of wind, sending the debris toward her, carrying flames upon the dry kindling of the forest floor. She laughed and began ripping the individually crafted feathers from her shoulder plates, revealing tips sharp as daggers. She chucked them toward him one by one, and he carefully maneuvered to dodge each one, thankful for the cover of the trees. But she slammed her invisible force into the tree he crouched behind, and he felt the roots begin ripping through the ground under his feet.

He dropped into the space that now opened up in the ground and rolled to the side, barely avoiding another eruption of fire. She was learning control and strategy, and he had to admit that he was impressed. After a few grueling minutes of dodging her variety of blows and sending quakes through the ground and wind through the trees, he decided to show her what he could really do. He rose to his feet and rolled his head back on his shoulders, listening to the crack of his neck. Then he stepped out from the rotting oak he had taken shelter behind.

He raised his hands in surrender, and as she threw her full power toward him, he began. She poured into him, and his body soaked it up, shattering the darkness into light. He held his palm up before him, twisting it to examine the back of his hand, and then flexed his fingers. She watched him in curiosity, momentarily pausing her offense.

He tilted his chin and hurled her own power back at her. She tried and failed to defend herself. He would not let her darkness harm his people ever again. The witch guardians had come—an entire army of them—to his valley, the very night he had decided to retrieve Ravenna from Oro. He had planned to save her, his betrothed. But the guardians had completely wrecked his valley and caught his people off guard while they slept. They had bypassed his guards and dropped from the mountainsides down into the village and began slaughtering even those who had not been cursed. It had not made sense to him then, and it still didn't.

The valley was full of gifted Embers, and as their leader, Leith had made sure every last one of them learned to fight after that night. The Ink Bloods were known for their legendary strength, but what outsiders did not know is where that strength came from. It was all from the Light—and now Ravenna knew that too. It was not that Leith was collecting Embers to steal their gifts as Degare had done, and it was not just that he was raising an army of them. He was one with them, and together, they were going to take back Arresia.

Perhaps if he had gone and gotten Ravenna out of the castle that very evening, things would be different. She would not be sired to the King of Oro, and she would not be filled with darkness. But he could not have left his people so soon after a loss like that, and he had chosen to remain in Ink Valley for months, instead, sending Cove as a spy.

Cove had meddled with the dark spell, and Leith could

not say he would not have done the same for Ravenna—seeing her in the state she must have been in. The darkness was cunning, made of shadows that lurked as unseen serpents, working to deceive those on Light's path. Cove should have never stepped off that path, but Leith knew why she was so desperate to put an end to the Kingdom of Oro. Once she had seen a potential route to Degare's destruction—the key to her husband's salvation—she had taken it without second thought.

Maybe he had been too late. Maybe it was best that he put an end to it now, before she could do any further damage. Perhaps all hope for the Dove had been lost.

Something slammed into him, and he rolled to the side, encasing himself in the flames he had taken from Ravenna. "You're killing her," Xan growled, towering over him. *He is still here?* Leith blinked and looked behind Xan, where Ravenna lay on the floor of the forest, still as stone. He backed away from her for a moment, letting her power stop curling around his fists, intertwining with his. Cove and Edme were emerging from the trees, and Cove rushed toward Ravenna, falling to her knees at her side. She pushed some stray locks of red hair away from her face, and Xan remained planted between her and Leith, his face like stone as his eyes dropped to the glowing lightmarks at Leith's chest. Confusion and irritation coated Xan's face in a grimace, and at the sight of Ravenna's chest rising and falling behind him, Leith let out a low sigh of relief and rubbed a hand over his face. *She is alive, but everything else is falling apart.*

Leith felt his second's presence like fire at his back before he heard her. "What is going on?" He turned slowly to look at Edme, who stood behind him with her arms crossed. "Looks like the secret's out," Edme muttered, nodding to his bare torso.

Cove's sights also fell upon his lightmarks, as if she had failed to notice them in all the commotion. The usual icy blue of her eyes appeared gray with the grief she had undergone in the last few days, and the colorless Dead Wood seemed to leech all color from her sunken cheeks. Against the grief that clouded her eyes, there was a glimmer of life there as she realized he was an Ember, too, and someone she should trust. Leith supposed it was a good thing he had come to trust Cove, since she could now put the pieces of his entire plan together if she thought long enough. The less people that knew his true intentions in Arresia, the better.

"I thought you'd killed her," Cove said in a hushed breath as she kneeled beside Ravenna, her shoulders sagging with a swirling storm of relief and uncertainty.

"He didn't?" Edme asked, as if disappointed. Leith frowned, glaring at Xan until he slowly stepped to the side to allow him to kneel next to Ravenna's weakened body. Her eyes were closed, and she almost looked *peaceful*.

Cove spoke slowly, as she was unable to remove her gaze from his glowing marks. "You told me two days ago you would kill her yourself if she threatened Ink Valley." He had been about to do just that. "But you didn't. You may have wanted to just now. . .but there is a hope you still hold onto, and that hope is not in vain. You want her because she is the Dove. Not just for her power. Not just to fight in your armies. Not just for the strength she would offer you against Oro. You are gathering the Seven." Leith stiffened and took a deep breath, bracing for the argument that was about to come from Xan, but surprisingly, he knelt in silent defeat beside Ravenna as his mind turned behind his eyes. "You need Ravenna to help lead Arresia to the Light," Cove realized.

Cove looked at the faces around her and smiled softly, shoving a paper into Leith's hand–a Light Scroll.

"This was in your satchel the night I found you," he acknowledged, examining the paper.

"I take it you didn't read it."

"I did," he said.

"Well, read it again," Cove said.

Leith narrowed his eyes, still standing over Ravenna as he unrolled the page. Xan was obviously listening, but he was taking what little time he had to gently smooth Ravenna's hair.

Leith breathed tightly and spoke the underlined passage aloud, *"When the Dove's wings turn black as sin, wash her with Light, and she'll be made pure within."* Leith looked at Ravenna, whose wings were blacker than a moonless night.

Xan looked up at him, pulling Ravenna into his chest. "She is not your Dove."

"He's right," Edme said, shifting on her feet. "She is not coming to the Light."

*I told you she would bring nothing but sin upon the world, yet you agreed to marry her,* Edme had once said to him. Leith's jaw twitched. Had she known of this specific prophecy when she'd told him those words? "It's hopeless," said Edme.

Cove looked at him. "I don't think it is, Leith. I know I made a mistake with the spell, but Ravenna's darkness was written in prophecy. I never realized it before, but is this not the hope we need, that she can be brought to the Light? She can still join us," Cove said, raising a brow at the marks on Leith and Edme's skin. Edme crossed her arms, and Leith nodded slowly. Cove did not speak for a moment, as if considering the consequences of what she was about to say next. "She *is* one of us. Can't you feel it?" Cove asked. Leith furrowed his brow, looking across Ravenna's body to where the Ember crouched next to her.

He paused, thinking about Cove's claim for a moment. *Did she finally know what he had suspected since the night he had found her washed up in Adullam?* "Even still, after she's been claimed by the darkness–chained to it–you think it is possible?" Leith asked. Where was the faith he had once so proudly borne?

Cove nodded. "It says it right there, does it not?" she asked.

Edme's footsteps approached from behind. "No way," she said through gritted teeth. Edme turned to Leith, arms still crossed over her chest, while Xan cradled Ravenna. Edme was tall for a woman, her height matched with Xan's, and she had a muscular build, fit for a warrior. Her attire was anything but practical out here in the Dead Wood. It did nothing to camouflage her against the colorless terrain, and instead, stood out like a flame in the night. She wore the gown of a queen, fashioned from bright oranges and yellows. Gold stitching lined the bodice, and her neck was clad in rare yellow jewels only found in Volcania. Leith looked back to Ravenna to avoid the conversation, but Edme would not let the words go unspoken.

"She cannot be one of us. Not after all she has done." Leith set his jaw.

Cove spoke up beside them. "Were we not all of the darkness once, before we came to the Light?"

Leith nodded. "We have all made mistakes, Edme. You included."

"I have not killed for a King of Darkness. I have not killed my own friend–"

"You have no right to speak of such things," Leith snapped with a cold rage, cutting her off before she could finish. Cove's eyes dropped to the ground that quaked beneath his feet, and her hand found a place on his shoulder, calming him with a soothing wave of power. Cove's gift of emotional manipulation was strange, and it was the only gift he had ever come across that he was unable to manipulate himself.

It was clear that Ravenna had cracked many times, but the moment in which she put the staff through Zephaniah was the moment that had cleaved her soul in two. Edme did not understand Ravenna like he had come to in the few encounters the two of them had this past week. Leith had felt the guilt that moved through her with each step, the emotions she tried to bury, the grief she felt but no longer understood. It was the reason for her constant drunkenness, and it was the very memory she tried so hard to forget. The Light within Leith was drawing the truth out of Ravenna. He could feel it. When she was near him, the sire was easier to resist.

He took a breath, and Cove spoke into the silence, "Ravenna has always been lost, she was not raised in the Light. But no one is destined to remain in darkness. She can still come to the Light."

Leith agreed. Ravenna was not of the darkness; she was another victim of it. She had not wanted to kill Zephaniah, but that had been the moment she stopped fighting. It was easier for her to give into the darkness than to fight against it when she was not equipped to do so. How is one to fight the darkness without any Light? She knew little to nothing about the Light and she was sired to darkness himself. It did not give her much choice in the matter, but Leith was going to change that. He was going to get her out of this.

Leith crouched down toward her, taking one of her hands in his palm.

"It is too much of a risk to leave her alive, Leith. She is sired to destroy Ink Valley," Edme said, inching toward him, toward Ravenna. Leith dropped Ravenna's hand and rose to step in front of her as Edme drew her flames. Xan rose to his feet at once.

"Stand down," Leith ordered her. Her flames did not die, and Xan took a step forward.

"I will not allow you to jeopardize the Kingdom for her," Edme said.

"It is only if you harm her that the Kingdom will be jeopardized. I will not allow it. This is my call. There is a reason you are not in charge here." Edme's stare turned to stone, and Leith allowed a burst of thunder to rumble through the sky. He readied himself to absorb her flame if she so much as breathed in Ravenna's direction, and he felt Xan's attention shifting wildly between the two of them.

Leith kept his eyes on Edme and took the dagger from its sheath—*Ravenna's* dagger—and examined it, just as he had the day in Ink Valley when he had taken it from her. Ashreya had known to take it with her when she had fled the castle with Ravenna as a baby—because she had known of the prophecy that Ravenna was meant to fulfill with it. Gerrin and Willa had known too.

Why had Leith ever doubted the prophecy? The Father always made a way, and whether or not Gerrin and Willa had tried to protect her so she could fulfill this prophecy, whether Ashreya had planned to hide her from it forever, whether

Degare had corrupted her and turned her to the darkness—the Light would still find a way to shine against the shadows. He turned from Edme and smiled at Ravenna, crouching to brush the hair from her cheek. Xan's eyes could not be peeled from the dagger in Leith's hand.

Where she laid on her side, the wings of her armor dipped into a vee at the top of her back leaving her skin exposed. Leith's lips fell into a frown at the sight of the brand on her skin, and he took the dagger and sliced across it with a clean, shallow cut. The dagger warmed in his hand. "What are you doing?" Xan asked, grabbing for the blade. Leith held it just out of reach, tracing the seven feathers that were etched on the blade.

"I am protecting her from the pain she'll feel if she uses her power to kill us all when she wakes." He slid his arms beneath her, readying to lift her from the ground. "Where do you think you're taking her?" Xan asked, his voice a low rumble amid the Dead Wood. Leith sighed, setting Ravenna back down and rising to his feet.

"I am taking her back to Oro. It is not safe for any of us, including my people, for her to be here."

"No," Xan shook his head, shoving Leith backward. Leith breathed tightly while clenching and unclenching his fist. "I am taking her far from here. Far from you."

Leith heard Edme sigh beside him, and he gritted his teeth. "For the last time, Xan, you cannot protect her."

"I was doing a fine job of protecting her until you came along," Xan snarled, encroaching on Leith, readying to draw the sword that had just been returned to him hours before. He was already betraying Leith's trust. Xan was a flight risk, and Leith could not guarantee he would not spill all of Ink Valley's secrets if it meant he had the chance to separate Ravenna from what he perceived as danger.

"Oh, come on. How do you think you two made it out of the Brunts alive?" Xan straightened as Leith allowed the ground to rumble beneath him. His face fell flat as he realized the quakes in the Brunts had not been some wild miracle. Edme took another deep breath beside him.

"Protecting her is not your job," Xan said. "It is mine."

"We can share the job," Leith said, holding his hands up in surrender and waiting for Xan to calm down. "We both want her alive."

Xan's nostrils flared, and he shook his head violently. "Why take her back to Oro, straight back to her sire?"

"It's easier to control her there. She listens to me. I'll figure out a way to break the sire. You need to trust me."

"I can't trust you with her," Xan said, and Leith watched as his brown eyes fell to the mark on Ravenna's back, where darkness was now seeping from the cut he had made. Using the dagger was not a permanent fix, but for the next few hours, she would be powerless. Just as she had been in the alley last night.

"Well, you are going to have to learn how to," he said, "because as long as I allow you to live, I make the calls." Leith drew from Edme's pit of fire gifts and surrounded Xan in flame. Cove jumped back in surprise, and Edme rolled her eyes at his display of power, then handed him a cloak to cover his marks. He draped it over his shoulders and fastened it at his neck.

"You're making a mistake taking her back there," Xan raged, and Leith closed his eyes for a moment, mastering control over those flames. For now, Ravenna would be unable to harm his valley, and he would take her back to the edge of the kingdom where he would convince her to resist the sire, to stop her from turning back to Ink Valley. She could do it if he asked. He had seen it time and time again. She had not killed him yet, though she had every opportunity to do so. She had kept his secret when she attended the king's dinner with only slight intervention from him. A part of her was still able to resist the sire–she just needed someone to remind her. He hauled Ravenna up against his chest to take her back to Oro, *for now*.

Before Edme could speak again and object to his plans, he looked her in the eyes. "Gather my armies and my people. Ink Valley is not safe anymore. You know where to take them." Edme nodded next to Cove, whose eyes were wide and curious.

"Oh, and we have a spell book to find," Leith said. He debriefed them on the disappearance of the book, and after a stern glare in Edme's direction that said *behave*, he turned to the grief-stricken blonde beside her and nodded his thanks as he looked at the scroll in her hand. It was all coming together, and though the truth about his mission was out, he did not fear. Because before him, in Edme and Cove and Ravenna, was a part of prophecy being fulfilled. *Seven bloods*. Ravenna's braid swayed as Leith turned to Xan, who watched helplessly from beyond the flames as Leith started on his way.

"She is not your Dove!" Xan yelled one last time.

*Yes, she had to be.*

# CHAPTER 60
# TRUTH OF THE BOND
### EDME

She hated bowing to a man—even more so when that man was Leith Fowler. But he had been successful in keeping this underground operation of rebellion going for nearly five years, and she had only joined a few months ago. She knew her place.

Leith respected her and left her in charge in his absence. Most of the time, he listened to her input. Unfortunately, that was not true when it had anything to do with the red-haired shield-maiden from Vestele. Edme watched as Leith left her in charge of his armies once again, while he carried Ravenna into the tunnels that he had constructed himself to deliver her back into the hands of her sire.

At least the Raven of Oro would be far from the valley while Edme prepared the Ink Bloods for the journey to their new haven. The Ink Bloods would be safe yet another night—though, the wretched witch guardians were still likely to pay them a visit. She would keep them at bay with her firelight while the Ink Bloods picked them off one by one and trained the new soldiers to do the same. They had been using the witch guardians as a training exercise each night they visited since the initial attack. Leith had been smart to ask her to head up the operation, and she had found she enjoyed training men and women in how to use their gifts in a warlike setting. She had a feeling it would be a necessary skill in the near future.

When the few men she had brought with her from Volcania had gone to Vestele and returned those months ago with a handful of survivors, she had not expected to be so impressed with the skills of their warriors. Only four of the nine were trained fighters, but even the healer–Tenille–had some knowledge on how to wield a sword. Edme could admit that they had done a pretty good job of protecting Ravenna all these years, even without gifts.

"Do you think you could allow me some space to breathe?" Xan muttered as they walked back to Ink Valley. Xan was still caged in flames beside them, and Edme could see the sweat forming on his brow.

She grinned. "Only if you promise to obey my every command. If I remember correctly, you are now permitted to train beneath me. I am the one in charge of Leith's armies." He glared at her and she dropped the circle of fire, allowing him to walk leisurely beside them without the threat of being burned.

"I'm thinking about going back to Oro," Cove said as they walked.

"Only a fool would do that," Edme said bluntly. Cove had been recognized by Ravenna, and she could be recognized again–by the king, his witch, or even another servant. To remain in the kingdom at all after Ravenna was bound to the king had been idiotic.

"Why would you do that?" Xan asked. Edme stared

straight ahead, but Cove was kind enough to include him in the conversation.

"My soulbound is in Oro somewhere–he has to be. Whatever you would do for Ravenna, multiply that by a hundred. I would do anything to get Elias back."

"Ravenna may as well be my soulbound. All these years, I have wanted nothing less than to love and be loved by her–to protect her with my life."

"Your version of a soulbond is quite different from the truth of it, I am afraid," Cove said. Edme wondered what she meant by that. Edme's parents had been far from soulbound, and she had little understanding of what the truth of it was. Though she understood little of the soulbond between Elias and Cove, she could nearly feel the blonde's sadness hanging in the air.

"What do you mean?" Xan asked, the slow steps of his boots crunching through the dead leaves. Edme listened carefully.

"You're not an Ember. You cannot have a true soulbond. It's a common misconception among Shades. Soulbonds are a gift from the Father of Lights. What you Shades call soulbonds, is a mockery. Whereas you bind yourselves through shadow and dark magic, Embers are bound through Light. It is a precious covenant."

"I am not a Shade," Xan argued.

"If you are not an Ember, you are a Shade," Edme muttered, continuing to stare straight ahead.

Cove continued. "A soulbond is not simply a marriage."

"I know there is more to it than that," Xan muttered.

"And what do you know of it?" Cove asked.

"I know that Leith wanted one with Ravenna when he

asked Ashreya for her hand right after her eighteenth birthday. He requested not only marriage–but a soulbond."

"Because he is an Ember, you fool," Edme muttered. That he had not connected the dots until now said a lot of his understanding of this world of Light and darkness. Perhaps he had been raised in the shadows just as deeply as Ravenna had, without even realizing it.

"Leith wanted the soulbond with Ravenna," Edme continued, "but he quickly realized Ravenna had been hidden from the Light, and a true soulbond would not be possible unless the truth was revealed to her and she became an Ember, too. They could have bound themselves through shadow in a faux soulbond, which is likely what Ashreya was imagining, but Leith would never have done that, and Ashreya would have never allowed Ravenna out from under the protections of Vestele, anyway. Leith would have settled for marriage, for an alliance, if only to get Ravenna out of that valley and to where he could teach her of the Light. She is the prophesied Dove, you know," she said with a mutter. "The Daughter of the Barren Queen."

Xan set his jaw beside her, and she understood the frustration that came with those words. "So what is in it for him? Why a soulbond?" Xan asked.

Edme looked at Cove, knowing she could better explain the details. Cove was clearly putting the pieces together in her own mind, realizing what Leith had been up to the very day she had been brought into Ink Valley after her time in the sea–when her husband had merged all his power with hers to keep her afloat–to deliver her to the only safety he knew from the scrolls. *Adullam.*

"Soulbonded Embers can share power. They can merge it. Together, they are a team, woven in Light."

Xan scoffed. "So he has always been after her power–from the very beginning."

"Leith is not who you've always thought he was, Xan. I thought maybe you'd have realized that by now," Edme said. "As infuriating as he can be, he does have her best interest at heart."

"Her best interest is becoming this Dove? This weapon for the Light? After suffering as a weapon for the darkness? I saw Leith using her power back there near the tunnels. Why would he need a soulbond for that if he can already use it?"

Cove spoke up before Edme could answer, her voice clear and confident. "Leith is greatly gifted, and it would seem he can utilize the powers of Ember or Despiri who are near him." Edme confirmed with a nod. "But to be soulbound to Ravenna–they would be a force. He would have constant access to her power, and she, his. They would not have to be near each other to do so. Figuratively, like marriage, you become one flesh, but in a soulbond, you also become one with your gifts. One with purpose. It is not something to enter into lightly."

"So you have access to Elias's power right now?" Xan asked.

"Elias quieted the bond between us by surrendering all of his power to me. By now, some of his own will have replenished, but I am guessing he is very weak."

"Why would he do that?" Xan asked.

"To keep me from coming for him. To keep me from endangering myself to save him." Xan looked at his feet, and

Edme stayed quiet as Cove's voice broke. "But he must be in Oro. I know he is still alive; I can feel it."

Edme took a deep breath. "I know you think he is in Oro, but if you've been over all of the inventory sheets and through the entire prison, he is not there."

"It does not make sense. Where else would he be?" Cove asked, and it was obvious she was holding back tears. Xan looked between her and Edme.

"I'd start with finding out who took the spell book from Oro," Edme said.

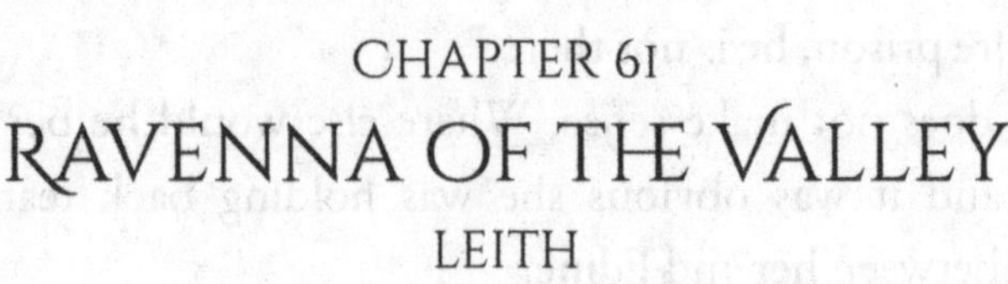

If she was the Raven of Oro, he had broken her wings. For the time being, she had no power against him. She was only Ravenna of the Valley, as she had been when he had first met her, though now with a little less of a conscience. He watched her sleeping face as he carried her through the tunnels until he had used up the last bit of fire he had stolen from her in the fight. When it got too dark to see, and only the faint glow of his lightmarks illuminated her face, he passed the time by whistling, listening to the notes carry for miles through the earth.

He had formed this very tunnel only months ago, cracking the earth and sending his power shattering through the hard stone. It had taken him four months of meticulous planning, mapping, and tunneling, careful not to hit any fault lines, and it had taken all of his energy. But it had given those Embers safe passage out of the Kingdom of Oro and had allowed them all to avoid the Valley of the Shadow, which was the only known path by land out of the kingdom. Leith knew Degare would send his search parties in that direction, maintaining the secrecy of the tunnels, but Ravenna. . .she was clever and had followed the echoes of his power, all the way to the opening on the beach.

Molding these tunnels had been a chore, because the entire time he worked, he only wanted to head straight into the kingdom and retrieve her. The vengeance he had once sought on Ravenna was not one that ended in death. It was a shallow anger, a disappointment in her betrayal of his clan. He wanted her to look into his eyes and see the hurt she had caused him. The deep, vengeful wrath that had drawn him to Oro, that had tempted him to ignore the voice that told him to *wait,* was the vengeance he wanted to release on Degare for taking her. But that still voice inside him had whispered *not yet.* So, he had distracted himself from the fact that she was in the castle being beaten, tortured, and sired, and only after he had restored his valley from the witch guardian attacks had he dug this tunnel all the way to the Black Sea in preparation for his next move.

The King and Queen of Ozanna were now safe with his army, tucked away where the darkness would not find them. But their heir—well, he was delivering her right back into the heart of Oro, where she was to stay until that sire was broken.

After a few minutes of sorting out his thoughts, Ravenna began stirring in his arms, and he felt the brush of her eyelashes opening against his neck. He prepared himself for the explosion of anger.

"Leith?" she questioned slowly, her raspy voice laced with a complicated weaving of hatred and confusion. He continued forward, glancing down at her. Her eyes were blinking quickly as she tried to adjust to the light that bled through the sliver of exposed skin between the edges of his cloak.

"Yes, Ravenna?" She squirmed in sudden frustration, and he set her down gently onto the stone, watching her struggle to gain her footing.

"What are you doing?" she asked. He could not see her well, but he could hear her rustling as she tried to summon her power. He assumed her first choice in the darkness of the tunnel would be flame, and he allowed her to search for a moment before his chuckle echoed through the tunnel.

"I've cut you again with your own dagger. I didn't want you trying to kill me again today." She looked to him and then quickly examined herself for the wound. She was still groggy and had not yet fully returned to her senses.

She reached for the sword at her side, and as she unsheathed it, he pulled her against his chest, knocking it to the ground. He did not release her. The sound of the weapon clanking against the stone ricocheted for miles, and she began to shake against him, as if the sound had triggered something deep within her.

She fought his touch, but Leith held her tightly.

His brows knit together as she trembled in fear—the same fear he had summoned with the deliberate clanking of the knife on his plate at the king's dinner. Relief flooded through Leith's body as she quaked against him—her remaining fear was proof that she was not too far gone. A proof of remorse, a proof that Ravenna Zenevieva Ozanne, the Dove, was still in there. Leith knew what the sound of the clanking sword meant to her. He had not been there, and though Cove had fled at first sign of the spell going wrong, she had still learned what Ravenna had been forced to do as Degare's puppet—that her first mission had been to kill Zephaniah Wilmore with the staff that was thrown to the floor beside her. Leith knew how trauma engrained itself into the mind, burrowing with its claws, leaving marks too deep to heal.

"Why am I still alive?" she asked. Her voice broke as she sobbed. "Why did you not kill me when you had the chance, when I couldn't stop you?" Her words were a mixture of disappointment and resentment. He kept hold of her wrists, holding her still against him.

She still wanted death. She begged for it–and it broke him.

"I am going to get you out of this, Ravenna," he promised. Arresia was counting on him.

She wriggled away from him, and he set her free, watching her pace a few steps ahead.

"I have been ordered to kill you. You should have ended me," she said, turning a slow circle with her hand on her forehead. Her skin was dewy with sweat, and her breaths were uneven. A few of her braids had been pulled loose, and a few stray strands now framed her face.

"He has demanded such things of you, and yet here I stand, breathing," Leith said, approaching her slowly. She did not retreat as he prodded at her and willed her to try again. *How far will she let me get with my blade drawn, metal shimmering against the light that glows from my chest? Can she truly resist it by will of her own?*

"Because he believes you to be Locke Carrington–whom I have been ordered to keep alive. Where do you keep all that bloodstone anyway? What do you use it for?"

Leith raised his chin. "I am not going to share that with you just yet, Ravenna. Do you not fear that if I did, you may have no reason left to keep me alive?" he asked, advancing toward her. "Or are you trying to find an excuse to kill me?"

She backed into the wall, and he stood only a breath away

from her now. "Locke Carrington is just one of my many names. I am also the leader of the Ink Bloods, leader of the rebellion against your king." Ravenna would not look at him. "There is a part of you that fights the sire, Ravenna. I am a threat to your king, and you know he would want me dead if you told him my true identity. Why haven't you, Ravenna? It is not because you search for my bloodstone. It is because you are still in there. You are not hopeless, and a part of you is protecting me—a part of you is working to sustain the rebellion against your king."

"I fight the sire and keep you alive because you may be my only chance at death," she said through gritted teeth. "I fight the urge to kill you as we stand here." She glanced to his drawn dagger. "I fight it every time you threaten my life, in hopes that you will finally grant my one wish and set me free of this sire." Leith stood in silence for a moment as he watched her wipe a hand over her face. "I protect the rebellion because I wait for the *Seven*." Leith went rigid.

"What do you know of the Seven, Ravenna?" Her eyebrows creased as she looked at him.

"I know that they are stronger than me. I know that no weapon formed against them will prosper. I know they can stop me, and that is what I long for."

Leith inhaled a long, shaky breath before he spoke. "You are one of them, Ravenna."

"What?" she asked, her wild eyes darting from the ground to his.

"You are one of the Seven. As am I."

She shook her head. "You're lying to me. You're lying."

"You are the Dove, and you are a part of the Seven—also known as the Munera. Five years ago, I sailed to Ozanna from my homeland of Remont, and I began preparing our armies." Ravenna quirked her head at the information he'd just offered her. *And where exactly is your homeland?* she had once asked him. His homeland was across the sea in one of the two remaining kingdoms of Light, where King Auden was gathering armies and preparing for war.

"The Seven have only recently begun emerging," Leith added.

"And who are they?" Ravenna asked. "How can you say with certainty that I am one of them?" He watched her for a moment.

"I will not give any names. But I suspect I know who five of them are, myself included. I am still waiting on the Father of Lights to deliver two more."

"And you think He has delivered me here, into this darkness?" she retorted.

"Your own choices and the choices of those around you led you here, Ravenna. It may seem unfair, but it was not Him who placed you here. It *is* Him who gives you a way out, though. It is His Light that offers you redemption." She shook her head, waving him off.

"I do not wish to hear it. There is no way out. There is not an ounce of forgiveness for what I have done. Kill me, Leith, before the sire forces me to end your rebellion. Kill me to save Arresia."

He would not kill her. He would give her anything–but not that. He could not.

He stepped forward, sheathing his dagger. The wetness on her cheeks gleamed against the glow from his marks. Leith placed his hand on the wall next to her head and leaned in close, speaking so that his words floated against her ear on a faint rush of his wind.

"I am going to test my theory one more time, Ravenna. And I will prove to you that you can resist the sire, that you do not need to be afraid to harm my valley." She watched him carefully as he hovered in front of her there in the darkness of the tunnel. Her hands were shaking against the sire, and he took them in his and brought them to his chest.

"Your king has done this to you, and I plan to kill him for it." At the rising of her chest against his own, and the sudden intake of relief, he vowed to kill Degare where he sat upon his throne. He would kill the king, and then he would take Ravenna far from this kingdom to join his people, where he could make sure she was cared for. She could be with her friends, and maybe then, she could recover. She would want to live again. He would teach her of the Light and the hope that drove him forward each day, and perhaps after hearing the truth, she would wish to help bring Arresia out of the darkness. Perhaps she was the key to the Kingdom after all.

# CHAPTER 62
## THE PROMISE
### RAVENNA

Death had been promised.

Leith was going to kill Degare. Ravenna could see the end of the sire nearing, and a weight had been lifted from her chest. She could resist the urge to kill Leith, not because her king had ordered him left alive, but perhaps because the two of them were part of the prophesied Seven. Perhaps the Light within him called to her and gave her the strength to resist the sire. Ravenna would use that newfound freewill to her advantage, and she would look the other way while Leith planned to kill the very king she had been made to protect, even if she suffered physical torture as a result of her disobedience. Now, she had something to fight for. A newfound hope—no pain would be too much for her. Degare's death was coming.

She was at the end of the tunnel near the beach, and Leith's hands were on her shoulders. His hazel eyes bored into hers. "If the king asks what happened, tell him you discovered that it was not Ink Valley who stole the spell book. Try to keep him off the topic of the missing Embers. Convince him to assign you orders to track down whoever stole the book. You are clever. You can manipulate the king. Ravenna, you *can* resist the sire." *Only when Leith is involved, it would seem.* But she would do her part until he was able to kill the king, even if the pain caused by her rebellion against the sire was excruciating. She would endure it for her freedom.

"Will you be staying in Oro?" she asked.

"My duties as Locke Carrington are not yet finished," he said with a smirk. Ravenna breathed tightly against the sire that prodded her to find that bloodstone. "You'll see me around," he promised.

"Miss, are you coming inside?" Ravenna whirled on the librarian, thankful that her gifts were temporarily inaccessible due to the cut between her shoulder blades by the strange dagger her mother had given her.

She was not planning on heading inside, but had only planned on killing the time until her gifts returned to her so Degare would have one less thing to question her about. She did not need him snooping around more than he was already sure to when she returned without the head of the Ink Blood leader. But as the doe-eyed librarian stared at her between the two oak doors awaiting her response, she figured, *What better way to kill the time?*

So, she stood and walked through the towering entrance between the two statues of witches and strange, winged beasts Ravenna had never seen. The witches' detailed gowns wound around the bodies of what she could only assume were dragons, and their hair flowed as if underwater. Even in stone, she could tell the goddesses were meant to be ethereal, just as the myths described them. The dragons were shrunken in size compared to the old stories she had been told around the fire in Vestele. Roarke had always been the one to tell those stories in particular. His voice would carry across the village, and his gin would slosh from the clay mug she had made him as he over-exaggerated his war stories of dragons and mystic men. Her mother had always rolled her eyes at the brute, saying he had too much to drink.

The librarian inched into the library on silent feet. "Let me know if I can help you find anything." Ravenna nodded her thanks and tried not to marvel at the vast number of books that stretched from wall to wall, floor to ceiling. She had never shown an interest in books, though she did know how to read, there were few in Vestele. She supposed she might enjoy reading stories that transported her to lands far away, if only she would give a chance to the books Degare had placed in her room.

The shelves were three floors high, and staircases wrapped and twisted throughout the entire building. Black stone floors stretched as far as her eyes could see, and fine engravings that told ancient legends and stories had been etched into every available flat space on the walls. She did not allow herself time to observe the depictions too closely, and instead, stepped forward, reading through the spines on the first shelf in front of her. She had never been in a library before and had no idea where to begin her search. Spell books, books on the origin of Oro, the elements of bloodstone, Degare's rise to royalty–there were many books to choose from. But none spoke of the Light she sought. The

Light Zephaniah had spoken of, and the Light Leith seemed to serve.

She gripped the worn scripture in her pocket and traced the book spines with her other finger, following the shelves to the back of the library. Of course, Degare would have *these* specific texts placed at the entry way–the ones that described him as an idol of the people who once had no power. Because of his accomplishments with bloodstone and the spell, darkness had found a way to manifest itself in the Despiri. Because of Degare, the Embers had someone to fear. Ravenna supposed she would fall victim to his punishments next if she were discovered lurking about the library for texts on Light. She could always claim she only wanted to know the enemy better, given that she was the king's sworn protector. Whether against her will or not, she was bound to him, and no matter the information found within the pages of these books, she would always be part of his darkness–until Leith freed her.

As she moseyed forward, she imagined Zephaniah in his late-night studies, searching these very walls to help discover her past. After over an hour of searching, footsteps approached behind her. She stiffened and turned at the gentle voice that followed.

"What is it you are looking for? Perhaps I can help you."

"I doubt you have any such thing," Ravenna said to the curly haired woman with youthful, green eyes. The woman was pale and probably close to Ravenna in age. She wore a brass band on her ring finger and an olive-toned apron over a linen dress.

"Try me," she replied in an inquisitive tone. "I'm Magdalene."

Ravenna bit her cheek and debated on whether or not to

tell the truth. She would not give Magdalene her name, but before she could stop herself, other words flowed out. "Anything on. . .the Light." *What could the woman do, threaten her?* Ravenna would kill her before she had the chance.

The young woman's face went cold for a moment as her eyes took in the armor of the King's Raven, and Ravenna could see the tension take root in her shoulders. "I thought it was you." Ravenna's shoulders straightened, and the woman spoke again. "He wrote and told me that you would come."

Ravenna had to focus on maintaining her balance as her sight went fuzzy. "*Who* told you I would come?" she said in a hushed voice.

The woman began walking, motioning for Ravenna to follow. Ravenna prepared herself for the name that she had once buried, but nothing could prepare her for the pain that followed when the librarian spoke it quietly, "Zephaniah Wilmore."

Every thought, every emotion attached to that name, returned at full force.

*Let go. Let go. Let go.*

Ravenna clutched her stomach, doing her best to collect herself as she followed Magdalene's hurried footsteps.

They scurried past the handful of librarians working the shelves—only one of which turned to greet her as they walked by. Their steps were choppy and quick, and they wove in and out of the rows and aisles of shelves that stretched to the ceilings. Magdalene pointed upward to a tiny loft lit by only a few candles and uttered under her breath, "There aren't many texts like that left here. . .I tried to keep some hidden where the librarians don't typically go, but over the years they have disappeared. Some are desperate for such texts, and I'm guessing you are, too, if you've come here to look right under the king's nose."

Ravenna's eyebrow twitched, and her fingers drummed against her thigh. "You wouldn't believe half of it," she said. She glanced around one more time to be sure they were still alone. "How do you know Zephaniah?"

Magdalene's eyes softened, and she tightened the linen hair scarf that kept the blonde coil of hair from her face. "He is one of the few good ones left in this kingdom. The other children of Light, we must hide. It is hard for us to find each other." Ravenna examined the woman, wondering if she was lightmarked beneath her clothes. She gritted her teeth against the sudden pain—the urging—in her spine. It was better that she did not know. Ravenna asked no further questions on the matter.

Ravenna swept some stray hairs from her own face as she began to ascend the steps, but Magdalene caught her arm. Again, for Magdalene's safety, Ravenna was thankful her power had not yet resurfaced. "How is he doing?" she asked, and her words circled around Ravenna, stirring up grief. "Zephaniah. He wrote to me from prison. How is he?" she repeated, after an excruciating moment of silence.

Ravenna's heart pounded in her ears. If her gifts had not been dormant, this entire library would be blown to dust. She backed up onto the step and plopped down. Magdalene stepped forward. "Tell me it is not so. Tell me he is alive."

"I cannot," Ravenna said quietly as his face hovered before her once again, threatening to summon her conscience. She blinked a dozen times, willing the memories away. *Let go.*

Magdalene brought a hand to her mouth. "No. No. No."

The brass wedding band on her finger glimmered in the candlelight, and Ravenna's eyes darted to the thicker ring she wore on a strip of leather around her neck. "When he wrote. . ." she choked on her words. "When he wrote, I knew he was in the tower, but he seemed hopeful. He was so hopeful. I–"

Ravenna cut her off. "There was never any hope."

"I never got to write him back," Magdalene whispered, clutching her stomach. "I never got to thank him properly." Ravenna studied her as she mindlessly brought her hand to her neck and twisted the wedding band in her fingers. Magdalene's green eyes were now swimming with tears, and Ravenna could not bear it–that she was the cause of so many peoples' pain. Ravenna was still crumpled on the stairs, and her gaze dropped to her hands in her lap.

"I am so sorry," Magdalene said suddenly. "I know he was helping you, too. I am sure you still grieve."

Zephaniah had committed his entire life to helping her, and what had Ravenna done with that kindness? "You owe me no sympathy," she said. "I beg of you, give me none."

Magdalene's eyebrows crumpled, and a single tear escaped her eye before she could wipe it away. "May he rest in Eternal Light. In the Kingdom that is to come."

Ravenna was tired of everyone speaking in ways she did not understand, of things she did not know. "What do you mean by that?" she finally asked.

Magdalene's eyes twinkled as she wiped her cheek with the back of her hand. "He said you had much to learn."

Ravenna's brows furrowed slightly, and the librarian motioned her up the stairs. She gestured to the far shelf; the one that was concealed to any potential onlookers below the loft. "Study here as long as you would like, but try to remain hidden. It is frowned upon to be researching such things, as I am sure you already know." She looked down at her hands, which twisted and turned with an anxiousness that was not there before.

"I must get back to my son," she said quietly. "I do not actually work here. I–" she stopped herself, and Ravenna did not pry. "Come back tomorrow at this time. I'll have some Light Scrolls to share with you."

Ravenna paused. "Light Scrolls?"

"Prophecy. Scriptures." She smiled again, and this time the joy reached her eyes. "And hope."

# THE LIGHT SCROLLS
## THE BOOK OF PROPHECY

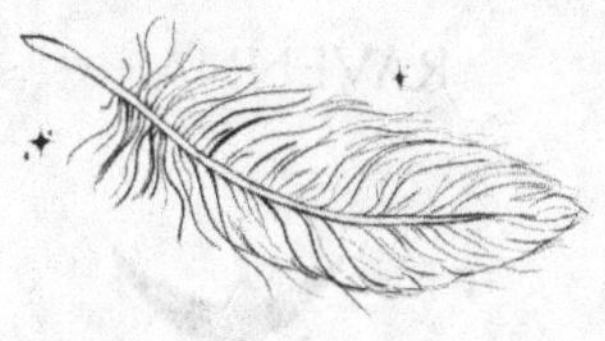

*In the latter days, when the Sun is soon to rise, the song of the Dove will echo across kingdoms carrying hope on the wind.*

# CHAPTER 63
# SELF-INFLICTED
## RAVENNA

There was hope all around her: in Leith, in Magdalene, in the prophecies, in the words that had been spoken to her by Galen and Zephaniah. There was light in the darkness, and yet, she hid.

She found herself in the comfort of her bed before she reported to the king. Yes, she was avoiding him. But only because she was not confident in her ability to lie straight to his face. After she had bathed, changed out of her tattered leathers, and lounged around for about an hour, Degare requested her presence.

She covered the cut on her back with a red cloak. It was exactly like those that the soldiers of Oro wore in the streets below, and it was her sire's favorite color. A reminder of the blood he had proudly spilt and the power it had given him. She hoped that the seemingly proud representation of his kingdom—her kingdom—upon her back, would be enough to calm his imminent punishments, but she did not allow her hopes to swell.

She listened to the clicking of her heels as she wandered through the hallways of the castle, winding down the stairs, and turning left toward the throne room. No escorts prodded at her sides to make sure she got where she was going.

In only a few short minutes, she found herself outside of the doors that she always dreaded opening. Nothing good ever lurked behind them. She sent a tendril of her power toward them, and as they parted for her, she was surprised to find Degare pacing in front of his throne. His eyes shot to hers with cold rage. His shoulders turned toward her, and his entire body went rigid with anger as his eyes fell to her empty hands. He looked as though he wanted to rip her to pieces, but Ravenna walked toward him anyway, obeying that beckoning sire.

She curtseyed but did not bow her head. She kept her eyes locked with his and her chin up. "Your Majesty."

He spat at her feet. "Ravenna."

He spoke her name like an order, and it twisted around her spine, leaving her body unsettled. She held the curtsey for a moment and then straightened. His gaze did not turn from her while he lifted a hand to clear the room. "Leave us!" he demanded. Ravenna felt Jara stiffen beside her, but the witch did not budge. The king's rage extended to her, and he said, "You, too, witch." Jara's face tightened, and before she could object, the king shot her a glare. Reluctantly, she obeyed.

When the room had cleared, he turned his back on Ravenna and walked up the stairs of the dais to his throne. The echo of his bloodstone staff tapping each stone step rang through her ears. "Tell me you did not fail me again." She could not look at him. She hated the way the disappointment coating his voice made her feel, as if she truly cared to please him. Every last cell within her had been programmed to do his bidding, and his disappointment was more punishment than the physical torture she knew was coming. "What happened?" he asked her, his voice laced with hatred.

*If the king asks what happened, tell him you discovered that it was not Ink Valley who stole the spell book. Try to keep him off the topic of the missing Embers.*

"Ink Valley did not steal the spell book. It was nowhere to be found." She had not even made it to Ink Valley, let alone searched their entire territory for the book. But she believed Leith, and the lie poured from her lips more easily than she had expected, though nausea now worked its way up her throat, as if her body were revolting–the sire working the truth out of her.

*Convince him to assign you orders to track down whoever stole the book. You are clever. You can manipulate the king. Ravenna, you can resist the sire.* Before Degare could speak again, she said, "I need new orders. I will find whoever has stolen from you, and I will make them regret it."

Degare narrowed his eyes at her, then tilted his chin upward a hair. "Very well. You are to find whoever has taken my spell book *and* my Embers, and you are to *kill* them on sight." Did he know she had not destroyed Ink Valley? Did he know he had allowed Leith Fowler, the very leader of the rebellion, a room to stay in his castle right across from his most powerful weapon? Ravenna kept her gaze neutral, remembering that freedom had been promised. She could hold on just a little while longer. "You do not leave anyone alive. Do you hear me?"

"Yes, Your Majesty."

"If you understand me so clearly, then why is it that my men march to Ink Valley as we speak, taking care to destroy what you left untouched? To retrieve my Embers, which I need for the trade that is to happen in less than five days?" She could not help the breath that caught in her throat at his knowledge of her betrayal.

"Aside from this betrayal, Ravenna, I have not seen Mr. Carrington in a few days. I hope you have not forgotten the mission—"

"No, Your Majesty," she said too quickly, cutting him off. His eyebrows raised.

"Well, lure him into your bed or something. He seems to be quite smitten with you. Use that to your advantage, and do what you must to find that bloodstone." Ravenna nodded and swallowed the knot in her throat. "He can help you to locate my Embers too. And the Ozannes, now that they are missing," he hissed, drawing out his words in exasperation, "I hope you understand that I am going to need you to prove your loyalty to me." She nodded again slowly, the picture of submission.

She looked around the empty room, quickly realizing that Degare had cleared it to remove all witnesses. Not because he cared to hide the atrocities he was about to commit, but because he would appear weak if anyone else realized that she had failed. Though she had been sired to wreak havoc upon the rebels, she had not taken any lives. She had returned home empty-handed.

The king nodded to her belt loop, where a small knife hung at her hip. She knew what he was asking of her. She removed it, holding it in her palm. Her grip was tight and sweaty, and she could not help but dig her nails into the wooden hilt. "I need you to make me believe it," he said. She nodded.

"Anything, Sire." He smiled a cruel and wicked smile.

"Cut your leg, ankle to knee." She held all the tension in

her jaw. As she slowly dragged the blade up the length of her shin, she bit down a scream. "Cut deeper," he said. She did. Red blood poured over the black stone floor, and she thought maybe she would sink into the puddle, but Degare spoke again. "Other leg." She could barely stand, and as the knife moved with a mind of its own, her wailing echoed through the throne room.

"Use your flames to cauterize those before you bleed out." She hated herself for the disappointment that rooted in her gut. His voice was coarse, and his anger palpable. At least her power had returned to her. She brought flame to her hands, then watched it sweep downward over her quivering legs. Screams billowed out of her, and though Degare appeared pleased at her pain, he immediately halted her screams with a command. *"Quiet."* She bit down on her cries of anguish—could not release them if she wanted to. She willed her flames to focus in on those bleeding veins, but she had little control, and the surrounding skin began blistering and mending together as it melted. She had not mastered her gifts well enough to give delicate direction to those inherently destructive in nature.

Ravenna listened to the ticking of the massive clock that had been intricately carved of dark wood and displayed on the north wall. A grueling hour of proving herself to him went by, with her fulfilling every command and choking down her screams so those outside would not realize she had failed in her mission to destroy the Ink Bloods.

"Fragment the stone, command it to rise." She tried and failed three times before she successfully sent a whisper of her power through the ground. Minuscule cracks willed their way forward, cutting bits of stone free. As they began to break off,

Ravenna raised a hand, wishing for the stone to rise. It did not obey her. She tried again. "Do it now," Degared urged her on. Sweat dripped down her temple, and she focused as she raised her hand again. Finally, the stones hovered in a group beside her. A hundred small rocks trembled midair, awaiting command. Ravenna concentrated intently on that outflow of power as she watched her sire, guessing what that command was about to be.

In torturing her, Degare was reclaiming his throne—restating his authority over her. She had damaged his ego in not following his commands, and she knew she would be reaping the consequences for weeks.

Degare's voice rang out through the throne room. "Stone yourself." She closed her eyes for a moment, breathing deeply before coaxing the stones to clash against every inch of her body. She would rather be whipped at the posts, or tortured on the table, than be forced to go against her every bodily instinct and follow the sire to harm herself. The infliction of pain no longer scared her, she deserved it. But to do it to herself took a different type of willpower. It was like a war within, between herself and the sire that had woven its way into her very being.

She braced herself, remembering the first time she saw a woman stoned in the streets of the Brunts for assumed infidelity. She was no older than thirty and had three young sons who cried for her at the edge of the crowd of people. Hatred had spread across the entirety of the crowd's faces, even from those who did not know her. It was made clear to Ravenna by the accusations of those in the crowd around her, that she had been disloyal to the commander, to whom she belonged against her will.

Ravenna's face had gone to the boys who stood crying as

they watched their mother cowering, and Ravenna noted by their clothing that they were probably poor, though heirs of the commander himself. Hendrik had done nothing to care for his own blood. The Brunt men had all wielded small pieces of sunstone with arms drawn back, ready to pelt her. Her dark hair had covered her face, but Ravenna had known she was crying and trying to avoid looking at her sons, who were about to watch her die.

As the darkness around her celebrated murder, Ravenna had wanted to waltz into the middle of that circle and shield her, *kill* every man who stood in judgment for what she had had to do to provide for her family. But Xan had been by her side, and he had pulled her away before she had even had the chance. *We cannot risk it. The Despiri of Oro are in town collecting Embers,* he had said. *We should not even be here. You need to stay in Vestele, where it is safe.* She was not an Ember, and therefore the threat of the Despiri never worried her. Of course, that had been before Ravenna had understood why she had always been so coddled and kept within the valley.

But, all along, she was a hidden heir. What good all those years of hiding had done. To this day, she wished she would have helped the woman. Xan's strong grip had pulled her away through the crowds, keeping his head ducked and urging her to pull her cloak over her head. Ravenna now knew that had been to hide her identity from the prying eyes of Degare's men, who might have noticed her uncanny resemblance to Gerrin and Willa. Ravenna would do anything to go back to two years ago, or even one year ago, when her life had not been ruined, and the people she loved were still alive–when their bones were not strung up on the wall before her. When she could ride Fintah with her arms spread wide like an eagle's wings, soaring across the open valley, welcoming the dawn on the horizon.

As the stones plummeted against her skin, she thought only of Vestele. It all came rushing back. Everything she had pushed aside so she would not have to feel. The clay pots she once molded in her hands. The tall grasses that seemed to collect the whispers of the wind and soothe her as she gathered berries. The way her mother had always cared so fiercely for her safety, though Ravenna had not appreciated it at the time. Xan's widening grin as he looked at her, racing alongside him on horseback. The way he was always there, no matter what. Even when she pushed him away. Even when she denounced him as her second, he had come to her door to make sure she got out of the burning valley alive. Even without the blood oath, she knew he still would have been there for her. Because he had chosen her, and they were not lovers, but they were more than friends.

She craved companionship. Seeing him in the Dead Wood had not registered with her until now, and she realized she missed him. She needed him, and he could not be here for her. *No.* She would not want him to be put in any more danger because of her. She wanted him safe and far, far from here. But he was in Ink Valley, where Degare's men were quickly approaching.

Ravenna swayed with dizziness as the last of the stones smacked into her. She could hear each individual impact as she stood there, and then another louder impact as they fell to the floor around her at once. Blood seeped from a new laceration on her forehead.

"Heat the stone, remove your shoes, then walk on it." Ravenna's legs almost collapsed from beneath her, but she shifted toward a small table with wine on it and tried to catch her balance, sending the wine and herself crashing to the floor. Red–both wine and blood–stained her cloak. "Get up!" Degare commanded. She hauled herself up, her body begging her to collapse again.

Her palms were on the cold floor, and she retched forward, trying not to vomit from the pain. Slowly, she kicked her boots off. Her knees dug into the stone, and she sent a wave of raging heat through the contact points, careful not to let the heat travel toward her sire–who she was still unable to harm. *You will not harm yourself unless I command otherwise.* So, this was one of the instances he had been preparing for when he had given her that command.

Ravenna crawled forward, hoisting herself up with all her strength. The ground did not yet burn her, but at Degare's impending command, she would let down her guard against her own power once more, and her flesh would burn upon contact. "Do not worry, Ravenna, dear. The healers will be called in soon." And then killed, because Degare could not risk them finding out about her shortcomings and ability for disobedience. He would not allow himself to appear weak and would not allow his weapon to appear rebellious.

"I will not accept a healer. I deserve the pain that will come with healing naturally, Sire." She nearly choked on the words, but she would not allow innocent healers to die because of her.

Degare smiled. "Very well, then. I feel that you have learned your lesson. You can rest after you have made it to your chambers." He gestured toward the ground, implying that he expected her feet to burn the entire journey to the west wing, and she nodded once, hobbling over to pick up her boots.

"Guard!" he called in his right-hand man and commanded

him. "Clear the halls. Ravenna is not to be seen." The guard shifted his gaze to where she could barely stand, broken and quivering in pain. Her cloak was three shades of red: fabric, wine, and blood. Blood from her face now slid down her neck, and not a hint of remorse flashed in his eyes.

Before the guard shut the doors behind him, he nodded his understanding to the king. Ravenna was not to be seen in this condition. It was not only that, but that the stone floors were about to be unbearable to walk on—like lava stone. She heated the ground before her, breathing deeply and preparing for the pain that would be sent through the soles of her feet. She wished for the power to stop flowing from her body or for it not to bend to her will, but it did.

When the route to her chambers had been cleared, and no person—not even a guard—stood in the halls, she advanced forward out of the throne room. "Walk slower," he called behind her, and she did, away from her sire, dropping her walls of protection. She imagined the reddening of her skin as she walked, each step gruesome. Maybe she was a fool to deny a healer. She knew firsthand that burns were no wound to be toyed with. The pain would only grow worse before it lessened. She willed herself forward, willed her power to stop heating the floor, but she could not. It was as if the sire had been strengthened—reconfirmed after a small bit of rebellion. Her face crumpled, and her body nearly fell forward onto the ground. The only thing keeping her upright was the fact that she did not wish for more of her body to be covered in burns.

When she had finally made it up the stairs, she entered the winding hall of stone that led to her chambers. She only had to make it a hundred more steps. The halls were empty, as ordered, and she held tight to the end of the railing at the top of the stairs, trying to avoid letting her body crumble and touch the stone. Most of her skin was protected by clothing, but she knew she would be unable to rise, and she would die there, slowly. The sire commanded her to make it to her room, and besides, Degare would not let her die. *She* could not let herself die, as much as she wished to.

As she struggled through the next step, and every ounce of pain shuddered through her, she heard a door crack open. She tried to move quickly, not standing in one place too long, but her body was slowing down, and her joints disobeyed her. Slowly, the clicking of boots graced the halls. She kept her head down, willing herself to make it the remaining seventy feet to her room, where she would collapse and rest until she was summoned again.

"Ravenna? What are you doing?" Leith's steps quickened toward her. As he neared, she felt herself begin to collapse against the sire, and it was freeing. Leith's eyes locked with hers, pained and confused, and then he dropped his gaze to her blistered, bare feet. "What is this?" He then noticed the heat rising from the stone, and before her body could hit the ground, his arms were lifting her, bringing her tight against his chest. He stared at her as his mind turned, and she could tell he was putting all the pieces together.

"Get me to my chambers," she choked out. He listened, carrying her through the door in an instant. Every bit of her body relaxed as the sire quit raging war against her own will, and Leith carried her toward the bed. He sat her down into the plush covers and went straight into the bathing chambers, his face laced with. . .*rage*? Ravenna tried to hold her eyes open, but she wanted to sleep so badly, and she found herself dozing off to the feeling of her power going out from her. The feeling was accompanied by a sloshing sound in the bathing chambers.

When Leith returned with a bucket of cool, clean water, he pulled her to the edge of the bed so her legs dangled over. He removed the cloak from her shoulders, and she did not fight him. As she sat up, he tucked a few pillows behind her back for support. One at a time, he rolled her trousers up and silently placed her feet into the bucket of cool water. As the bloody fabric was pushed from her legs, he noted the cuts she had been forced to make down her shins, and he grimaced. She did not dare look at the wreckage. The coolness of the water soothed her burns, and she could feel unattached skin, mangled and melted away from its place. Leith worked silently, his hands gently grazing over the tender burns and washing her feet. She could only see the top of his head, his dark hair veiled his face from view.

"Why are you helping me?" she asked him. He would not look at her. She had caused the deaths of his people when she had turned the witch guardians onto him. She had tried to stop him from rescuing those Embers just two nights ago. She had come to destroy his village, and she would have done it if he had not stood in her way. When he did not answer her, she began to speak again, "I don't understand why you are going to such lengths to help me."

"And I do not understand why I have not yet killed him for what he has done to you," Leith snapped, his voice shaking the walls of her chambers. He looked at her with intensity for a moment and then redirected his concentration to her wounds, as if distracting himself before he marched out the doors to end the king now. Ravenna kept her mouth closed. The tension around him was near tangible; she could cut it with a knife. "I should have never brought you back here. I should have known Degare would pull something like this." Despite the bite in his tone, his touch remained gentle on her skin. The faint sound of movement in the water and the rippling effects from the quaking stone filled the room.

Ravenna breathed deeply against the pain. "There is no other option for me, Leith. This is my life now."

"I will not accept that," he said brusquely, and the walls shook again in response. She shuddered. *Why does he care so much?* He pulled her left foot out of the water, and at the pressing of a cloth against the burns, she winced.

"Caring about me will only get you killed," she bit out against the pain.

"I do not think so," he said. "Degare is nothing without you, and you are not his *puppet* any longer." He rose to stand up and grabbed her chin, forcing her eyes to meet his. "Do you hear me?" he asked, his hazel eyes burning into her own. They watched each other for a moment before his mouth moved again. "I will not watch you destroy yourself." His eyes danced from bruise to bruise, wound to wound, and then back to her eyes. "You are *done* doing his bidding." She scoffed as he barked the orders like she had any choice in the matter.

"As if it is that easy!" she retorted. "You have no idea the hold he has on me, Leith." His face was mere inches from hers. She tried to rip her chin away from his grip, but his fingers tightened, constraining her.

"Maybe not, but I do know the hold *I* have on you," he said, closing the distance between their faces until only an inch separated them. He breathed tightly, as if restraining himself. She did not pull away, and instead, whispered.

Her words were barely audible. "You have no hold on me."

"Is that so?" he countered and softened the grip on her chin slightly. She felt his breath on her lips. "I know you feel it too, Ravenna."

"Feel what?" she asked, a faint quiver in her voice.

"The pull between us. The force that keeps you from driving that knife through my heart." His gaze flicked downward, toward the blade that rested against his chest. She dropped it at once, breath hitching in her throat. *When did I grab that?* Degare did not want Locke Carrington dead yet—not before she had the bloodstone—but he did not know Leith's true identity or the threat Leith was to his life, and Ravenna was to protect the king at all costs. *Could that include going against the sire?*

"I—"

"The rules of the sire demand that you kill me, and you have proven my point time and time again that harming me is the one thing you will not do. There is a reason for that, and we are going to use it to our advantage."

# CHAPTER 64
# STAY WITH ME
## LEITH

Leith's power writhed under his skin as he looked upon Ravenna's wounds. Degare was still breathing after all that he had done to her, and though Leith knew it probably made him some primal, possessive idiot, it was all he could do not to barge out the door of Ravenna's chambers and head straight down to where the king lounged unbothered on his throne in the castle below.

Leith knew they needed a plan, and he was working on it. Day and night.

He kept reminding himself that Ravenna was in no way, shape, or form, his. She did not belong to him, but she was one of the Seven. They were forged for the same purpose, and the rage and hurt that came with seeing her harmed was that of a man whose very soul had been shredded. He could not relax, and every time he spoke, a little of his power crept out through his voice, rumbling through the streets of Oro. Leith would not allow Degare to harm her ever again. They would get the spell book back, and then he would kill the king.

"My general sent word about an hour ago," he said. Ravenna's brows cinched together, in confusion or pain, he was not sure. "By dove," he explained.

He knelt before Ravenna, taking her other foot out of the water. The flesh was destroyed, and it would take hours to heal her, to knit her body back together. Two poorly cauterized cuts had been sliced down her shins, and her body was bruised all over, as if she had been beaten repeatedly. He focused on the plan, breathing long, unsteady breaths.

"She was relaying a message from one of my spies. We suspect we know who has the spellbook."

"Who?" Ravenna asked, propping herself up on her elbows. Her body trembled now, the aftereffects of the adrenaline. Leith looked away from her and focused his attention back on the cuts.

He blinked, clenching and unclenching a fist. "The King of Edmaria."

"Idris," Ravenna stated slowly, as if working out something in her mind. After a long pause, she spoke again, "Yes, it was him."

"How can you be sure?" Leith asked. They needed to be positive before they acted against him—making this war an even bigger one.

"We danced, he showed off, and he disappeared. He did not come to the king's dinner," she said.

Leith tilted his chin up to look at her and added to the thought. "And it was that evening that the spellbook was stolen from Jara's chambers—while everyone was occupied with the ball. He caused his distraction, and then you did not see him again?"

"That, and his ship had disembarked by morning. I even

heard Jara mention another missing ship–assumed to be shipwrecked. That one had been sailing with Embers from the Dawn Islands. Perhaps it finally docked in Edmaria, but Idris reported it shipwrecked so he could keep the stock for himself." It was plausible, and smart.

"Wait, the Dawn Islands?" Leith asked. She nodded, face scrunching against the pain, and he let up some of the pressure he had on her leg. He needed to send word back to Cove immediately.

"What are you doing?" Ravenna asked hastily, pulling her leg from his grasp. Her power recoiled from his own, where he had been using it to begin stitching and healing her injuries.

He held his hands up. "Healing you. I don't have the power on my own. . .but yours, I can use to help you–"

"No," she said, wriggling away from him. He paused, perplexed.

"These wounds will take weeks to heal on their own," he said slowly.

"I do not care," she said, still leaning back on her elbows.

"Is this because you still think you somehow deserve this?" He could not help that his voice grew louder. Her stubbornness was enraging, and he could not stand the fact that she still did not see that none of this was her fault. She did not balk at him but instead leaned forward to the edge of the mattress. She said nothing, only looked at him with an inquisitive look. He continued. "Here is why you are going to let me help you, Ravenna Ozanne. Because in a few days, after you've rested, you are going to receive new orders from Degare. He is going to send you into Edmaria to wreak havoc upon Idris and his kingdom and stop him from creating any of his own Despiri. And while you are far from here, I am going to kill him." She studied him, and still, he could not read her. But then, she nodded slowly, as if agreeing to the plan despite the pain it caused her to know that he was to kill her sire.

"How do you plan on telling Degare of Idris's crimes?" she asked. Leith's lip ticked upward.

"Leave that to me." The king still foolishly trusted him and had no idea of his true identity. He did not even suspect that it could have been one of the foreigners he had allowed to stay in the chambers straight across the hall from his greatest weapon, who had depleted his stock of Embers in one fell swoop and had stolen Gerrin and Willa from their executions. Degare thought him to be a fellow man of darkness, a Despiri who was interested in purchasing more Embers–and Leith would keep it that way for now. Degare was after the bloodstone Leith had spent years collecting in his tunnel digging endeavors, and that was fine by him, if it meant he was allowed the time to coax the king's Raven into the Light.

Leith looked at her, motioning toward her cuts and burns, awaiting her permission to continue.

"Degare will not allow it," Ravenna said.

"Did he tell you that you were not allowed to heal yourself?" Leith asked.

"No. He offered healers and I refused them because I knew he would end their lives."

"Well, you do not have to worry about him ending mine, sweetheart. I am still a valuable piece in his games. Tell him you healed yourself–it is your power, not mine."

Reluctantly, she nodded, and he began pulling from her power, intertwining hers with his own and allowing it to whirl within him. Her darkness entered him, and he willed his own light to caress it and cover it. When her power had bloomed inside him and felt like oxygen to his lungs, he began channeling it outward toward his fingertips, where he massaged that healing power into her broken body. She breathed a sigh of relief as he willed the power to course through her, bringing some of her pain upon himself.

His breathing became heavy, and his shoulders sunk forward as he continued working, willing those horrible cuts to mend together. Her agony plagued him. Leith knew she was strong, but he did not expect her strength to be immeasurable.

When only two thin scars painted her skin, he moved his hands down to her feet where the burns had melted and destroyed her skin. His hands shook with exhaustion. He would not let himself stop. Drawing all that power from her in the Dead Wood and then expelling it back into her all at once had nearly depleted his own reserves for the rest of the day, and he had not had much rest since then. He still had his own power, but drawing from another source was exhausting. Ravenna needed to heal so she could begin preparing for her long journey to Edmaria, where Leith had big plans for her once he had killed Degare.

About an hour later, once her skin had mended itself, he rose to his feet, preparing to move onto the bruising on the rest of her body. She caught his shaking hand. "No more. Not tonight." He looked out the window and realized night had fallen. Under the light of the three moons, the streets were empty. Everyone had long since gone to sleep. He did not pull away from her gentle grasp.

"Stay with me," she said, the fingers of her other hand tapping slowly against her leg. Her face was unreadable, as if she was trying too hard to maintain its neutrality. Leith's forehead creased as he looked at her, and he began to protest, but then something like sadness settled in her eyes.

She had lost every friend and all the family she had ever known. She had nothing–not even her own freewill. She scooted back toward the headboard. There was a near indecipherable mixture of nervousness and guilt in her expression as she invited him to join her on the mattress with a gentle tap of her palm against the fur hide.

Leith swallowed, his body remaining still as stone as he studied her beneath creased brows. Her pleading face was like a thorn to his flesh, pricking and prodding him to come closer. The loneliness behind her eyes called him and his shallow breaths to join her. He backed up, jaw tightening as he sank into the chaise across the room, counting the nervous, mindless tapping of her fingers as she watched him.

A sigh left her lips as she sank into the pillow, legs curling up into her chest. She looked away from him then, allowing her distant gaze to fall to her restless fingers at the mattress beside her. A comfortable silence encompassed them, and it did not take long for her body to relax in sleep. She had invited him to stay. She trusted him, and *finally*, she was beginning to let him in.

Before her morning servants could enter, Leith quietly rose from the chaise and stretched his legs. Ravenna was fast asleep, her red hair flowing behind her over the plush pillow. He guessed she would sleep into the afternoon–as she should. He poured some water into a glass from the decanter next to her bed and dumped the wine down the drain of the bathtub.

He tucked the satin covers around her and brushed the hair from her face before exiting into the hall. Thank the Light the guards had stopped posting outside of her chambers. It had made his coming and going quite difficult. In his chambers, he washed Ravenna's blood from his hands and quickly changed his clothes to something of higher status. Today was a big day for Degare. It was the day that marked the start of his downfall–or perhaps that day had already happened when he had stolen the Dove.

Leith hid Ravenna's golden dagger with the ruby in the hilt at his waistline. As Degare was with his staff, Leith was with that dagger. It never left his body and would never be left in his chambers unguarded–especially not in Oro where Degare would order it destroyed if he knew what it was. Leith would use it when he killed the king, and if the opportunity arose today, he would gladly take it.

Leith came upon the king in the courtyard where he threw darts with his favorite Despiri, whom Leith assumed was the mindreader he had heard of from his spies. He had the passing thought to siphon Jio's power and use it against the king to read his mind, but it would not be covert. Jio would notice and Leith's cover would be blown.

Leith built a fortress around every precious sliver of information in his mind and surrounded it with lies before he called out to them. "Ah, a good game of darts!" he said, spreading his hands open as he approached them. Degare turned to Leith with a wicked grin, noticeably drunk only two hours after sunrise. Jara watched the game from a distance, examining her nails and reading a book–which Leith assumed was a book of spells and darkness. She threw Degare a look of disgust and went back to reading.

"Join us!" Degare exclaimed in drunken joy, motioning him over.

"Gladly," Leith said. "But I won't go easy on you just because you're the king." He winked, though his insides boiled with rage as Degare laughed.

"I would not expect you to, boy. I'll show you the ropes." Leith heard Jara angrily flip a page as he gathered a few darts in his hand. Jio stepped to the side, happy to watch the game between the two of them—happy to use the opportunity to silently attempt his way into Leith's guarded mind. He would find nothing but a fictional story of Locke Carrington, who had spent his childhood and early teen years in the south of Oro mining bloodstone, only to find himself in the Brunts. Years of the backstory of his fake identity swirled in his mind: all the bloodstone the king so desired, stowed away somewhere far; conversations that had never happened with Commander Hendrik of the Brunts; the dozens of Embers Leith had delivered into his hands; the gold that filled his pockets as a reward for his hard work; the Summer Trades when he had collected his shadowmarks; the first time he used that power; the day he married none other than Lila Carrington, who happened to look a lot like Cove. He made sure not to show her face.

Degare threw the first dart. It found its place a couple inches outside of the bullseye. He huffed and shrugged, slurring his words. "I may be a little off my game this morning."

"Early morning wine I smell?" Leith asked, nodding to the red liquid in his glass.

"Would you like some?" Degare lazily raised his glass as if in a toast.

Leith shook his head and smiled. "No, I prefer whisky. But thank you." Another angry page flip echoed behind them, and this time, Degare rolled his eyes.

Leith took the opportunity to stir up just the conversation he had come here to have. "What has her all doom and gloom today?" he whispered, gesturing toward where Jara lounged. Degare did not even try to hide his response, speaking loudly in return.

"She searches for a spell to locate the man who ruined my trade and made me look like a *fool*." His tone changed at that last word, and he spat on the ground, probably remembering the reason why he drank.

Leith tilted his chin up as if in realization, though he had already known the answer. Degare threw another dart, this time missing the target completely.

Jara's annoyance called out behind them. "I search for solutions while he gets drunk and plays darts."

Leith was careful not to acknowledge that statement or the king's retort when he threatened to throw the next one at her head. He doubted the king could hit the mark from a foot away in his condition. Leith faced the target, nailing a bullseye. The king grimaced.

"You know, I have my suspicions about a certain royal who was visiting the night of your ball," Leith started.

The witch looked up from her book, and Degare threw another dart. "Oh?"

"Idris of Edmaria," Leith said nonchalantly, hitting another bullseye.

Jara spoke first. "You should be careful accusing one of Degare's trusted allies of such heinous crimes against the crown," she hissed, rising from her chair. But Degare threw a hand up in her direction, motioning for her to sit back down.

"I'm listening," Degare said, awaiting further explanation.

"He and I spoke at the ball. We were to meet up for a game of cards in the tavern before dinner, but he never showed." Leith examined the dart in his hand, tapping the tip with his index finger. He felt Jio studying his every move.

"He was invited to the dinner party, and he did not show up for that, either," the king noted in realization.

Leith hummed, pretending to be perplexed. "Yes, it was his seat I filled."

Jara cut in. "Why would Idris bother with a spellbook if he has no clan to cast the spells?" Leith raised a brow as he realized her sudden angst. Her mind was turning, and Leith wondered if this new information put a damper on the schemes she had made with her daughter in the Dawn Islands. "You realize that if you accuse him of this crime, we will lose the alliance," Jara said to Degare. Leith did not know if he would consider whatever was between Edmaria and Oro an *alliance*.

"Technically," Jio cut in, "there is no alliance. We have a verbal agreement that they sell their stock to us. The written treaty is that the bloodstone in the mines is sold to His Majesty. If they have kept any for themselves for the creation of a weapon. . ." Degare waved him off.

"I'll send my Raven to find out if it is true or not. If it is, she'll destroy his kingdom, and a treaty will not be necessary. We will *own* them." Jara visibly gritted her teeth, and Leith turned his back to the king, throwing again. He had to keep the contentment from his face–the pride that came as this fool was falling right into his trap.

"And how do you know she will actually succeed–" Degare

cut Jara off with a sharp look, and Leith felt the king's attention shift back to him.

"The Raven of Oro has never failed me," he insisted. Leith shrugged and collected the darts from the board. He tallied the points in his head, and Degare spoke again. "I will send my armies with her for transport, in case she locates my missing Embers and needs a way to. . .control them."

Leith could not help the tension that settled in his jaw. "I win," he said, shaking the darts in the air. Degare frowned, and Leith continued with his plan. "I did not think your Raven would ever need the help of an army–"

Degare gave a quick defense of his beloved weapon. "She doesn't." The king pondered the thought for a moment and then looked back at the witch. "She will go alone."

Jara rose from her chair and marched toward the king, ready to object, to argue that Ravenna could no longer be trusted and needed to be escorted to Edmaria. *Why doesn't she want Ravenna to go alone?* She shot Leith a dirty look, and he raised his brows, handing the king half of the darts for another round. "Do not forget our discussion at dinner. I am willing to work with your Raven as your new mercenary. I do hunt Embers for a living, and I hear you are missing many."

The king looked at Jio, and he nodded in confirmation of Leith's words. The king shook a dart in Leith's face and laughed a loud, drunken chuckle. "I like you! Of course you are willing to work with my Raven. She is lovely, isn't she?" Leith forced a smile at him.

A heavy storm was rolling in from the Black Sea, and it was no coincidence. He would kill the king right here if he did not get a grip. With the memories of last night flooding his mind– of Ravenna's mutilated skin, the bruises, the pain that had bled from her body into his own when he had healed her–he was losing hold on his power. He had never felt anything like the pain he had leached from her. Not only a physical agony but an inescapable agony of the mind.

He needed to speed up the process of getting her out of this kingdom so he could enact his plan and end Degare. Before Leith could kill him, Ravenna had to be gone, retrieving the spellbook and playing spy in Edmaria until Cove could arrive to help her. Once Ravenna was gone, he would need at least a few days to bring in his own Ink Blood soldiers and infiltrate Oro's forces so he could get the king alone. Leith had no doubt he would be extra guarded in Ravenna's absence, but that would be no issue. With her gone, Leith would not have to worry about her getting injured in the fallout. Because there would be fallout. His men would do all they could to get the Embers and followers of Light who may be hiding in this kingdom out before it crumbled under his wrath.

"Edmaria is a far distance to travel by horse. It will take her over a week to get there," Leith said, tossing a dart. And since she had no ship, she would be forced to travel through the Valley of the Shadow. Leith did not like the idea of that. He supposed she could travel the tunnels, but that would force her to leave her horse and travel on foot. "In a week, Idris will have already made it back with the spellbook and might have his own weapon crafted by then–if indeed he has a witch." Leith looked at Jara, who was calculating in her mind.

"Are you my new mercenary and *advisor*, Locke Carrington?" Degare asked. Jara blinked up at him.

Leith chuckled. "I have difficulty straying from my old duties."

Degare raised his brows, pausing mid-throw. "You *advised*

Hendrik? Why, the two of you must have made one heck of a team to bring in as many Embers to Oro as you did." Leith's stomach churned with disgust as he nodded. Thunder clapped in the west, and the witch's attention was drawn to the sea. Leith never truly worked for Hendrik, but as the Ink Blood leader, he did provide the Brunts with bloodstone nearly every year, and every year as a part of his facade, he was the one to take it back home. Every year except for the last. Leith had rescued many Embers from that city, but not as many as had been taken. "I see you and my Raven have been spending much time together. To discuss your new position as mercenary, I hope."

"Ravenna and I are very excited to get started in finding those missing Embers," Leith said. "In fact, I can help you expedite that, if you'll hear me out." Degare motioned for him to continue. "It is my understanding that in the first war, Gerrin Ozanne had the ability to *teleport*." The king's chin tilted upward. "As the heir of his power, does your Raven not also hold that gift?" Degare had announced his defeat of the Ozanne family at the ball and had gone into great detail to anyone who would listen about how they had tried and failed to fool him by hiding their gifts. It was a known fact that Ravenna held the power of both her parents, the gifts she had inherited through the stone, and those of every Ember Degare had killed with the staff. But Leith did not know if she even realized that she also had the power of every Vestelian who had grieved their gifts to live a normal life in Vestele, shielding and protecting her from the truth and the world of Light and darkness.

"Indeed, she would," Degare smiled, clearly mapping out a plan in his head. The corners of Leith's mouth curled upward.

"I suggest she begin training so she can utilize that gift." Leith began tallying points again. This time, he was positive that his plan would work. Degare was falling right into the palm of his hand.

"Jara, find someone who can train her in teleportation," Degare said. Leith smirked, running a dart between his fingers. The king turned to him. "How long will you be able to stay with us, Mr. Carrington?"

"I am all yours, Your Majesty. I have sent my wife home, and she is quite supportive of my duties here. I will stay in Oro for as long as it takes."

# CHAPTER 65
# SHADOWS OF THE PAST
## SABRINE

The doorknob jiggled, and Sabrine sprang up in bed, quickly looking to the floor where Merrick's blankets were sprawled about. She rubbed the soreness in her neck as he entered the room with breakfast, and she groaned against the movement she made to take it from him.

"Thank you," she said quietly. They had been here for two nights, and both mornings he had brought her breakfast.

"How are you feeling?" he asked, setting a glass of juice on the table. She nodded as she chewed and looked at the desk by the window.

"You were up late again," she acknowledged, looking over the curious notes he had made.

"Couldn't sleep," he said. Sabrine rose from the bed and went to the mirror. She hooked the gold jewelry into her nose and ears and then pulled her hair into a thick braid before stepping behind the dressing screen to change her clothes. Her gown from the trades was torn and stained with blood, so she opted for the purple ball gown.

"Where are you going?" he asked as she stepped out.

"I am going out again. To see if there has been any news."

"Dressed like that?" he asked, amber eyes surveying her jewels.

She scoffed. "What is it with you and the way I dress?" She tugged on her sleeves, making sure to conceal the many bruises on her arms.

"Well, for one, we're in the slums of Oro. That jewelry is guaranteed to get torn from your face in an instant."

"You are welcome to join me if you are so concerned," she said, motioning to the door. He had not allowed her to go out alone once, and though she was used to finding solitude in the woods near the cabin and on her walks to the Thickets, she did not think she missed it. But he was only a placeholder—a voice of reason until she could find the twins. He was a means to an end. Nothing more.

She knew he would come with her, and hopefully together they would be able to find some information on the twins. She refused to sit around and recover for longer than necessary. Despite her probable broken ribs and the soreness that plagued her body, she was capable of working to save the twins' lives. Nothing would stop her.

She buttoned her cloak at her collar, covering the jewelry at her neck, and began to remove the gold rings from her nose and ear. Merrick sighed and kept his eyes fixed on her as he collected his embroidered jacket from the bedpost. When he tugged it on, his face twisted in pain. Sabrine straightened her shoulders.

"What was that?" she asked.

"What?" Merrick returned, fastening the gold buttons of his jacket and hiding another wince.

"You're hurt."

"I'm not hurt," he argued, refusing to meet her stare.

"Yes, you are," she insisted, stepping toward him. He backed away from her, and she grabbed for his shirt. "Show me." Her hands ripped at his tunic until she lifted it just enough to see a purple bruise spreading across his abdomen. He stepped backward and she followed. "When did that happen?" His jaw set, and he refused to look at her as he tried to pull his tunic down. "When, Prince?"

He looked to the rafters of the stone ceiling. "When I was trying to get to you in the crowd, I suffered a couple of blows," he said with a shrug. "It's nothing."

Sabrine shook her head as she examined the welts. "You should have told me. You've been taking care of me, and you have at least one, or maybe two, broken ribs." She took two fingers and gently pressed around the swollen skin. "The bruising is spreading all the way to your shoulder." She lifted his shirt up to assess the damage, and he stepped backward quickly, trying to cover himself. His shoulder hit the wall, and as he flinched in pain, she saw exactly what he was trying to hide.

"You're shadowmarked," she said, and this time it was her backing away from him.

"Sabrine, I–" he stepped toward her, pulling his tunic back down, covering the darkness that crawled across his upper chest and shoulder, and possibly all the way down his arm. *He always wears long sleeves,* she realized. *He had always ensured his privacy when he dressed those nights in the alleyways.* She had only thought him a private person, or perhaps someone who lacked courage, but he was much worse than that.

"You're a Despiri." She choked on the words as her heart thundered in her chest. He grabbed for her, but she stepped just out of reach. "You're one of them. You-you've killed before. You *tricked* me." Nausea worked its way up Sabrine's throat, and she reached for the bag of coins that sat on the desk. Merrick grabbed for it at the same time, and the bag spilled, sending all the gold onto the floor. They both stood there for a moment, watching it scatter, and then Sabrine ran, dodging his grasp one last time before she made it out the door, down the steps, and into the streets of Oro.

# CHAPTER 66
# FRIEND
## RAVENNA

It was the first night Ravenna had slept through in ages without the help of alcohol. Her body was entirely exhausted, wiped out from the torture and the strenuous healing. Her eyes looked to the empty chair beside the bed, and then she felt the neatly tucked sheets beside her. It was late afternoon, and she had slept the day away.

Had the servants not come? Or had she been sleeping so soundly they had left her to rest? She could not imagine Degare wished to see her after last night, and she could guess it would be a few days before she was allowed to be in his presence again.

Suddenly, she remembered the meeting she was to have today with the librarian. She groaned, rubbing her forehead. She was so tired. Would she get another chance to view the texts Magdalene had promised her? She would go back to the library at her first opportunity today—after she got some more rest.

Just as she was about to doze off again under the blanket that had been laid on top of her, she heard the skitter of talons on the windowsill parallel to her bed. She rubbed her eyes and rolled her face over into the pillow, groaning again, and her stiff arm blindly searched the bedside table for a knife to throw. *Someone had moved it.* She peeked an eye open. *No. Someone had tidied my entire chambers. And moved the bottles from my table.* She shook her head, reaching for the dagger and the note on the far side of the table.

It read:

*I wouldn't leave you without a blade, Little Dove. You're not ready for the one your mother gave you, but in time I trust you will be. For now, here is a dagger to replace the dinner knife I returned to the kitchens—and the many curious blades and forks I saw in the streets beneath your window. Your chambers were a mess, perhaps you should allow the servants in to clean every now and then.*

*Your friend,*

*Leith*

She looked around at her tidied chambers and rolled her eyes. There was no hint as to when he might return or when she would see him next. At the shuffling sound at her window, she quickly examined the new dagger and deemed it nothing special, then chucked it toward the bird she knew rested there.

Though she had expected to see the black of a raven's wings out of the corner of her eye, she saw a glimpse of white feathers right as the blade left her hand. She hastily sat up as a gust of ruthless wind rushed through the open window, fortunately shifting the blade midair and sparing the dove. In its talons was another folded paper, a more recent note from Leith. *How had he trained his birds to come to her window?* She hurried to the sill, and as she took the message into her hands, she peered down to the pit of dead ravens and bones where a small, feral cat was scavenging, carrying away the shadows that plagued her in its teeth.

She unfolded the page.

*I've got your sire wrapped around my little finger. You'll start training for your new mission in two hours. Remember our deal.*

She collapsed back onto the mattress, sighing and listening to the distant thunder and the beat of the rain drops on her windowsill. She did not feel like training today. What did Leith have up his sleeve?

From the bed, she caught sight of the box of letters she had hidden beneath the wooden chest. She had not touched them since before she had given into the sire. She mustered the strength to crawl out of the bed and plant her feet on the cool stone floor. Reluctantly, she selected one she had not yet read. In Zephaniah's neat handwriting, she found an ounce of comfort.

*Ravenna,*

*I spent many days in the torture chambers, but the Father got me through. I hope you can find rest in His Light, too. I try to keep my mind fixed on Him, but it often wanders to you and the darkness you face. Being locked away, helpless, when I should have prepared you better, that is more torture than the chambers could ever be. I feel as though I have work that is not yet finished. I need to see you.*

*I will tell you everything I know from the Light Scrolls, of prophecy and truth. For now, remember this, Ravenna. No darkness in Him resides. No death, no sin, no lies. His words are true, and He brings healing. From the grief you drown in after the loss of your people, to the guilt that gnashes at your heels, there is a peace that can cover it all.*

*Zephaniah*

Ravenna bit her cheek and unfolded another letter. When she saw it contained more writings from the Scrolls, she tossed it to the side and picked up another. She skimmed over the words, assuring there was none of the prophecy she was trying to avoid, and a couple of sentences caught her eye.

*In our days in the tower, I noticed something. Your fingers are calloused like my father's were. From a fiddle. I think I'd like to play someday.*

Ravenna's thumb swept over her hard fingertips, and for a moment, she was transported to a time before the darkness had come after everything she held dear. She could see the village dancing in the night, every face claimed by joy and nothing less. She could almost hear the quick-paced melody, feel the warmth of the fire on her skin. She blinked, hurriedly snuffing out the flames that had been fueled by the aching in her chest.

*Zephaniah would never learn to play, and she would never play again.*

Ravenna swallowed the knot in her throat and made her way to the bathing chambers. She debated on ringing in her servants but decided against it. She did not wish to have them scurrying about, poking and prodding her in the bath and rushing her along. Above the tub, the window was wide open, and the rain was coming in sideways. She grimaced and leaned in to shut the panes. But then she remembered Cove, and she paused to focus on the clear water.

She felt the power moving within her, and she projected it toward the rain. At first, the droplets recoiled, as if her first burst of power had been too much. She tried again with an imitation of Cove's gentleness.

At first, she could only focus on moving one drop. Very slowly, she used her eyes to direct it into the tub. She was not sure if she was using gifts of water manipulation or the ability to move items with her mind, as she had discovered the day of the executions. She smiled, looking back out the window for more.

Next, she moved three drops and then a handful. Before she knew it, she was moving glasses worth of water, the rain sucking right through the window and obeying her command to slosh down into the tub until it was filled. She smiled broadly and without restraint, then sank her tired body down into the water.

In a tub encased in the gentlest flames she could muster, she enjoyed a nice, warm bath. At least for about twenty minutes, that is until two healers rushed in, expecting to find her dead. She heard them before she saw them. When her chamber door slammed open against the stone wall, and their quick footsteps followed, she grimaced.

"Ravenna? My lady?"

She sighed, rolling her head back on the edge of the tub. "I do not need a healer," she groaned from the bathing chambers. There was whispering outside of the door, and another sheepish voice responded.

"King's orders. You're to start a new round of training today and–"

"I do not need a healer," she reiterated. The healers went quiet as they debated on their next course of action. They did not dare open the door without permission–probably in fear of being incinerated.

"What is all the fuss about?" A voice that drove needles down Ravenna's spine echoed through the door. She immediately straightened, putting the guards up in her mind.

Before the healers could answer, the witch flung the door to the bathing chambers open.

"A knock would have been nice," Ravenna said, lazily rubbing a bar of soap in circles on her shoulder.

"Where are your wounds?" Jara snarled. "Degare said you'd need healers." She could already feel the witch trying to worm her way into her mind in search of answers.

"Didn't you know? I have all the king's power. Part of which is the ability to heal myself." It was not a lie. But if asked to replicate the events of last night, she could not mend her wounds without Leith's help. She had no clue how to utilize that gift, and every one she possessed was different. Learning each gift was like teaching herself a new language. She would be better off focusing and mastering one before she learned any others, but where Degare was concerned, if she had the ability to cause mass destruction to his enemies, she was doing fine. It did not matter if her flames often wandered outside of the bounds she had given them, or if her darkness enveloped the whole kingdom instead of the room she had assigned it to. In his eyes, that was raw power—and the strongest type of power she could have.

Ravenna longed to control it, though, and at today's lesson she would do just that. She would learn and *try. Because now, there was hope.* If she did this and mastered whatever gift was in store for today, she would leave on this mission, Leith would have the opportunity to kill Degare, and she would be free.

"The king had no such gift. That must come from. . .your bloodline," she said in disgust.

"Towel, please," Ravenna said, holding her hand out toward Jara. The witch scoffed, grabbing her towel from the vanity and slamming it down into her hand.

Ravenna scrunched the towel around the ends of her hair, careful around the small braids that were always with her. "Why so grouchy? Is the king not treating you kindly?"

Jara rolled her eyes and ignored her comment. "Dry off. We're going to the opposite side of the kingdom for training today, since you destroyed the coliseum." Ravenna ignored her statement.

"You know, I don't understand why you stay with him. It is not like he holds any power over you, anyway." Ravenna was just being nosey now. She did not actually care about the affairs of the two most evil people in the entire world. But she was curious as to why the witch had not killed Degare the moment he held no physical threat to her. *What makes her stay?*

"It is none of your business, but just like you would have risked your neck for your own people while they were still alive, I suffer for mine." Ravenna pondered on that for a moment, wondering what kind of deal Jara had made with Degare for the benefit of the Delle Witch Clan. Perhaps Locke Carrington's bloodstone had something to do with it.

"He betrayed you. He is a liar," Ravenna said. A slap of cool, malicious power swam through her, and in just a split second, Jara was seething in her face.

"You do not speak poorly of your king," the witch reminded her. It had not been an order given by her sire, it was more out of respect that she had not been openly degrading his character in front of everyone. She had mostly wanted to avoid punishment. Ravenna chuckled, no longer caring. Unless the order came from Degare himself, she was not bound to it.

"You love him," Ravenna said nonchalantly, shrugging and stepping out of the tub in only her towel. She walked to the vanity and began to comb the tangles from her hair. "Must be horrible."

Ravenna could not imagine what it would be like to love someone so awful. And then she remembered that she was Degare's weapon, and she was all his darkness multiplied by a hundred. She could never be deserving of love either. There was a time when she had avoided it. She had kept Xan at arm's length, never letting him in. Always turning away when she feared he might kiss her. Standing here now, she regretted not allowing herself to feel what it would have been like to be loved, just once, by someone who was not obligated to. Her mother had loved her, and the parents she had never known had loved the idea of her. What did they think of her now?

If Zephaniah, who had come to be her friend, could see her now, he would not recognize her. Xan had looked at her that way in the Dead Wood just a day ago—like he didn't recognize her—and he had watched in brokenness as she had tried to kill him.

She was darkness, and she needed to stay far from anyone who might come to care for her. Because of her, most of her village was dead. Zephaniah and Galen had suffered the same fate. Xan and Tenille had both come close to death because of her on multiple occasions. Her parents had nearly been executed, but they had been rescued by Leith.

Leith had helped her last night, only to ensure she was ready to leave for her mission. If she was out of the kingdom, he would have a clear shot at the king. He could claim it was to free her, but it was only because he knew Ravenna would kill him in his attempt if she was present. He was using her, and she did not blame him. After her betrayal with the witch guardians, she would expect nothing less of him. He could pretend to care for her well-being, and to enjoy her company, to believe her to be the Dove and not the Raven, but he was only weaving his schemes together to kill the king.

It was because of this common interest that she would help him.

# CHAPTER 67
# HER CHOICE
## XAN

Tomorrow at dawn, the Ink Bloods were leaving Ink Valley. It was no longer safe, because Leith had been a fool in letting Ravenna–and now Degare–find out his plans for Oro. Xan should have been there for her. Leith had waited too long, and now Ravenna was no more. Xan should have broken out of Ink Valley the first day he had gained the strength to stand after the fires and the poison. But Tenille, she had shown up on the edge of death, and he could not leave her alone. Not after knowing she had no one left after her mother and most of Vestele had been killed by the Despiri.

"Xan, we'll get her back," Tenille was saying beside him as she finished up braiding his horse's mane. Tenille's black hair shone with a hint of honey in the afternoon sun. Xan shook his head. When he had seen Ravenna in the Dead Wood, his hope in getting her back had dwindled. The Ravenna he knew was gone. "For now, we should help where we can. The Ink Bloods are not like we always thought. They are strong, yes. And Leith sought Ravenna for her power, but Xan, these are good people," she said, gesturing around them. Tenille had been enjoying her time with the other healers in Ink Valley, and to see her content here gave Xan the peace he needed to leave.

"Leith still wants Ravenna for her power. He'll do anything to get it, and that includes putting all of Ink Valley in danger. It is not wise for us to stay with them any longer," he said. "Us Vestelians need to stick together; we need to find a way to get her back and keep her away from Leith, or he is going to lead her to her death." If Leith succeeded in getting Ravenna away from Degare, she would remain a weapon, but for the Light, and Xan did not think there was a flame left that could withstand the darkness in Arresia.

"Come on, you can't keep her locked away forever," Nilo butted in. Xan was grateful Nilo had survived the fires, but he could care less for his input. "We tried, Xan. It didn't work. She knows the truth now, or at least part of it. How can you be so sure she wouldn't choose to fight for the Light if she had the choice?" Nilo asked, crossing his arms. The feather tied at his bicep swayed.

Xan set his jaw. "I'll give her the choice," he said. "But Leith won't." Xan shoved his rations into the saddle bag on his horse.

"I don't think he's as evil as you make him out to be, Xan." It had been easy for Xan to see Leith as evil when he'd been going around Ink Valley calling himself the *Shadow* to newcomers, and when he'd been covering up the truth of his mission from everyone he claimed he didn't trust. He had painted himself in faux shadowmarks to play a part, but Xan wasn't convinced of his integrity. Especially not where Ravenna was involved. "We're all trying to do the right thing here," Tenille said. "He cannot force her to become an Ember."

"I say we stay here with the Ink Bloods," Nilo said as he munched on a fruit. "With them we have the numbers and strength, and we aren't starving. I think I've gained twenty pounds," he said with a grin. Physically, Xan felt stronger too. "The last thing Ravenna was going to do for Vestele before she was taken was unite us with Leith's clan," Nilo continued. "I don't think she made that decision lightly."

"I never should have let her be the shield-maiden," Xan muttered as he fastened the saddle bag.

"I told you to challenge her for the position," Tenille reminded him as she added a white feather to the horse's braid.

He gritted his teeth. This really was all his fault, and it looked like he would be fixing it all on his own.

Since he had returned to Ink Valley after his little altercation in the Dead wood with Ravenna and Leith, Edme had assigned him the task of training Ink Bloods and Embers in hand-to-hand combat. Most of the Embers who had just come from the holding prison in Oro were too weak to participate in much training, but there were about two dozen who had joined him today. Cove—the blonde Ember who had been with him and the others in the Dead Wood, and who Xan knew to be a spy in Oro—was training a few of the new Embers to utilize their gifts of water in both offense and defense. It came as a surprise to Xan that not many Embers knew how to fight with their gifts. Not many had even used their gifts since before their captivity, and Xan guessed Cove had somewhat of a similar background. Her empathy with the other Embers was palpable, and he admired her for it. The art of empathy was not something he was skilled in.

Xan was leading his new warriors through a pattern of maneuvers when the Volcanian general approached him. She stood at the same height as him, and her strength was made known in her calculated walk.

"Oh, spare me," Xan muttered.

"You're teaching them wrong," Edme said, marching toward him and reaching for the blade in his hand.

"Easy there," he said, drawing back and keeping his hold on his sword. "It took months for you to allow me to touch a weapon, I don't think I'll be letting go anytime soon." He had finally gained some trust, and that would make saving Ravenna easier. Edme rolled her eyes, still waiting for him to hand the blade over. He examined the sword in his hand, suddenly feeling the need to prove himself equal to her, whether she bore the title of general or not. He was second to the shield-maiden, and he had spent the last years training Vestelian men and women to fight. It was time she stopped with her blatant disrespect.

"Why were you so reluctant to give me a blade all this time?" he asked. "Was it because I'm better than you with a sword?" He twisted the sword in his hand again and tossed it, drawing attention to his skillful hold.

Edme crossed her arms, waiting for him to hand over the blade. He did no such thing.

"Admit that my techniques are better than yours, and that you have no right to try and correct me," he said, holding the blade out of reach.

Edme scoffed. "I am no hypocrite. I could beat you in a fight."

Xan laughed and looked her up and down, taking in the marks on her skin that glowed orange like molten lava. "Without using your fire?" he asked, remembering the times she had used her flames to prod him into submission.

"Easy," she said, face neutral.

Xan's brow ticked in satisfaction. "Then it's a duel." Nilo cracked a broad smile beside Xan and spit the seeds of his fruit onto the ground, then offered Edme his sword. She took it without taking her eyes from Xan, and for a moment, he was reminded of Ravenna's stubborn determination to win every challenge and of her incessant need to prove herself best. He blinked and took a deep breath. "When I win," Xan said, turning his blade again, "what is my prize?"

Edme shook her head. "Don't worry about it. That's not going to happen."

Xan let his lips fall into a faux pout, and then he smiled, coaxing her toward him with two fingers. A young girl that Xan had learned went by the name of Kaida encouraged Edme from the sidelines. "You'll have him pinned in less than a minute, Ed. I know it." Edme was Kaida's mentor in all things fire.

Edme said nothing, only stepped slowly from side to side, sizing him up. Within a matter of seconds, all of Ink Valley had gathered around to witness the duel in the crisp autumn air between mountains. Xan smiled at his audience and at the few familiar faces that had been with him since he was a boy—the ones who had watched him grow into his purpose. *Protect.*

"When I win," Xan said, "you entertain the idea of helping me get Ravenna back. Without Leith." Edme's glare at Xan was intense, but a corner of her lip tugged upward.

"You'd be better off partnering with him. I am the one who wanted your girlfriend dead." Xan narrowed his eyes on her.

"Just fight already!" Kaida yelled. And with that, Xan jolted forward with his blade.

Xan could admit that even without her fire, Edme was still a strong warrior. She fought with pent up anger though, and he quickly learned that she was not methodical, but rash in the decisions of where to swing her sword. Xan was always three moves ahead, mapping out the fight in his head, and she fell into every trap, unaware that he was the one leading this dance.

"Think before you swing," he told her as he ducked low. She grunted, pulling her sword down as he rolled through the dirt. *Is she truly trying to kill me?* He could have swiped his sword across her shins easily in that moment, if he wanted to. But this was just a way in which Xan was to earn her trust, along with the other warriors of Ink Valley. Killing her would get him nowhere, and that was not what he wanted anyway, as insufferable as she may be. Xan was not sure if he would be tagging along in their travels tomorrow, or if he would abandon Tenille to go his separate way toward Ravenna. But he had come to realize that trust from the general of Leith's armies would bring him far.

"Come on, Xan," Nilo yelled behind him.

Edme's eyes flashed, and he saw fire behind them. "Ah ah ah," he said, circling her with his blade pointed inward. She lunged forward and he sidestepped, bringing his forearm down on hers and knocking the blade from her grasp. Edme watched the dust scatter as it fell, her lips in a flat line.

"Looks like I win," Xan said as Nilo came between the two of them and collected his sword from the ground.

"Get back to training," was all she said, waving a fiery hand over her shoulder as the crowd that had gathered parted for her. Xan shook his head, smiling to himself as Nilo clapped him on the shoulder.

At dawn, Xan found himself following the many Ink Blood warriors and their families, the Embers, and all the wagons, horses, and cattle through witch territory toward the Hollow Coves. He was not sure if traveling this territory was worth the risk, even if there was a supposed haven awaiting them at the other end. Over half of the Embers they'd just liberated were physically ill, malnourished, and incapable of defending themselves, and the other half were nearly as useless. If they were to cross a witch clan, what would become of them? Would it be execution to all who bore no Light and straight back to Oro for the ones who did? Did the witch clans work for or against Degare? Xan set his jaw as he surveyed the forest around them, watching for any movement outside of the crowd of Ink Bloods.

Ashreya was the only witch Xan knew, and if she had been able to temporarily disable a group of Despiri in Vestele that wretched night, what more could an entire witch clan who were not out of practice do to these people?

"Relax, friend," Nilo said beside him. "I don't see any witches, do you?" Xan rolled his eyes. Leith claimed he had not seen any witches in this territory in months, and Nilo believed him. *But if they aren't here, where are they?* "Even if you could, I doubt they could see us. See that warrior over there?" Nilo pointed to one of the Ember soldiers that had escorted him to

Vestele, where Ravenna had told him she never wanted his protection.

"I know all about his cloaking abilities," Xan muttered. It was how they had transported all of these Embers from the trades and the prison to the tunnels unseen, and it was how Xan and Tenille had made it away from Ravenna alive when she had destroyed what was left of Vestele.

"Pretty neat, huh? There's one for every hundred people. They have to rotate out when they exhaust their power, but we should be able to make the journey undetected."

"I still think Leith is making a mistake in letting his armies travel through these territories."

Nilo smiled. "I kind of respect the guy. Look at this army he is raising, and at the clan he has built. He has an abundance of warriors who, honestly, could crush us in a battle." Nilo jokingly swung a blade through the air, and Xan glared at him. "What?" He sheathed his dagger. "I am just stating the obvious. Most of them are gifted by the Light. We would be hard pressed to find another clan that offered us more strength."

*If only this clan was not the one that was to bring Ravenna's death or to force her to fight.* Ashreya never wanted this, and Xan did not either.

"Some of these new Embers can barely walk. I've seen three collapse already," Xan said as his feet crunched through the leaves where he walked amid a thousand men and women.

"Well we can't stay in the valley. I'm thankful Ravenna is still alive, but you have to admit, she has endangered all of these innocent people. My guess is, Oro's Despiri will leave nothing but ash between those mountains." Xan's eyes fell as the thought of smoke clouded his mind, bringing with it everything he wanted to forget.

Nilo was right. They were safer traveling through witch territory for a few hours, than to wait for Degare's wrath to come upon the valley where he believed them to be.

"We'll return to Ink Valley when it is deemed safe," Edme said from behind them. Xan turned around, eyes immediately drawn to the vibrant color of her dress, which contrasted sharply with her rich skin. Her hair was styled differently every day. Today, it was pulled across her shoulder in a thick set of braids, and he could see a yellow topaz earring peeking out from beneath it.

"What makes you so sure?" Xan asked, shifting his attention forward as they traveled on foot. "You're not in charge here. But I think you could be, if Leith was out of the picture."

Edme chuckled. "Believe it or not, Xan, Leith still has my respect. I do not wish him gone. You, however, still lack my respect. Perhaps make yourself useful and take this letter on up to Cove." Edme waved a letter in the air, pointing it toward the back of Cove's head, where the woman's platinum hair reflected daylight like a moon. Xan's eyes wandered to the seal of the letter, where he recognized Leith's signet from the ring he always wore on his finger. Xan raised his chin as he took it into his hand. He wanted nothing more than to tear it open and read the secrets inside, but something told him this was a test, and it was one he refused to fail.

"I can do that," he said with a shrug.

"Good. I need to check in with the two men cloaking the flank." She looked at Nilo. "See if you can't get everyone to pick up the pace. We don't need to spend the night out here if we don't have to. My cloaking Embers are tired."

With that, Edme left, and Xan and Nilo exchanged a glance. "Finally, an assignment. This place is feeling a little more like home every day," Nilo said proudly as he set forth to encourage the tired people to set their weaknesses aside and trek faster.

Xan looked to the letter in his hands and then at the thousands of unfamiliar faces around him. Even if it meant he had to join in the Ink Blood's fight for a time, he would use Leith and his resources to get Ravenna back, and then he would take her far from here, from this place that was not their home.

# CHAPTER 68
# FAIR FIGHT
## COVE

"A letter came for you," a familiar voice said from behind her. Cove halted her humming and spun around to see Xan. He was tall and rugged, and if he had been a bit cleaner with curly hair, perhaps with a bit more shine, he might have reminded her of Elias. She pulled her navy cloak on. He noticed her attention to his stained tunic and brushed some dirt from it.

Cove spoke up. "Well, since you won the duel, did Edme agree to help you save Ravenna from the evil Leith?" she asked, smiling at him. He grimaced and clutched the letter a little tighter.

"Who is it from?" she asked, nodding to the message in his fist. Currently, all of Ink Valley was traveling east toward their new haven, where they were to hide from Degare's army and his Raven while they waited for new orders from Leith. He handed it over silently and watched her break the seal as they walked.

507

"Whatever it is about, I want in." Cove's forehead creased, and she stifled a laugh. His lips fell into a tight line.

"Sorry, it's just, you aren't gifted, are you? What do you plan to do against the shadows we fight? I don't see how–"

"I'm a warrior. I trained all the Vestelians, and you have seen what is left of us." Xan nodded to a tawny man that watched them from a few feet away with a wide grin. Cove waved, and Xan continued, "I won against Edme. I am good with strategy. I'd make a good general or whatever you need, as long as it involves getting Ravenna back."

"We have a general," Edme cut in from beside them. Cove and Xan turned to face her. "I sent you to deliver a message, not barter for my position," she grumbled. Xan blew out a breath and looked to the sky. "Come to me if you're not satisfied with your work. I'm in charge here."

"Okay. I am not satisfied with staying back and training the Ink Bloods in hand-to-hand combat. I want to bring Ravenna home." Cove chewed on her lip.

Edme smiled, summoning flame to her palm, and said, "No." Xan scoffed. "Look, you're not being kept under lock and key anymore, and you have your weapons back. If you really wanted to, you'd be gone by now," Edme muttered.

Cove shrugged at Xan. Edme had a point, but Cove doubted the general would let him leave that easily. Not with the information he had about Ink Valley. But the Ink Bloods had men inside the castle with Ravenna, and Xan would be a fool to leave before trying to use that to his advantage. Cove saw what he was doing, and she understood far too well. Men like Xan could be dangerous. Unstable. She could see that he would do anything for Ravenna, just as she would do anything for Elias.

"What does the message say?" Xan prodded, reminding her of the letter that had traveled all the way from Oro. Xan hovered in front of her, trying to catch a glimpse of the words as she unfolded it.

*Cove,*

*Elias might be alive in Edmaria. Ravenna spoke of a ship that docked there and never made it to Oro for the trades. We suspect Idris is holding Embers there. To write to you my plan is too risky, but go and find your husband and bring him home to the Ink Bloods. You have a home here now. You know your purpose. In the desert lands, watch out for the King's Raven. She will be in the territory soon on Degare's orders until I can put a stop to that sire. Aid her where you can. Tell Edme to send a hundred of our best men to the outskirts of Oro through the tunnels and to wait there for my signal.*

*Leith*

Cove's heart thrummed in her chest at the newfound hope that flooded her.

"He aims to kill the king," Edme said flatly from where she read over her shoulder.

Cove nodded. "It would seem so." *Elias might be alive in Edmaria.*

"By now he must have had a million chances to kill that girl, and he has yet to succeed," Edme muttered.

Xan stiffened. "It's time to move," he said to Cove. "Your husband is in Edmaria, and Ravenna is about to be there." *And likely on orders to retrieve or kill Elias.* "You and I, let's go."

"Absolutely not," Edme said quickly.

Cove pondered for a moment. "No, he's right. I am going, and you have no right to keep him here any longer either." She would go anywhere or face anyone for Elias, and if Ravenna was on her way to him now, Cove needed to get there sooner.

"We cannot just let people leave, he knows too much." Cove shook her head and sighed as Edme continued. "And, apparently, we're about to move our armies toward the border of Oro. We'll need all the warriors we can get."

Xan scoffed at that. "You think my skills are needed now? Only after I beat you yesterday?" He tilted his head and flames curled around her fists. "Sorry Ed, but I won a fair fight. You owe me this. Where Ravenna is, I'm going. If you need me, I'll be in Edmaria, ready to bring her home."

# CHAPTER 69
## STOLEN STALLION
### SABRINE

Sabrine had spent two nights in the streets, sleeping beneath the ominous fog of this wretched kingdom. Degare's trades had been delayed, yet again, and Sabrine was thankful that with each passing day, the probability of them happening seemed to lessen.

Merrick was searching the entire kingdom for her, but she was good at hiding. *How could I have been so foolish as to trust him? I have been working with a Despiri this whole time.* Sabrine watched from the docks, where she had gone to sit for the day, as many of the ships were disembarking. She had hoped to catch wind of the plans for the trades, and information where the Embers could have gone, but she heard nothing other than complaints and backless speculations.

"Degare is a fool," a woman from Brinland was saying in a shrill voice. "His kingdom has obviously fallen under attack, and he tries to hide it from us? I refuse to stay here any longer." A few ships and boats still swayed in the sea of blood, and Sabrine watched as the lady and her friend climbed aboard.

"The Autumn Trades are not happening. He needs to call them off."

Sabrine positioned herself next to the tiny sailboat, which they were brave to take across the waters of the Black Sea. By the looks of it, it had already suffered damage in the hailstorm and had been poorly repaired. Sabrine adjusted the fabric around her face and cleared her throat. "You believe the trades will be canceled all together?" she asked, pretending to be disappointed.

The two women looked at her as if they had not noticed her there. "Degare said one week, and it has been four days without news. I bet he hasn't reclaimed his stock yet. By the time he does, everyone will have left."

Sabrine nodded, considering, and the brown-haired woman spoke up. "We have experienced nothing but grief in this kingdom. First, we had to travel through a raging sea of *blood*. Next, the king's weapon stole my favorite dress straight off my body." Sabrine raised her brows. "Then, the hailstorm damaged our boat, an earthquake followed, and suddenly the Embers I came to purchase are missing?" *Shallow, uncompassionate woman, to long for and celebrate murder.* It was disgusting. Sabrine needed to find the twins. The woman held tightly to her hat against the unforgiving winds that hovered over the Black Sea, which had begun fading from red back to a deep blue that was nearly black. Sabrine backed away as the boat left the dock, and the woman called to her over the sound of waves breaking against rock. "Oro is not the kingdom it once claimed to be. If I were you, I'd leave the first chance you get!"

Sabrine bit her lip and took toward the markets, where she hoped to find some food for the day and some actual information regarding the location of the twins. Most of the vendor stands had been destroyed, but a few remained in the square. She swiped a strange orange vegetable from a basket and shoved it into her cloak, then reached for a piece of fresh bread from another table. Swiftly, she took a few steps west, and with her back to the vendor, she tore a piece off the bread and took a bite. She was starving.

"Hey! Are you going to pay for that?" the vendor yelled. Her chewing halted as she froze in place, heart thundering in her chest. *Have I lost my touch?* This kingdom was not one to be caught stealing in. Sabrine began searching her empty pockets, keeping her eyes on the Despiri guard whose attention was now on her. She had the money sack tied at her thigh, but she refused to spend it on anything other than the twins. There was an alley to her left, and if she could make it to the end and out of his sight, she had a decent chance at escape.

"Yes, she was," a familiar voice said, and Sabrine's face flushed. She turned to see the Prince of Edmaria, just as he flipped a coin toward the grouchy man. It was gold, and worth far more than the tiny loaf she had stolen. The Despiri guard who had been ready to pursue her relaxed. Before the vendor could thank him, Sabrine turned to run, but Merrick caught her arm, sending her heart into her throat.

"I thought I'd find you here sooner or later," he said. She tore her arm from his hand and whipped a dagger from her cloak.

"I'll make a scene," she warned, glancing at the vendor and the Despiri who had both turned their attention elsewhere.

"Just let me explain," Merrick said, stepping toward her slowly. He looked dirty, as if he had spent his recent nights on the streets, too, and his amber eyes portrayed a faux gentleness as he reached for her. She hated the way he cringed as she continued to retreat.

"No amount of kindness will undo what you've done," she hissed. There could not be redemption for him. He had killed an Ember, and then he had pretended to care about her and her siblings' safety. "What was really in it for you? Why did you offer to help me?" she spat, shoving him away from her. He stepped forward once more, hands raised. She kept the dagger pointed at his chest while she slowly backed away, and then she fled again.

The streets were slick with rain, but he was fast. She heard his steps thundering behind her. "You won't survive on your own!" he called after her. "You need me!"

She said nothing and pushed onward as fast as her legs would take her. She aimed for the east side of the kingdom, where she hoped she could hide amongst the crowds in the slums. She glanced behind her and saw him falling behind, then saw him take to the left, probably planning to circle the building to trap her. When he disappeared around the corner, she slowed and removed her cloak, discarding it in an alley. She began walking in the other direction, watching her surroundings carefully. She joined a group of women who were heading back toward the square carrying buckets of clean water. She worked her way into the midst of them, hoping their frail bodies were enough to conceal her. After a few deep breaths, she allowed herself one brief glimpse behind her.

She had lost him, for now.

She remained near the group and only paused when she saw the witch and the king's weapon traveling on foot in the other direction. Gradually, she separated herself from the other women, and they walked mindlessly on, ignoring her coming and going completely. Sabrine made her way toward the King's Raven and the witch, following closely enough behind them amid the crowds so she could eavesdrop on their conversation.

"What is my new training to be?" the Raven asked. Her hair was a deep copper, perfectly matching the rust that had formed on the iron gates of Oro. It was pulled back into a thick braid made up of many smaller braids–a style Sabrine had seen before on some of the native valley dwellers near the old kingdom of Ozanna. The Raven was clad in custom armor of black steel, fashioned to resemble the bird whose name she bore, and a wooden bow, much nicer than the one Sabrine had left in the cabin, was strung over her shoulder.

The slender, black-haired witch paused for a moment, pondering the Raven's question, as if carefully choosing what information to give. After a moment, in a cruel voice, she said, "Our king is to send you to Edmaria. . .alone." Sabrine's mouth went dry. "You are to use your gift of teleportation to travel there and stop Idris before he can forge his own bloodstone weapon." Sabrine stopped in her tracks. *Edmaria? Idris is forging his own bloodstone weapon?* Sabrine recalled seeing the many Embers coming off the ships in the Thickets all those weeks ago. She recalled the strange way they were being sorted; the way some were being sent to the mines, and the way most of the others seemed to remain off the ships when they should have been continuing to Oro. Idris had been overworking the bloodstone mines lately. *What if he was collecting his own bloodstone for a weapon. . .and his own Embers? What if Neah and Risley had never made it out of Edmaria?*

Like a spooked horse, Sabrine took for the gates of Oro without a thought, the purple satin of her gown flowing behind her in a kingdom full of black. She did not care that everyone was looking at her, or that the Raven of Oro was just around the corner. She locked her sights on a Despiri guard who stood next to his stallion unaware of her approach and readied her dagger.

With one fell swoop, the Despiri guard fell, the horse's reins were in her hands, and she was climbing up, sending the stallion racing toward the rusty iron gates that led into the Dead Wood. She was a murderer now, too, but she did not care. Over the blood rushing through her ears, she could make out the faint sounds of yelling behind her as some of Oro's men trailed after her. She urged the stallion to go faster, thankful for the lessons she had been given when she was younger. She squeezed with her legs and held tightly to the reins as they whipped through the brittle branches of the lifeless forest.

*Had Merrick known all this time that his father was keeping the twins in his kingdom?* It didn't make sense. *Why would he have gone through all of this trouble?* Sabrine thought her adrenaline had all been spent during her recent endeavors in Oro, but her head pounded with it now. She did not look behind her as her horse dove further into the blackness of the woods, hooves squishing into the mud and leaving prints all the way to the Valley of the Shadow.

# CHAPTER 70
# A NAME THAT ECHOES
## RAVENNA

"Why must we walk all this way?" Ravenna whined, trying to annoy Jara. "Don't you have a royal carriage or something for this?" Her body was sore and tired, and she was carrying the extra weight of her sword and bow and arrows. She hoped she would have time to brush up on her skill before the mission.

"The king is occupying it, for his trip to the Black Temple." Ravenna guessed he was still pleading with the goddess of the sea to bring his kingdom clear water.

"Our kingdom is the most wealthy and powerful of all of Arresia and we only possess one carriage?" Jara rolled her eyes at the snide comment. Her dark hair was sleek today, its shine extending just below her shoulders. Typically, she wore it up and neatly pulled back into a twist. Today, Ravenna had done her own hair, a style made up of loose strands and about seven tiny braids. Each a small reminder of the lives she had taken and the vengeance she was finally on her way to achieving.

"We have many carriages. *I* did not request use of one today to keep the king in high spirits."

"One wrong move and it'll set him off, huh?" Ravenna said, listening to the clacking of her boots against the stone. Jara muttered something under her breath that sounded a lot like agreement with her statement. Ahead, the air was dense with a gray haze, and the rain clouds covered much of the east side of the kingdom. They had rolled in over the Black Sea and were now moving east, toward the outskirts of Oro. She wiped the rain from her face and continued forward, not bothering to avoid the puddles. With a mile to go before they reached the edge of the kingdom where she was to begin her new training, she would be sopping wet anyway.

"What is my new training to be?" Ravenna asked.

Jara informed her that she would be going to Edmaria alone, using the gift of teleportation. It was this first bit that Ravenna guessed Leith had especially negotiated–that Degare's armies be left behind. Because if they were left behind, Ravenna would not be held accountable for whatever she was to achieve in Edmaria, and there would be no witnesses if she failed to do so.

With the armies staying back, there would likely be a war in Oro the moment Leith tried to assassinate Degare. But Ravenna knew Leith would have his own armies of Ink Bloods, and possibly vengeful Embers, waiting to engage in the destruction of Oro. He was hoping to take out all the Despiri along with Degare. Leith was going to wipe out Oro in its entirety. The king and all the king's men. Ravenna tapped her fingers against the hilt of the sword at her side.

Jara continued forward, disgusted that the hem of her expensive black dress was dragging through muddy puddles.

Ravenna wondered exactly what *teleportation* was and how she was to use it to travel and stop Idris before he could forge his own bloodstone weapon, when he had likely already started crafting it. She was days behind him.

"You'll have four days maximum to master it. Then you must be on your way," Jara said. Ravenna looked to the tall, black stone pillars that towered high above the prison. She could not help but look to the prison walls and try to glance inside to see how many Embers still suffered there. There was a ruckus in the streets behind them—likely just an altercation among the slum-dwellers—so Ravenna stayed focused and let the Despiri guards handle it. As she and Jara made their way toward the pillars, Jara spoke again. "This building is similar to the prison because there is bloodstone built into the walls. I can spell bloodstone to work how I want it to. In the prison, it keeps the Embers from being able to use their gifts. It weakens them along with the shackles. In this new training center, I've spelled it to assist in control and magnification. I got the idea after you struggled before the ball, and Degare approved the idea to add bloodstone into the walls. We used what little supply Edmaria brought in on their ships. The final touches were made the day before the earthquakes. Thankfully, it suffered only minor damages and needed few repairs. It will be announced in the Winter Trades, and only the Despiri who purchase kills will be allowed entry." Ravenna admired the building, noting the minuscule slivers of bloodstone that had seemingly been melted into the natural black stone of this land and crawled all the way to the roof, which was the height of three mature oaks stacked on top of one another.

"Is this why the king searches for Locke Carrington's bloodstone?" Ravenna asked. "For things like this?"

Jara shook her head, her face smug. "Not quite."

Ravenna reached out a hand to touch the wall, and sure enough, her power seemed to sing and thrum against the bloodstone. She pulled back, ashamed that she had liked the feeling so much. Jara smirked at her and pushed the dark wooden door open, revealing a vast empty room with a towering, dome ceiling crafted of thick glass. Raindrops gathered on the other side, and Ravenna watched them trail down until they met the stone walls that held the dome up. There was movement across the room, and from the shadows, a man began walking toward them. He raised his hands, calling to her.

"The Raven has finally made it!" He smiled a little too broadly for her liking. He was too chipper for this kingdom. One moment, he was thirty feet from her, and in another, he was within arm's reach—as if he had vanished into shadow and willed himself to materialize right in front of her. *This must be teleportation. Is this what I am to be learning?* He grasped Ravenna's armored shoulders, and she resisted the urge to knock him on his back. "Welcome!" he said, shaking her slightly and looking unreadably at Jara.

She willed her skin to produce flame and heat the steel feathers, and in only a second, the man was releasing her and checking his hands for burns. He staggered back as his skin began to blister. Ravenna raised a brow at him as if to say, *Do not test me.* The man should understand his boundaries before they began, and rule number one was: *do not touch the Raven of Oro.*

Ravenna wiped her hands on her pants and adjusted her leather corset. She had worn such things in Vestele to protect her body while fighting, but the armor she had been given here in Oro was far more luxurious and slightly more comfortable. It probably worked better, too, though, she had not been involved in much hand-to-hand combat lately to test that theory.

The man smiled nervously at her, extending a hand for a handshake. Ravenna looked at his blistered palm and waved him off. "I-uh, my name is Marcus," he stuttered, dropping his hand. Even Jara rolled her eyes at his sudden nervousness. Jara slapped him on the shoulder, and he jumped.

"Well, Marcus, get to it. We don't have all day," the witch said, locking eyes with Ravenna for a moment that seemed to say, *Good luck with this fool.* A corner of Ravenna's lip tugged upward, and she returned her attention to the blubbering fool. He was not the typical hardened Despiri she had come to expect out of Oro's gifted men, and though slightly too optimistic, it was almost like a breath of fresh air.

"Are you going to teach me how to teleport or what?" she said, flashing him the whisper of a grin.

He danced on his feet for a moment while he tried to find his words. "Why, yes. I-I. . ." he started and then cleared his throat. "I apologize," he said slowly, taking a deep breath. "I am no teacher, I–"

Jara cut in. "He's been selected out of the prisons to teach you. Teleportation is rare, and he is the only one in Oro well versed in the skill. He's our best hope," she muttered. Ravenna narrowed her eyes on the witch and then looked to Marcus. When she really *looked* at him, she recognized the hollowness in his eyes that would come with years of persecution, malnutrition, and probably slavery in the mines.

He was an Ember, and she had just been cruel to him. She had the strange and sudden urge to apologize, to right the wrongs she had just done to this person who deserved nothing of the evils that had pursued him. But she could not risk her neck like that, not in front of Jara, and not before this mission—*her only hope at freedom*—could be complete.

Marcus being an Ember explained his nervousness and Jara's presence. She was chaperoning not only Ravenna, but the prisoner as well, to be sure he did not pull any stunts. The witch sauntered to the other end of the room to take a seat, and Marcus began.

"Excuse me if I am unpracticed. I have not been allowed to use my gifts in. . ." he paused as if he were counting. "Well, probably years," he said with a sad smile. "I have lost track of the time." His blue eyes shimmered with tears, and Ravenna noticed a slight shake in his arms. He was probably about forty years of age, and between the mines and the prison he had been trapped in, his body had aged and broken down to complete exhaustion.

Ravenna offered him a small smile, and as he braced himself on the back of a chair when Jara wasn't looking, Ravenna went to rest a gentle hand atop his. As he pulled away in fear, her eyes fell to her feet.

Marcus started with his instructions. "To teleport, you need to have physically seen or been somewhere before." Ravenna narrowed her eyes, and Jara looked up from her book from across the room.

"What do you mean, she needs to have been somewhere before, Marcus?" The witch stood up, and before Ravenna could register it, a flash of darkness plummeted into her Ember mentor. Ravenna lunged forward, helping him to his feet, and stared at Jara, who was now raging with anger.

Marcus rubbed the shoulder he had landed on and began

to explain. "She cannot move to unknown locations, she has to be able to picture where she wants to go," Marcus said quickly.

"And how do you think she is to get to the Sand Palace of Edmaria? To breach its walls undetected?"

"Well, uh, once she makes it to the kingdom, she can move within range. Every gift is unique to its wielder, and she is probably stronger than I–"

"Spit it out," Jara said, stomping toward where they stood in the center of the training room.

"If she can get close to the palace, she should still be able to breach the walls without knowing what is on the other side. Moving small distances at a time is not difficult, but it is draining." Jara looked to Ravenna then back to Marcus, who continued speaking, "To move a distance that is exceptionally long–like she will be doing from here to Edmaria–is draining, too, and she must know where she wants to land. She needs to be able to picture it, or she could get lost in the state in-between." Ravenna pondered what that might mean, and her body shivered at the thought.

"And how is she to get to Edmaria if she has never been there before?" Jara hissed, and Marcus retreated a few steps.

"I know a place in Edmaria." Ravenna said, earning the looks of both Marcus and Jara.

Jara raised her brows. "And how far is this place from the Sand Palace?"

"Two days' travel, maybe," Ravenna said, picturing the tranquil scene in her head.

"One day's travel," Jara said. "You'll make it from there to the Sand Palace in one day. You now have only *three* days in Oro to master this skill, and then for *you*, Marcus," Jara turned toward the frightened Ember, "it'll be back to the prison."

Ravenna took in a deep breath, wondering how she was going to learn to teleport a hundred miles to the Edmarian border in only three days, and how she was going to protect Marcus in the process.

"I must notify the King of our change in plans," Jara muttered. She looked back over her shoulder as she walked toward the door. "I trust that you remember our deal, Marcus?" Marcus nodded.

"My family's safety relies on my allegiance," he said, as if he had repeated it a hundred times. Jara nodded, then slammed the door shut behind her, leaving them in the quietness of the training room.

"You have family," Ravenna said quietly.

"Yes," Marcus replied, still rubbing the soreness out of his shoulder with his blistered hand. Ravenna cringed, wishing she knew how to command her healing gifts like Leith had so she could take that pain away from him. "A daughter and a wife." She guessed that explained why he did not just teleport away from this kingdom while he had the chance. His loved one's lives depended on his obedience to the king.

"They are in the prisons?" Ravenna asked.

He shook his head, voice shaking. "The mining camps. My daughter was born there. I haven't seen them in years. . .since some of the king's men discovered the rarity of my gifts. We were separated when I was transported to the Dawn Prison in southern Oro in wait for the Ember Trades. I was recently transferred here," he choked on his words. "At least when we worked the mines, we got to be together." He smiled a sad smile, and Ravenna felt a tear slip down her own cheek. She wiped it away, willing her conscience to suppress itself just a little while longer.

"I'm sorry for what has been done to you," Ravenna said. "And I am sorry I burned you." Now she wished she could take it back.

Marcus slowly reached for her hand, and when she gave him a nod, he grasped it. "I am sorry for what has been done to *you*," he said, clasping her hand between both of his. She was only sorry that she had allowed herself to surrender to the sire. She could have made a difference for him and his family. For so many. "Your name echoes through the prison," Marcus said. Ravenna's eyes darted to his. "They say you could be the one that will help restore the Light to Arresia."

She pulled her hand away. "It is too late for that."

"Oh, Ravenna," Marcus said through a teary smile, shaking his head.

"They know not what I have done," she said. "If they did, my name would be forever buried within the walls of that forsaken cage."

# CHAPTER 71
# THROUGH THE VALLEY
## MERRICK

After hearing the commotion and guessing that Sabrine had been the one to kill a Despiri and swipe his horse, Merrick tracked her all the way to the Valley of the Shadow. *Has she gone insane? Where is she going?*

He had paid for his horse–well, he had not given the owner much choice. But he had shoved a gold serpent into his palm and basically dragged him from the mare's back. The mare was not as quick as his Edmarian stallion back home, but she was quick enough to gain on Sabrine as the evening faded into night.

The prints were fresh and had not yet been flooded by the rain that came down quickly. He halted there at the edge of the crevice between two mountains. He had never been through this valley as a Despiri, and he did not want to find out if the valley was hungry enough to feed on his sins. But the thought that pushed him forward was that Sabrine had just killed a man a few hours before, and now she was deep in that narrow valley on her own.

The horse refused to walk into the narrow canyon, and Merrick sighed, aiming his torch forward until the glow of it illuminated the tracks Sabrine had made. He rubbed his neck as he watched the shadows that seemed to dance in the firelight, inviting him in. The marks on his shoulder and upper chest seemed to grow cold and hollow, and the feeling within him was that of empty darkness. There was no light to cling to.

The narrow canyon before him stretched to the rainy skies, and he watched the raindrops scurry down the jagged stone walls at the entrance. Finally, a breath of courage filled his lungs.

"Let's go," he said softly, petting the mare's neck. The horse stomped, and Merrick climbed down, pulling her by her lead. She tugged back, and he slowly coaxed her forward and kept his eyes on the torchlight in front of them. The valley truly did leech fear from the deepest parts of one's soul.

*Sabrine, Sabrine, Sabrine. You are doing this for her,* he said to himself.

She was in the depths of this canyon somewhere, thinking he had betrayed her. He would not rest until he had explained himself. Memories of all the evil he had done beneath the rule of his father threatened to resurface, and he suppressed them, pushing them down into his soul, hiding them from the hungry shadows. *Think of something else. Anything but your sins.*

Eerie noises echoed through the canyon: the dripping of water and the sloshing of his steps through the rainwater. As he continued forward, the water deepened to his knees, and he waded through, tugging his mare along behind him. Beneath his feet were piles of what he could only guess to be bones of those who had passed through before him. He pushed each leg forward, carcasses scraping at his ankles.

"Where are you, Sabrine?" he muttered, holding back a gag.

She had to be in the blackness just ahead of him, but the valley swallowed up all light, and his waning torch only lit a few feet in front of him against the fog and the rain. There was a scraping of talons and a flapping of wings as a colony of bats took off from the cavern screeching. The hair on Merrick's arms rose as he ducked, avoiding the mysterious shadows that seemed to creep across the stone walls and grab for him.

When the water became shallow, he breathed a sigh of relief and then took toward the skinny opening he could see on the night horizon. His horse whinnied with joy as she saw the stars before them.

That was when he heard it. A scream like no other, thundering through the valley and into his soul. It nearly split him in two, and he recognized it in an instant.

"Sabrine!" he yelled, tumbling forward toward the exit. She had to be somewhere along the way. "Sabrine?" Another scream, and his horse spooked, throwing him against the stone and knocking his torch into the water, leaving him in the narrow valley with no light. He dragged himself up.

The shadows of myths had been awakened. Merrick stumbled forward, feeling his way along the wall. It took about two hundred steps before he tripped. His heart plummeted into the pit of his stomach, and he reached down, feeling the body. He knew her by her hair. The shadows had gotten to her first. There was a strange howl down the canyon, the call of a wolf, and if Merrick did not know better, he would have believed it to be real. It was only the valley playing tricks. He collected her body into his arms, unable to see her against the darkness, and carried her forward through the final steps of the valley.

A deep breath whooshed through him as they reached the other side, and he fell to his knees, watching the moonlight caress her face as his fingers searched for a heartbeat.

"Merrick?" a voice said from behind him. He staggered back on his hands and feet, watching Sabrine's body turn to black sand in front of him. *What is this?*

"Merrick?" the voice said again. He shook his head and blinked, willing the shadows away. He rose to his feet, drawing the sword he never liked to use, and spun in a slow circle. Beneath the fog and the rising sun, the land was becoming brighter, and he could see a few feet in front of him. "Merrick, I'm down here."

"This isn't real," he said loudly, still spinning slowly until he saw her small figure crumpled against a rock.

He went to her side, quickly kneeling. "What happened? Are you hurt?"

"No, but you are," she said. He looked down to where blood was gushing from his side, and his hand found the gash in an instant, stopping the flow of red. He looked back to her, and she was no longer there. He took his hand from the wound and examined it in the dim light; the blood that stained his hands turned black and started creeping up his arm to mesh with his shadowmarks. He jumped backward at the sight, then watched as the black fell away like grains of sand. He had to get away from this valley. Now. He turned to run south, anywhere that wasn't here. The tree roots of the Dead Wood tripped him as he fled the strange hallucinations of the shadows that dwelt in the valley. He had to find

Sabrine. *What if she was experiencing the same? What if she was–*

Merrick's eyes spotted the boot he had bought for her that day in the Thickets. He trailed the set of footprints that went out from it, and sure enough, there she lay against a tree. Her breathing was ragged, and the blood that seeped from the wound in her leg did not turn to sand when he touched it. He felt her hair. Her dress.

"Merrick?" Her voice was different this time. Quiet and frail. Merrick watched her for a moment longer, studying the way the blood flowed from the wound on her leg before he tore his shirt and made a tourniquet with a stick around her thigh.

"What are you doing? Leave me alone," she said with as much grit as she could muster in her weakness.

His eyebrows sank. "You'd rather die than accept my help?" She said nothing, only stared at his chest where she had seen his shadowmarks days before. He shifted where he crouched, suddenly feeling small in her presence.

Her throat bobbed. "It was your kind who murdered my parents, and your own blood who took the twins from me."

Merrick shook his head as he tightened the fabric around her leg, and she squirmed beneath his touch. "Hate me all you want," he said, "but I know your pride isn't so great that you'll risk the twins. If you don't let me help you, you'll die here in these woods, and they'll die too." He tightened the makeshift tourniquet. "What were you doing out here anyway?"

She huffed, and her sapphire eyes finally settled on his face. Even in her injured state, she spoke to him with unwavering ferocity. "Your father is holding Embers in Edmaria. He has been collecting bloodstone. And now he aims to create his own weapon. I suppose you knew nothing of this?" She did not allow him to answer. "If you must know, I am going to save the twins."

He gawked at her. "You think you can just march into my father's kingdom and take them? You'll need strategy. Stealth. Something you won't achieve with that leg." It had been torn near the artery, and she was lucky to be alive. He looked up to her pale face. She was beginning to drift away from consciousness. "What happened anyway?" he asked, trying to keep her alert.

Her head fell to the side, and she nodded to something Merrick had not seen there before. "I'm guessing that is a witch guardian," she muttered as Merrick hesitantly rose to examine the beast. It was two times his size and had rugged skin black as coal with an exposed heart, where Sabrine's dagger was nestled right in the center.

"You–you killed it?"

"It must have been after my horse," she said quietly. Merrick shook his head, looking at the stallion that stood a few yards away.

"How could your horse have been cursed? It wasn't your horse. I–they don't come after you unless you're cursed." She perked up a little at his sudden concern.

"Well, I've never killed one. I can assure you, I wasn't cursed."

Merrick rubbed his fingers over his eyes and took a deep breath, then pulled the dagger from the beast's heart. He turned to Sabrine and crouched beside her, slipping his hands beneath her body.

"What are you doing?" she asked angrily, trying to scoot away from him, but her strength had waned.

"Getting you out of these woods," he said, rising to his feet with her in his arms. She winced, and he adjusted his hold on her leg, shifting so her weight was favored to one side.

"No. Put me down, Prince."

"And leave you for the witch guardians? I cannot live with that on my conscience too, *Duchess*."

# CHAPTER 72
# SABOTAGE
## RAVENNA

As Ravenna stepped out into the dark streets of Oro, she groaned. To be out past dark was not what she had hoped for—especially not with the witch guardians still out for her blood. At least she shared that curse with a dozen of the Despiri now, and they did not visit every night.

Marcus had turned out to be an incredible teacher. She had mostly just watched him teleport very small distances within the building most of the day, and had seen how it had exhausted him. She was only successful at teleporting a few feet one time throughout the entire evening, but she was confident she would do better tomorrow.

When their dinner was delivered, she had ordered one of the many guards stationed outside to retrieve a pillow and blankets, and when he had returned with an armful and some questions, Ravenna had shut the door in his face. She made a bed for Marcus in the far corner of the training room, trying to bring him a little comfort so he could rest well. At least he had been granted a few nights outside of the wretched prison. When she left, she had made sure he had eaten his meal and had plenty of water to drink and bathe. Fetching the water had been easy because clean rain had fallen all day.

To her surprise, the guards did not question her further about her kindness and did not escort her back to the castle. They remained to keep Marcus within the training dome and did not pay her a second glance. She preferred it that way.

With about a mile left on her walk home, she heard the first witch guardian. She kept walking, hoping to at least make it to the kingdom square without attracting too many. But her wishes came unanswered. She heard the clicking of locks on the doors of the homes in the slums and saw the curtains being yanked shut. This was her chance to brush up on her skill.

One by one, the guardians came out of the shadows until they were surrounding her. They had been sneakier tonight, and she had to admit she was impressed with their stealth. They were so dedicated to killing her, they were evolving to increase their chances of success. The seemingly dumb, brute creatures were not dumb at all. They lived for a purpose, and that purpose was to return witch bodies and the power within them to the ground, and to kill those who tried to stop them. *But where had they come from, and in what way did their loyalty to the witches benefit them? Did they serve some invisible master?*

No guards were in sight, and she huffed a breath, pulling an arrow from her quiver and nocking it onto her bowstring. It flew right into the heart of the closest beast, and its large body fell forward, smacking the stone with a thud. She heard the crack of her wooden arrow breaking in two beneath it. She spun, releasing another arrow into the eye of the tallest beast, and it staggered backward as she shot another into its exposed heart. When she was out of arrows, she drew her sword, twisting and turning through all the maneuvers she had learned in the valley.

Pushing that blade into the open chests of the guardians brought her back to that night in the Dead Wood, when one had cornered her on that limb and Edme's fire had flown in on Leith's wind, engulfing them wholly. She guessed she could use her own gifts, which were just as powerful and more vast than those of Leith and Edme, but what was the fun in that? She smiled, continuing to swipe and fight with her blade until she was surrounded, trapped in the midst of six of the giant beasts. They closed in on her until she had no room to twist with her blade, and instead of blowing them to bits with her darkness or melting them with fire, she tried her hand at teleporting.

Though she had only been successful once during today's training, she willed herself to the other side of the circle they had formed so that she would be at their backs. A sharp bone jutted toward her, and she fell backward into the arms of one of the beasts. She squinted her eyes, focusing on the location she wanted to go. When her feet hit the ground, she spun to see them all confused as to where she went. She swayed in exhaustion, but could not help the laughter that bubbled from her chest. *Again.* She moved to the other side of the circle. This time, she hit the ground on her side with a loud smack. Their heads all turned in an instant, and they were moving to attack her at once. She lifted her arm, but her sword was not in its grasp. It had not moved with her. She cursed under her breath, rolling just in time to avoid being staked by one of those protruding bones that acted as spikes on their arms. She tried to summon her flame or her darkness, *anything* that could be of use, but it was like her reserves were empty. She had exhausted herself. She rolled again, scrambling to her feet. She tried to teleport again, this time willing herself somewhere further, like *safe in her bed*. Nothing happened. She stumbled as she retreated, and her legs would not move fast enough.

She was suddenly yanked backward by her braid and landed again amid a circle of guardians ready for vengeance. She was not looking forward to the part where they ripped her to shreds, but Arresia could thank them for it.

As they closed in on her and she took one final breath, a wind strong enough to send them tumbling backward into the streets whooshed through the air above her. Leith stood there, offering her a hand up, and she rolled her eyes. *Why is he always saving my life?*

"I am glad to see you made it to training today. You seem to have a knack for killing the messenger," he said dryly, in reference to the dove she had almost killed before seeing his note. "Birds are a very important line of communication, Ravenna. You should allow some of them to live," he said, waiting for her to take his hand.

"What are you doing here?" she asked, looking over his shoulder at the quickly approaching witch guardians.

"Can't let you die yet," he said, smiling. "We've got a job to do." She took his hand, and he pulled her up until she stood on her two trembling legs. He furrowed his brows at her as he helped her gain her balance with hands on her arms. The beast's snarls echoed through the streets behind them. "I would have pulled from your fire gifts, or really anything that could have killed them, but I'm working with little to nothing here," he said, motioning to her. "You've completely exhausted yourself."

"Who knew teleportation could take it out of you like this," she said, catching her balance on his arm. "Why are there so many? Where are the guards?" Usually the Despiri guards would at least take the brunt of the fight.

"I may have sabotaged the guards tonight," he said slowly, pushing her behind him and backing away as the witch guardians neared with rage behind their black eyes.

"What do you mean?" she asked over his shoulder, drawing the sword from his back.

He smirked at her before answering. "They're dead."

"All of them?" she stuttered out. Leith might have just ruined their plan before they had even begun.

"Relax, I made it look like the witch guardians did it."

"How?" Ravenna demanded.

"Let's just say I disabled the guards and then let the witch guardians wreak their havoc."

"Clever," she said beneath her breath, still retreating from the guardians.

She kept the sword in front of her, and with another gust of heavy wind, Leith steered the beasts south, over the kingdom walls, and toward the vast Dead Wood that stretched from the edge of Oro all the way to the edge of Vestele. Ravenna stumbled after him as he followed the tumbling guardians and continued to command the winds.

"What are you doing?" she called over the roaring air.

"Watch and learn, Ravenna. It's called improvising." His hands directed the gusts, and they continued walking south, all the way out of the castle gates into the Dead Wood. "Splitting the earth when I've spent all that time crafting and creating my secret tunnels is too risky. So, I'll use my gifts of wind," he said as he halted the winds and let the guardians get their footing.

*What other gifts did he possess?* She had seen him manipulate wind and earth, and utilize the power of those around him. *Was there more that he could do on his own accord?*

As the guardians stood up and began to move toward them again, Ravenna stood there, sword shaking in her hands. She was going to collapse from exhaustion. *What is he doing?*

The beasts were a few hundred yards away, and as they began running toward where she and Leith stood at the edge of the rotting forest, Leith raised his arms, and the black, winding trees of the Dead Wood began swaying. His wind dove through the trees, weaving in and out, breaking off sharp-pointed limbs.

Ravenna thought she was hallucinating. The broken limbs plummeted toward the ground at such a speed that they became deadly spears impaling the guardians. One by one, the beasts fell, until there was only one left. It kept coming at nonhuman speed, dodging limbs, eyes locked on Ravenna, who was swaying in dizziness. She kept the blade in front of her from where she stood next to Leith, changing her stance to hold more steady. With one last crack, and a limb spiraling through a wind tunnel into the guardian's back, Leith threw his arm in front of Ravenna, pushing her back a step as the guardian fell perfectly onto her sword.

She stumbled backward and released the blade as it penetrated the guardian, then she looked to Leith before she collapsed onto the floor of the Dead Wood.

# CHAPTER 73
# HE LOVES ME

## JARA

She stirred the soup in her small porcelain bowl with her spoon, then leaned back into the chair. Degare was across from her, sipping from his wine and making a point to ignore her presence. She opened her book, hoping to escape from his presence for a moment, to escape from the overwhelming essence of him that lived and breathed in her mind.

Lately, it had been impossible to think. Aside from the fact that Degare was about to take Edmaria as his own and ruin her backup plan with Celeste, Jara could not think about anything other than his coldness toward her. She could not help but think maybe she had failed him in some way or could have done something else to please him better. She needed him to look at her longer than a second, needed him to want her as much as she wanted him.

When she had chosen him some twenty-five years ago to help bring her plan of overthrowing the Ozanne's to fruition, she had chosen him because he had appeared weak and easy to manipulate, and he already had possession of his village's valuable bloodstone. The bloodstone was what kept her clan powerful and able to tap into their magic. Bloodstone got its power—its connection to the darkness—from the blood of the original witches that was offered upon the highest mountain in Oro a thousand years ago. When their blood was spilled, they placed a spell upon the ground, that their magic would forever run through it. As their blood spilled down the mountain, that magic seeped into the crevices of the earth, forming miles long channels of darkness that spread throughout Arresia. All in hopes of one day putting an end to the reign of the Light. From the beginning, the witches longed to claim Arresia as their own.

Jara's mother, Delle, left Jara with the witch clan while she seduced Arne Ozanne—who was prince at the time—in hopes of fulfilling the original witch's wishes and producing an heir with the prince. Unfortunately, Queen Isa had seen through Delle's schemes and manipulation of her son, and after sparing the child, had poisoned Delle, leaving Jara as a young orphan. The child her mother bore with Arne was Ashreya Ozanne—who had turned from the destiny their mother had given her.

It made Jara sick—that Ashreya could disavow her heritage—that she could deny herself as a witch and follow the Light instead. It was heresy. Jara vowed to fulfill her mother's wishes and planned on one day placing herself on the throne as Witch Queen of Ozanna, but she knew it would not be easy.

Upon discovery of the power the bloodstone gave the witch clans, the Ozanne's began mining the bloodstone from the ground in hopes of ending the practice of dark magic and taking out all threats to their bloodline and the Light. With nearly every inch of bloodstone removed from the channels in the earth, the witch clans grew weaker. Wars broke out amid the clans, and witches of both land and sea fought each other to possess and stockpile the most bloodstone to maintain their power against the gifted Embers.

After a defeat and loss of all of the Delle Witch Clan's bloodstone, Jara was in her early twenties and vowed not only to become Witch Queen and find more bloodstone, but that her clan would reign over every witch clan, Ember, and anyone else in Arresia. That was when she had started her search for bloodstone and had come across Degare near her old territory.

Degare's village had been burned by the Ember Prince, Gerrin, and his armies, and Degare had been left entirely alone. His mother had died years before from old age, and his betrothed had been taken out of the Hollow Coves during the attack—*saved* by the hands of Gerrin himself. Jara had struck gold in finding him; someone who hated the Ozanne's just as much, if not more than she did. Someone who had possession of just enough bloodstone to fuel her clan's magic.

But now, Jara could see that he had been the one playing her all along. He had risen to the top, and she had been the steppingstone for him, the shoulders on which he stood. But her back was breaking, and she did not know how much longer she could hold him, how much longer it would be before she snapped.

He had once promised her clan their land back with enough bloodstone to keep them above all other clans. It was an agreement among her clan to invest what little bloodstone they had in the formation of the staff. It was to be a mutually beneficial agreement. If all the bloodstone were ever destroyed, Degare would still reign over the Embers by possession of their power through the staff. But it all fell on this one condition:

when bloodstone was found in Degare's mines, it was to go to the Delle Witches. Degare was to have reign over the Embers, and Jara was to reign over the land and all that was in it.

But with the creation of the bloodstone staff, Degare only grew greedier for power. He kept every ounce of bloodstone for himself, and the witches never saw his promise hold true. It was because of Jara's continued loyalty to Degare that her clan had shunned her.

"Do you ever remove yourself from those books?" They were the first words he had spoken to her all day. They ate breakfast together every morning, then lunch, then dinner, and dinner was the first meal at which he had spoken to her. She did not look up from the pages.

"Why would I?" she said coldly, secretly hoping the tone of frustration would strike a nerve in the king, and he would perhaps show enough care to fight with her. To fight *for* her.

He took another swig of his wine. "Invite Locke Carrington for dinner tomorrow, would you?" She looked up from the book this time.

"Have Mirren do it. She is standing right behind you, ready to wait on your every need." Jara's servant did not so much as shift on her feet.

"I asked you to do it," he said sternly. She grimaced, smacking her book upside down on the table and rising to her feet. She was keenly aware of the steak knife to her left and the king's lack of guards. She was also aware of the dark magic she held in the palm of her hand and of the spells she had been studying. But the thought passed through before she could make up her mind, and Degare grabbed her wrist and led her around the table to where he sat. A smile—both cruel and charming—spread across the mouth that had once been surrounded in wrinkles from the power that had writhed within his body. The body she had restored and returned to him, along with all the power he could dream of.

He reached a hand toward her cheek. The same hand that had once been unsteady and aged, had become smooth and sure. Its twin found her own hand and led her away from that place in her mind. Forgotten were his follies against her, once again.

"Invite Mr. Carrington to dinner, so I can do my best to get that bloodstone for you, dear," Degare said. "I have reopened old mines. You know I search diligently. It is all for you, Jara."

Fingers traced from her cheek and over her shoulder, then down her spine, removing every ounce of hate from within her. When his mouth found hers, she did not hate him any longer. They were young once again, traveling the continent in search of more bloodstone. The two of them were a thousand shades of darkness woven together. Perhaps Degare was still feeding her empty promises, but she could give him this one last chance.

Jara laid beside him while he slept, wrapped in the sheets of his luxurious bed. She had missed this bed, but mostly, she had missed him. His hair had darkened in the months since the Raven had taken hold of his power. Though Jara hated the pride and attention Degare now bestowed to his beloved Raven, she was thankful his body was no longer dying.

She traced a finger across his chest, wishing to stay in this moment forever. At a sudden knock against the thick wooden door, she pulled the covers to her chest and began to order them away. But Degare pulled her in close to him and placed a kiss upon her forehead, then called to the guard to enter.

"Your Majesty." The guard lowered his head in a bow and made it a point to look to the left of the bed and avert his eyes from Jara's indecency, though she was covered with a blanket. Degare kept her close, rubbing her arm with his thumb while he conversed with the guard.

"Speak," he grunted.

"You have received an anonymous tip that Locke Carrington was seen exiting the Raven's chambers in the early morning hours twice this week." Degare stiffened and his thumb halted its tracing. Jara lifted her head to view his reaction.

"Thank you," Degare said. "You may exit." At the shutting of the door, Jara whipped her head back to him.

"Perhaps you should have made it clear that she is not to have men in her bed if you care so deeply," she said, spitting frustration. Her cheeks heated with jealousy.

Degare looked at Jara and grasped her face in his hand, then moved it back to cup her neck. He chuckled, and she could not tell if the laughter was genuine or of the cruelty she was so familiar with, but then he spoke, "I love *you*. Jara, my witch. I love *you*." Her breath caught in her throat at the sudden words. She had waited a lifetime for those words, and they had still caught her off guard. *He does not mean it. He cannot.*

He had never said those words to her before—had never used those words on anyone in the twenty-five years she had known him. She looked at him in confusion, and then he pulled her forehead to his and they rested there, breathing in each other's air. *He does not mean it.*

"Why do you think I placed him across the hall from my Raven? She is to *use* him. She is only doing her job. I assure you; she is only working to find the location of his bloodstone. When Ravenna finds the bloodstone, I promise you, it is yours." Jara smiled slowly.

"Mine?" *He loves me.*

"*Yours,*" he said with a wicked smile, kissing up and down her neck. "And these are not the only plans I have for my Raven. We are going to siege Edmaria, and you, Jara Delle, will find yourself quite pleased with the plans I have for you."

*Perhaps I will rule the witches after all.*

# CHAPTER 74
# NO TRUST

## MERRICK

errick held tight to the reins of the horse, Sabrine's body slack against his chest.

"Try to sleep," he said into her hair, which kept getting in his mouth. She tried to inch away from him, but there was nowhere to go. "You're going on night two with no sleep, and your leg is getting infected. You need the rest."

"You haven't slept either," she said, and as she grew weary, he could hear the usual sarcasm fading from her voice. They were making their way south around the mountains and hills before they'd cut east toward the twins in Edmaria.

"One of us needs to be awake. It may as well be me, since you couldn't do much to protect us with that leg," he said. They had tried to stop for rest during the day yesterday, long enough for the horses to eat and sleep. He was thankful they had two horses to switch between when one became exhausted from carrying all the weight. Sabrine would not admit it, but he could see pain written all over her face, and when she had tried to ride on her own, she had nearly fallen off. She was fading fast, and Merrick was beginning to worry. He could not tell if she was just in need of sleep or if the infection was beginning to take hold.

"You think you could protect us against a witch guardian?" Sabrine muttered. "With what weapon?"

Merrick rolled his eyes. "I am capable of using your bow," he lied. He could use it, but he doubted he would do much better at injuring a witch guardian than Sabrine had done with that deer. He blinked and reached into her sack, pulling out some of the jerky he had forgotten was there. "Eat," he said, waving it in front of her, waiting for her to take it.

"Those are my rations," she said.

"And rations are for when you need sustenance. I'm not stealing any of them, so you can relax about that. Eat." She snubbed her nose at him over her shoulder and slowly chewed on the jerky. She was as thin as his mother had once been, and the sight of her hollow cheeks put him in the rocking chair beside his mother's bed all over again. "I think we need to get you to a healer," he dared to say.

"No," she said. "And there is no *we.*" Merrick inhaled as they bobbed up and down on the horse's back. He was not sure how much longer they'd be able to travel through the night, and he only hoped as night fell that they would not be crossing paths with any witch guardians. He had never spent a night in the forest alone, and though maybe Sabrine had, and maybe she had been lucky enough to kill one guardian, he doubted they could survive another attack. "I do not wish to continue on with you. We should go our separate ways," she said.

"Our separate ways?" Merrick could not help but release a breathy laugh. "Where will you go, Duchess?"

"I know my way to the Sand Palace," she said. "I can get there without you. I do not know why you are helping me anyway, because I no longer want it." She curled her lip at the shadowmarked arm that held the reins beside her, and he recoiled so she was no longer pressed against him.

"I understand why you do not want my help." His words came out slowly. "I do. But you will not survive on your own, and some part of me feels responsible for you."

"You are not responsible for me. I have been on my own for some time now. I do not need help from anyone. Especially not a Despiri."

Merrick's throat bobbed, and then he halted the horse.

"What are you doing?" she asked quickly.

"You don't need my help," he said with a shrug. "So take your horse and go to the Sand Palace, where I am sure the twins are not." He had figured up every possibility. Merrick knew his father best, and he thought he knew where he was hiding his secret stock of Embers.

"What do you mean?" Sabrine asked, unmoving atop the horse in front of him.

He spoke to the back of her head. "I can get you to the twins, but you need to let me help *you* first," he said. "Sabrine, you need to rest. You need time to heal before you go trying to break them out of their chains, or you'll end up dead. You can barely walk."

She was silent for a long moment, and then she whispered, "I almost trusted you." Her voice cracked with a disappointment that nearly cracked his heart along with it. "I cannot trust you. Not with those," she said, nodding to his marks and inching away from his touch. Redemption was something he had searched day by day for, and with her, he thought he had found it. But for him, maybe there was no such thing.

"You can trust me," he said, and he meant it. He would meet his end before he let her die from that wound, and he would dedicate all his breaths to bringing her family back to her if that was what it took. "You have no reason to believe me, but I will prove it to you." He would earn it.

"We travel south to the cabin. There, we will have water and a proper bed for you to rest in. We recoup for a day or two while you heal and make the plans. We have time. It is better to be prepared than to go into something like this without a plan. It'll be you and I against who knows how many guards, and–"

"Since you know where the twins are, and I am guessing you won't tell me in fear I will go alone, fine. Take me to the cabin. But do not speak to me unless it is about getting them to safety."

# CHAPTER 75

# A Nightmare Bound
# with Honey

## RAVENNA

er bed had never been more comfortable. The silky
sheets wrapped around her, the coolness soothing
to her skin. She felt as if she had been dragged
behind a horse, and the quietness in her veins from
depletion of power was relaxing. Her eyes shot open.

*How had she gotten here?*

The last thing she remembered was that she had been in the
Dead Wood with–*Leith.* He was quite intent on keeping her
alive. She ran a hand through her messy hair and found herself
looking to the nightstand, expecting to find a note but there
was nothing.

Some hint of disappointment flooded her body, and she
crawled out from under the blankets and pulled on a robe. Out
the window, the day was made of clear gray skies. She would
need to learn very quickly how to teleport without it ending in
her collapsing on the floor of the forest. Especially at night–
when the guardians would be sure to find her. In two days she
would be on her way to Edmaria, and on her way to offering

Arresia a tiny bit of peace, an apology for all that she had done. Ravenna dreamt of a world safe for Embers, and that world could only come to fruition if she were not the Raven any longer.

Her fingers thrummed on the vanity as she looked out the window. She waltzed to her wardrobe, pulling the doors open and revealing a handful of leather training outfits and a dozen beautiful gowns she had yet to wear. It was not practical, but she slipped into one of the olive-green gowns and did a spin before adding some gold jewelry to complete the look. Her spirits were high today. She was ready for this mission. But first, she had an errand to run.

Ravenna's feet were killing her by the halfway point, and she found herself removing the heels and walking barefoot before she could even see the library roof across the kingdom. A familiar voice called out behind her, and she found herself hiding a smirk as she kept walking.

"Glad to see you're able to walk yourself today." She turned so he could see her eye roll, and he gave her bare feet a curious look. She kept moving forward, letting him trail her. "Where are you off to in such a rush? Is your training not in the other direction?"

"Are you stalking me now?" she asked in a facade of annoyance.

"It's hard not to, when I do not quite trust your motives and you hold so much vital information in that pretty little head of yours." She looked him up and down, but she did not hide her smile as she shook her head. He wore a bone-colored tunic with a tanned hide jacket over a brown trouser, and he could use a shave.

"Oh, you still don't trust me? I thought we were past that," she retorted. He followed her up the steps of the library.

He smiled, stepping ahead to hold the door open for her. His hair was the deepest brunette, and sometimes under the dark skies of Oro, it was almost black, falling in textured waves just above his eyes. "It just so happens that you and I crossed paths. I was already on my way to the library."

"And what exactly are you here for?" she asked, moving past him through the doorway. She felt the soft graze of his hand against her back as he ushered her forward. She quickened her pace until she was just out of reach.

"I'm here for whatever you are here for. Whatever it was you and Magdalene discussed three nights ago," he said, putting his hands in his pockets. Her breath caught in her throat.

"You are stalking me, then," she said flatly.

"I was just in the right place at the right time."

She hummed, beginning to search the rows of books for the familiar woman who had helped her earlier in the week.

Leith leaned down to whisper, the stubble on his cheek grazing her ear. She inched away. "Straight to the back, last door on the left. Secret passageway by the bookshelf with the brightest red book." She turned to face him in confusion, but he motioned her forward, and they ducked silently into the depths of the library until she found the back wall. Sure enough, through the last door on the left side of the winding hall was a small bookcase with a bright red book against the wall. Both surveyed their surroundings before slipping behind the tapestry and into the peculiar passageway, unseen by any prying eyes.

They did not speak for a moment. The darkness was completely noiseless. Leith spoke first. "If you're not going to summon a flame, I will," he said. She felt him pull from her power, and it was a strange feeling. It was not uncomfortable, just new. Like a piece of her shadow was being mended with light. In the blink of an eye, he was holding her flames in his palm. The passageway lit up around them. Leith ran his finger along the jagged wall, taking in the details of the tunnel she assumed he had not made. "Such poor craftsmanship," he muttered before turning to her, flame still in his hand. He watched it wind around his fingers. "You seem well rested. Your reserves have replenished themselves overnight."

"I feel better today than I have in months. Since I broke the stone," she said.

"The power will build up inside you and eat away at every ounce of nutrients and energy you have. You must keep it in check," he explained, shrugging. "Slowly releasing and using your power in controlled environments over time is better than letting it all build up and using it at once. Last night, your body finally crashed. Your body houses so much power, you should be releasing bits of it near constantly, or your body will keep crashing like it did last night. Teleporting should not take *that* much out of you–though I have found it to be one of the more draining of gifts."

"So am I to constantly encase myself in flames, or what?" she said, wandering forward through the passageway. *Where are we going?*

"If you want to show off, sure," he said, and she liked that she could hear the smile on his lips. "But perhaps something a little less daunting."

"*So* not my style," she said, and he chuckled. They continued forward for a few minutes by the light of her flame in his hand, and when they finally came upon a door, he halted in front of it, then whistled so clearly that if anyone had passed by, they would have believed it to be a bird.

After a long minute, Magdalene answered the door and quickly ushered them in.

"I did not expect to see the two of you together," Magdalene spoke slowly, her green eyes wandering curiously between them.

Leith answered before Ravenna had the chance. "We ran into each other. Quite peculiar, how that works."

Ravenna started, "I'm sorry I missed our. . .meeting a few days ago, I–" Leith cut in.

"She and I lost track of the time," Leith said, as if he had not spent that evening healing every inch of her body from the damages done by her sire. *Is he trying to redirect my thoughts from that wretched torture?* She shook her head as Magdalene's brow twitched knowingly.

"Well, let me show you what he left behind," Magdalene said to Leith, while turning to console her weeping infant. "I was very sorry to hear of his death," she said, stealing a glance at Ravenna as she swayed her infant son. One handedly, she began laying a few pieces of parchment and some scrolls across the table.

Ravenna felt Leith's eyes following her as she walked around the table to study the familiar handwriting on the pages. She looked up at him. *Why had he been asking questions about Zephaniah?* She crossed her arms, watching him across the table as he began to examine the pages too.

"Zephaniah was a courageous man. He left these with me for safe keeping. He was unaware he had the gift of prophecy until a few days before his death—when he was in the prisons. But when it came. . .it was overwhelming to him." Magdalene gestured to the messy table. "Galen Bauer was a good friend of his," she said, and Ravenna's heart sank. "I met her once." Magdalene's hand fell to her womb. "I assume it was she who delivered these to the loft for safe keeping. She knew Zephaniah collected and concealed scrolls and books here."

Ravenna looked around the small room where it was obvious Magdalene and her child lived. Books filled a small shelf to the left, and there were no windows. Just a torch and some fruits and bread, and a makeshift fire pit where she could cook. Above it, there was a small hole bored through the stone for the smoke to rise without drawing attention outside. Magdalene must have noticed Ravenna's curiosity because she explained. "My husband Henry was hanged when I was pregnant. Zephaniah witnessed it and brought me here before they could decide to kill me too. I have been in hiding ever since. He brought us rations, he kept us alive. When he didn't return, I had to start going out on my own to get food." Ravenna surveyed her, searching for the lightmark she was sure she bore. "I hear Galen suffered the same fate as my Henry." Ravenna's throat bobbed. "To live in the Light is to be willing to die for it," Magdalene said.

Leith looked to the side at Ravenna, monitoring her as Magdalene revealed a faint lightmark on her wrist. Ravenna swallowed and distracted herself by letting her fingernails press into the palms of her hands until there was red. Magdalene continued, "I named my son after his father, and I dedicated him to the Light when he was born. His glowing marks–a reminder that the Father shines upon him–have since faded, but until he is able to live without me in the case I am killed for my own allegiance to the Light, we will remain here."

"Why would you dedicate your child to the Light, knowing the target the lightmarks would put on his back?" Ravenna asked, trying to collect her sudden anger. Leith shifted on his feet, worry lines beginning to spread across his forehead.

"They are called lustermarks," Magdalene explained gently. "I dedicated Henry to the Light because I trust the Father, and I wanted to show Him that trust. It was an act of faith. The marks come and fade in a matter of weeks. Placing all my trust in the Father was easy after I met Zephaniah. He was a gift, and he reminded me of the Light when I sat in the darkness of grief after losing Henry." Ravenna's face flushed. "Zephaniah kept us alive here–he helped me through labor and birth and those first months of my son's life. He was planning to help us flee." Ravenna tried to sway her thoughts away from Zeph, away from the throne room and the day she had delivered him into death, when all he had ever been was kind. Not just to her. To everyone it would seem.

Leith narrowed his eyes on Ravenna, watching her closely as he spoke to Magdalene. "Flee where?"

"Eswen. My husband has family there. Remont would have been fine, too, I suppose," Magdalene said. "King Auden is gathering Embers there, to fight for the Kingdom. Finding a safe voyage to either kingdom would be a challenge, though," she said.

Leith dipped his head and nodded, considering. "There are

other ways you can help. There are things here in Ozanna that we can do."

Ravenna lifted her eyes to Leith and shook her head. *Do not coax this poor woman into your schemes where she will be in danger.*

"But as long as you feel safe here, for now," he added, "you're doing plenty."

"You said Zephaniah had the. . .gift of prophecy?" Ravenna asked, changing the topic. Leith glanced at her across the table and picked up one of the pages, then flipped it over, quickly scanning the words. Ravenna ran her fingers across one of the pages, where Zephaniah's pen had once scrawled.

"I haven't read them all yet, but after you left the other day. . .I read this one," Magdalene said, handing Ravenna a page. "I think he knew about his death." Magdalene frowned, and Ravenna held her breath as she read Zephaniah's words.

It was titled: *The Rise of the Raven.*
*Through wild eyes of sea and jade,*
*a nightmare binds like honey.*
*A torture crafted like a blade,*
*the dark of night turned sunny.*
Ravenna swallowed, continuing down the page.
*Spilled wine in a kingdom of black,*
*a clanking staff, a sounding siren.*
*The Dove falls under attack,*
*the darkness, met with defiance.*
*He, unmarked for his time,*
*brought to her, a payment for crime.*
*She who bears wings of sin,*
*his death ushers in.*
Ravenna staggered back, gripping the page tightly. Leith

stepped around the table, concern swelling in his hazel eyes, and took it from her. Before he could process it, she was turning away, holding herself up on the back of a chair as her breaths came rapidly.

*Zephaniah had known I would kill him.*

His last words to her echoed in her mind once more, and as she turned back to the table, steadying herself with her arms on the solid oak, a page right before her read: *There will come a time, when seven bloods from seven kingdoms will come together in the Light, and no weapon formed against them shall prosper.*

She choked, remembering the four words he had added onto that sentence, the four words that had flowed from his mouth as *prophecy—as hope.*

*Not even you, Ravenna.*

Beneath her hand, a flame bloomed, quickly spreading across the table. Leith acted quickly, sucking the oxygen from around her in a wind tunnel. He pushed her backward from the table, gripping her shoulders, and Magdalene shielded her infant with her own body, willing to suffer the burns of a dozen flames in exchange for his safety. Leith's hazel eyes bore into Ravenna's, and he shook her softly.

"Control it," he said calmly. She inhaled, digging her nails into the skin of her palms. She squeezed her eyes shut, willing that power to settle. *You will be free soon. Remember his promise.* She looked at him, eyes wide. Magdalene was hovering over her baby in the corner of the room, watching the two of them closely. Ravenna focused on Leith's eyes until she began feeling the wild power nestle back down inside of her, and she wondered if he had helped her—if his power could work in that way, too.

Leith's eyes remained on her for a long moment while he

decided if she was going to burn up everything in this room or not. She gave him a nod of reassurance, one that said she was fine, and then pushed him away from her. She settled against the wall, putting as much distance as possible between herself and Magdalene and Henry.

Magdalene's mouth had gone agape, and her words came out rapidly, "I must go to the markets. I'm in need of a few items for dinner." She looked at Leith. "You're welcome to stay and look through these, but keep an eye on her," she said, nodding toward Ravenna. Ravenna's cheeks heated, and she thumbed through a few scribbled pages as the woman kept talking to Leith. "Dinner won't be till late. I'd offer some, but I know those beasts search for you in the night. Be gone by sundown." Leith nodded his thanks as the door closed in haste behind her.

Ravenna said nothing, suddenly aware of his gaze on her. She hated it when he looked at her like he wanted to know what was turning in her mind. Her face burned hot as fire, and a wave of dread washed over her. She turned from him, leaning her back against the table to examine another page.

To her surprise, he did not pry for more information about how she killed Zephaniah in the throne room nearly four months ago. She was sure that he had already known, anyway. But to fully spiral in front of Leith, to learn that Zephaniah had seen his death coming–was too much. So, she stared at the page in her hands and pretended to read.

She could not bring herself to process another one of Zephaniah's words. She refused to learn anymore about herself, anymore about what horrors she might commit under Degare, and what darkness she might become. But she did hold on to that promise Zephaniah had made her, that no weapon formed against the Seven should prosper. No matter what Leith said, Ravenna was not the Dove–she was a Raven. She was not one of them. She was the weapon formed against them, and there was no amount of Light that could undo her darkness. Even without the sire bond, Ravenna could never be the Dove. She was not worthy to bear that title.

# CHAPTER 76
# DOVE'S ASCENT
## RAVENNA

Ravenna left for training shortly after Magdalene fled from her own home in fear of Ravenna's lack of control. Ravenna could see it on the woman's face, and though she had tried not to care, that, mixed with the shame of the words she had just read, had her exiting back through the tunnels only moments later. When Leith tried to follow her, she had insisted he stay behind and study the texts. She was not sure what he was looking for, but she would not stand in his way.

As she walked across the kingdom now, the thought of Zeph having written anything else about her–and Leith coming across it–had her in a near sprint, her heart beating into her throat. She found herself at the edge of the cliffs, where she had watched the hailstorm roll in over a week ago. She paced there on the edge, thinking of all the times she had considered and wished she could leap from her balcony. The water was now fading from red to its natural black color, and she let her eyes glaze over as she watched the waves crash into the boats at the now near-empty docks. A raven cawed as it took flight into the gray skies from one of the ship's stearns, and her eyes darted to it in an instant. It was those wretched birds that seemed to watch her, prey on her, and laugh at the torture she underwent in this kingdom. She had once wondered if they were warning her, but now it felt like they were taunting her.

She was The Raven of Oro. Ravenna had become something she never wanted to be.

She let out a bellowing scream as she ripped her bow from her back and knocked an arrow, pulling back the string to aim for no more than a second before she let it twist through the air toward those wings black as sin.

As the arrow met the bird, sending it descending toward the dark waters below, she exhaled, and a flock of pure white doves ascended up the edge of the cliff, knocking her backward onto her back. The flap of their wings cut through the air in a symphony of hope, and she laid there, mesmerized, as they filled the clouds above her.

She was still as stone until they dissipated, and then she wondered if she had imagined it. When the morning turned to afternoon, she forced herself to rise and head toward the training dome where Marcus would be awaiting her. She needed to pour her emotions into practice today, and she needed to master teleportation without using up too much of her energy. She would not end up unconscious on the forest floor again—especially not in the middle of an unfamiliar territory.

Marcus greeted her with a smile.

"Sorry I'm late—I had some errands to run," she said, hurrying in through the door and hoping to get started as soon as possible. She released small bits of those dark shadows, letting them seep from her skin and calm the thrumming in her veins. She remembered what Leith had told her–that it could weaken her and harm her in the long run if she kept it all bottled up and released it all at once. She let go of the hold she had on her power, letting it out for a few seconds like a breath, then reigned it back before she lost control.

"Ah, don't worry about it," he said, waving her off as he examined her shadows. "I enjoyed sleeping in. And in the comfort of a bed–a makeshift one–but a bed nonetheless." He gestured to the blankets in the corner. She was sure the blankets were much cozier than what he would sleep on in the prisons, and she offered him a small smile.

She was grateful for his kindness, and she was grateful that she did not have to deal with the gruffness of a Despiri soldier, no matter how brief their training was to be. She had today and tomorrow left with Marcus, and then he would be forced back into the prison, and she would be on her way to Edmaria.

"Today, we will start where we left off," he said, not hiding his glance down to the shadows that still crept across her skin and wove between her fingers. "You were exhausted after yesterday's session, yes?" She nodded, twisting her hands against herself and trying to hide the darkness within her. "You have the right idea, slowly bleeding your power out. It teaches you to master control, and you'll need expert control to make it all the way to Edmaria."

She took a deep breath. "My Despiri trainers never teach control," she said. He chuckled.

"Of course they don't. They do not know the first thing about the gifts they steal from my kind. They kill and steal with only destruction and power in mind; many do not ever learn to properly utilize the gifts they take." He disappeared from in front of her and she spun, meeting his smile where he now approached at her left. "When a Shade kills an Ember with the spelled bloodstone weapon and becomes a Despiri, the power which was once of Light–given by the *Father* himself– disappears. It remains with the soul as it enters into Eternal Light."

"What is the power that is received through the bloodstone then?"

"It is nothing more than a mockery, created by the darkness. It's a power fueled by death. The Despiri do not see, but the power they attempt to steal is always tenfold compared to what they receive. The darkness creates the illusion that it is overpowering the Light, but that is not the case at all."

"I don't understand," Ravenna said slowly.

"The bloodstone staff is simply a tool the darkness uses to draw from death. Darkness cannot draw from the power of Light that has been placed within the Father's followers. The power received by the Despiri is pure darkness, created by death. The darkness tries to mimic the power of the Ember, but it is never exactly the same. It is never as powerful. Especially with improper training on how to use it."

Ravenna raised a brow. "That is why the King of Edmaria holds the power of wielding darkness; the Ember he killed wielded the gift of light manipulation," Ravenna realized.

Marcus nodded. "Darkness will often try to masquerade itself as good, as Light, but the truth will be revealed. Light always wins."

"So, you're saying that Embers are more powerful than any Despiri?" There could be hope for her freedom after all–hope that Arresia could return to the Light.

"Most are." He looked at her. "You," he motioned to her shadows, "are an exception." She clenched her jaw, remembering that hundreds of Embers had to die for her to possess this power that she never wanted. "You may be a Despiri now, Ravenna. But I believe you could change the world if you chose to serve the Light instead."

She nearly burst out in laughter. "I cannot do anything whilst sired to the king."

He clicked his tongue as if not believing the words she was saying. "Is the Father of Lights not stronger than any dark spell or sire?" She studied him for a moment.

"And where is He in all of this?" she blurted angrily. Marcus stepped back a foot as fire poured from her palms and crept across the ground, but there was no fear in his expression. He was confident in the statements he made.

"He has been here since the beginning. He is in this whether you are blind or actively seeking." Why was everyone always speaking in riddles that she did not understand, of a god who she did not see? "Why do you think the witches and the Despiri—who serve the darkness—try so hard to destroy all Light? Because they fear Him. Because they *know* it is His kingdom in the end."

"What are you saying?"

"It is because of the shadows that His true Light can be revealed. . .that we can come to realize just how marvelous and unlike us He truly is." She stared at him until he continued. "Look. There are scriptures and Light Scrolls and prophecy—"

"I know all about that," she said, even though she understood nothing. Her hand mindlessly reached for the pocket of her cloak, which always held that worn piece of paper she had kept.

"I should not speak of these things to you, for they have been banned since Degare's reign. It was his way of keeping the Light from shedding on the sins of those who dwell with him in the darkness. His way of ensuring a long-lasting reign for himself." Marcus rubbed his forehead with his hand. "Look, what I am trying to say is that even the darkness fears the Light. Open your eyes and you shall see the truth. I cannot make you see. You only see when you *want* to."

*Do I not want to see the Light? Do I not demand to know where this god is while I am drowning in darkness?*

Ravenna stared at him incredulously for a long moment, and then he added, "Look around you. You better choose the side you want to be on soon. Because the darkness is quickly passing, and His true Light is already shining."

"I don't have time for this," she said, and he frowned. "I need to be able to teleport a hundred miles the day after tomorrow."

Marcus stuffed his hands in his pockets and shrugged his shoulders. "Okay, then," he said after a long moment. "Let's make it happen."

She changed from the dress that was far too luxurious and obtrusive for training and entered back into the dome. Marcus was sitting in a chair hurriedly eating his breakfast. He looked up to offer her some.

"No, thank you," she said, waving a hand at him, curious as to why he would offer her any of his food when this was probably one of his last decent meals. He had probably not eaten so well in years.

He slapped his palms down on the table. "Well, we better get to it," he said with a bright smile. He was happier than he had been yesterday, and he no longer feared her. "Why don't you start by going from the west wall to the east wall," he suggested, gesturing between two sides of the dome. She made her way to the west wall then very carefully observed every detail of the exact point she wanted to travel to. "Remember to conserve your energy. You may feel that you need to use a sudden and big burst of power, but that is not the case. Moving from here to there—while still draining after you do a lot of it—can be quite simple if you are careful."

She focused solely on that point at the east wall and on the same power she had tapped into the day before. Searching for that familiar piece of power was like searching for a single fiber in a tapestry of a hundred shades of red. There were so many unfamiliar and strange powers within her, it was nauseating to wade through them all in search of the right one. She could always find fire—she held many gifts of flame, and where they dwelled in the tapestry, it was warm and bright. She understood why it had been Degare's favorite, since he was always cold and in darkness it was natural to be drawn to it. As she strayed from that place in her mind and dove deeper into the core of the mosaic of powers, she grew colder, like a space in between. She plucked that fiber and pulled from it, thinking of the spaces she could move to by will of her own mind.

*Calm. Control. Conserve,* she reminded herself as she moved her fingers down that invisible fiber. She pictured the east wall made of glass, the place where the rock jutted from the earth on the other side. She looked at it and willed her body to fabricate there, slowly strumming that tiny thread until she felt it start to work. She was careful not to take too much of that power. She conserved it and was in complete control. A smile grew on her face as she looked at Marcus from where she now stood on the other side of the room. He clapped in celebration of her success, and then she moved again, tapping him on the shoulder.

"Well done!" he said, spinning around to meet her with open arms. She nearly walked into them but caught herself and backed away before he could embrace her. She rubbed the back of her head as he dropped his arms.

"Okay," he said, still smiling at her. "Try somewhere that you know now, without being able to physically see it." Her first thought was Vestele, but she pictured how it used to be. Full of life and sunshine and green grass that had not been smote into the earth by her raging fire. Then, Marcus added, "Somewhere close." She thought of Galen's house, where she had felt such warmth despite wrestling with death.

She pictured it, and it appeared around her, though all the warmth and color had been leached from the home. Because Galen was gone, and the flowers and green herbs she had filled the walls and baskets with were now brown, the tapestry on the wall was now covered in a layer of dust from the earthquakes, and the small dining table had been moved in front of it. Ravenna's hand found the woven artwork. She loved its colors so much, as well as the depiction of what she only imagined was the palace of Ozanna before it had become abandoned and decrepit. Its walls were covered in climbing vines and flowers of pinks and yellows, and the Edmarian River ran around the base of the mountain in a crystal blue. The palace climbed the heights of the mountain—the highest mountain in all the land. Its gates were made of pearls, and the streets of gold. She could not imagine what it would have been like to see the kingdom in all its glory.

She would be punished if the king ever found it in her chambers, but she did not care. She ripped it down and beheld a hole in the wall that opened into the stone. It was like the passageway in the library, but the opening was smaller and did not reach the floor. She blinked and moved the table immediately, then lit a flame and threw it forward. The light traveled for only a few feet before contacting a pile of stone and dust where the tunnel had caved in and was now blocked from entry. *Did this tunnel once connect to all the others that led to Ink Valley? Had Leith dug it, and if so, how had he known Galen?* Ravenna deemed her questions unimportant in the grand scheme of the mission she was currently training for, but she would get her answers when all of this was over.

She quickly rehung the tapestry and made a mental note to return later, then teleported back to Marcus. He looked at her with amusement. She forced a smile and nodded. "It worked. I can do it."

"And how do you feel?" She thought for a moment, then nodded slowly.

"A little out of breath but fine."

"I do not want you to overdo it. You have learned much quicker than any Ember or Despiri I've ever seen, though, I *have* been in the prisons the recent years of my life and have not seen much." He winked, attempting comedic relief on the dark subject. "I have confidence you will be just fine. For the rest of the day and tomorrow, you should rest. Prepare for your long journey. Though, I will be here if you need me," he added gently.

"Thank you," she said, gathering her cloak and sword. It was only the afternoon, and though she wanted to return to Galen's empty home to explore the mysterious tunnel system, the Despiri guard outside of the dome informed her that Degare had requested her, and she could feel the tether between her soul and the king's tightening, as if he were tugging her leash. She grimaced, hiking toward the castle where her sire awaited her.

She found the king not in the throne room, but in his chambers with the witch. Both appeared tired but pleased with one another for once. They were having brunch together on the balcony, and it appeared they had just gotten out of a bath. Ravenna stared through them as she spoke, stepping over the scattered clothing amongst the floor.

"Is this mission top secret or something?" She looked to the messy bedding for a moment then back to her sire and Jara. Strangely, Jara was smiling, and her face was almost unrecognizable. She did not look at Ravenna for even a second but kept admiring the king as if he had just given her the entire world. "Why must we meet in your private chambers?" Every other time, she had been commanded in the throne room in front of an audience.

"Because, Ravenna. You failed me with your last mission. Succeed with this one and perhaps I will not fear embarrassment in front of my men in the possibility you return empty-handed." She supposed he had a point. It had made him look weak when his own sired weapon did not obey him. She bowed her head again in reverence. "You will not humiliate me again."

"No, Your Majesty. I will not," she said. And it was not a lie. Because he would not live to feel the humiliation that would come with her betrayal. This was her keeping her promise.

"Good. And besides, this mission is *highly* secret. None shall know until you have completed it. It stays within the walls of this room. Though, there is one other who knows a small bit about it." Ravenna narrowed her eyes. "Locke Carrington—with whom you spent the night with two nights ago."

Getting Leith to stay in her chambers had been easy, though Ravenna had not expected him to sleep on the chaise. As hoped, someone had seen Leith coming or going and had assumed that meant she had seduced him. The king smiled, looking at the pleased witch. "I am glad to know that the mission is going well, at least. Tell me, Ravenna. Have you found the location of his precious bloodstone yet?" She had not. Something like dread whistled through her.

Leith, *Locke Carrington,* was a threat to her kingdom, and she was letting him walk freely. The room spun around her as that tether in her soul pulled tightly, reminding her of everything she must do if Leith failed at ending her sire. She swayed and braced herself on the table. Degare cocked his head to the side, and Jara stilled, her face going back to stone.

"Not yet," she said slowly. "I just need a little more time. I have almost gained his trust." The words caused physical pain as they fell from her lips, and she stood up straight again. That tether burned, seeming to brand her in two from the inside out. Pain shuddered down her spine, urging her to find Leith, find the bloodstone, and end the threat that he was to her king. Degare had no clue that the man he was playing for a fool was actually playing him. Leith will have killed him by this time next week, if she was lucky.

Could she deal with this pain for that long? Would she even be able to leave the kingdom now, with this crushing sensation driving through her, ordering her to end him?

The king did not even know Leith's identity as the Ink Blood leader. *How have I avoided telling him this long?* Suddenly, in the presence of her sire, it all threatened to come crashing down. She needed to leave before she let that information slip. Keeping these secrets for the next week was her only hope at freedom. *Fight it, Ravenna.*

"I expect that bloodstone in my witch's hands before the end of the month." Ravenna narrowed her eyes, studying Jara for a moment. *What are they up to?* Jara smiled and tilted her chin up as she looked down her nose at Ravenna. "If you have any chance to inquire with him about that stone, take it. And as soon as he tells you, *kill him.*" Ravenna had to stop herself from staggering back.

"Why must he die?" she asked, attempting to remain unbothered, though her veins felt like a thousand knives were flowing through them, cutting her up with each pump of her heart. It was becoming hard to breathe.

"Why shouldn't he? He is useless to me. I only hired him to help find my Embers and to keep him around so we could find his bloodstone. You are capable of retrieving my stock on your own, aren't you?" Ravenna nodded slowly. "I was hoping he would at least invest in my trades, but due to recent events," he grimaced as he recalled the day of the executions, "it does not look like my Ember Trade will likely happen before you have obtained his bloodstone and killed him. Not that I need more riches," he gestured to the luxuries around him, "but while you're at it, go ahead dand retrieve his gold as well." Ravenna could have told him—ached to tell him—that Leith was not who he believed him to be. That Leith was leading a rebellion, and that he was powerful—perhaps even a match against her power—at least until she learned to properly use it to its full extent. And that was precisely why she needed Leith to kill Degare. *Soon.*

She was biting back a wince against the pain of the sire as Degare spoke again. "Anyway. You are here for your new mission. I have all the documents you'll need to prepare." He gestured to the papers on the table. "Blueprints, maps, and a few portraits of some men I'd like killed if you happen to come across them. Your focus, however, is of course retrieving the stolen book and the bloodstone weapon, which I am guessing has already been forged. If not, do not leave that wretched desert land without every ounce of bloodstone and the book." Ravenna knew the bloodstone was powerful for witches and could help Degare hold power over the Embers, but that he was suddenly stockpiling so much, when very little had been found in the mines over the last few months, was concerning.

*What would he be able to achieve with so much of it?* Leith's plan had to work.

"Do not leave Idris alive," Degare added. "We are to begin besieging his kingdom. With him dead, it should go rather quickly. Remember, I will also need you to find the location of the Embers they stole from me."

"Yes, Your Majesty," she said, taking in every word, every order, though she hoped the sire would be broken before she had the chance to obey.

"And Ravenna." She looked back to the king. "When you find them, just kill them all." *What?* "Whatever you do, do not allow Idris to use his weapon on them."

"There will be even more bloodstone than I imagined," Jara said in whispered amazement. Degare smiled.

"Enough for your clan to come running back to you in time to help us take Edmaria as our own." He smiled at Jara like he *loved* her, so convincingly that even Ravenna almost believed it. Jara may have seemed cold and calculating on the outside, but on the inside, she was simply a blind fool.

"Kill them. . .all?" Ravenna questioned, needing clarification on his last orders. He tossed her a chunk of bloodstone, this one a deeper tone of red than she had ever seen and heavier. *Pure and probably spelled.*

"With this bloodstone in your hand, yes. Kill every last one."

# CHAPTER 77
# A LONGING FOR LIGHT
## RAVENNA

She had not seen Leith since they had searched through Zephaniah's notes at Magdalene's. It was a good thing. She needed space–and distance–from him. She winced, gripping the window sill, stone crumbling beneath her touch as her knees buckled. If Leith walked through her chamber door right now, she was afraid she would not be able to stop herself. The pain that now slithered down her spine like a snake was too harsh. She would kill him just to relieve it.

Her conversation yesterday with the king had reignited that sire, that somehow kept dwindling the more time she spent in Leith's presence. But right now, her hatred burned for him so brightly that she feared she would lose herself and ruin this entire plan. So she locked her chamber door and did not exit until she was called to the throne room by her sire.

Clad in a red, sleeveless, trailing dress, she followed halls all the way to where he lounged on his black velvet throne with the dark-haired witch in his lap. Her nearly translucent skin was pale against his, and her deep red lipstick had stained his mouth. Ravenna hid her disgust as she approached them, her heels clicking the entire length of the vast, empty throne room.

Before she could bow or address him, Degare waved his hand. From behind the curtain came a ghostly woman. She was purely flesh and bone, and as Ravenna's attention fell to a tiny lightmark beneath her left eye, breathing became difficult. It almost looked like a scratch. She had golden blonde hair and big, doe eyes of gray.

Degare shifted his gaze between her and the Ember and smirked. Ravenna wanted to turn and run far away from here. She wanted to teleport to a land where he could never find her. But she could not. That tether that bound her would always exist, and it would always call her home.

Degare raised his staff and extended it toward her. She took it in her hand.

The metal was cold, just as she remembered it.

The frail woman, who looked as if she had been plucked from the prisons just moments ago, walked down the dais to meet her where she stood. Ravenna watched her come closer and did not miss the tear that slipped down her cheek. Her mind was racing, and at Degare's command, the bond started its work.

"Kill her." Ravenna's arm seemed to rise on its own, and no matter how much she wanted to fight it, she did not. Because she remembered the plan, and if she drew suspicions of her allegiance now, she would not get to leave on this mission tomorrow and would not get her freedom. Many more would meet their demise if Leith's plan did not work. So, it was the life of this one Ember—who would be killed by someone else anyway, if not by her right now—or the lives of a thousand saved.

Ravenna knew better than to look into her eyes as she put the bloodstone staff to her chest. The soft gray hues would only stir the memory more, and she had been running from it the moment she had set foot in this room.

Only Degare and Jara stood witness to the sin. As the woman slumped forward and Ravenna withdrew the staff, she looked to her sire—a picture of pure dedication to her master. There was a time when that would have come easy for her, just after she had been branded and given into the sire completely. That was before the Light within Leith had reignited the fight in her.

Everything had grown more difficult then, like she was constantly fighting the sire—fighting against her own flesh. Though guilt bloomed in her now, and she could barely stand, she wore the mask of a faithful servant and soldier ready for battle, standing with utmost respect for her king.

"Very well," Degare said. He took the bloodstone staff back from her and wiped it clean with a rag. She refused to look at the floor where the woman's lifeless body had crumpled.

"Why her?" Ravenna asked. The woman had held only a drop of power, barely any at all.

Degare chuckled. "Not for her power, Ravenna. This was one last test to ensure I can trust you with this mission." Ravenna swallowed, and she tried not to visibly sway where she stood. Jara whispered something in his ear, and his eyes lit up. "Ah, yes, about your mission. Do not bother returning to me until you have the spell book, the weapon, and Mr. Carrington's bloodstone all in your possession. I expect you back in a month."

Ravenna vomited the moment she shut the door of her chambers. For a few hours, she laid on the floor unmoving. Her vision was unfocused, and her hands shook. She was in this space again–the one where she could not think or breathe.

When the servants brought dinner, they smacked her with the door. Only then did she peel herself from the floor and allow them inside. They cleaned and left, and then she wrecked the room again. She emptied all the wine, and when she would finish a bottle she'd throw it, allowing the glass to shatter across the room in pieces. Her wardrobe was on its side, spilling red onto the floor. Another braid found its way into her hair.

A braid for a life. It seemed hardly sufficient. She barely recognized her shadowmarked reflection in the dim light of the candles. She had been watching the flames for more than an hour now and recognized a change in pattern, as if a slight breeze had entered the room. Then she felt her power starting to leech from her body and return in a gentle caress. *A warning.*

She threw a wall of flame up as Leith opened the door.

"Leave," she said.

"I will not leave you." His voice was calm and steady, and in it there was no fear as he shut himself in the room with her, eyes scanning the broken glass and empty bottles.

"You must, and you will," she said, the flames raging with her voice. "I will hurt you."

"You won't," he assured her. She felt her power intertwine with his as he moved through her flame without even a wince. He paused before her with a pained look on his face and waited for her to say something. His eyes darted to the scattered books and the upside down furniture.

*He is a traitor and a rebel, with plans to kill your king.* The tether within her seemed to saw back and forth, willing her to end him where he stood. She shut her eyes and tried to breathe. "Ravenna," Leith said softly. She refused to open her eyes. "Ravenna."

"What?" she snapped. His lips tightened as he inched toward her.

"You will not hurt me," he said again.

She breathed deeply once more. "I want to," she said.

"*You* do not want to. That is the sire bond talking."

"I just killed an innocent woman," she said, and the words came out as a sob.

"That was not you. Again, that was the sire. That was Degare." She shook her head. Her hands had done it.

Leith acted as though he wanted to move toward her, but she threw a hand up, halting him. "Why do you try to help me?" He looked hurt at the question, and before he could answer, she spoke again, realizing the pain from the sire bond had subsided to something she was able to ignore. "Why can I resist the sire when you are present?" She refused to believe she was one of the Seven.

"It would seem that I am your only weakness," Leith said with a soft smile.

"It is weakness that causes me to kill."

"Then let me be your strength, Ravenna." With those seven words, he moved toward her another inch, the expression on his face pleading, his hazel eyes melting into her. She stood up from the vanity and backed away, shaking her head. She would not let anyone else get hurt; she had been here too many times. She would not let anyone care for her ever again.

"You are a part of this plan, Ravenna," he said gently. "You are doing well in this endeavor. Whether it is the sire bond that drives you to Edmaria, or your will to do right by the innocent people as a *princess,*" he paused, a gentle expression gracing his face, "you need to trust the Father has a plan. He can use you. Just make it to Edmaria, Ravenna. Make it there, I'll break the bond, and without the sire, you'll be able to free the Embers." She ran a hand down the new braid in her hair. So many things could go wrong with this plan.

But if everything went right, it was her one last chance, perhaps a chance at atonement. She sat on the windowsill across from where Leith stood staring at her with his arms crossed in front of his chest. It was getting late, and she needed to rest. He offered her a drink of water from the decanter by her bed. After a moment of hesitation, she took it and hoped she was sober by dawn.

Tomorrow morning she would blink and begin tunneling through that in between space toward Edmaria. She would have about three days worth of traveling on foot once she arrived, but she could lessen her time by teleporting short distances. She wanted to be well rested since she would not only be trekking on foot and teleporting but would likely be using many of her other powers to complete her mission.

Killing Idris, retrieving the spell book, finding the bloodstone weapon and the location of the Embers—all lined up with Leith's wishes for his own mission on *saving* those Embers and returning Arresia to the Light. She would achieve those orders, and by then, hopefully Leith will have killed Degare. If Degare remained alive, without Leith present,

Ravenna knew in her soul that she would not be able to resist the sire bond. She needed Leith to succeed, or the sire would force her against the Embers, either to deliver them to Oro or to kill them.

"You cannot fail," she said, examining the back of her hands.

"The plan will work, Little Dove. Do not worry."

"No. You *cannot* fail. If you do not break the sire in time, I will be forced to kill thousands. I cannot *live* with that." His brows sank. If he failed, she would completely surrender to the sire once more, just so she did not have to feel. And she did not know if he would ever be able to pull her from the shadows. "Marcus thinks I may lose a couple of days teleporting such a long distance. We did not even bother telling Degare. It will take me a few days to get into the heart of the kingdom where Idris resides. Then, give me three more days to find the book and the weapon, and you may kill him."

Leith narrowed his eyes on her. "Why must it wait? I could have him dead tomorrow." He crossed his arms, studying her.

Ravenna swallowed and looked to the ground. "Let me stop Idris first. Get the bloodstone weapon and the book. Let me do that much before you kill him." Leith tilted his head. "Look, if you end the sire bond too soon, I am afraid I'll abandon the mission." She looked away from him. "I do not trust myself. You need me to stop Edmaria from becoming the next Oro, do you not?"

Leith's brows met in the middle. "You won't run, Ravenna, you can do this."

"You don't understand, Leith. I want to help you. But I don't know what breaking that bond will do to me—"

"What are you saying?" Leith asked, stepping forward once.

Ravenna quickly shook her head. "It drained me when the king and I were bound, and it will probably drain me when we are unbound. I want to be sure I can finish this mission for you. I need to do this. For you. . .and for me. For Arresia."

Leith continued watching her, and then he sighed. "Fine. So, you need a week?"

"Six days. No more, no less," she said. She had been over the blueprints and the plans. With her ability to teleport, six days was enough, and then Arresia would be on its way to freedom from her darkness.

"Sounds like you have thought it all through," Leith said. "Sometimes I forget you are the clever shield-maiden who beat me in the Gauntlet and took my stone."

A faint smile crept across her mouth. "What do you do with those stones, anyway?" she asked, and the words burned coming out. "I mean, what is the point of supplying them if you're just going to take them back?"

Leith grinned. "It is more for sport than anything. But each year, I can maintain the people's fear of my clan. They see me run the Gauntlet and win time and time again, and they assume the Ink Bloods have the power of a dozen bloodstones. They never dare to stand against us, and they never suspect us to be Embers."

"The *Ink Blood* title does sound pretty ominous," Ravenna realized. "It is a name you'd never suspect."

"Yes, well I got the idea from your parents, Ravenna." She looked at him inquisitively and then remembered Degare's comment those months ago. To hide her from Degare, her parents had named her after Degare's royal crest–the raven.

Though they and Leith all believed she was destined to be the Dove, she was the Raven of Oro.

"Keeping the truth behind Ink Valley concealed has greatly contributed to the success of my mission," Leith continued. "Our enemies do not know we are Embers. They hear about the bloodstone. We are a threat to them because they know we are strong. The guards at my gate are not friendly to outsiders. It is all a ploy." Ravenna chewed on the inside of her lip.

"So, what do you do with the bloodstone?" she asked again, fingers tapping against the sudden shredding pain that threatened to knock her off her feet. His lip tugged upward into a smirk as he tilted his head.

"I destroy it."

"All of it?" she asked quickly.

"Every single ounce."

She took a deep, shaky breath as she fought the sire. It pressured her to end him now that she knew of the bloodstone's fate, and he cocked his head at her, sly smile widening–like he enjoyed this game that had her fighting not to kill him at the drop of a pin. Like he knew what he was doing in leading the conversation here.

*You will not harm him,* she said to herself, but her blade had found its way into her hand again. He looked down at it then examined his nails. *Do not trust me so easily,* she wanted to say.

"You think I do not know you have been sired to steal my bloodstone? I am the one who spread the information that I possess such things. It is a strategy, Ravenna. The king knows what I allow him to know. I am the one who sent a servant to tip the king off that Locke Carrington was seen leaving your chambers. He thinks you are succeeding in your hunt and in your ways of seducing me—and you can bet he does not know that I first came to this kingdom with plans to kill *you*." He looked up at her, raising a brow.

"You never should have told me that," she said slowly. Now there was not one reason that Degare would have for her to keep him alive.

"You shouldn't have asked," he said smugly. Ravenna blinked. "You thought you had me, but I have never been tricked, Ravenna."

"I tricked you into an alliance," she said, still holding the blade tightly in her hand. "And even though it was never completed, it still resulted in the loss of innocent men, women, and children, all because you are insistent on protecting me. I deceived you before I was ever under the king's reign. What makes you think I will not do it now?" As the burning in her spine became fierce, she breathed small, tight breaths.

"There was a time when I blamed you," he admitted. "But in coming here, I realized the anger that consumed me was not for you. I was angry at myself for not acting sooner. For leaving you in the shadows. I cannot go on allowing you to take the blame for the deaths of my people any longer. I take full responsibility. I entered into the alliance with you willingly. I knew you were cursed, and I knew that made you a threat to Ink Valley. But all of that was overshadowed by the fact that you are the Dove."

"Not anymore," she said, and then she corrected herself. "I never was." Leith's gaze was that of a broken, tired man. "Whether you believe I am at fault for the death of your people or not, I am still at fault for the death of dozens." She could show him every tiny braid and name that each one had been woven for. The knife trembled in her hand as it fought for her to close the distance between it and his flesh. *Would he soon be another braid in her hair?*

Leith's eyes flicked to the blade. "I am trying to prove to you that you still have the freedom to resist the temptation to kill me," he said slowly. "You can resist darkness. But it will be much harder if you try to do that on your own."

"What do you mean?" The tether was cutting through her, catching fire and burning everything in its wake. She held her breath against the pain, bracing herself on the bedpost.

"You must choose the Light. You must stop running from it. Quit hiding in the shadows because of your shame."

"You know nothing," she shouted, backing into the window.

He ran a hand over the stubble on his cheeks. "A part of you longs to be near me, because when you are near me and the Light that is within me, you feel like you can catch a breath." He stepped closer to her, where she had collapsed onto the window bench. "It is not me, but the Light within me that is your strength or your weakness–whatever you want to call it. And then there is the part of you that hates me because you feel the need to kill me. I am a threat to your king, and I threaten to light up the darkness within you." He stepped toward her again. "Let it happen, Ravenna. Let go." Ravenna stood from the bench before he could trap her, and she stepped to the side. "This is the dawn of something bright, Ravenna. You are the Dove. The sooner you accept that, the easier things become. I suggest figuring out which side you're on before you leave for Edmaria." Marcus had said just as much.

"It is not that simple," she snapped, advancing toward him.

He held his hands up in surrender and backed away.

"You think I want to do the things Degare demands? You think I enjoy being sired?"

"When I first arrived in Oro, yes. A part of you enjoyed it. I am only trying to make sure that doesn't happen again."

"I have been miserable since you arrived," she said.

"I am sure you have been. But I refuse to let you wallow in the mire any longer."

She narrowed her eyes at him and felt that power thrashing beneath her skin.

"When I kill Degare, and you are freed of the sire, which side are you going to be on?"

Ravenna closed her eyes for a moment. "You think I would start killing Embers of my own will?"

"I think you'll be confronted with a choice. A decision that you have not yet made. Light, or the easy route?"

"Do not worry about such things," Ravenna said, rolling her eyes and waving him off as she collected another bottle from the wine cart.

Leith ripped it from her hands and guided her into the wall. "Now, Ravenna, do not disappoint me," he uttered low, his hand beside her head. "Can I count on you?" he asked, ducking low as he fought for eye contact. Something within her stirred, and she pushed him to the side, grabbing the water decanter from her bedside instead. Leith tilted his chin up in approval.

"Promise me you will kill the king on the evening of the sixth day," Ravenna said. "No sooner, no later." The timeline needed to fall perfectly.

He arched a suspicious brow at her, but he said, "You can count on me. That will give me enough time to move my armies—"

She cut him off. "Do not tell me your plans. I do not need to know." Wisely, Leith shut his mouth and nodded. "Get Marcus out. And Magdalene," Ravenna said. At that, Leith looked at her with hope.

"No Embers will be harmed in the fall of this kingdom," he assured her. "You can be hopeful now, Ravenna. Because all of this," he gestured to the castle around him, "all of this is just mist. And it vanishes with the coming Dawn."

"Well, then, bring me the Dawn, Leith."

# THE LIGHT SCROLLS
## THE BOOK OF PROPHECY

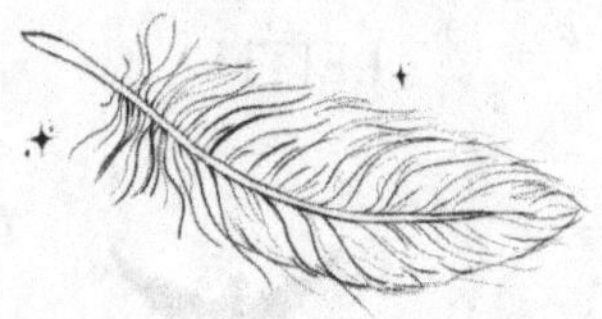

*A once barren queen shall birth a daughter, and she shall become a bright light, a crackling flame. Burning brighter than any Ember before her.*

CHAPTER 78

# REMEMBER THAT

LEITH

Leith had never been more ready to kill Degare, and this time next week, he would do it with Ravenna's Dagger of Light. It only seemed fitting, since she could not do it herself.

Leith only left Ravenna's chambers after he had disposed of all the alcohol, which her servants seemed to supply without question. One more week, and she would be free. Free of the sire, but not of the shame of what she had done. That would linger, and Leith needed to be sure she was ready. She would need Light. He would go to her in Edmaria as soon as he could, as soon as he had freed her from the sire, and they would liberate those Embers together.

He rubbed a hand over his face and poured a bit of whiskey into his glass, but he did not drink it. If he was her strength, she was his greatest weakness. Ravenna was sleeping now, and he lay awake across the hall in his own bed, sending his gifts of wind weaving through her chambers, feeling for any hints of stirring in her sleep. Her gifts seemed to call to his, coaxing them across the hallway and through the door. He allowed them to explore, sorting through the plethora of powers she held. Not even Ravenna realized all the gifts she had, the abilities she had acquired.

Leith's own power, the ability to wield the powers of anyone–Ember or Despiri–swelled as he searched through the pieces in the mosaic within her soul. Where Light should be shining through, it was only dark and colorless. If she were to come to the Light, a warm, golden glow would encompass this mosaic as it was burned up and made new. Leith had a feeling it would increase. She was the Dove, and she had only skimmed the surface of her potential.

He ran his fingers across each piece of that mosaic, feeling the power bleed from each one. *Fire–warm to the touch–and the only piece with a faint glow. The ability to move things with her mind–the power Leith had drawn from to stop the executions. Strength. Teleportation. Shadows. Lightning. Water manipulation. Earth manipulation. Thunder.* Leith remained there for a moment, listening to the storm in her soul. She stirred in her sleep, and he quickly sent a bout of light between them, sending it skittering across the mosaic of a hundred pieces, lighting up the many colors in the shape of a dove.

*You are the Dove,* he whispered to her soul. *Remember that.*

PART THREE
THE DAWN

# PART THREE

## THE DAWN

# CHAPTER 79
# EVEN STILL
## XAN

"So, you and Ravenna, are you. . .together?"

Xan sighed. This woman never stopped talking. Her mood had turned hopeful in the past few days riding toward her husband in Edmaria, and for both of their sakes, he hoped Elias was there. It was not that he did not like Cove, but he was thinking up strategies, and she was asking him questions he did not want to answer.

"No, we're not," he said, not looking back at her but maintaining his sights on the map in his hands–the one that belonged to Ravenna.

"But you want to be?" she asked. *Yes, even still.*

"Ravenna and I are only friends," he said, shooting her a glare that said *drop it.*

She lifted her hands from the reins in surrender and nearly lost balance. He rolled his eyes. "Have you never ridden a horse before?"

"This is my second time," she said proudly. "In the Dawn Islands, I walked the kingdom. The land is quite easy to travel."

He watched the knuckles of her dainty hands turn white as she collected the reins again.

"What was it like there?" Xan asked, skimming the map of their route along the Edmarian River. The bottom corner of the map was signed with the initials, *Z.W.*

Cove chuckled atop the white mare that reminded Xan of Fintah. "Do you want the long or the short version?"

If he could keep her on the topic of *her* and not him and Ravenna's lack of relationship, he would take it. "We have at least two more days on the road," he said. "Tell me the long story."

"I'll start with my father then."

"Bad man?"

"Very," she said with a huff.

"So, he is not an Ember, I take it?" Xan asked.

"He is far from the Light. As far from the Light as I thought was possible, until I met Prince Andreas of Edmaria." Xan remembered something he had heard about the Prince of Edmaria's death, and before he could ask, Cove continued.

"Marinos, my father, is cursed with greed. He forced me into performing as a way to earn income." Xan's jaw set, and she quickly explained. "I am a singer. He brought me to the palace in Oriana when the princess was searching for ladies. He thought my talents might earn me a place as a lady and also give me the ability to earn a wage—which I was then to send to him if I wanted him to keep my secret." Xan knew she was gifted, but he had not yet seen any sign of a lightmark. She smirked at his visible curiosity. "I keep it hidden," she said, pointing to her collarbone. "It's just a small mark, here. I am not as brave as Edme, marching around with it uncovered."

"Brave, or stupid?" Xan muttered. "I am surprised Leith

allows her to do that, with how secretive he is about his mission."

Cove shrugged. "Edme is loyal to the Light, but when it comes to Leith, who I believe has been chosen to lead us into the Light's return, I think she is a little rebellious."

"Jealous, maybe. She seems to take pride in her position as general. Maybe she wants more."

"Maybe," Cove said. "Pride is a dangerous thing. It can easily be one's downfall."

Xan hummed. He could agree with that. "So, you said your own father was willing to blackmail you?"

"Well, he is not my father by blood. I was orphaned at twelve," she said, looking at the path ahead of them.

"Me too," Xan said. "At five."

"Young," she said. "I am sorry."

Xan shrugged it off. "I am sorry about yours, too."

"Don't be. Something good came of it, at least."

"What good could come from that?" Xan asked.

"On the night I fled my parents' murderers, I came to the Light. My parents were Embers, so maybe I still would have come to the Light if they had lived, but in that state–all alone– I learned trust. I realized what my parents had been trying to show me all along."

Xan said nothing. He could not understand the hope everyone seemed to have in this Light. His father was killed defending it, and his Ember mother was killed in the fires started by that same war.

"Anyway, as I got older," Cove continued, going back to the original topic, "Marinos planned for me to marry into wealth and make him rich–"

Xan looked at the shine of her hair in the sun, and the eyes that were a bright, piercing blue. Xan set his jaw. Marinos must have seen her beauty and decided to make money from it.

"What?" she asked.

"Nothing. Go on," he said, waving a hand at her to continue.

She shrugged. "So, I was dealing with all of that, trying to figure out how I could keep my secret in Marinos' mouth, and how I could marry and keep my life with a lightmark that was bound to send me to the trades. Then, Elias came along. He is an Ember, as you know. We fell in love rather quickly, but I was expected to marry an Edmarian Lord. Lord Arlo," she said with a shiver. "Prince Andreas found out about my secret, and he was going to kill me–so I killed him first," she said quietly. Xan's eyes darted to hers, and she gave him a shameful look. He never would have pegged her as a killer. "I lost control," she explained.

"The world is safer for people like you without him," Xan offered.

Her eyes softened. "That's what Elias told me," she said. "He covered up the murder for me, and we started making a plan to save the Embers who were about to be shipped from the islands to the trades." She paused, thinking. "Now I know that Andreas was there to retrieve Embers for his father. They were never going to go to Oro."

Xan could not fathom that there was about to be another kingdom with power like Degare's. How did Leith expect to get Ravenna through this alive? Xan would not watch her risk her life taking on the kingdoms of darkness. When Leith freed her of this sire, she was done. Xan would protect her as he always had.

"So how did Elias end up on that ship?" Xan asked. "Where did it all go wrong?"

Cove took a deep, shaky breath. "We bound ourselves in marriage the night before we were set to free the Embers, on my father's boat." Xan's forehead creased. *How had they ended up on her father's boat?* "It is a long story," she said, waving him off. "My father would not have approved of my marriage to Elias, because he was a servant, so Elias offered to work for my hand for seven years. I was furious." Xan raised his brows and held tighter to his horse's mane as they went across the rocky ground along the Edmarian River. "When we docked in Oriana," Cove said, "the Edmarian Lords were waiting to take him away." Her voice was becoming unsteady. "They thought he was the one who killed their prince, and they took him from me."

"And how did you end up here, with Leith?" Resentment bled out of his voice at that name, and Cove rolled her eyes as if she could feel the tension in the air.

"Elias's gift is also water manipulation. When we were soulbound, we became able to pull from one another's wells of power. He used all of ours to send me to Adullam, where he thought I would be safe."

"As in the Adullam where Lumes found refuge in the Witch Wars?" There was much Xan did not understand, but he knew that Lumes were what the followers of the Light were called before the Father put His Light and power within them.

Cove nodded. "It is abandoned now. Leith found me there and brought me back to Ink Valley. He did not really share much with me then, but I know now, that the Ink Bloods are the new Adullam. Embers flee to the old caves in search of protection, and he offers them a haven. Ink Valley offers hope."

Xan scoffed.

"Hate him as much as you want, Xan. But he has been chosen by the Father of Lights–just like Ravenna."

"Chosen for what, exactly?" he called over his shoulder, as he and Alf led the way, weaving in and out of the trees.

"Don't act so oblivious, Xan. You're scared because you're lacking in trust, but you don't believe the darkness is stronger than the Light. You know the Light wins in the end. You know of the Prophecy of the Seven. You see it all coming together. That is why you hid Ravenna all those years. It wasn't because you have no faith, it is because you want the Father of Lights to choose a different way. Keeping her from His plan is selfish."

Xan said nothing. He had no rebuttal, because everything she said was true.

## CHAPTER 80
# GOOD LUCK, LITTLE DOVE
### RAVENNA

A dove flew into the windowsill, stirring her from sleep. Ravenna needed to wake anyway. The sun would be up in less than an hour, and she had planned on getting an early start. Her head was pounding, and her body stiff and sore from the wine. As she turned over, something soft grazed her face. There, on her pillow, was a white feather. She collected it, smoothing it between her fingers for a moment.

*To protect you while you sleep,* she remembered. She smiled softly at the memory and realized that all this time, this Vestelian tradition had been a subtle hint at those prophecies that told her she was someone she was not.

She rose from the bed, grabbing the decanter of water and pouring some into a glass before continuing to the window, where the dove retreated and left a small note for her. As she unfolded it, wind like the breath of dawn caressed her cheek.

*When the sire breaks, remain in Edmaria. I'll meet you at the Sand Palace, and we will find and liberate the Embers*

601

*together. Degare may have other plans for them, but you and I will not allow that.*

*Good luck, Little Dove.*

She inhaled. This was for the best.

Ravenna dressed and collected the spelled bloodstone from her vanity. She flipped it over in her hands, willing herself to leave it behind, but when her hand started to shake and her spine began to send that burning sensation all throughout her body, she tucked the stone into her pocket along with Leith's note.

Her clothing was appropriate for chilly nights and would also protect her against the beating sun of the deserts of Edmaria. She did not know what weather to expect in the autumn desert, but by the looks of the clothing the king had sent up with dinner last night, she was to experience both cool and hot days. The cloak he had given her was a golden beige tone, one that would likely blend her into the sands and keep her camouflaged. It reminded her of the sunstone-colored cloak she'd often worn in Vestele. He had also sent one of deep purple with the crest of a curled-up serpent between the shoulder blades. She was to go undercover in the palace, acting as one of Idris's soldiers if needed. She stuffed it into her pack along with jerky, bread, and some water. Her sword slung across her back opposite of her quiver, and her bow was at her side. She had never been to the deserts of Arresia but had heard plenty of stories from the warriors in Vestele.

Ravenna made sure to eat a filling breakfast, though her nausea was strong from last night's wine. She walked to the edge of the kingdom where the Dead Wood started and waited for the morning light.

The sun was red, like a cleansing fire raining down upon

the treetops, ushering in the mercies of dawn. Soon, the world would be free of the darkness that had consumed her under the sire. She practiced envisioning the place she was to go in her mind, the only place she knew in Edmaria. As that cleansing, fiery light fell upon Oro and graced her skin, along with a gentle breeze, she closed her eyes and went.

# CHAPTER 81
## THE FACE OF ORO'S PRIDE
### SABRINE

Somehow, Merrick had gotten her to the cabin in the woods in one piece. Her skin was covered in a layer of sweat, and she had been laid on the bed where she had slept with the twins many nights, snuggled together for warmth with their sweet little arms wrapped around her.

She remembered her nights spent in the forest with Merrick, listening to the sounds of witch guardians tracking their every move as they traveled south, but somehow, there had been no more attacks. She had fallen in and out of consciousness the last day of the journey from blood loss and exhaustion.

"You're shaking," Merrick said.

Her eyes darted to the corner of the room where he sat. "Do not touch me," she warned as he started to rise from his seat. His shadowmarks were covered, but she could not help but envision them there, creeping up his arm. He sat back into the wooden chair and grimaced.

"Fine, I'll wait until you pass out. But we cannot wait this out any longer. You're coming to the country home. There is a healer there who can help you." If Sabrine had ever allowed the twins to practice their gifts of healing, and if they were still here, perhaps they could have helped her.

"You're not taking me anywhere," she spat, trying to lift her head. "I am not letting your Despiri healer touch me."

"Dareen is not a Despiri."

"An Ember, then?" she asked, assuming Dareen would be dead soon, if so.

Merrick shook his head, and his lips fell into a tight line. "She is neither. She is a regular healer who uses herbs and medicines–"

"I do not need a healer; I only need rest. I lost a lot of blood. I'll be better by morning."

Merrick rose from his seat and closed the distance between them. He stared at her for a long moment before bending to rip the sheets from her body, revealing the nasty wound on her leg.

"It is infected," he said. "You'll be dead by morning." His eyes did not leave her face as she examined the purpling skin around the wound. He had done a poor job of stitching it while she was unconscious, and the flesh which was touched by the gruesome bone shard of the witch guardian was revolting.

He was right. It was worse than she realized.

"The cabin was only supposed to be a resting spot for you to heal. You're doing quite the opposite. It is less than a day's travel to the country home. It is best to go now, before nightfall. The guardians may not have returned yet, but they will."

If she laid here any longer, the breath would leave her body, and the twins would have no hope of survival. *Fight. For them.*

"Okay," she said. "Help me up."

Merrick breathed a loud sigh of relief and threw his sack over his shoulder, then assisted her out of the bed. "I can walk," she said, pushing him away from her once he had gotten her onto her feet. Even as her vision began to blur and her body began to give way, she avoided his touch. He stood there, arms extended, awaiting permission to carry her. She shook her head. "Go wait by the door." Reluctantly, he exited the room. A few seconds later, as she was blinking against her tunnel vision, she heard the door creak open.

Merrick's voice rang out into the cabin. "What the–"

"What is it?" Sabrine asked, steadying herself against the wall as she crept toward the front door with all her strength.

"Stay here," he said, and she heard the door shut behind him, followed by the quick pounding of his footsteps across the wooden porch. Sabrine nearly fell into the door, but she caught her balance on the doorknob. She breathed deeply for a moment, collecting herself before she pulled the door open to see Merrick in the yard, leaning over a sleeping red-haired woman.

Sabrine squinted against the sun, blinking rapidly until she could make out the raven's crest of Oro woven into the back of the woman's cloak. "Merrick. . ." she warned. He did not look at her but remained examining the strange woman outside the cabin. His fingers felt the thin metal armor she was clad in–the black armor that draped over her shoulders and chest that was made to look like feathers.

"Merrick. . ." Sabrine said again, keeping herself upright on the railing of the porch. She stumbled down the steps, nearly crying out from the pain, and quietly unsheathed the dagger from her belt as she approached him.

"Sabrine, what are you—"

His hands disarmed her of the blade, and as she lost her balance, he laid her gently on the ground. She turned on her side, looking into the face of Oro's pride. "That," Sabrine said, "is the Raven of Oro."

Merrick nodded. "I recognize her from the ball."

"And you're just going to wait for her to wake up and end you? Kill her," she barked, dragging herself backward to lean against a tree.

"I can't," he said slowly.

"What do you mean, you can't?" she asked incredulously.

"I-I don't know. I planned on it, I just. . .can't."

"Give me the blade," Sabrine said, reaching for the dagger in his hand.

He pulled it away from her and tucked it into his cloak, shaking his head. "We're doing this my way."

She watched from against the tree as he pulled some old rope out from beneath the porch and began binding the Raven's hands and feet. The prince had lost his mind.

# CHAPTER 82
# VERY
### RAVENNA

"She is the most powerful Despiri there is, do you not think she is going to take offense when she wakes and realizes you've taken her captive?"

Ravenna's eyes opened slowly, and she took in her surroundings. She was inside a small home built of wood, and the air inside was musty. There was a stench that met her nostrils, and as she noticed the man and woman from whom the voices belonged to, she pegged the smell as coming from the woman's obviously maimed leg. Ravenna would know that type of injury from a mile away.

They kept arguing as she collected herself, feeling the binds they wrongly assumed would hold her. She blinked against the utter exhaustion that crept through her. Out the window to her right, she could see that she had teleported to the correct place, but the cabin was not vacant as she had assumed. Out the south window, the Edmarian river flowed with water, and just across that river was Brinland, where she had traveled with

Xan and some Vestelian warriors in the spring to bury her mother.

Ravenna tried to keep her head upright as she quietly watched the interaction between the two. They argued as if they were enemies on a similar mission, each fighting to complete the next task their own way. The woman was severely ill but still feisty. Ravenna thought she would make a strong warrior, with a little more nutrition, perhaps. The man held his head high despite her insults, but his arms stayed crossed over his chest, as if a part of him wanted to hide. The circles beneath his eyes were a deep brown, and he looked as though he had not slept in a week.

Ravenna cleared her throat. They both turned in an instant to where they had tied the Raven of Oro to a wobbly wooden chair. She refrained from smiling. Even without her power, she could have broken free in a matter of seconds. The man holding the ropes knew little of tying knots—or stitching wounds by the looks of it.

"What is it you want with me?" she asked, watching the woman tremble—not from fear but weakness.

"Merrick, why don't you tell her what it is you want? Maybe we can both learn," the woman muttered, barely moving her colorless lips. Ravenna's eyebrows raised as she looked back to the man whose demeanor was calm, even when the harbinger of death was before him.

"Merrick, you say. As in Prince Merrick?" Ravenna asked wryly.

It was then that he took a step back, and the woman next to him shook her head. Ravenna smiled between the two of them, and then she willed what little power she had left to burn through the ropes at her wrists. Smoke filled her nostrils, and she bent to slowly untie the ropes at her ankles. Neither one of them were stupid enough to use the blade at the prince's side, and Ravenna gave them points for that.

"What are you doing in my kingdom?" the prince asked.

"What is Edmaria's only heir doing in a rickety old cabin with no guards?" Ravenna retorted, looking around but staying seated.

The woman stepped forward as if to speak, and Ravenna tilted her chin to examine the way she limped, and the way the prince caught her elbow.

"I wanted to kill you when you showed up here," the woman said matter-of-factly, yanking her arm away from the prince. "But Merrick thinks you can help me."

Ravenna raised her brows. "Well, thank you for your honesty," Ravenna said, still studying her. "And you are?"

"Anya," the woman said too quickly.

Ravenna narrowed her eyes. "The honesty didn't last long."

The woman took a breath and rolled her eyes as Merrick gently elbowed her. "Sabrine. My name is Sabrine."

"Look, I know you have the ability to heal," Merrick said, stepping forward. "Is that something you could do for us?"

"In exchange for. . .?" Ravenna asked. She had fallen into a bucket of luck, coming here.

Sabrine pushed past him, and he steadied her again.

"I believe we want the same things," Sabrine said. "He will help you in order to repay me for what his father stole."

Ravenna's heart began thundering in her chest as she began to paint the picture of what Merrick's father could have stolen from Sabrine, and she quickly stopped her from elaborating.

"I am here on orders of King Degare—to kill the Embers

which were stolen from him. Do not breathe another word about what exactly has been taken from you," she said sternly. "Because if you do, it could be dangerous for all of us."

Sabrine stiffened. "You really just do whatever Degare tells you, huh?"

Ravenna nodded.

"Then I am hoping he told you not only to stop King Idris–but to kill him." Sabrine did not break eye contact, and she held her chin high as the prince gave her a pained look, as if she had just betrayed him.

Ravenna nodded again, and Merrick's panicked eyes darted between Ravenna and Sabrine, the latter refusing to look at him.

"You asked what I was doing in your kingdom," Ravenna said with a shrug. "Now you know."

"I heal her and you help me into the castle. You work with me on locating the Embers your father keeps, and you help me to retrieve the bloodstone weapon. Deal?" Ravenna asked, sipping the tea he had made her. Sabrine was in the bedroom, withering into death. It had been a couple of hours, and Ravenna's power was slowly replenishing. Merrick glanced through the doorway where he could see Sabrine's sweat soaking through the thin sheets on the bed as she shook with infection. Ravenna rolled her eyes. "I'll kill your father myself. No need for you and your conscience to get in the way," she muttered.

Reluctantly, the prince agreed to her stipulations with a slow nod.

"Good," she said, wondering how this woman had come to mean more to him than his father's life. "I'll hold you to it." Merrick swallowed as Ravenna rose from the dining table and took toward the tiny bedroom.

He followed closely behind her. "How do I know I can trust you? How do I know you're not just going to kill us both after you've gotten what you need?"

Ravenna pulled the sheets from Sabrine and laid a hand on the exposed skin of her leg as Leith had recently done for her. "You don't," she said. "But I don't see myself killing *her*, at least. I kinda like her spirit." Sabrine fought to live, and Ravenna could appreciate that. There was a time when she, too, had something–someone–to live for.

Merrick bit his lip. "Yeah, I kinda like her spirit, too," he said softly.

"She won't last long with the witch guardians on her tail, though," Ravenna said as she searched for the same healing power Leith had pulled from her just days ago.

"How'd you–"

"I've seen my fair share of injuries from the witch guardians." She looked down at Sabrine, who was fast asleep.

"You're cursed?" he asked.

"Very," she said.

"How?"

"They came to retrieve my mother. I got in the way," she said, allowing the power within her to begin weaving through Sabrine's diseased flesh. She studied the damage, trying to figure out where to start. It was refreshing to use a part of her power for something good, and she had not told them of her lack of confidence in using this gift that she had not been trained in.

"Is there any reason one would just. . .come after you?" he asked.

"Never heard of one," Ravenna said. "They are harmless if you're not cursed. But once you've killed one. . ." Ravenna trailed off and her head snapped up to Merrick. "You're saying she wasn't cursed?"

He shook his head. *The guardians had attacked her with no motive? As if they were now killing for sport?* "Strange," she said. *Very strange.*

Ravenna examined the stitches on Sabrine's leg and held her hand out toward the Prince of Edmaria. "Give me your blade," she said. He was slow to grab it, so she reassured him. "I need to cut this hacksaw job of stitching loose before I can continue." The hilt of the blade met her hand, and she dumped a bit of alcohol from her canteen on it, careful not to use too much. She would need it later.

Sabrine stirred and began pulling her leg from Ravenna's touch. Ravenna held pressure on her warm skin and looked at Merrick. "Hold her still," she ordered. Merrick's brown eyes grew wide, and for a moment, Ravenna saw Xan. She cleared her throat. "Do it, now."

"She does not want me to touch her, I–"

"Do it or these stitches aren't going to come out too cleanly," she said, hooking the tip of the blade beneath a stitch, just as Sabrine jolted in her sleep. The stitch tore through the skin before the blade could cut it, and Ravenna watched as Merrick paled at the sight of the blood.

She rolled her eyes, grabbed his hands, and placed them on Sabrine's shoulders. "I've got her leg. You hold here." Merrick was uncomfortable with his hands on her, as if she may wake up any moment and usher him into death. Curiously, Ravenna looked between the two of them one last time before she went down the line of uneven stitching, cutting each one with the dull blade.

"She'll have a scar, but it won't be as bad as the one she would have had if she would have survived an injury of this magnitude with only your help," Ravenna muttered, eyeing the way the stitching had pulled her skin taut unevenly. "Her muscle was sliced in two. She'll likely have a few days of recovery even after I finish." Ravenna set the last stitch on the table.

"Days?" Sabrine said, opening her eyes and shaking off the prince's touch. "I need to be better by tomorrow."

Ravenna chuckled. "There is no way. I hardly know what I am doing. I am convinced that even a master healer, or even someone who is doing this for the second time and not the first, would tell you the same."

"What do you mean you hardly know what you are doing?"

Ravenna gave Merrick a glare. "I can stop, if you want. Leave her open right here?"

Sabrine laid back in the bed. "No. I am already feeling better. Just finish, please." Merrick stepped forward, readying to hold her still once more. "I'll manage without you," she said to him, and Ravenna raised her brows as he sat back in his chair and watched.

Ravenna sent her power weaving through the infection, and it was as if her power knew what to do. She balanced on that thin thread within her soul that held the gift of healing, and she focused on maintaining that balance. As Ravenna grew dizzy, the color seemed to return to Sabrine's cheeks. The infection had spread throughout her body, and Ravenna felt it becoming less and less, but with each caress of her power against it, her own body waned. She had exhausted her power from teleporting here, but it was not just that. It was as if her body was beginning to absorb the effects of the infection. She could feel an echo of pain that came with each pulse of power, as if her body were pulling the affliction out of Sabrine.

She remembered the way Leith had paled as he had used her healing power on her a week ago, and the way he had grown weak. *He had continued through this? For me?*

Ravenna paused, and Sabrine sat up in the bed to look at her leg, which was still cut open and was now seeping blood, but the infection was visibly lessening. She swayed and blinked through the dizziness in her head.

"Lay back," she said to Sabrine, who was watching her closely. "I am almost finished."

Sabrine obeyed, and Merrick stayed silent in the corner of the room as Ravenna willed herself to continue pouring from her shallow well of power. She would need to rest and replenish before she made it to the Sand Palace. Perhaps a day would be enough.

When Sabrine's leg was back to its natural brown tone, and the only thing left to heal was the open stab wound, Ravenna breathed a sigh of relief. "This might hurt," she said to Sabrine, and the woman braced herself by gripping the sheet next to her. Merrick rose to his feet to monitor Ravenna's work, and she took her fingers and squeezed the flesh of Sabrine's thigh back together. Sabrine groaned in pain, and Ravenna sent out one final burst of power, taking shallow breaths until the muscle and the flesh had knitted itself back together.

"Done?" Sabrine gasped.

"Done," Merrick said with a grin beside her, and she sat up

to see her leg. Ravenna swayed where she sat, but despite the exhaustion, she felt relief, because she had done something good. *I helped someone.* In exchange for information. But she had saved a life instead of taking one.

"Thank you," Sabrine said to her, and there was genuine gratitude behind her voice. A smile graced her face, and it almost seemed unnatural on her. Ravenna could not imagine her laughing, but Ravenna had not laughed much in the last six months either.

"You're welcome," Ravenna said, and then she looked at Merrick.

"I guess I owe you some information," he said, and his voice was quiet–dreadful.

Ravenna stood slowly, listening to the call of the sire bond. "It would seem you do."

# CHAPTER 83
# PLANS IN PLACE
## LEITH

Leith walked the tunnels beneath Oro, marking them with carvings into the rocks. Five years ago he had made it one of his missions to continue the work of the Ozannes in mining the bloodstone out of the ground. For the last few years, as he had sent his power weaving through the rock, he not only searched for bloodstone, but crafted the tunnels in the process. He made it his mission to continue the tunnel system beneath Oro when the Dove had been taken.

The Delle Witch Clan was weakening because of lack of power within the earth, and they continued in their diligent search for bloodstone. The Ozannes and Leith had not been able to rid the land entirely of it, but the tunnels that had come from his search would benefit the Kingdom of Light greatly. These tunnels would aid him in the liberation of all Embers.

The tunnels all stemmed from the abandoned Kingdom of Ozanna, where select servant passages and cave systems in the golden Sunstone Mountains creep beneath the land to provide transport across kingdoms.

Leith ran his hand down the black rock and then stopped to carve an arrow that pointed toward Ozanna–toward the Kingdom of the Dove.

Soon, Oro would be no more. In the coming months, Leith planned to return Gerrin and Willa Ozanne to their thrones, where the Ink Bloods would be the first of their new people. Then, Leith was to return to them their heir–the Dove. He would bring her to the Light, no matter how long it took. This was the beginning. This was the dawn before the Dawn.

Leith smirked as he eyed the tunnel to his left, the one that would collapse the throne room where Degare sat. Not all the tunnels were to be used for travel. This one would crumble–a fault line strategically placed beneath the kingdom. On the day of the ball, when Ravenna had sent the room quaking, he'd been worried she would trigger it. There were many tunnels, and Leith had memorized them like the back of his hand. After much study, most of them had been crafted during the quakes he had sent out at the time of the executions, and Edme had ushered the Embers through the many he had already crafted–the ones that took them toward Ink Valley and allowed them to avoid the Valley of the Shadow.

In all his rage, Leith often had to be reminded of the importance of the preservation of life among those who had not yet turned to the Light. Though the Shades and Despiri of Oro walked in darkness and wished death upon Embers, it was not right for Leith to condemn them to Eternal Darkness. The Father of Lights, in all His sovereignty, was the One who made that judgment, and the blood water He had sent had succeeded in conveying His message. Through the red waters, the foreigners that were present for the trades and the people of Oro knew that their kingdom was being plagued by something their shadows and false goddesses could not overcome, and many of them had fled, meaning their lives would be spared in the fall of Oro. Even after all they had done to the Father of Lights and His children, they had been granted more time for repentance. *He is merciful—more merciful than me*, Leith thought as his mind shifted to Degare and all he had done to Ravenna. *Degare deserves the death you are about to deliver*, he assured himself.

Leith knelt and whispered a prayer through the tunnels, then rose to his feet and followed the warm glow that lit them. Edme's wild power was a beacon to him, drawing him out of the darkness. When he was within range, he drew a small flame from her and held it in his palm, lighting the rest of the way.

She stood there with a legion of men—ungifted warriors and Embers—awaiting orders. "I brought the best of the best," she said.

"You didn't bring Xan Dollery," Leith noted, eyeing the four dozen men and women—some of whom he recognized from the night he'd liberated the Embers in the Brunts. Xan was nowhere among them.

"He is not the best of the best."

"Debatable," Leith said. "He is quite talented with a sword."

"Better than Edme!" one of the men said aloud, earning a shooting flame to the arm. Leith raised his brows.

"Oh? Did something happen in my absence?"

"We had a duel, and now he thinks he should be a general."

"You lost a duel against a Vestelian?" Leith teased, crossing his arms.

Edme didn't answer. "Xan Dollery," she said, "is on his way

to Edmaria with Cove. Thinks he can save Ravenna. Not only from Degare, but probably from your influence, too."

"Xan believes me to be a poor influence? I was unaware," he said sarcastically. "I hope I can kill the king before Ravenna gets her hands on him, or he will think nothing at all."

Edme shrugged, nodding to the tunnels beyond him. "Is everything set?" she asked.

"All is ready," he said with a nod. "Follow me." The legion followed him through the tunnels, and he led them directly beneath the Ember prison, to the tunnel he used several days ago to free two hundred prisoners. "This tunnel enters straight into the back of the prison. I want four men on the ground outside of the main entrance, and four entering here through the tunnel. Take out the Despiri guards. They won't be expecting anything. They'll be too caught up in the trembling ground to notice you. When they do, it'll be too late. Once they are dead, use their keys to release the Embers. You'll have under a half hour to get them all out of the prison and into the tunnel. Follow the arrows, toward Ozanna. You can find rest there, but do not stay long. You'll use the tunnels to continue west toward Adullam. The others should be there by now, getting settled."

Leith turned to look at Edme. "I'll need you on the ground. There are Embers outside of the prisons. There is one–a woman and her infant–in the back of the library. Get them out." Edme nodded.

He turned to another gifted Ember, one who would take Edme's place as general if both Leith and her were ever absent at the same time. "Gideon, take seven men and go to the prison. It will fall an hour after the first shock. Get the Embers out and take them out the side entrance to the slums. There is an inn there on the corner, owned by an Ember couple in hiding. They know you are coming. They'll usher you inside, where a tunnel awaits. They are to accompany you to Ozanna."

Leith turned to survey his army. "All of you, listen closely. I kill the king before anyone moves. I need my full focus to be on him first, and then I'll shift to falling the kingdom. At first shock, go, and make it fast. Degare's armies will deploy on their own orders, and it will be chaos. With the cover of the tunnels, I expect limited combat, but prepare yourselves either way."

The men and women nodded, and each began forming their mission groups. "Those of you that are left, I want you dispersed throughout the kingdom. Search for any sign of Embers. We get them all out. You hear me? Look for candles in windows, look for ducked heads and seemingly empty houses. Check every nook and cranny, and salvage what Light this kingdom has left. My spies will be doing the same." Leith looked upon the many glowing faces of his warriors who stood in Edme's firelight. "This," he said, holding up a chart, "is a diagram of all the tunnels. Study it. Know which ones to avoid. The red ones will collapse—the ones in black are safe to travel through. Find where you'll be and make note of the two tunnels nearest to you. Once you're underground, follow the arrows." Leith pointed to the carving on the wall.

This was going to work. He had come here to retrieve the Dove, and that was exactly what he planned to do. He'd fight for her til Kingdom come.

He looked upon his army, pausing on Edme. "Let's bring the Dawn," he said.

# CHAPTER 84
# BOTH CALLING MY NAME
## RAVENNA

While Sabrine was resting, Merrick and Ravenna sat at the small table, and she wondered how many meals had been shared between Sabrine and whomever she was missing. Merrick brought her a stack of papers.

"I have been working on this plan for nearly ten days–since the earthquakes in Oro–thinking up every possibility and every outcome," Merrick said quietly, as to not wake Sabrine. *Did he say the earthquakes, the ones that happened on the day that was supposed to mark the trades, had been ten days ago? That meant Ravenna had only lost two days traveling.* "These are the blueprints," he continued as he set the papers before her. "I am sure your king provided you with some, but these are updated. My father is a strategic man. There will not be an easy way into the kingdom. You're not just going to waltz into the palace. He does not let anyone–even me, his own son–know of his plans. I had no clue he was planning all of this until I noticed he'd left after the ball and was not in attendance at the trades."

Ravenna rubbed her forehead as she leaned over the table, looking at the pages. His handwriting was scribbled over every square inch of paper, a hundred jumbled thoughts crowding each page. "I am going to need you to sum it up for me," she said dryly. "I do not have time for this."

"Here is the entrance to the Sand Palace. This is where we are," he said, pointing to the tiny, wooded area by the Thickets. "Here, is where my father has guards and checkpoints." Merrick's finger bounced around the page, and she noted each of the two dozen locations between them and the palace. "Maybe even more. I have been absent for a couple of weeks."

"That is a lot of checkpoints. Why is he so paranoid?" she asked.

"I am guessing it has all been in preparation for his mission in stealing from the most powerful kingdom in Arresia. I saw him dancing with you at the ball. He was sizing you up–seeing what he needed to be afraid of."

"I must not have impressed him," she said, since he had gone through with his plan anyway.

"I'd say you impressed him very much. So much so that he decided it is worth it to create his own weapon. He just has to be stronger than you. Hence, why he is gathering so many Embers."

"Degare really thought too highly of himself with that one, didn't he?" Ravenna muttered. Her sire always thought it would be impossible for any to surpass her, but Ravenna could see Idris surpassing her power in a matter of days–if the immense power did not kill him. Sired or not, she could not let Idris achieve that.

"I am only helping you to help Sabrine, and because we want similar things regarding the destruction of my father's weapon. I want to keep that power away from him just as much as you. I do not trust you, however, and there are things I will not share regarding the Embers in my kingdom. I believe we—or at least your sire—want different things when it comes to their safety. I am sure you can understand," he said.

She nodded. He was smart to keep the location of the Embers secret from her, but it would only delay her for a little while. She hoped Leith succeeded with the plan before she found them.

Merrick continued. "I have a friend that shares your power of teleportation. You said yours also only works as far as the eye can see or somewhere you've seen before?"

Ravenna nodded. "That is why I came here instead of directly to the palace. I suppose it is a good thing I did not wind up unconscious on the throne room floor in front of your father, though."

Merrick huffed a breath and said, "Yeah. I would say so." He studied the maps in front of him and shuffled through the hundreds of notes. "I can get you into the palace. But you'll need to teleport. I am sure my father has given his men your description, they'll be on the lookout for you, and you're not hard to miss," he muttered, looking at her vibrant hair and metal-feathered armor. He began circling points on the map. "Take this path. Teleport from here, to here, to here. You should be able to see this distance. Staying concealed will be hard, because near the palace it is open desert. I recommend you wear something different, and cover your hair and your face. Most of the people here cover their heads against the sun anyway. You'll blend right in."

Ravenna looked over the dozen circles on the map. "Once

you're within the kingdom walls," he said, "and the palace is to the east, take this entrance." His finger tapped at a point on the map. "Now you're in the palace. I don't know what to suggest from there," he said.

"I can manage the rest," Ravenna assured him. "Once I'm in, I'll find the spell book and the weapon. If your father is anything like Degare, they will not be far from him. I'll have them both in my possession, and take his life, before the next morning."

Merrick cleared his throat and began gathering some blankets from the chest beneath the window.

"I am glad we are on the same page," he said, tossing her one made of wool before he began making his bed on the floor.

The sire bond kept Ravenna awake all night, tugging her from sleep. Urging her to move. Sabrine was still in the bed resting, and Ravenna was on the floor of the cramped dining room. Merrick was on the floor in the small hallway that connected the two rooms, and by the sound of his anxious breathing, he was not sleeping either.

"You hate your father enough to help me kill him," she said. "Why?"

The prince was silent for a long moment, and just as Ravenna began to wonder if he had fallen asleep after all, he spoke.

"I hate my father, but I do not want him dead. I only wanted her to live."

"You owe her a debt that great, huh?" Ravenna asked.

"A debt too great to pay. I am afraid no good deed could ever right it."

Ravenna knew the feeling. "I doubt whatever you did was intentional. You don't seem like the type," she muttered. Merrick turned on his side and looked at her. The room was dark around them, aside from one flickering candle.

"Is what you do intentional?" he asked.

Ravenna sighed and scooted back against the wall, pulling her knees to her chest. "I don't know what is me and what is the sire. The king's soul and mine are entwined, stitched together in darkness."

"And how tight are those stitches?" Merrick asked, glancing down the hall to Sabrine.

"The ones that are left. . .I couldn't get a blade beneath them if I tried. Some have been broken loose. Some part of me has been freed of that hold he has over me. But until every stitch is undone, I cannot trust myself."

"Are you saying if it were up to you, you would fight for the other side?" Ravenna shrugged, and Merrick spoke again. "Yeah, I think I would too."

"I just-I do not know whose blood to spill and whose to save." She had spilled so much. Ravenna twisted her hands in her lap. "There are two armies, two men calling my name. One calls me Raven, and one calls me Dove."

"And which do you wish to be, Ravenna?"

She thought for a long moment.

"Dove."

Sometime in the night, she had fallen asleep. She was awake now, looking up from the floor at the millions of stars she could see through the window–the same stars that used to light the way home to Vestele. Ravenna took a deep, calming breath.

She avoided those places in her mind like a plague.

Sabrine was snoring in the bedroom, and sometime in the night, Merrick had moved his bed from the floor in the hall to the floor at her bedside. Ravenna sat up at the sound of a stick snapping outside and stiffened when a horse nickered. Her heart leapt in her chest, but then she remembered Sabrine's stolen horse was tied to the porch, and she relaxed. Until she heard a whisper that sounded a whole lot like the quiet order of a soldier.

"Go around the back, wait for my signal," the voice said.

Ravenna rose to her feet slowly, careful not to creak the floors as she shuffled to the bedroom at the back of the cabin. Sabrine was the first to wake. Ravenna pulled her from the bed in an instant, slapping a hand over her mouth as she brought her to the floor next to Merrick, who woke abruptly too. Ravenna brought a quick finger to her mouth and pointed toward the window.

Merrick listened, his brown eyes wide.

"I recognize one of the voices," he whispered. "My father's men."

"Are they looking for you?" Ravenna asked quietly. Merrick and Sabrine exchanged a glance, and Sabrine reached beneath the bed for a knife.

"Me, or her, or both," he said. "By now, they'll know I am a traitor–" Ravenna motioned for him to be silent.

"They cannot know for sure that you are here," Ravenna

said. "They are only guessing. Let me handle it." This, she could do. The sire allowed it, and she wanted to do more good. Merrick nodded, and Ravenna left them there, huddled by the bed.

# CHAPTER 85
## BIG PLANS
### MERRICK

The Raven of Oro was defending them, as if she were on their side. Merrick crouched by the bed, trying to peek out the window, and Sabrine yanked him down and out of sight.

"You're going to get us killed," she hissed beneath her breath. She released his shirt as quickly as she'd grabbed it, wiping her hand on her cloak, as if he had a disease. Merrick rolled his eyes and glanced out the window again. There was movement–some sort of altercation going down–and he saw shadows twisting into the air and around Ravenna's arms. It took him a moment to realize they were not her own, but that they belonged to one of his father's men, a Despiri. Ravenna was not moving, as if she were unable to fight. She had looked exhausted after teleporting and healing Sabrine but–

"Don't tell me this is the Raven of Oro," the Despiri soldier said. "How could we have gotten so lucky? Idris will be pleased." He slapped some shackles onto her wrists, which

Merrick assumed were spelled. "The prince is inside, go get him."

Merrick quickly sank below the side of the bed again, looking around for any way out. Sabrine's eyes were bulging in fear. "They don't know you're here," he said. "I'll go out to meet them. You need to hide."

"What? I–"

"The twins, Sabrine. I don't know what they want with me. But you stay alive for the twins." Merrick assumed his father had finally come for his head. Merrick was a prince, and it was not hard to guess that he had strayed from allegiance to his father's kingdom. This time tomorrow, he would likely find his place in the darkness of the afterlife his deeds had earned him.

Sabrine turned and began pulling up three floorboards, where he assumed the twins had hidden those weeks ago. She motioned him in, as if she cared to save him.

"There isn't room for the both of us," he lied. The soldiers would not stop searching until they had him in shackles. "Get in," he said as the doorknob began to wiggle. "Quickly."

Sabrine hesitantly stepped into the hole, putting her weight on her good leg, and then she peered up at him with those sapphire eyes. If he could bottle the color of her gaze–like the blue-hour sky of twinkling stars–he'd carry it with him into eternity. Nothing good awaited him there, but if he possessed just one reminder of her, he would consider himself blessed far beyond what he deserved. He was nothing to her, but she had allowed him a chance at redemption, and for that, he was grateful.

"Goodbye, Sabrine," he whispered, before he covered her with the floorboards. She said nothing. He slipped a paper into a crack in the wood. "Get them back," he said beneath his breath as the Despiri guards entered the cabin.

He met them by the dining room table, arms raised, surrendering to his imminent death. The Despiri guards slapped shackles around his wrists without a word, and then they collected his many notes from the table. "Looks like you had big plans," one said. "Using the Raven of Oro? I think that is your father's job now." Merrick swallowed, not looking back as they marched him out of the cabin and into the night.

# CHAPTER 86
# DO NOT LET ME DIE

SABRINE

The night hours were long. When the rustling of leaves and the whisper of voices had finally gone, they were followed by the groans Sabrine had come to recognize as witch guardians. She remained frozen beneath the floors while they wandered aimlessly around the cabin. Sabrine heard the front door push open, followed by the heavy footsteps of the wretched beasts. She gripped the note Merrick had left until it was moist with sweat. As dust crumbled into the dark space around her, she willed her breaths to quiet.

She envisioned the massive guardians filling up the tiny room of the cabin above her, and she squinted her eyes shut. She heard them push the bed to the side as if it weighed nothing at all. She was grateful that the wound on her leg was no longer festering and open, or they would have located her in a moment. By pure luck, they exited the cabin, defeated.

When dawn broke, and the sun began shining through the cracks of the floor above her, Sabrine quietly pushed up on the floorboards. This hiding place had not worked for the twins, but it had worked for her. She released a shaky breath as she stepped up into the bedroom with her weak leg. The sun was rising, and there were birds singing their melodies outside the window. She was alone, and once again the twin's safety relied solely on her. She unfolded the paper Merrick had slipped through the crack and into her hands.

The paper was a hand-drawn map, and there were a few circles dispersed throughout it. All but one circle was black. Sabrine studied the lone red circle, realizing that it was near an active mine where there was known to be much bloodstone in the ground. Merrick had circled the nearby caverns. It would be a prime location for holding Embers captive. From the location of the cabin to that red circle, there was a dotted line.

The prince had left her with every possible location of her siblings, and the route to get her there safely through all the guards and checkpoints. As she remembered the way she had treated him these past few days, a pang of guilt settled in her stomach. Shadowmarked or not, he had done more for her than anyone ever had.

Sabrine needed to leave immediately if she wanted to spend less than two nights in the woods with the guardians that were now out for her blood. Quickly, she rummaged through the Raven's sack, collecting rations of jerky and fruit, and a cloak with the Serpent of Edmaria on it. The Edmarian soldiers had stolen her horse, and with only her knife and an old bow, she headed north, toward the caverns where she hoped the twins awaited her.

She had no plans other than to somehow slip in alone and out with two others. They would be shackled, so she would have to monitor the guards that surely surrounded the prison, and find out which of them held the keys.

The woods seemed to be never ending, but after eight hours on foot, she reached where the soil turned to sand. Sabrine was thankful for the shoes on her feet, which Merrick had bought her in the Thickets nearly six weeks ago.

Her breaths grew tight as she exited the cover of the trees and entered the vast desert. For the twins, she could do it. She willed her feet forward, finding peace only when the thick sand dipped into low divots and sank deep enough to conceal her from any onlookers. The desert stretched for miles, but she pushed forward in the heat of the day, her newly reconstructed muscle growing taut. She stopped to rub it, wincing against the pain, and took out the map Merrick had drawn. She would be walking for at least twenty more miles, and between here and the caverns, there would be no shelter. She really could have used a few days to recover as Ravenna had warned. Her muscle had been completely rebuilt, and it was weak. But she was able to compensate for that weakness with her other leg, and she dragged herself along, hour after hour, keeping her mind on the twins.

Well past sunset, she continued forward in darkness. The stars above were many, and she found a sort of peace in gazing at them as she trudged forward in silence. Until she was knocked from her feet by a witch guardian.

Sabrine's entire body went rigid as she lay in the sand beneath the navy skies, searching the horizon line for any sign of that dooming silhouette. From the divot in the sand, rose the beast, and it came toward her slowly, delighting in the chase.

She crawled backwards, not having the strength in her leg to rise. She had gotten lucky with a guardian once, and for the twins, she hoped she could manage again. She held the knife out in her shaking hand, and as the beast crawled toward her, she prayed aloud to the Father of Lights for the first time in years.

"If You care about Your children as the Embers all say you do," she said breathlessly as she watched the beast approach her beneath the light of the stars, "make a way for me to set them free. I cannot do it on my own. Do not let me die."

She did not expect anything. She did not even know why she said the words. But as the guardian took a final leap toward her, thunder rumbled through the clear, starry night, and a bolt of pure lightning came down into the sand, sending a shard of glass plummeting into the chest of the beast.

Sabrine shielded her eyes against the light, dropping her knife to the sand.

"I said I'd find you when it was time, but I did not expect I was being drawn here to save your life."

Sabrine's eyes darted to the glowing lightmarks that now shined through the darkness before her–on the man from the Thickets. *Nakoa.*

"How did you find me?" she asked, mouth agape.

He chuckled. "The Father of Lights works in mysterious ways. Believe it or not, you aren't the first woman I've saved from those pesky beasts. They originated in my territory, but they seem to love it here near Ozanna."

Sabrine watched him silently, then looked to the fallen monster beside him. *Is this man truly claiming the Father of Lights had led him into the wilderness to aid me?*

He offered her a hand up, and she took it, wincing as she put pressure on her leg. She looked back to the stars above and then to the lightmarks that covered his abdomen and chest, glowing through his thin tunic against the night.

"What are you doing all the way out here, Sabrine of Brinland?" he asked, pushing hair from his eyes.

She brushed the sand from her cloak. "My siblings were taken," she said. "They are likely being held in the caverns about twenty miles north of here."

"And you travel in the night, alone? What is the plan when you get there?" Nakoa asked.

"I am very good at thieving," she said. "But I was hoping I would come up with a more detailed plan along the way."

"I guess I showed up at the perfect time," Nakoa said. *That, he had.* "I've been here in Edmaria, monitoring Idris's every move. I'll help you get them back."

"What's the catch?" she asked, crossing her arms. *Why would he help me?* There was a strange confidence about him, and something in his eyes reminded her of the man she had spoken to outside of the castle in Oro.

"No catch," he said with a shrug as he started to walk forward. His body was a large silhouette in the night, strongly built and burly. "Are you coming or not?" he asked. *What other option do I have?*

Sabrine limped after him, following the light of his marks, and they embarked on their mission to save the twins.

*The Father of Lights truly does work in mysterious ways.*

# CHAPTER 87
# FREEDOM FROM THESE CHAINS
## RAVENNA

After an entire day on horseback, the Edmarian soldiers delivered Ravenna to a little cavern in the desert. Merrick had been taken on to the Sand Palace by orders of his father, but she had been shackled and chained to the smooth sandstone of the cavern with a hundred other Embers. She could be more easily contained here within the bloodstone walls and with spelled chains, which temporarily disabled the gifts of both Despiri and Embers.

Quick and shallow breaths overtook her as she was surrounded by those she had been ordered to kill. The shackles on her wrists that kept her from using her power were the only thing preventing that sire bond from pushing her into a massacre. If she were not physically restrained, even without access to her power, she would be forced to do the unthinkable. Her hands shook in her lap as the cold bloodstone in her pocket weighed against her leg, reminding her of that very command.

"It's okay to be scared," a small voice said. "But whether we

637

die in these caverns or not, Eternal Light awaits us." Ravenna lifted her head to see a tiny set of hands reaching toward hers, and she pulled away as far as the chains would allow. The little girl was no older than ten, and she had a lightmark on her cheek. Her eyes were a deep blue against her brown skin. Beside her, a little boy, similar in appearance, peered at Ravenna. His mark was just above his brow, and Ravenna wondered what his gifts were.

"Our mama always used to tell us that. Sabrine doesn't really believe it, but we know it's true."

"Sabrine?" Ravenna asked, heart leaping at the name.

"Our sister," the small girl said, tears fighting to escape down her hollow cheeks. "I miss her."

"I hope she is okay," said the boy quietly from behind her, his voice cracking.

Ravenna looked around the cavern, among the hundred faces that were illuminated beneath torch flame and the glow of lightmarks. She was the only one chained in this entire cavern who bore shadows where light should be. *What were the odds of her being chained next to these two?*

"Your sister is okay," she offered. She would not give them hope in telling them she was coming for them; she had seen the security around the prison on her way in. Sabrine would have to be a master at concealment to be able to break through the walls of this prison.

"Do you know her?" the girl asked hopefully, looking back at her brother, who was wiping his wet cheeks.

"I do," Ravenna said, keeping tension on the chains that separated them. "I met her once. She is a strong woman, and she would do anything for you." Ravenna thought back to the days when she was shield-maiden over Vestele. She would have done anything to protect her people and her home. She had once known pure devotion like Sabrine had for the twins. She lived it, long ago. She cleared her throat. "Your sister loves you very much."

Both children smiled at that, and Ravenna's gaze fell to their little hands, joined together.

"I'm Neah," the girl said to Ravenna.

"And I'm Risley."

Ravenna did not offer them her name in fear they and the other Embers inside this prison might recognize it. Though, if her feathered armor did not give her away, she did not know what would. "It is nice to meet you," she said, peering across the caverns. There were over a hundred Embers here, chained together, backs against the cavern walls. "How many guards patrol this area?" she asked, taking in her surroundings.

"I counted eight today," Neah answered. "Yesterday they were talking about taking us to meet King Idris soon." Ravenna bit her cheek, watching the only guard in sight walk up and down the rows of Embers. *Does this child know what it means for them to meet the king? Had his weapon been completed?*

The sire bond whispered against her mind, haunting her. *When you find them, just kill them all. Whatever you do, do not allow Idris to use his weapon.*

Ravenna nearly choked as that order was made fresh in her mind. She resisted the urge to feel the bloodstone in her pocket. She was surprised the guards who had brought her here had stopped searching her after they'd confiscated her sword. "How many of the guards are marked?" Ravenna asked. If she could keep the spelled shackles on while she killed the guards before they could move the Embers for transport, perhaps she could buy herself some time until Leith could break the sire. But if these guards were Despiri, they would have more to use against her. Ravenna was a warrior, but without her power, and against multiple Despiri, she would fail.

"The Despiri are marked, like you?" Risley asked, looking at the shadows on her arms.

"Yes," Ravenna said, attempting to cover the back of her hands.

"At least half of them, I think," Risley said.

Ravenna sighed, leaning her head back against the wall. She could fight the sire as long as she was chained because here, against the wall and without her power, she had no choice. All of these Embers were going to die, either by Idris's hands or hers. She weighed her options and then offered a weak smile to the twins as she fought the burning in her spine. As long as they kept her shackled until Leith could kill Degare, these Embers would be safe.

"I guess we shall visit the Sand Palace together, then," she said.

# CHAPTER 88
# GOING SOUTH
## XAN

Xan had determined that while it would be difficult, he would honor his word to Nilo. Where Leith planned to give Ravenna no choice in the war, Xan would. He would allow her to choose whether or not she wanted him to take her far away, or if she wanted to stay and fight. He only hoped she did not choose to side with the Ink Bloods. There was no alliance, and she could still take her people back, if she so desired. With the power she now held, Xan believed it would be quite simple.

Xan and Cove had been traveling on horseback for five days, and they had finally hit the sands of the Edmarian desert at nightfall. Lightning struck in the south, lighting up the sands as they traveled east toward the Palace. The warrior in Xan wanted to suggest they rest for the night under the cover of trees, but the thought of Ravenna being nearby had him continuing into the darkness of an unfamiliar country without a second thought.

With the quick flash of light, Cove perked up as if she had seen something.

"What is it?" he asked, scanning the horizon. He waited for another bolt, but none came.

"Up ahead," she warned under her breath. Xan followed Cove's line of sight to the barely visible silhouettes that stood around a handful of tents, standing between them and the direction of the Sand Palace.

"Looks like some sort of checkpoint," Xan said. Cove halted her horse.

"I'll never make it through. We'll have to go around."

Xan surveyed the vast miles of dunes and sandstone hills, then his eyes fell to their exhausted horses. They had both assumed the King of Edmaria was holding the Embers and Elias somewhere near the Sand Palace, meaning Ravenna would be there, too, carrying out her mission from her master. Xan's jaw set as he sized up the men. There looked to be three, maybe five at the most.

"I can get us through," he said with confidence.

"I cannot defend myself here in the desert with no water to draw from. I am not going to let you get me killed before I can ever save Elias."

"They will not be the ones doing the killing," he said, feeling the weight of his sword at his side.

"Some may be Despiri—"

"Be brave, Cove. The sooner we get through, the sooner you hold your husband again." *And the sooner I am reunited with Ravenna.* He thought of her alone all these months, forced to do the bidding of evil, and it broke him. Losing her had been the equivalent of losing his purpose. If this had been him and her coming up on a potential group of Despiri, he would have insisted they turn back, but she would not have listened, and he would have followed her into the fight.

He thought of Ravenna for a moment longer: her determined spirit, the strength she held in her stride, the way her laughter, even among a crowd of many, had always been the one to carry through the valley as if it had wings of its own. He remembered the way her heart softened for the young children, and the way she had always longed for freedom—only to have it all stripped away before she could ever truly taste it.

*Be brave for her*, he told himself as he started toward the checkpoint in the open sands beneath stars. Cove dug through her satchel and reluctantly followed behind him, gripping a knife in her fingers with the reigns.

"Try not to draw attention to that," he said. "And loosen your shoulders. Follow my lead."

The sound of the guards' voices and laughter echoed across the dunes, and Xan mapped the land around him for the quickest exit. They had strategically placed themselves in the path easiest to travel by, a valley between the stone hills and slippery dunes. Avoiding every checkpoint in this country would be impossible.

"What is your business here?" one called out in a gruff voice as they neared. Xan could count four men total. Two sat on upside down buckets, unconcerned with their approach, and the others stood tall with their hands on their undrawn weapons.

Xan looked to the side at Cove, whose hands were shaking against the reigns of her mare. He took a breath before giving his response. "We travel east to the shore. We are looking for work."

"What kind of work?" the man called.

"I'm skilled in swordmaking. And my sister is a seamstress." He gestured to Cove who still sat stiffly atop her horse.

"Let us see her handiwork, then, to be sure you are not lying," one said. All four men were on their feet now. "Stay there, and send her forward." Xan got ready to protest, but as he looked to the side at Cove, she was already stepping down, and the sand was shifting beneath her feet. Her throat bobbed, and she held the skirts of her linen dress as she walked with her shoulders back, hair like silver in the moonlight.

Xan watched closely as she approached them. His muscles were rigid with tension as he fought the urge to accompany her. He could not hear the words they spoke as she neared, and he could not see her face, but the fingers that gathered the skirts at her side were trembling.

With her back to him, her voice was muffled, but Xan could make out some of the conversation. They watched her longingly, as if they had not seen a woman in ages. Thankfully, they made no moves to close the distance between themselves and her, but as they peered upon the dress she wore, that they believed she had crafted herself, Xan began to grow uncomfortable. He was sure Cove was having the same thoughts. *What if they check for lightmarks?*

Xan kept his eyes on them as he stepped down from his horse. He lurked through the night, trying to keep his silhouette in line with that of the mare behind him to draw less attention. As he neared, he could make out the words of their conversations. "What are you fine men doing all the way out here?" she asked in a hushed voice, as if she was embarrassed for Xan to hear. "Surely you have wives at home who miss you?"

The man in the center smiled, taking a slow step forward. Xan could not decipher whether it was a threat or evidence of enticement. She was distracting them with conversation, and being that she was desirable, it was working.

"King Idris has placed many checkpoints throughout the country. Here, we only check for Embers."

"Embers?" Cove placed her shaking hand on her chest as if shocked, and Xan watched the trembling cease as it rested there above her heart. "Ah, yes," she said, as if remembering something. "And then you ship them to Oro."

One of the men shifted on his feet, and Xan halted, waiting for the perfect opportunity to strike. None of them looked his way as Cove stood before them. "No, miss. Between us," he stepped forward and whispered low, and Xan took one step forward, "if we come across any, we shuttle them to the southern cavern, where they'll stay until our king can take their lives for his own." Cove's breath visibly hitched in her throat, and Xan took the leap. She backed up, allowing him room to strike from the shadows. Two men laid breathless at her feet before the others could react. The tallest grabbed his sword and lazily swung it forward, eyes in a crazed panic. Xan dodged it and grabbed the man's wrist, forcing his blade to the ground. He jammed the hilt of his own sword into his nose, knocking him unconscious. When Xan spun to end the other, his eyes first met the blue of Cove's, piercing the night.

She stood with her hands raised, faced with a guard who thankfully bore no shadowmarks. His blade was pointed at her, and its tip scraped the linen of her dress as her chest rose and fell. She did not break eye contact with the man, but blinked violently, squeezing her eyes shut and back open as if she could will him away.

"Let her go," Xan demanded as he watched her stand in fear. "Take me." Xan put his own hands up in surrender and laid his sword at the man's feet. He turned on him in an instant, freeing Cove from the threat of his sword.

"Take you? I am going to kill *you*." He moved forward, blade pointed, and Xan retreated a step. His mouth fell dry as he looked death in the eyes. "*Her*," the man said, shifting his blade toward Cove for a moment, "I am going to take." He looked at Cove for a moment. "You belong in those caverns, don't you? What is your little trick? How did you get Burhan to tell you secret information about where we keep them? What is your game?"

Cove was still as stone, and while the guard was distracted, Xan took the opportunity to duck and ram his shoulder into his torso, pushing him to the ground. He placed his foot on the man's wrist, keeping him from raising his sword in defense.

"Cove," Xan said, "knife!" She tossed Xan the knife and he palmed it, bringing it to the man's throat in an instant. As Xan ended his life, Cove turned away.

He climbed to his feet behind her. Her shoulders rose and fell with quickened breaths, and she held up a hand to wave him off as he laid a hand on her arm. "I'm fine," she said. "Search the tents for supplies. We're going south."

Her face was pale and her legs unsteady, but Xan nodded and left her there to collect herself. He gathered water canteens from the tents, a few knives, maps, and a sword for Cove, though, to think she could use it was irrational.

*The Embers are being held in the southern caverns. And where the Embers are, Ravenna will also be. Finally.*

Xan loaded up the saddlebags on the horses and waited for a few minutes before Cove had gained her composure. Silently, she pulled herself onto the back of her horse and headed south by way of the constellations Xan had never cared to learn.

"I'm sorry I almost got you killed," he called from behind her.

"Don't be," she said. "We'd still be headed in the wrong direction if you hadn't."

"Still," he said, "I won't let it happen again."

# CHAPTER 89
# NO REST
### SABRINE

"Are you sure you don't need to rest?" Nakoa asked over his shoulder as Sabrine lagged behind, trudging through the cool sands of the night. She lifted her knees high as she walked and attempted to breathe quietly so he would not hear the exhaustion that had overcome her. The dune they climbed now was the highest yet, and Sabrine longed to touch the starry horizon as they trekked upward. She struggled on her weak leg for a moment longer until Nakoa turned to face her completely, still awaiting an answer.

"I do not need to rest," she said. Her breaths were deep as she hungered for air. The usual bite in her voice was nonexistent. *I need to get to the twins.*

"A few minutes is not going to hurt anything." Above his brown eyes, his thick brow ticked. "We'll still make it by daylight if your map is correct," he said, unfurling it and holding it up to the moonlight. She knew he was right. The land was turning from sand to hills of golden stone, like that of the caverns. "Where did you get this anyway?" he asked, examining all of the checkpoints on the map. She bent over, bracing her hands on her knees for a moment.

"The Prince of Edmaria, strangely enough."

Nakoa's eyes shot to hers. "You know the prince?"

"He is the reason the twins were taken," she said, immediately regretting her rash words. A piece of her had begun to trust Merrick as a friend. He had spent nearly two weeks proving himself to her in trying to save the twins, and he had spent another few days trying to save her life after her injury. But he was shadowmarked, and she no longer knew what was real. Nakoa thought for a moment.

"The Despiri Prince of Edmaria was trying to help you save your Ember siblings?" he asked, rolling the map back up and placing it into his satchel.

Sabrine was quiet for a moment. "Yes. He was." *Not because he cares,* she told herself, *but because he is looking for a shot at redemption.* She started back up the dune, and he paced himself beside her.

"Where is he now?" Nakoa asked.

"Enduring the wrath of his father, I suppose." Her stomach twisted with a strange guilt.

Nakoa fell silent, and when they made it to the peak of the dune, he pulled her to the ground with him. Sand embedded into her elbows and she winced, turning to glare at him. A finger at his lips warned her to be silent, and she followed his gaze out to the pacing silhouettes on the horizon.

At least four Edmarian guards patrolled the small encampment that was nestled in the sandstone hills before them.

"This checkpoint was not on your map," Nakoa said, scratching his head as they laid on their bellies, ducking behind the peak of the dune. "Are you sure the prince isn't trying to get you killed?"

Sabrine pondered on that for a moment, and as she saw a few unraised tents at the edge of the camp, the tension in her shoulders released. "No. This camp is new."

Nakoa studied the guards for a moment, his eyes narrowing against the distance.

"We'll just go around," Sabrine whispered.

"The caverns are just over the next hill. They have been placed here as an extra measure to guard the Embers. They are using the sandstone hills as cover. My guess is, that cavern is surrounded by guards." Sabrine's heart plummeted into her stomach.

"Surely we can get through under the cover of night, I–" Nakoa looked down to his glowing chest, and she paused. "I can get through," she said.

His brows knit together as he shook his head. "What will you do if you make it across?" She knew there was no way she would be able to free them of their chains and sneak them out on her own.

Sabrine sighed and watched the guards and sleeping camp below. "You can use your gifts. Strike them with lightning," she suggested.

"And risk waking the entire army?" he said, shifting on his arm to look at her. "We'd both be dead in a minute." He surveyed her and added, "Well, me shackled, and you dead."

"Fair," she said. "Then take out the whole camp. You can, can't you?"

He blinked at her. "I don't know who they are holding in those tents. I am not risking the lives of innocents. I fight against darkness, but my goal is not to kill every one who stands in my way. We do not repay evil for evil, but there is such thing as justice. And it is justice that my God will bring. There will be death and war along the way, but the Embers want to salvage life where we can, Sabrine. We want to bring hope to those lost in the shadows. Our goal is to deliver a message. A promise of life eternal with no suffering or pain, filled with all that is good through the presence of the Father and His marvelous Light."

Sabrine was still as she stared straight through him, reliving all the moments her parents had ever tried to force those very words into her brain. The very Light he spoke of was the same Light she had always blamed for her parents' deaths.

"We do this my way," Nakoa said sternly as he fought for her agreement. *Does the Father of Lights truly care for His children? The ones who bear His Light upon their skin like targets in this world of darkness? Is all of this a coincidence, or had He truly heard my desperate plea in the wilderness?*

She looked upon Nakoa's lightmarks and the hope they were supposed to bring. Reluctantly, she nodded. She would not blindly trust, and she did not know if any amount of evidence that the Father of Lights had heard her would ever suffice, but she would give the benefit of the doubt, just this once. For the twins.

"Are you a good shot?" Nakoa asked, nodding to the bow on her back.

She huffed a laugh. "No."

"Me either," he said. "I'll have to sneak down there and take them out with a sword."

"They'll see you coming," she said as she looked at his marks. She reached for the sack at her side and pulled out the purple cloak with the gold serpent of Edmaria embroidered on the back. "Wear this."

He twisted it in his large hand, and she wondered if it would fit him, being that it was supposed to be worn by the Raven of Oro. "Did the prince also give this to you?" Nakoa asked, puzzled.

"Long story," she said, urging him to put it on. He narrowed his eyes on her and slid down the back of the dune so he could stand without being seen. Sabrine looked between him and the camp. He tugged the cloak over his shoulders, and though it was too short and barely buttoned at his neck, at least it would cover his marks while he approached the camp under the cover of night. He rolled his shoulders and took his sword into his hand. "The Edmarian soldiers' hair is all cropped," she said as he freed his from beneath the collar of the cloak.

"No," he said. "I'm not cutting my hair. By the time I am close enough to see, they'll be dead." Sabrine chewed on her cheek. "Stay here until I give you the signal. When I've taken care of the night watch, you can join me at the well." He pointed to a small stack of stones at the edge of the camp where she assumed the soldiers retrieved their water. "We'll continue through together."

Sabrine nodded and nocked an arrow into her bow as he hustled up and over the dune toward the camp that separated her from Neah and Risley. She watched the guards closely as he made the descent, keeping her arrow aimed in their direction, but having little faith she could hit one if she tried.

None of the guards looked Nakoa's way, though, and as his burly silhouette made its way toward them in the blue hues of the night, Sabrine lowered her bow and prepared to run. When she had first seen him coming off of the boat in the Thickets, she had guessed that he might be a warrior. Tonight, she knew it.

He moved flawlessly through the guards, carefully targeting each one as their backs were turned. No noise escaped them as he took their lives by the sword, and when he had fallen each one, he began dragging them to the well. When all four bodies were stacked by the stones, the remainder of the camp still asleep, his face turned to the height of the dune where she crouched, and she snuck across the sands.

He was lowering the bodies gently into the well when she arrived. "What are you doing?" she whispered.

"Hiding the evidence that we were ever here. We need to sneak into the caverns undetected, and this entire battalion will be on high alert if they suspect someone killed their guards." When the final body had been released into the hole, Nakoa took careful thought to cover their tracks and to smooth the disrupted sand near the entrance to the camp. Slowly, they made their way through.

They avoided the light of the few fires burning brightly in the midst of the brown tents, and instead, they traveled along the outskirts of the camp. Nakoa had collected one of the fallen soldier's swords, and he wore it boldly on his back across his own blade. They were careful to leave no trace as they moved toward the hills where the caverns were nestled behind.

"I'll watch your back," Nakoa said. "Stop when you get to the top."

She started up the hill, and he walked backward behind, keeping an eye on the silent battalion below. They reached the top and peered downward together. The hills continued as far as the eye could see in the night, and had it not been for the warm glow of the fire in the hillside about half-mile north, she would have thought the map had been incorrect.

"There," Nakoa said, pointing to it. "That's the cave. We

will need to move quickly, but we can make it by sunrise." He offered her a hand and led her down the steep face of the hill. Rock rumbled beneath her boots, and she slipped once, only to be caught by his arm. "Let's make it to that peak," he said, pointing northwest. "We'll be able to map out a plan from there. We need to see how guarded this cavern is, and we need to find a way to move however many Embers are in there out, without being caught."

Sabrine halted. "You never said anything about rescuing all of the Embers." *How could that even be possible?* They'd be discovered in a minute.

"Idris has returned from Oro, and his weapon is complete. If we leave them, every one of them will be dead by the end of the week." She swallowed, following him up the hill despite the burning in her legs.

"How are we going to sneak so many out without being seen?" she called behind him as he stopped at the highest elevation amid the hills. "Or tracked and captured all over again?" She supposed it was doable, since someone had done it at the Ember Trade just two weeks ago. But strangely enough, she found herself needing to know the strategy now.

"With the Light," Nakoa said, " all things are possible, and there is much of it in that cavern."

"That's not a good enough answer for me," she said, breathing heavily as she ascended the last few feet to stand beside him. She crossed her arms. "What's the plan?"

His lip tugged upward as he studied her. "I'm going to break them out, and you're going to do what you claim you're best at and sneak them away. I'll follow up at the rear, making sure we are not followed. Tell me, Sabrine. Which of these routes," he paused, motioning outward across the lands, "would you take a hundred Embers to flee if we were taking them west, toward Adullam at the western shore of Ozanna?" *What was this Adullam that he had mentioned twice now?* He waited patiently for her answer as she calculated, her eyes drifting from the glow in the cavern across the lands at her left.

She pointed toward a rocky path at the base of the hill they stood on. "I suppose I would take them west to where the sea cuts between Oro and Edmaria. From there, under the cover of forest and mountains, I'd go south until we hit the river. Then we could travel along it toward the shore. But the mountains would be treacherous, and even under the cover of trees, the Despiri would track–"

"It'll be a long journey," Nakoa said. "But even if you took only the twins and fled, you cannot protect them on your own. Not in this world. There is safety in numbers."

Sabrine thought for a moment. "Fine. I'll lead them west, but if I feel like the twins are in the least bit of danger, you're on your own." There was a twinkle in his eye with an unspoken thought, and she wondered if he thought her a coward.

"You cannot be a shield against darkness when you wallow in the shadows yourself," he said.

Sabrine forced her mouth to stay shut. *You need his help. Do not let his remarks get to you.* She looked past him to the reddening desert horizon. In only two hours, heat waves would be visible across the Edmarian sands. She was thankful she'd be traveling west into the forest.

"We need to move quickly," she said. Nakoa looked to the cavern below, and then to the east, where the sun would soon rise.

"That, we do."

# CHAPTER 90
# SHADOWS UNCHAINED
## RAVENNA

At sunrise, when the golden desert sun began to shine into the hidden cavern in the dunes, Ravenna awoke to Neah and Risley snuggled together. They had gravitated toward her in the night, and Neah's head was now resting on Ravenna's shoulder. Ravenna sat still as stone, careful not to wake her. Some of the other chained Embers were beginning to stir with the daylight, and the sound of shackles shifting across the stone filled the cavern. The air was dry, and there was a new soreness in her throat. The smell of sweat and waste wafted through as the people around her stirred. Her eyes watered, and she longed for a sip of water.

Ravenna figured the guards would be bringing sustenance soon, being that they would want the Embers alive for their king. In the hundreds of scattered tin plates and empty jars, there was evidence that the prisoners had at least been fed well enough to maintain strength so they could travel on their own two feet. A family of four huddled together by the entrance. Their chains kept them close, but so did their hands, which were joined so tightly their knuckles were white against otherwise brown skin. They all leaned together against the south wall, opposite of Ravenna. The way they watched her with little emotion behind their eyes was unsettling.

There were only two guards patrolling the inside of the caverns, and being that it was morning, Ravenna assumed they would be rotating shifts soon. But when the two guards exited the caverns too quickly for it to be a routine shift change, Ravenna knew something was out of the ordinary. There was a distant sound of metal clashing, and she tilted her head to peer out the exit of the cavern and into the brightness of day.

"What is it?" Neah asked beside her, her head lifting from Ravenna's shoulder.

"Nothing," Ravenna lied as strange thunder echoed outside. "Go back to sleep." Neah didn't, and instead, she shook Risley awake too. Ravenna watched as a large brute of a man rounded the corner, wearing an ill-fitting cloak with the serpent of Edmaria embroidered on the back. He was built like Roarke, and in his hand, he held a ring of keys. Though his back was to the sun, there was a radiance behind his eyes that she recognized. She had seen it in Zephaniah, Galen, and Cove. But they were not the three her mind fixated on. There was another, whose likeness she could swear she looked upon now.

"That guard is new," Neah said. "I haven't seen him before." The Ember family against the south wall turned their attention to the right as the guard entered. He surveyed the room, and Ravenna kept her head ducked away from the light. The beat in her chest intensified, and she watched silently as he bent and began unlocking the shackles of the father in the family on the south wall. He uttered something in a low voice, and a sort of light—a hope—blossomed behind the father's eyes.

He looked upon his family with assurance, clasped each of their hands in his, and then took toward the exit where he stopped and peered out, as if he had been ordered to keep watch.

Ravenna's eyebrows sank in curiosity as she watched them; the strange guard came down the line, examining the locks on each of the Embers' wrists and tried to find the right key in the dozen on his ring. The Embers were chained together with the strange spelled shackles, and each key undid the shackles of about ten prisoners at once. "He is releasing us," Neah said with a bright smile. Ravenna was connected to Neah and Risley's chains with a handful of others.

*He cannot be,* Ravenna thought. The bloodstone in her pocket became heavy on her leg, and her body churned with sudden anxiety as she tried to distance herself from the twins. She clung to the shackles on her wrists, willing them to stay locked.

*Do not allow him to free you, or you'll kill every Ember in this cavern. Either without your power and by the sword, or outside of this cavern with your power as they flee. The sire bond demands you kill them all.*

She would not allow this man to free the shadows that had finally been tamed.

She studied him, trying to place his face, trying to place the strange energy that seemed to surround him and draw her in. It was almost hypnotizing, the way it taunted her, almost bringing her back to a place she had encountered in Oro. The place where she had found strength.

His familiarity distracted her, and when she had finally blinked it away, he was at the end of her row, key in the lock. She opened her mouth to stop him, but before any utterance escaped, Ravenna's shackles fell to the floor along with Neah and Risley's.

*No.*

She could suppress it no longer. The demands of the sire came rushing back, begging her to get out of this cavern, to restore her power beyond these bloodstone walls, and to wrap her fingers around her own bloodstone as she took every life for herself.

It was all encompassing. Nauseating. Uncontrolled.

*When you find them, just kill them all.*

"All of you, follow me out." Ravenna shuddered back into reality as his words cut the air. "I am getting you to safety. There is a haven in the west. We have a long journey ahead, and the Edmarian soldiers will be on our tails." Her fingernails cut into her palms, and she willed herself to collect the shackles and place them back onto her wrists. The sire allowed no such thing.

"Are you coming? Let's go!" Neah said, grabbing Ravenna's arm to tug her toward the exit where the man was headed to lead the Embers out.

Ravenna backed away from Neah's touch, pressing herself against the wall and fighting the pain that was creeping up her spine, burning where that brand was, urging her to end every life in these caverns.

"Go without me," Ravenna choked out. Right as the twins were about to argue, a familiar voice echoed through the room, calling them by name.

"Neah! Risley!" The man looked surprised—or maybe irritated—to see Sabrine bolting into the cavern, favoring one leg, but when he turned to see the twins leaping into her embrace, his eyes softened. "You're okay. You're okay," she whispered into their hair. Ravenna held her breath against the pain radiating through her back as she watched in horror of what she was about to strip away from Sabrine.

The man and Sabrine were oblivious to the war unfolding in Ravenna's mind—the one the sire was winning. "I couldn't wait," Sabrine said to the guard as the children wept in her arms. "I told the Embers where to go. I'll catch up to the front, I just needed to know they were here." She turned her attention down to the twins and pulled their chins up so their eyes met hers. "You're safe," she said. "I am so sorry." Ravenna shut her eyes tightly, willing the sire to quiet.

*Kill them all.*

She could not fight Degare's demands much longer. She needed Leith to kill him.

She turned toward the wall, pounding her hand against the stone in protest of the voice in her head. Today was day six. She only had to hang on a little while longer. Leith would break the sire. He would do it. He promised.

*I am not the Raven any longer,* she said to herself. *Soon, I will be set free.*

"What's wrong? Are you okay?" the man asked from behind her, finally noticing her presence. Ravenna turned to him, gritting her teeth through the pain.

"Get them out of here," she barked. "Get them out of my sight, now." He raised his hands in surrender, and caution painted his face as he tiptoed toward her with his hands low, as if he were approaching a rabid animal. The pain jolted down her spine, pushing her to pursue the Embers—to *kill them all.*

She looked to the ground for anything she could use as a weapon against this man before her. *No.* She fought the desire to reach for the shattered glass shard from a broken jar at her feet. *Do not kill him.*

*Yes, kill them all.* She was lucky her power could not return to her within the confines of this cavern.

"Come on Leith," she muttered. "Now. Do it now."

"What did you say?" the man asked, still creeping toward her, trying to calm her. "How do you know Leith?"

Ravenna's eyes shot up to his. They were brown, but shaped like Leith's, and the structure of his face was similar.

Sabrine's voice echoed behind him. "Nakoa. She is the Raven of Oro, she has been sired to kill the Embers. We need to get out of here," she urged him, concealing the twins behind her body. When Nakoa spotted the shadowmarks on Ravenna's arms, he halted.

"Leave it to my cousin to get wrapped up in such a mess," he muttered, not taking his eyes from Ravenna. "You have the map, Sabrine. Do as we discussed. I'll hold her off."

Sabrine did not hesitate. The caverns were empty in a heartbeat, aside from Nakoa and Ravenna. "You cannot hold me off," Ravenna said as she grabbed the glass shard at her feet. "You need to kill me."

"You're Ravenna of the Valley. You're the Dove. I know better than to kill you. Leith will have my head," Nakoa said, circling her. He drew one of the two swords from his back and pointed it toward her, as if the threat could subdue her. She tried to focus on his lightmarks, on the Light within him that was also in Leith–the only thing that had ever succeeded in quelling the sire. She begged it to calm her, she begged it to overpower the demands in her mind, but it did no such thing.

Ravenna was shaking with the pain that rattled through

her. "If you do not kill me, all of those Embers you're working to protect will die."

"Leith is working on breaking the sire as we speak, correct? I'll keep you at bay until then," he said, assuming it would be easy. She swiped toward him with the glass, and he dodged it.

Nakoa did not take his eyes from her as she began to circle him, aiming for the exit where the dormancy of her power would end. He could try to stop her, but the side of Ravenna which held the title of warrior had never met its match. He would meet death at her hands, and her pursuit of Degare's beloved Embers would ensue.

"Keep me in the walls of this spellbound cavern, and your job will be much easier," she said through gritted teeth, stepping toward him again. "But even then, you are only prolonging the same outcome. It is me or them."

*Please, Leith. Free me, now.*

# CHAPTER 91
# WASTED TIME
## COVE

Cove allowed the beat in her chest to soothe her as they traveled into the sandstone hills. The sun was coming up in the east, and Cove was thankful they were no longer traveling in that direction. The day would be hot, and their long sleeves, cloaks, and hoods protected them against the powerful rays of desert light.

*Elias. I am on my way to you.* She willed the words down the bond. She could barely remember what it had been like for those brief moments of bliss, when he could hear her and she, him. Could he hear her now? *I will be there soon.* She clenched her fists, trying to stop the anxiety from manifesting in her bones.

"Cove?" They were the first words Xan had spoken since his apology to her hours ago. He eyed her hands. "You said you were defenseless in the desert with no water to draw from. But what I saw back there—"

"Yes?" she asked slowly.

"How did you distract those men? It was like they suddenly became docile toward you."

"Only for a moment, and then I failed," she muttered. Cove did not want to talk about such things.

"Failed at what, though?"

"I have the ability to manipulate emotions, to a degree. But I am not skilled in it." Cove kept her body turned from him as shame colored her cheeks. *Why had I even tried to use such a power?* The guard had been aware of her antics. She had not been subtle enough. The dangers of using this power were far too great. "My fear got the best of me I am afraid."

"So the Father of Lights gifts some people multiple gifts? Not just one?" Xan asked.

Cove nodded. She knew Leith had more than two, and Xan had witnessed that in the Dead Wood. How many would Ravenna have, if she came to the Light?

Xan hummed in wonder. "How much farther do you think we have?" he asked from behind her. The map she could hear him examining now had led them into the hills from the east, and there were no more checkpoints between here and the cavern. There was one north of the holding place that they would need to avoid, but Cove had a plan to get Elias home safely. To the Ink Bloods. To *Adullam,* where he had sent her with such care all those months ago after his promise to keep her safe. Now, hand in hand, they would return together.

"Not far," Cove said over her shoulder. The air was beginning to feel heavy, and with that gift she hated, she could feel something stirring in the valley: *distress, anticipation, anguish, fear, relief, longing.*

*Freedom.*

"Let's go," Cove said, urging her horse to a sprint.

"Cove, wait! What are you doing?" Xan called behind her. His voice faded into the dust, and she kept her eyes forward, toward the emotions that spilled into the valley ahead of her. Something was happening. Someone was freeing the Embers.

As Cove rounded a hill, and the source of those emotions was revealed, a sob broke from her throat. She leapt from her horse, and her feet took her forward into the crowd of Embers that moved west. Their backs were to her, and as she plowed into them, she spun, scanning the faces of every victim there.

*Elias, I am here.*

*Elias.*

*Elias.*

"Elias!" Her voice was pleading, cutting through the shallow canyon, alerting the silent Embers of her presence. Many turned to look at her, eyes wide. Someone grabbed her shoulder and spun her around.

"Quiet!" the old man said beneath his beard. His cheeks were hollow, and he shook her back into reality. "You are going to get us all killed!" Cove's chest rose and fell, and she turned to the masses, watching as they were shuttled out of the caverns.

*Leith should not be here yet. Who has freed them?*

She turned again, but the man was gone. She grabbed the shoulder of the woman in front of her. "Miss. My husband, Elias. Have you seen him? Blond hair, gray–" she paused and corrected herself, "blue eyes." She ran her hand through her hair, looking from left to right at every Ember who walked past her.

*Elias, where are you?*

The woman shook her head. "I haven't seen him, I'm sorry." Cove pushed through the crowd, desperately asking everyone who would listen if they had seen her husband.

"Elias," she said aloud. "Elias, please." Her voice was a broken plea, and the weight of the ocean on her chest threatened to steal her breath.

"Did you say, Elias?" a voice said behind her. Cove turned at once, meeting the green eyes of a petite man who looked to be from her homeland. His skin was like leather, and his hair was matted and coated with dust.

"Yes, yes. Do you know him?"

"We were on the ship together. You are the one who jumped into the sea after him–he was so worried about you."

"Where is he now?" she asked desperately. "Tell me."

"When they escorted us off the ship, they said they were taking him to the palace. Said he was the prince's murderer. He never denied it for a second. It was the reason for his *special treatment* on the ship." Cove's head was spinning. The valley became nothing but darkness around her, and she struggled to hold her own weight. She felt the man's hand on her arm, and she swayed forward, pushing through the masses to find her horse. "Miss!" he called behind her. She did not respond.

*He is in the palace. He is going to be executed for the murder you committed,* she thought to herself. *You have wasted time coming here. He is going to die because of you. You are a killer. It cannot be undone.*

# CHAPTER 92
# ALL FOR YOU
## XAN

He watched as Cove plummeted into the crowd, dust flying beneath her feet. There were no guards in sight, and about a hundred Embers were traveling west, no chains or shackles weighing them down. The only noise was the sound of Cove's strangled cries echoing throughout the valley as she searched for her husband. He rushed forward to quiet her, but halted as he heard a familiar voice inside the cavern at his right.

Slowly, he turned. *Is she already here?* He entered, hands low so as to not appear as a threat. Her voice carried through the caverns, and Xan's chest tightened in anticipation. In what state would he find her? Sired, or as the woman he had fallen in love with?

"It is me or them," Ravenna said. *Who is she talking to?*

Xan rounded the corner with a deep breath before laying eyes on the Raven of Oro. Before her stood Leith's cousin, a defensive wall between her and the Embers. Ravenna's eyes flashed as she noticed Xan, and then she lunged forward, knocking the sword from Nakoa's hand with a move the two of them had practiced a hundred times in Vestele. He tried to picture her as the shield-maiden, loyal to her people, her friends, but standing here in the midst of her oncoming attack, the image of Ravenna of the Valley, Ravenna Zenevieva Barrett, fiddler, potter, warrior of Vestele, faded away. Her hands trembled and her palms were bleeding, as if she had used pain to distract herself from the voice in her mind. Xan could see she was fighting a losing battle within herself.

"I know you don't want to do this, Ravenna," Xan said.

She laughed, but it was a solemn sound. It was not the same laughter he used to work to draw from her in a life not too long ago. Nakoa drew the sword from his back as Ravenna picked up his other.

"I have no choice," she said breathily, wincing against some hidden pain.

Nakoa spoke over his shoulder, not taking his eyes from Ravenna.

"You and I, warrior. We keep her in these caverns and away from those Embers until Leith can break the sire." Ravenna looked painfully at Xan, shaking her head.

"Leave, Xan. Do not let me hurt you." The torment in her voice broke him. "I gave into the sire for you. I did it to protect you. Do not let that be in vain."

Xan's throat bobbed. *Was she telling the truth? What did she mean, she had done this for me, to spare me?* He kept his hands low as he approached her. He did not draw his sword.

"No, Xan," she said, shaking her head and backing away. She cried out in pain, and it was all he could do not to rush to her side. She hit her knees, but her grasp held tightly around the sword. "Do not put me through this again."

"Through what, Venna?" Her eyes welled with tears at the sound of her nickname, and she blinked them away as she looked up at him.

"I kill for the king," she said, rising to her feet. Nakoa stiffened before her, keeping his sword extended but out of her reach. "I have no choice."

Xan's gaze fell to the free hand that now slid into her pocket. Out came a bloodstone, and she gripped it tightly in her hand before swinging her sword low. Nakoa blocked it with his own, and at the sound of metal clashing on metal, Xan drew his own weapon. In this cavern, he was guessing she did not have access to her power, making her the same warrior he had always come second best to in Vestele. With he and Nakoa united against her, there was a chance they could hold her off. But with the unruly rage behind her eyes, and the sire that drove her, Xan feared the outcome.

The Ravenna he knew was still inside her, though, buried deep in heavy soil, and she could not handle anymore blood on her hands. He stepped forward, blade drawn.

*Stay alive for her, Xan. Do not let it be in vain.*

# THE LIGHT SCROLLS
## THE BOOK OF PROPHECY

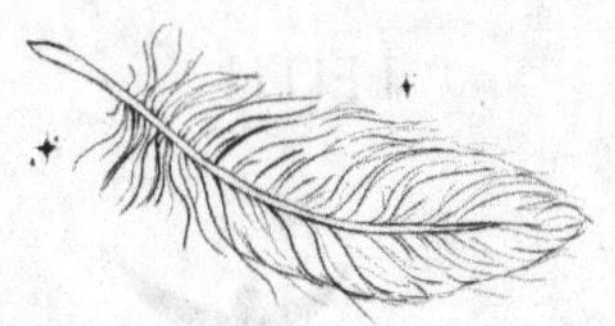

*The Dawn will come, and on that day, even the kings will bow.*

# CHAPTER 93
# WHAT FREEDOM MEANS
## LEITH

Leith had checked and rechecked every tunnel beneath the kingdom. He had studied the diagrams and sent his power weaving through each one, finding each fault point, just to be sure he remembered everything correctly. This plan was going to work. He was going to kill the King of Oro, and he was going to free Ravenna of the sire bond.

Leith touched up the faux shadowmarks on his neck, spreading the charcoal paste evenly with his fingers until there were no clumps. When it had dried, he tugged the collar of his tunic upward and smoothed his dark hair before tugging on his jacket. His late nights worrying over Ravenna had cast shadows beneath his eyes, and he needed a shave, but it would have to wait. He laced his boots and strapped a knife to his ankle before studying the diagram of the tunnels one more time. Then, he burned the evidence.

He still occupied the room across from Ravenna's, which was now empty. He wondered how she was faring on her mission and if she'd fallen back into the claws of the sire. Today was day six, and she was counting on him. He checked his watch and then slipped Locke's wedding band onto his finger. His eyes fell to the ring on his pinky and he blinked. *Time to go.*

Although he was well-trusted by the king as Locke Carrington, alleged Ember mercenary, he was unable to get a private meeting today. Degare was surrounded by an unusual amount of Despiri guards with Ravenna gone, and his witch seemed to have a newly ignited admiration for him. She was exiting the throne room as Leith entered. *Perfect.*

The throne room was Leith's preferred place of meeting. The tunnel that ran directly beneath it would greatly benefit him in escaping if all went wrong.

"Mr. Carrington!" the king said happily. He was drunk on wine, and he was unsteady on his feet as he came down from his throne to offer Leith a glass. Leith watched half of the alcohol spill onto the ground as Degare stumbled, and then he took it, as to not turn down an offer from the king.

Leith dipped his chin. "It is good to see you, Your Majesty. Any word from your Raven?"

Degare chuckled. "I assume everything is going well. It would not be easy for her to fail me. I thought about sending you with her, but I wish to see how she does on her own."

Leith smirked, taking a sip from his glass and wondering if Degare was telling the full truth about why he had not sent him on the mission, too. *Was it because he had expected Ravenna to have killed me already? Or was it because he was catching on that Ravenna had seemed somehow distracted lately?*

Ravenna would be counting on his perfect timing to free her of the bond. He needed this to work. Leith surveyed the room, taking in each Despiri guard and carefully exploring each of their powers. *Strength. Mind-reading. Fire. Wind, similar to mine, but weaker. Manipulation of shadows.*

"I could have greatly benefited her in Edmaria," Leith said to the king with a shrug. "But, since you decided to hunt the Embers for the kill and not to bring them back, she did not really need my help, did she?"

Degare shook his head. "My Raven needs the help of no one. She is quite capable on her own, and you've helped me here in Oro immensely." Degare raised his glass. "I thank you for that, Mr. Carrington. You are wise beyond your years. Your clever ideas helped me to make leeway on this mission. I am sure I will be keeping you around for at least a little while longer—whether to aid my Raven or not." Leith recognized the tone of his voice and knew the king thought he was hiding something. But Leith was well aware of Degare's plans to lay claim to his bloodstone and swiftly end his life.

Leith gave an honest chuckle. "Well, I am glad to hear that. Though, I must say, I will miss working with the lovely Ravenna."

Degare smiled smugly, as if all had gone according to plan. The king believed Locke Carrington was unable to resist the temptations of his Raven, and that sooner or later, she would use that to her benefit, laying claim to his bloodstone. Leith refused to acknowledge how much of the former was true. Ravenna had become something more to Leith than he had expected—a weakness, perhaps.

"I am sure my Raven will continue making time for you, Mr. Carrington. Do not fret."

Leith allowed his power to silently sweep the room one more time, pinpointing each power and noting which Despiri guard it dwelled within. "I hope she will," he said.

Leith wanted to spend all the time in the world with her. He wanted to know her beyond the sire and to learn which parts of her were true and which had been fabricated. The woman he had met months ago had carried enough pride to endanger his clan for her own selfish gain. She had been cunning, and she knew the ways of manipulation. There was a darkness in her even before this sire had planted its roots, but what of the Light? Had any of its seeds fallen on fertile soil within her mind, or had they all been choked out by the weeds of this bond she now had with Degare?

Ravenna had done much wrong under the influence of the king who stood before him, and she had wronged Leith before it all. But Leith had wronged her, too, in not telling her the truth sooner. In the mask that he wore to keep her from it, just as everyone in Vestele had. He had planned on telling her everything of the world she had been hidden from, and he had planned on sharing the Light with her the night she returned to him to be wed—when he was sure she could be trusted to know of his mission in Ink Valley. But that night had never come. Leith's eyes fell to the ring on his finger and he wondered, if that night had come, would the Dove have trusted the words he was saying?

Now she knew everything, and she was trusting him to set her free.

"To Ravenna," Leith said, holding up his glass and taking one last sip of his wine. As Degare smiled and raised his own glass to his lips, Leith said a silent prayer before he ripped every ounce of power from each of the Despiri and sent it flying back into them as pure Light. Leith plucked that tether that connected him to the fire gifted Despiri, and before the last flame could snuff out with the Despiri's final breath, an inferno engulfed the throne room.

Degare began yelling, ordering the guards that no longer breathed. There was no one to help him. Leith tilted his head from where he stood among the flames and turned to the king, unsheathing the dagger from his side.

"Jara told me not to trust you," Degare snarled, stumbling toward him. "It was you. The plagues, the attacks. Ink Valley. It was all *you*."

Leith smirked, running his finger across Ravenna's dagger, then tapping it on the tip. "Yes, well, perhaps you should have listened to your witch for once," Leith said. "She really is an intelligent woman."

"As is Ravenna," Degare said with a grimace, as if he had just realized something. "You are here to free her of the sire, am I correct?"

Leith shrugged, sending a burst of wind through the throne room that knocked Degare flat on his back. The king's head crashed against the stone, and Leith leaned over him, dagger to throat.

"For what you've done to her, I have promised to kill you," Leith said matter-of-factly.

The wry smile did not leave the king's face, and Leith pressed the dagger against his neck until it drew blood. *Finally, my Dove will be free.*

"You think she will be yours when I am gone?" Degare said, chuckling. "Foolish man! Can you not see? She played you." The pressure on the blade lessened where Leith knelt over the King of Oro. Degare burst into wicked laughter. "*She played us both.*"

"What are you saying?" Leith asked. Thunder traveled

across the seas, and he could not help the burst of power that poured from his body into the stone beneath. It rumbled through the kingdom, no doubt falsely alerting his soldiers, mimicking the signal they had set to mark the beginning of the war. *No.* The tunnels below began to shake, and Degare raised his brows, impressed. Soon, all of Oro would be under attack.

"You wouldn't kill her, so she went with the only other option," Degare said through clenched teeth. A dozen Despiri soldiers rushed into the throne room behind him, failing to fight their way through the flames. Leith kept the blade to their king's throat. *What is he getting at?* "Foolish, foolish man," Degare muttered from where he was pinned to the stone.

"Spit it out," Leith said, his voice a thundering threat as he added force to the blade.

Degare coughed and spoke again. "Ravenna and I are bound. Not only by sire, but by life–if you kill me, she dies. She knew that."

# EPILOGUE
## MERRICK

errick did not fight as the guards took him to his father. They ushered him along toward his father's chambers in the Sand Palace, and when they arrived at the door, Jamila exited.

"Merrick?" she said quietly, surprised to see him. Her eyes fell to the chains at his hands, and as the guards looked between the two of them, he gave her a look that said, *Go.*

"Bring him in!" his father grunted from the other side of the door as Jamila hurried down the hall, looking back a few times. Merrick was ushered in to the king. "It is just like you to run off to the country home when things get tough," the king muttered, rising from his chair. His face was in a permanent grimace as he approached the doorway where Merrick stood. The guards turned to leave them alone, and to Merrick's surprise, he waved at the shackles on Merrick's wrists. "Remove these," he said. They did, and his father motioned for him to have a seat at the small table across from the bed.

"Are you not going to ask me about my trip?" his father

asked. His father enjoyed playing games like these, and Merrick breathed tightly, knowing where this conversation was heading.

"How was your trip?" Merrick asked dryly.

"Delightful. But I am sure you already knew that, being that you were there." Merrick stiffened as his father held up the plans he had spread across the dining table in that small cabin two nights ago with Ravenna. If he had no reason to kill him before, he certainly did now.

He remained silent as his father spoke. "What is it you were doing there? And what is it you were doing in my own kingdom, conspiring against me with the Raven of Oro?"

Merrick had known this conversation was coming, yet nothing could have prepared him.

"You are my only heir, Merrick. And you have disappointed me."

"I never wanted to disappoint you. But it is not your approval I seek," Merrick said.

"And whose approval do you seek?" the king asked.

"One day, when you die, Father, your deeds here will have earned you eternal darkness. Is that what you want?" Merrick spat, rising from his seat and slapping his hands down on the table.

His father cackled. "To finally hear you say it–to know that it is the guilt that eats you alive. You are just like your mother. *Weak*. You seek the approval of the Light? It is too late, Merrick." He reached forward and tore Merrick's sleeve, revealing the sin that crept up his arm. "You are marked with darkness. You are *my* heir. You are *my* son. You do as *I* say," the king spat.

Merrick did not care if he was too far gone. He was done cowering; he was done serving the darkness. "I will not stand by and allow you to dictate my life and my decisions," Merrick said. "I will not complete our alliance with the Dawn Islands, and I will not voice my support of your new weapon," he said. "If you wish for that, you're not going to get it," Merrick said. "You forced my hand once," he hissed, looking at the shadowmarks that now painted him, "you will not do it again."

"Do not speak so soon," his father grunted. "You'll be on a ship before spring to seal the alliance with The Dawn Islands. In the meantime," he motioned to one of the guards Merrick had not seen approach the doorway.

"What is this?" Merrick asked, looking between the guard and his father. *Where is the death I expected?* His father held up a finger, and Merrick watched as the guards brought in an unfamiliar, foreign man, with golden curls and eyes like a storm. From the shackles on his wrists, Merrick knew that he was an Ember. His clothes were worn, tattered, and stained with blood. His skin was nearly the same drab gray as his tunic, and his body beneath the tunic was frail.

"I thought you were keeping your Embers in the caverns," Merrick said sheepishly.

"Son, the Embers in the caverns are for me. This one, is for you," he said, extending a sword toward him. In the hilt was a bloodstone, and Merrick's heart plummeted. His father had already succeeded in forging the bloodstone weapon. It was as if he were back in Oro, at the first trades, in front of an audience, making the kill his father had bought for him. *Not again.*

"Merrick, this is Elias. He is a wedding gift from your bride to be. A sort of. . .offering." Merrick shook his head, wishing this wasn't real. "It was he who killed your brother. If you desire the throne which Andreas was to inherit, you will kill his murderer."

Merrick thought his chance of inheriting the throne was long gone. He believed that his father's hatred for him had far outweighed the fact that he was the only heir. Standing here now, Merrick knew that he *did* want to inherit the throne, if only to do something good for Edmaria. To right his wrongs. *But this?*

His father spoke again, urging him to take the new bloodstone weapon. "A life for a life."

# THE LIGHT SCROLLS
## THE BOOK OF PROPHECY

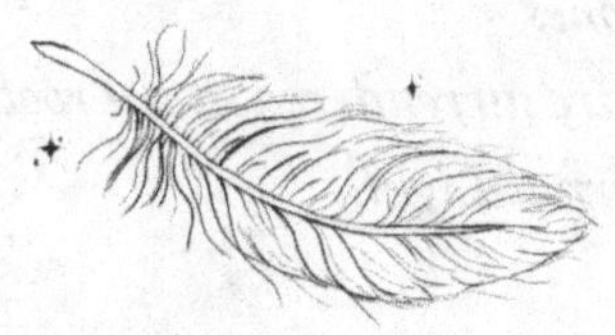

### *Prophecy of the Seven*

*In the days of darkness, there shall come,*
*those who fight, and those who run.*
*But from the Father, a gift to be found,*
*Seven wrapped in light, crafted and bound.*
*Two sons of thunder and a mourning dove,*
*a peaceful serpent and the one in love.*
*Upon them a wolf, to be dressed in sheep's clothing,*
*the other, an Ember of fire and loathing.*
*Among these seven you shall find,*
*the promise of Light—as they remind.*
*No weapon formed*
*against them shall prosper,*
*They are armed with Light—there is no weapon sharper.*
*Armor of Light, made from the tree,*
*crafted in gold, to protect thee.*
*Each piece made for one,*

*each one made for the Kingdom.*
*Kingdom of Light,*
*clothed in might,*
*the weapons collected,*
*the kingdoms elected.*
*Placed on their thrones,*
*Light in their bones,*
*til the weapons are surrendered at the roots of life,*
*Ushering in Eternal Light.*

# AFTERWORD

Dear reader,

By now you are starting to see how deep the darkness runs in Arresia. It is the same in our world today, but like in Arresia, there is a light. There is hope. Keep your eyes fixed on Him—Jesus Christ—and the shadows will fade away.

This book has been my most challenging project yet, but I believe it is my favorite. Watching my characters walk through darkness and saying goodbye to some of them was *hard*, but so necessary for the story I am trying to tell. I have been a bundle of nerves and excitement in anticipation for this release. I don't want to break hearts, I want to show broken hearts that they can be healed.

Much of this book was inspired by the grief I experienced in 2022, which led me to a deeper faith and true relationship with Christ. When it was too difficult for me to walk through that valley, He carried me.

By my experience and the experiences of friends, guilt seems to go hand in hand with grief. Guilt over words not said, time spent elsewhere, mistakes that cannot be undone. I began diving deep into this story during this time of mourning, and when these themes showed their faces in my outline, I knew I could use them for good, just as God did for me. I hope that through these characters and their struggles, you can see yourself and know that you are not alone, that you can watch their journeys unfold and see how all things work together for the good of those who love Him.

Turn your face from the shadows and look upon the Son. You are never too far gone for His light to reach.

With love,
Abigail Brier

# Acknowledgments

It is with immense gratitude that I write this:

First, I want to thank my Savior, Jesus, for pulling me out of the darkness and into His marvelous light. It is because of His goodness and grace that my chains of grief and sin have been broken. In Him, I am free indeed.

Thank you to my husband, for leading our family in faith, and for speaking truth and encouraging me daily.

Thank you to my family and friends, for listening to me ramble about this series for years now and for supporting me with excitement through the process.

To my editor and proofreader, Chelsey: for not only being an incredible editor, but a dear friend who dedicates endless hours of work into this series and cheers me on all the way.

My deepest appreciation to: my alpha and beta readers, for helping to shape this story into what I dreamed it could be.

Lastly, thank you from the bottom of my heart to those of you who have supported in any way, whether that be through an Instagram message, comment, share, or by reading these books. Your support does not go unnoticed.

# ABOUT THE AUTHOR

Abigail Brier is the American author of the epic fantasy series, *Til Kingdom Come*.

Aside from writing, Abigail enjoys quiet time in nature, bird watching, flower gardening, and spending time with her family in the midwestern United States. She finds herself very busy with her many creative hobbies, which include painting, design, and photography. She can often be found sticking post-its on the walls or working on her laptop to the background noise of cinematic music or worship songs, snuggled up with her cats and dogs.

Abigail's love for storytelling blossomed when she was in middle school. She started (and abandoned) many stories until she came to the idea for the *Til Kingdom Come* series. In the midst of grief, she was reminded of the hope she has in Jesus, and this story became an outlet for her to share the good news with others. She began pouring little pieces of her own story into her characters, many times unintentionally, until the story came to life. If readers take away anything from this series, Abigail hopes it is this:

There is light in the darkness. There is hope in despair. There is joy in the midst of grief. There is redemption when you feel irredeemable, and you are loved beyond measure.

# MORE BY ABIGAIL BRIER

Rush of Ravens, book 1 in the Til Kingdom Come series.

Sea of Sorrows, book 1.5 in the Til Kingdom Come series.

9 798989 718153